SALVADOR DALI MURDER

ROCK N ROLL BOOKS BY HOWARD A. DEWITT

Van Morrison: Them and the Bang Era, 1945-1968 (2005)

Stranger In Town: The Musical Life of Del
Shannon (with D. DeWitt) (2001)

Sun Elvis: Presley In The 1950s (1993)

Paul McCartney: From Liverpool To Let It Be (1992)

Beatle Poems (1987)

The Beatles: Untold Tales (1985, 2nd edition 2001)

Chuck Berry: Rock 'N' Roll Music (1981, 2nd edition1985)

Van Morrison: The Mystic's Music (1983)

Jailhouse Rock: The Bootleg Records of Elvis
Presley (with Lee Cotton) (1983)

HISTORY AND POLITICS
Obama's Detractors: In The Right Wing Nut House (2012)

The Road to Baghdad (2003)

A Blow To America's Heart: September 11, 2001, The
View From England (2002) (with Darin DeWitt)

Jose Rizal: Philippine Nationalist As Political Scientist (1997)

The Fragmented Dream: Multicultural California (1996)

The California Dream (1996)

Readings In California Civilization
(1981, 4th edition revised 2004)

Violence In The Fields: California Filipino
Farm Labor Unionization (1980)

California Civilization: An Interpretation (1979)

Anti Filipino Movements in California: A History,
Bibliography and Study Guide (1976)

Images of Ethnic and Radical Violence in California
Politics, 1917-1930: A Survey (1975)

NOVELS
Stone Murder: A Rock 'n' Roll Novel (2012)
Elvis Presley Murder (2014)

SPORTS
The Phoenix Suns: The View From Section 101 (2013)
The Phoenix Suns Turnaround (2014)

SALVADOR DALI MURDER

By Howard A. Dewitt

Horizon Books
P. O. Box 4342
Scottsdale, AZ. 85261-4342

Horizon Books
P. O. Box 4342
Scottsdale, AZ. 85261-4342
(925)-202-6005
E Mail: Howard217@aol.com

First Published 2014

Copyright Howard A. DeWitt

ISBN: 1495273806
ISBN 13: 9781495273803
Library of Congress Catalogue Number: 2014903188
CreateSpace Independent Publishing Platform
North Charleston, South Carolina

A Precaution

I no longer believe anything I am told or for that matter
what I read in books, particularly in books I write.
If the text states clearly that every word is made up, that it
is the product of the author's imagination, I would hesitate
and think about it. The novelist often uses the disclaimer
"Any resemblance to actual persons, living or dead, events,
or locales is entirely coincidental," don't believe it.
In fiction there is an element of truth not available in the
non-fiction book. It is truth in some rather elegant form.
The rather dusty facts, arcane phrases and the historical
bin of information are woven into the fiction tome to
produce a history, if a somewhat fictional one. Fiction
is often closer to the truth than non-fiction.
Fiction sheds light on people and events. The danger
is that you look into a soul or an event with insight.
Often what you see is dark. It is still the truth.
In the following pages you will see the truth of fictional people.
Keep in mind you are not in the book. It is fictional. Trust me.

PART I:
SALVADOR DALI INSPIRED TERRORISTS

"Surrealism is destructive, but it destroys only what it considers to be shackles limiting our vision." Salvador Dali

Acknowledgements

The characters and plot in this book sprang from my imagination. There are two books that I have written, **A Blow To America's Heart: England Reacts To 9-11** and **The Road To Baghdad** that are important starting points for this volume. A lifetime of reading spy and mystery books makes it imperative to thank the giants in this field John Le Carre, Len Deighton, Eric Ambler and more recently Dan Fesperman. They have all written serious espionage thrillers. My take has a more comic tome but they spurred my interest in the genre.

None of my friends or for that matter relatives-in laws appear in the book. Even though five of them asked me pointedly if he or she was in it. My brother and his wife saw themselves in a previous novel. These are wonderful relatives with a sense of their own importance. They were not, are not and will not be in the novel. So Dennis and Janette don't worry. Duane you are not here either. At the Paradise Bakery a large number of people have listened to my ideas, thank you Claude, Peter, Sandy, Arnie, Ron, Jim, Paul, Phil, Mike, Charles, John, Yvonne, Will, Buffy, Jay, Nilda, JJ, Mike, Graciella and George. In Seattle my brother Duane was an excellent critic. My other brother Dennis is a marvelous writer and a wonderful person. He is never critical or gets mad at anyone. In Seattle, Dave, Marc, George, Gaby, Warren, Grady, Dennis, Neil and John all provided inspiration. No last names are used to protect the innocent.

At Scottsdale's Starbuck's Jamie, Mr. W., Ron, Dr. Howard Axelrod and the Chicago detective turned novelist listened to my ideas. The coffee served by Sarah helped as I listened to these folks. Thank you. In Mesa, Jackie and Joe, Ed and Jean and Big Hair Rebecca and Jerry who were all sympathetic to my endeavors. My in laws Barb and Ken listened to me more patiently than anyone as did my children Darin and Melanie. My good friends Bert H., Homer K. and Jim K. are gone but they remain in my memory. Thanks to all of you. You are not responsible for the writing and ideas, you are simply good friends whom I treasure. Thanks for listening to me. Or should I say struggling through my written words.

This novel has its genesis in a number of my college classes. When my mentor and late history professor, August C. Radke said to look at history from all sides he introduced me to literature. When Professor Earl Pomeroy taught me about the American West, he used artists. Then when Professor Herman Bateman corrected my laborious PhD dissertation, he told me to read some books on art to relax. My three former professors unwittingly set up this book.

If you like the book send me a note at Howard217@aol.com

CHAPTER ONE

A Dali Mystery

"Have no fear of perfection-you'll never reach it." Salvador Dali

At the entrance to La Gare de Perpignan train station the small man with the large moustache was dead. He looked like Salvador Dali. He wasn't. Dali had been dead for twenty-five years. The dead body blocked the front entrance. People milled around. The police arrived. They took out his passport. It read Salvador Dali. There was a second passport. The name on it was Johnny Hallyday. The third and final passport read Khalid Tomah. They all had one thing in common. The passports were traced to Pakistan. The dead body was the first wave of al Qaeda terrorism. It was more than a decade since 9-11 brought al Qaeda terrorism to the forefront. There was now an American al Qaeda cell dedicated to the triumph of the Muslim way of life. It was based on the work of Salvador Dali.

The unique terrorist cell founded by an African American who converted to Islam was in Alabama. There was also a smaller cell in New York City. It was called the Doc Pomus cell. Pomus was a Jewish songwriter. No one would realize that it was a radical Muslim terrorist cell. Its members were educated, multi-millionaires and connected to the core of American capitalism. They were also African Americans angry at affirmative action, hostile to President Barack Obama, and they regularly sent money to Bill O'Reilly to support his books. In a nation that prided itself on political correctness, no one suspected college educated, Democratic Party voting, rich African Americans as terrorists. They did exist. They were also former college athletes who despised the special treatment that athletes received on university campuses.

This terrorist cell dedicated to the memory of Salvador Dali was intent upon promoting Muslim radicalism. When Dali proclaimed he had: "Arab lineage," the terrorists took note. They loved his self-congratulatory phrase: "My descendants are an offshoot of the Moors." Then Dali said: "I have a fear of too much democracy and too little spiritual truth." The terrorists translated this into a virtually invisible al Qaeda cell. The al Qaeda intent was to introduce Muslim terrorism in Barcelona and San Francisco. This fractured, incoherent idea was the product of fuzzy thinking and misplaced loyalties.

There was one African American who was intent upon attacking his country. He was plotting to bring the triumph of the teachings of the Quran and the clean, wholesome Muslim way to America. In Alabama, this youthful university student quietly adopted the Muslim credo while earning All American honors in basketball and a Phi Beta Kappa degree in finance.

In Alabama, this young man hated the slave name that he was given, James Smith. It was an innocuous last name. Smith was a name for those who didn't belong. He was quiet, thoughtful and possessed a near genius IQ. The road to a superior education was due to his basketball skills. The slave masters at the University of Alabama didn't keep track of his straight A's in the classroom. They believed that the professors liked him for his quiet dignity and work ethic. He grew increasingly radical. The finance major obscured his real interest. Middle Eastern Studies dominated his class work. No one paid attention to his serious academic interests.

When he starred for the Alabama basketball team, he hated the term "roll tide." He embraced the "roll tide" nonsense for his education. He despised the term "Negro." Everyone used it. The world made African Americans second-class citizens. He minored in Arabic Studies and since 9-11 Smith felt vindicated. In the aftermath of 9-11, James Smith, All American basketball player, quietly founded an al Qaeda cell. He would wait a decade to destroy capitalism and imperialism.

There was one difference between Smith and other homegrown American terrorists. He based his al Qaeda cell's activities on the writings, the lithographs, the jewelry, the drawings, the ceramics, the screenplays and the paintings of Salvador Dali. In Dali's art and writings, there was a message to the West. Be ready the Muslim way of life is coming.

When he traveled to San Francisco on business, a local well-connected entrepreneur angered James Smith. The San Franciscan was a good Catholic. He was also a staunch American patriot. His name was Don Gino Landry. He had a number of legitimate businesses. It was rumored that he was a Mafia Don. Dubbed the purple Don for his flamboyant dress, Gino Landry was seen around San Francisco in the best restaurants, the most exclusive social gatherings and the opening night of the San Francisco Opera and Symphony.

Don Gino Landry was also famous worldwide as a Salvador Dali collector. The story of Don Gino's road to become a renowned art collector began when he was a young child. He traveled with his dad to Spain when he was six years old. It was there that he met and shook the hand of Salvador Dali. It had been more than forty years since Don Gino Landry spent a few minutes basking in Dali's glow.

It was a hot day on August 27, 1963 when young Gino walked into the La Gare de Perpignan and met Salvador Dali. Now a decade after 9-11, a terrorist dressed as Dali was preparing to blow up this small train station that Dali once declared was "the center of the universe."

As the handsome man in the purple suit stood to the side of the La Gare de Perpignan, he watched with a detached interest. There was an al Qaeda terrorist disguised as a Sikh.

The man in the purple suit watched the turbaned terrorist. He carried a large batch of papers in a manila folder. He looked concerned. The man in the purple suit lit a small cigar. He walked over and plunged a knife into the terrorist. No one seemed to notice. The purple knife that killed the terrorist was back in his pocket. Don Gino Landry watched with interest as the local police cordoned off the crime scene. It was a typical small town French police force. They had limited training. They had little knowledge of murder. The so-called murder book would turn out to be a joke. Don Gino looked on with curiosity. In the background, six large Samoans looked over the crowd. One went up to Don Gino and whispered something in his ear. The Don walked over to the police commissioner. He stood a respectful distance and watched.

The local commissar frowned. He was tired of men dressed up as Dali dying in front of his train station. Why? The answer was simple. When Dali declared La Gare de Perpignan the center of the universe, people came to die. Most of these people hoped to die of natural causes. This man was different. He was a Muslim. He had a note. It read: "The first of Allah's triumphs, more to come." He was the new breed of al Qaeda terrorist. He wanted to make a statement. The police around the world weren't prepared for publicity seeking terrorists Even ones without turbans who were in disguise.

The police commissioner walked up and stood next to the dead turbaned man. A handsome gentleman in a purple suit walked over.

"Good afternoon, Mr. Commissar," Don Gino said.

"And you are, Sir?"

"Only an interested American tourist."

"Did you see something?"

Don Gino paused and said: "Yes I did."

"And!"

"The man was stabbed by a man wearing a Turban."

The police commissar looked agitated. "Muslims do not wear Turbans."

"Not always."

"Is there a point here my American friend?"

"Yes, my men have found the culprit." Just then six Samoans brought in a frightened little man. The police commissar searched him. He found a purple knife. He saw blood on it. He also found a crumpled turban. The commissar bagged both for the evidence technician.

"Thank you, Sir. I believe that I have solved the crime."

"You have, Commissar, I am simply an interested tourist." Don Gino smiled. There were more radical Muslims headed to Barcelona.

Some came from Europe. Some came from the Middle East. Some came from America. Don Gino was ready for all of them.

"Your name, Sir."

"Gino Landry."

"My good friend," the commissar continued. "You have made a friend for life."

"Thank you." Don Gino left as the frightened little man was led to a flic van.

The commissar was aware that Dali's life appealed to a wide variety of people. Some were political. Some were artistic. Some were commercial. Some were dilettantes. Some were just plain crazy. Some were al Qaeda terrorists.

Don Gino watched as the police processed the scene. His thoughts were on the eccentric Salvador Dali. Terrorists lionize the artist who is long since dead.

His Catalan roots influenced Salvador Dali's eccentric lifestyle. This incident at La Gare de Perpignan defined his early life. This small train station was where Dali would sit for hours imbibing local French culture. On August 27, 1963 Dali declared that the train station in Perpignan was a source of inspiration. As each train arrived at this small, but magnificent, station Dali would sketch people and events. One day with the press present, Dali remarked: "I have found my artistic center, it is here in Perpignan." That not only brought the small French town fame, it inaugurated years of petty crime, imposters showing up disguised as Dali and the myths grew around the artist. La Gare de Perpignan was the symbol of surrealistic creation.

Don Gino had strong images of the Perpignan train station. He remembered the clean sparkling platform. The magnificent trains rolled into the station as the crowds watched in awe. The shiny engines, the sleek sleeping cars, the bright dining cars and the well-dressed porters created a special travel aura. It was magical. The men who got off the trains wore stylish Paris cut suits, they carried expensive leather monogrammed brief cases, and they were in a hurry. Salvador Dali had a different persona. He was calm, relaxed and playful. As a young boy, Don Gino didn't understand this behavior. Dali was so different from the other men. Don Gino wanted to be like him. He wanted to think like him. He wanted to make statements like Dali. Some things that Dali said hadn't made sense to the young boy. Now the mature Gino Landry understood the ribald nature of Dali's genius.

When Dali recalled standing outside that station he wrote: "My penis sprang to attention with joy and ecstasy." La Gare de Perpignan is a short distance from Figueres. This is where Dali established his Theater-Museum to display his life's work. When Dali proclaimed that Perpignan was "the center of the universe," it brought fame and fortune to this small French village. It also brought more interest than the locals could tolerate. Don Gino recalled the time in 1963 when he visited Perpignan with his father.

That day, as Dali stood in the train station, a seven-year-old boy walked up and introduced himself.

"Hello, I'm Gino Landry." The little boy smiled at Dali.

"Young man," Dali said. "You will grow up to be rich and famous." Then Dali took out a small pair of scissors. As he did a massive arm seized Dali.

"Don't!" the little boy screamed.

Dali looked in horror at the six foot five 280-pound Samoan bodyguard. "Sir, unhand me."

A handsome man in a purple suit stepped in. "Signor Dali my apologies." Dali looked straight into the eyes of the huge man and realized he was talking to Giuseppe Landry, a Sicilian Mafia figure, who controlled San Francisco's North Beach entertainment industry. He was also a major figure in money laundering and protection. Don Giuseppe was also a good Catholic. Dali smiled. No one made the Don unhappy.

Dali said: "Let me talk to this young boy." Don Giuseppe bowed and smiled.

"Mr. Dali, the boy is fascinated with everything you say and do." Dali smiled.

Dali took a piece of paper out of his brief case. He quickly sketched a pencil drawn figure and he handed it to Don Gino. Then Dali took scissors and cut the picture into an irregular pattern.

"There young man, you have Dali's no one possesses." Dali patted the boy on the head and smiled.

"Thank you sir, I will cherish it." The little boy smiled.

"You will be a powerful, rich and principled man, Gino," Dali said. "This sketch is a Dali original to start your collection, one day you will have the money to be a Dali collector. You will purchase originals and you will be admired." Dali patted the boy on the head. He looked at the father. Dali hoped that this satisfied him.

"Thank you, sir," the little boy said. He watched Salvador Dali walk around the train station. Why did Dali consider Perpignan to be the center of the universe? The little boy was curious. He watched Dali talk about the philosophy of cosmogony, which is the notion that this small French village was where world civilizations gathered to solve their problems. "This seemingly insignificant train station," Dali said, "has so many different energies it typifies creation and life." The little boy listened in awe. He didn't understand Dali. He would.

Don Gino looked back upon this time as one of inspiration. He became a patron of the arts, a fiscal supporter of the Catholic Church and San Francisco mafia figure intent on purging the streets of drugs and prostitution. He made his money the old fashioned way. Protection. Unions. Legitimate business. When Don Gino laundered his protection and union dues through his legitimate businesses, they became even more profitable. He found that crime didn't pay as well as legitimate business. He also remembered the lessons he learned in college.

By the time Gino Landry entered the University of California, Berkeley, he majored in philosophy. After he became San Francisco's most notorious Mafia Don, he was the only criminal with a master's degree in philosophy. He was also the only criminal to be a Pac-10 First Team Basketball All Star. Don Gino was accomplished in many ways.

When Don Gino killed you, it was in a philosophical way. He did it in a humane Catholic manner.

When Don Gino Landry emerged as a thriving and honest businessman, as well as a Mafia Don, he remained a good Catholic. He was also San Francisco's pre-eminent Salvador Dali collector. He also supported American democracy in the Middle East. These forces coalesced to bring him into the midst of a terrorist plot. Don Gino followed the terrorist's infatuation with Dali. He found it strange. He also found it insulting. He always looked back at that day at Perpignan station as one of inspiration. He would guard Salvador Dali's legacy.

After Dali painted **La Gare de Perpignan**, the sketch for the master was missing. In San Francisco, Don Gino purchased the stolen sketch. He built a special viewing room in his home for it. A few days after the sketch was sold, the criminal who masterminded the sale to Don Gino was found dead. He had a purple gag in his mouth. The case remains unsolved.

Perpignan Station was the nearest major French railroad station to Port Lligat. Dali and his wife Gala left from it each autumn to travel to Paris. Every September Don Gino arrived in Perpignan and took the train to Paris. Don Gino bought a home in Paris at Rue Gauguet. This is where Dali and Gala moved in the spring of 1930. It was a modest working-living space. The studio brought Don Gino close to Dali's creative efforts. He could feel the surrealist creativity.

For Don Gino 7 Rue Gauguet was his retreat. It was down a small cul de sac. There was a patisserie around the corner and every morning fresh, hot baked goods were delivered to his door. The bakery had just gone through a painting, furniture replacement and all new ovens. **Architectural Digest** featured the bakery in a special issue, as it was the only one in Paris with purple ovens.

Don Gino's infatuation with **La Gare de Perpignan** took him to Germany It was here that he discovered another priceless Dali.

The Museum Ludwig in Cologne, Germany received the rough sketch for the large oil on canvas painting, "La Gare de Perpignan." It was wrapped in a silk, purple sheet. The sketch is displayed side by side with the original. Each year, Don Gino Landry takes a brief vacation in Cologne to view the rough sketch of magnificent Dali. Then Don Gino looked in disgust at Picasso's **La Femme a l'Artichaut (Woman With Artichoke)** from 1941. Picasso's work paled in comparison to Dali's. Don Gino was intent on making the world aware of Dali's greatness.

Over the years, Don Gino walked around Cologne; he noticed the large number of Muslims. He also disdained the attack on German holidays. The same thing was happening in San Francisco. One day he would take a stand against Muslim radicalism. It was increasing each year. He remembered his youthful trips to Europe. That was a safe time.

While vacationing in France and Spain, young Don Gino was aware of the prominence of the Catholic Church. He vowed to maintain his Catholic faith. He also continued collecting Dali's art. He was intent upon maximizing Catholic prominence. There were a number of Catholic priests in San Francisco charged with crimes against children. Don Gino saw to it they disappeared. San Francisco had no known pedophiles among the Catholic clergy. No one likes to make the Don mad.

It had been fifty years since Don Gino Landry met Salvador Dali. Now he was one of the world's premier Dali collectors. He was also a notorious San Francisco Mafia figure. He controlled restaurant unions, he had a series of legitimate businesses, including the most profitable dog canning company in the world, and he was making more money legitimately than from his criminal activity. This bothered Don Gino. He considered his Mafia activity as a means of purifying the San Francisco economy.

Don Gino's fiscal contributions to the restoration of San Francisco's Mission Delores, and his funding of Catholic pre-schools made him a regular at dinner with politicians and business leaders. The Roman Catholic Archdiocese of San Francisco presented Don Gino the Saint Francis of Assisi Award twice for service to the church. There was no one more respected than Don Gino Landry. There was also no one more patriotic. Since the 9-11 attacks, Don Gino had given more than a million dollars a year to fight the war on terror.

It had been sometime since Don Gino thought about his country. He knew that there was an al Qaeda cell in the South. He tracked it to Alabama. He looked at the Southern politicians, like Rand Paul of Kentucky or that other dimwit Mitch McConnell, also from Kentucky; Don Gino realized that they didn't have an ounce of common sense.

He would have to find the terrorists and eliminate them. He needed Trevor Blake III as his front man. The young private eye would help keep Don Gino in the midst of the action while allowing the San Francisco mafia figure to maintain his cover.

The al Qaeda terrorist threat increased daily. Don Gino's CIA contacts, his friends in the FBI and the Department of Homeland Security consulted with him daily. He was asked quietly to investigate words picked up in an e-mail by the National Security Administration. They had found the key words "Mission Delores," the number "3," as well as "Don Gino Landry" in an encrypted message to a San Francisco al Qaeda sympathizer. The person sending the e-mail from a New York Internet site signed it "Wilt Chamberlain." The big dipper had been dead for years. Then NSA picked up another encrypted message from Chamberlain to a Barcelona Mosque. It simply read: "Everything is fine at Sagrada Familia." Something was up, and it was Don Gino Landry who had to discover a means to foil al Qaeda.

Don Gino reflected. In Dali's work, he saw a ring of truth. That is his paintings told one more about history than those who wrote the boring historical tomes. He also realized that al Qaeda terrorists so badly misinterpreted Dali's work that one had to protect civilization from their irrational thoughts of a dominant Muslim world. They were using the myths, not the realities, of Dali's life to perpetrate violence. Don Gino would end this blasphemous misrepresentation.

CHAPTER TWO
Habbibi And Al Qaeda Terrorism

"What is important is to spread confusion, not eliminate it."
Salvador Dali

A bullet narrowly missed Habbibi's head. He dove into the rocky ground next to Salvador Dali's museum home. The Port Lligat home was Dali's only permanent Spanish residence. Habbibi looked at the series of small fishermen's cabins that Dali used to form his house-museum. The artist's workshop, the library and the work-rooms were shabby and inconsequential to Habbibi. He was going to blow up the Port Lligat home. Why? He had no idea. Allah instructed him to do it.

Habbibi had been well trained by his benefactor, the American Negro known as Hammadi. His real name was James Smith. He was a basketball legend at the University of Alabama. When they played Wake Forest, Smith scored thirty-five points and held future NBA legend Tim Duncan to five points. He graduated cum laude with a dual major in finance and Middle Eastern Studies. Somewhere in his education, Smith converted to Islam and took the name Hammadi.

He recruited Habbibi, who was not very bright, to fail in his attempt to blow up the Dali home. As Hammadi watched events unfold, he smiled. He would throw Don Gino and his minions off by leading Habbibi to a failed terrorist plot. In this way, Habbibi would obscure the real target. That target was the Barcelona Sagrada Familia. It was the church that the Pope consecrated in 2010. The infidels would suffer. Then Don Gino could watch as his most precious San Francisco monument was blown to pieces. That target was a secret! Salvador Dali, Hammadi thought, would be proud of this American al Qaeda cell.

The al Qaeda Dali organization used his paintings, his drawings, his jewelry and his books to proclaim the triumph of the Muslim way. Dali was a good Catholic. Habbibi knew that this was a cover to obscure Dali's Muslim leanings. By blowing up the Port Lligat House-Museum, it would remove all suspicion of Dali's flirtation with and following of the Muslim way of life. Habbibi didn't know that he would soon be in the company of 300 virgins.

Habbibi planted dynamite around Dali's foundation. Allah would be proud. The Dali home was a landmark for the religious heathens who threatened Islam. Or rather it was the place where Dali pilgrims came to worship at his altar. Habbibi had his own stilted view of Dali. Unlike many of his Middle Eastern radicals, he didn't see the Arabic roots that Dali claimed. He realized that the al Qaeda terrorists, who followed Dali, had a plan to blow up Barcelona's Sagrada Familia and a San Francisco landmark.

While some members of his al Qaeda cell loved Dali's paintings, Habbibi hated them. When Hammadi hired him, he realized that Habbibi would deflect attention from the real plot. Habbibi believed that Dali's Catholic presence was blasphemous. Until the day that he died, Dali professed strong faith for Catholicism. Habbibi was incensed. It was Dali that he hated. This was insane. Dali was a heathen. Habbibi would end this al Qaeda flirtation with Dali by placing the dynamite around his Port Lligat residence and destroying it. Not all Muslims think alike. This was the message of the satanic American media. Habbibi would see that they had evidence of this notion.

Someone was nearby. Habbibi quietly eased himself into the bushes. He looked. He saw no one. His detonator, a small transistor radio, was in hand. He would witness Dali's home erupting into flames. Allah would be proud of his warrior. Then Habbibi heard gunfire. Then another shot.

Who fired the bullet? He saw no one. Then he heard an authoritative voice. "Habbibi, prepare to meet your maker." He turned. A tall, slightly effeminate figure, stood in front of him. The man was dressed in a purple suit, he wore a purple cape, and his white shirt and purple tie made him look like a fashion plate. He even had on purple shoes. He carried a gold and purple cane. He smoked a small cigar. He was alone. So it seemed.

Habbibi said: "I will kill you. You are no more than some old faggot." Habbibi pulled out a knife. "I'll gut you, you bastard." The tall handsome figure had no weapon. In a lighting move the man in the purple tuxedo kicked the knife out of Habbibi's hand. The second blow disabled his left leg. Habbibi howled on the ground.

"Tell me my friend, why would you be placing dynamite around the small cottages that make up Dali's historic Port Lligat home?"

"You swine, I will say nothing."

The man in the classy purple outfit lit another small cigar. "We need to talk." He stood looking at Habbibi with disgust. Then the man in purple kicked Habbibi in the ribs. He wrapped the ends of his purple cape around Habbibi's neck. He had a perfect garrote. He squeezed to the point where it hurt. Habbibi could still speak. But not very clearly.

"Now I would like some answers about what you have in mind as a San Francisco terrorist attack."

"My men will kill you instantly," Habbibi hollered. The man in purple suit smiled. He snapped his fingers. A group of six large Samoans came out of the trees carrying dead bodies. Habbibi's six Muslim suicide warriors. Then a midget came out of the trees. He smiled. He wore a purple suit. He carried a battery, some cables and some pliers. He also had a brief case filled with small knives.

One of the Samoans brought a table, a chair and a thermos of coffee. Habbibi was tied to the chair. The mysterious man in the purple suit sat down.

"Please a coffee, cream, no sugar." The man in the purple cape took a small knife and a larger one from the brief case

"We can do this simply or we can make it prolonged."

"You will never get me to talk." Habbibi smiled.

"Do you know who I am?"

13

"Yes, I do. You are some old faggot."

Don Gino smiled. He cut off Habbibi's middle finger. Then he lit another small cigar.

"Now Mr. Habbibi, we need to know the source of your San Francisco contact."

The meticulous precision that the man in the purple tuxedo employed was one indication that he was experienced in torture. Habbibi broke down. Soon Habbibi was talking fast and furious. He looked exhausted.

Habbibi admitted that al Qaeda was on its last legs. It still posed a threat to the U. S., but they had no effective network. They had only one direction. That was to pursue extremism. The death of Osama bin Laden ended al Qaeda's organizational genius. The man in the purple suit talked quietly to one of the Samoans. They tightened the clamps on Habbibi's wrists and legs. He screamed with pain as the electricity soared through his body. He blurted out everything.

Habbibi said: "Al Qaeda will pose a threat to the U. S. and its interests for some time." Don Gino smiled. He walked over and he began to make small cuts on Habbibi's legs. He told the Don everything.

Habbibi said: "There is a mole. Someone working with you is a traitor. You will never find him. I don't know his identity." After more torture, Don Gino realized that he would have to find the mole.

An hour later, Habbibi was crying, he was missing three teeth, four fingers, and he had burns over much of his body. He continued talking furtively while holding his middle finger.

"Yes, there is a terrorist cell in Barcelona." Habbibi shook with fear.

Don Gino said: "Tell me about it."

"I know very little, there is an American Muslim, a Negro, he has a perfect cover. He is targeting a San Francisco landmark. His American al Qaeda warriors will destroy it. I have no idea what they will blow up in San Francisco."

"What is the connection to Salvador Dali?"

"I only know that they are counterfeiting Dali's art to raise money for Allah's final victory."

"What do you mean Allah's final victory?"

"You will never get me to tell you," Habbibi said. "That's because I don't know." The battery and pliers were set up with the cables attached to Habbibi's private parts. He looked on in horror. Don Gino turned up the voltage and smiled.

"I still have some secrets and I am willing to die." Habbibi slobbered. He was going to be strong.

Don Gino said: "The 300 Virgins are going to have trouble servicing you in Nirvana." It took another hour. Don Gino learned the convoluted plot. A repositioning cruise on the Carnivolet line from Florida to Spain would raise the money for the Barcelona and San Francisco terrorist attacks. Don Gino smiled. He had all the information that he needed. There was one missing piece to the puzzle.

Don Gino took off his jacket. He folded it neatly. He smiled. One last chance for Habbibi.

Don Gino said: "Who is the leader, the man working for al-Qaeda?" Habbibi spit at Don Gino who took out a purple handkerchief and wiped his face. A bottle of hand sanitizer quickly cleansed his face. He glared angrily and pulled out a small pistol. He shot Habbibi in the forehead. The midget started a fire threw Habbibi into it and the bodies of his helpers. They were burnt beyond recognition. Then the Samoans swept up the teeth and any other potential DNA evidence and placed the fragments in trash bags. The remains would be ground up and shipped to Pakistan in cans of Don Gino's Gourmet Dog Food.

The man in the purple suit had a mystery to solve. Al Qaeda terrorists were counterfeiting Salvador Dali's drawings. They were also operating with a Las Vegas firm, Park Avenue Artists, to tarnish Dali's reputation. The man in the purple suit was San Francisco's, if not the worlds, pre-eminent Dali collector. He didn't take kindly to someone attempting to devalue his collection.

Don Gino opened his cell phone. He looked at the pictures of his key Dali's. He saw another clue. Dali left a small clue in several of his paintings. That clue was on Don Gino's cell phone. He looked intently at a reproduction of Dali's **The Metamorphosis of Narcissus**. This painting symbolized death and petrifaction. In the corner of the painting there was a small church, Don Gino realized that the Barcelona attacks were to take attention away from San Francisco. Both terrorist plots were directed at the Catholic Church. He would stop those violent attacks. Petrifaction gave him the clue to realize that Sagrada Familia was being targeted for destruction. He would foil that plot. In San Francisco it would be more difficult. He had no idea what al Qaeda targeted in San Francisco.

Then Don Gino studied Dali's final drawing, **Head of Europa**. There it was again, a small drawing of something that looked like it belonged in San Francisco. When Dali gave this painting to Spanish King Juan Carlos, it was a thank you for the King awarding Dali the title, The Marquis of Dali de Pubol.

As Don Gino closed his cell phone, he smiled. He loved to look at his collection. What angered Don Gino were the smugglers and terrorists. He would take care of a problem that the CIA had trouble solving. He would make sure that the forgers, the illicit businessmen, and the Park Avenue Artists, who made money from dealing with Muslim terrorists, were punished. Death was the ultimate punishment. For terror minded Muslims, it was the ultimate reward.

Don Gino was on vacation in Spain when he came upon the plot to discredit Dali's art. He discovered how and where the new al Qaeda cell was ready to strike. There was one problem. There was a mole inside his operation. Don Gino would pretend that he knew little, if anything, about the abortive plot. Once he discovered the plot, he began to plan its demise. He had to find the money source. That was no problem. Like most criminals, the al Qaeda terrorists used the banking system in the Grand Cayman Islands.

Don Gino flew from Spain to Grand Cayman. When he checked into his Georgetown hotel, the usual obnoxious tourists from a Carnivolet ship were purchasing the trash known as souvenirs, or they were snorkeling. The tourists were fat Americans from Iowa with names like Beth, Brad, Bill, Bud, Ken, Barb, Lyn with one N, Bob or Sue. If you had a name over four letters you were a liberal.

When the cab dropped Don Gino off at the Caribbean Club on Seven Mile Beach, he relaxed. At a thousand dollars a night, his suite was perfect. Bob and Sue from Des Moines couldn't afford the place. He was safe. It was time to figure out how the money in Grand Cayman was being used, and how it was funding al Qaeda.

There was a mysterious figure coming to the islands to fund the terrorist plot. His name was James Smith. He registered into a Georgetown hotel. He would check on the money the next day. As Don Gino arrived in Georgetown, he called his Grand Cayman banking friends. They were on the look out for the stranger arranging for al Qaeda terrorist funds.

After relaxing in his hotel, Smith went to dinner at Agua. This Cayman Island seafood restaurant was the hip spot with an updated aquatic theme. It was some distance from the hotel. Smith had time to think. The local banks were not easy to deal with, and they were unfailingly security minded. So he dressed in his best clothes. Those of an English gentleman. He wore an expensive double-breasted sport coat with charcoal grey slacks and tasseled black shoes. A Hermes tie offset his starched white shirt.

When the terrorist leader walked into the Butterfield Bank, he failed to notice the small, polite Asian man working as a teller for a day. The Vietnamese teller's nametag read, Emilio. He smiled profusely. He helped the handsome man in the sport coat to arrange a sizable cash withdrawal from a huge bank account. As the teller graciously helped load the money into a briefcase, Emilio also stuck a tracking device no bigger than a toothpick into the briefcase lining. He now had a direct line to the terrorist money.

Don Gino and Emilio prepared to fly back to Barcelona; they talked at length about al Qaeda. When they arrived, a pair of official police eyes followed their every move. A high ranking and decorated policeman was curious. Emilio vanished into Barcelona. Don Gino was driven to Port Lligat to pay homage to Salvador Dali's home. The policeman followed in a nondescript car.

As Don Gino's entourage drove to Port Lligat, he reviewed what he knew about the terrorist plot. His notes pointed to two sites that would make al Qaeda even more of an international threat. Don Gino began elaborate planning to foil these nefarious plots. Then he smiled and thought about Port Lligat.

He had fond memories of this area. It was in this remote terrain that Dali arrived in 1916. He was a young man barely twelve years old. That summer as Dali wandered around the Spanish countryside, he discovered modern painting. He was on vacation with Ramon Pichot's family. Mr. Pichot was a local artist who brought back paintings from Paris. Dali later established a permanent Paris residence. It was during a summer traveling throughout Spain that Dali's fascination with modern painting blossomed into an obsession. Don Gino was protective and territorial concerning Dali. He didn't like killing the Muslims. He was a good Catholic His conscience bothered him. The will of God was to preserve the Catholic Church. Don Gino would work to that goal.

While Don Gino walked around Port Lligat, a Barcelona police detective Hector Alfonso Domingo-Mercedes, head of the Guardia Urbana de Barcelona, watched him. Domingo-Mercedes headed a unit that looked into suspicious foreign activity. He knew that the man in the stylish purple outfit was a Mafia Don. He wasn't sure why he was in Spain. There was a reservation at a Barcelona hotel. But that was sometime in the future. Detective Domingo-Mercedes needed to get to know the man. That would not be a problem. When Don Gino arrived in Barcelona, Domingo-Mercedes would ingratiate himself with the well-known San Francisco crime figure. Until that time he would observe his habits.

Just a few blocks from Dali's Port Lligat home, Don Gino found a Catholic church. He went into the 17th century Church of St. Mary and walked into a confessional. A priest came into the darkened space. In the back of the church a police detective took a seat on a wooden pew with small droplets of water. He watched as Don Gino entered the confessional.

The ornate wooden confessional was laden with carvings of saints and the sunlight bounced off the lacquered wood. The priest entered his separate compartment. He looked at Don Gino. This was the American who was so important to San Francisco Catholics. He was well dressed, if slightly effeminate, and he looked concerned.

"My son, you may begin your confession."

"Forgive me, Father, I killed one man today and six others had their lives ended. My men did that at my direction. It was all due to me. Is it possible to achieve forgiveness?"

The priest could barely hear Don Gino. He was obviously troubled. The Church of St. Mary recently had installed a red light to let those who wandered through the church know that a confession was taking place. The patrons politely stayed away from the confessional.

The priest breathed heavily. "No, my son, the Lord doesn't forgive murder."

"Thank you Father. Is it possible Habbibi will go to a different heaven?"

The priest paused again. He continued breathing heavily. "God does forgive those who protect his kingdom. There is only one Heaven. Habbibi will not go there. Go to mass for the next six months and perform twenty-five Hail Mary's each morning. We live in extraordinary times my son and we need your help. You are a warrior of the Catholic Church. Go in peace Don Gino."

When he left the confessional, Don Gino was amazed. How did the priest know his name? Was this a sign to continue his vendetta against al Qaeda terrorists? It was! Don Gino smiled. It was time to plan his response to al Qaeda. He needed to make some plans to end the terrorists' attack on Catholicism.

But he wanted to enjoy the Port Lligat experience and the Cadaques countryside. Don Gino needed a courtside view of the countryside to think. He knew the place. The finest hotel in Cadaques, the Hotel Playa Sol.

Cadaques was not only the town next to Port Lligat; it was a two and a half hour drive from Barcelona into another land. When Dali came to Cadaques, he felt a sense of artistic and personal freedom. Don Gino experienced the same rush. He had been to Cadaques many times. He had donated large sums of money to make the confessionals modern with green and red lights. The money to maintain two local Catholic churches came each year from an anonymous San Francisco donor. The priests knew that it was Don Gino. It was not uncommon to see a priest eating with him when Don Gino was in town. No one seemed to notice that in addition to the six Samoans who traveled with Don Gino, there were locals around to make sure that the Don was comfortable. They also made sure he was protected.

Father Miguel Santos, the local Catholic priest, presented Don Gino with a charcoal sketch by a local artist Eliseo Meifren. He was the first nineteenth century modern artist to live in Cadaques. Don Gino valued the charcoal, as it was the foundation point for Dali's artistic emergence. He thought of this magnificent charcoal, as he traveled to his hotel.

Don Gino Landry checked into the Hotel Playa Sol. He dressed in a white tuxedo for dinner and decided to take a walk. The Hotel Playa Sol was his favorite. The tasteful rooms, as well as the view of the manicured grounds, brought peace and contentment. While the rooms and the food also were superb, the tranquil atmosphere was the draw. He walked around the grounds. A cat came up, rubbed against his leg and purred. Don Gino stopped and looked at the cat. He recalled that Dali's cat, Ocelot, was an integral part of the artist's life. This stripped cat looked much the same.

His men had gone to Dali's house and removed the explosives. He prepared to return to San Francisco. He would need the help of San Francisco's private investigator, Trevor Blake III. He also had to contact his friend Bennie. They were both integral to the plan to defeat the terrorists and prevent the Salvador Dali murder. It was the murder of Dali's reputation. The besmirching of his art angered Don Gino. It was a mistake to make the Don angry. No one lived through his wrath.

He also sent encrypted e-mails to FBI agent Chastain Johnson, Emilio, and the retired CIA agent Matt Luman. He also had a secret weapon the Three Amigos. They were already in place. They would all be on the Carnivolet cruise from Tampa to Barcelona.

While Don Gino was in Port Lligat, a tall African American shadowed him. This nondescript figure did not draw attention. He didn't stand out. He was tall but unassuming. He watched Don Gino's every move. This man led an al Qaeda branch of terrorists organized to honor the memory of Salvador Dali. They were based in of all places the American South. They called themselves "the al Qaeda brothers for Dali." If questioned, they would say it was all a joke. They were serious terrorists. Salvador Dali inspired them.

Why did they love Dali? It was Dali, who in his youth castigated Christianity, it was Dali who was critical of the Democratic process, and it was Dali who supported Spain's General Francisco Franco, Italy's Benito Mussolini and Germany's Fuhrer Adolph Hitler. There was no active al Qaeda in Dali's time. James Smith told everyone Dali would approve of and support al Qaeda.

The solitary figure watched every move that Don Gino made. He would make this blasphemous Mafia figure pay with his life. He was gay. He was Mafia. He was a protector of the Catholic Church. When Don Gino got aboard the Carnivolet line for Barcelona, he would be watched. He would also die.

The mysterious Muslim stranger from America was scheduled to be on board the Pearl of the Ocean. He was a millionaire. He was politically connected. He was a friend of President Barack Obama. He was in the University of Alabama Athletic Hall of Fame. He wasn't suspected. He was part of an Alabama based al Qaeda cell that planned to blow up cherished American and Spanish landmarks. Salvador Dali would be the instrument in destroying a monument to San Francisco's past.

The Salvador Dali murder was planned by al Qaeda to bring praise to Allah's mission, as well to destroy a key portion of the capitalistic west and the Catholic Church. Dali would approve. He would also support al Qaeda financially. He was doing so without realizing it. The sale of his art on the Carnivolet ship, the Pearl of the Ocean, funded terrorist attacks.

Hammadi smiled. He knew the end of the mystery. The CIA, Don Gino Landry, that bumbler Trevor Blake III, the beautiful but immoral FBI agent, Chastain Johnson, and that God damned magician with the martial arts skills, Bennie the Beneficent, as well as the guy, who played piano in the lounge, Matt Luman had no idea what Smith planned. They thought it was about Salvador Dali. They had FBI files, CIA files, private intelligence but they didn't realize that there were two targets. The other one was in America. Smith knew that they were simply too inept to realize it.

Smith watched as Don Gino and his repulsive Samoans beat the truth out of the oaf that he set up to fail in the Port Lligat bombing. Abdul Habbibi was sacrificed to obscure the grand plan. Habbibi confessed to a bombing scheme. None of it was real. Smith-Hammadi's plan had fooled them. Allah had three hundred virgins waiting. He remembered Habbibi's smile, as he drew his last breath. Paradise was just around the corner.

"I don't like Habbibi's confession," Don Gino remarked to one of the Samoans. He grunted. "There is something I am missing." Don Gino lit a small cigar. "We need to get rid of the body."

The midget valet said: "Boss, I am on it."

Don Gino said: "Don't worry, I have special eyes on the Pearl of the Ocean. The Three Amigos are aboard. They are specially trained."

"Boss, they are a Judge, a defense lawyer and a prosecuting city attorney. What do they know?"

"They know terrorism. They are former Navy seals." Don Gino smiled. The Three Amigos were his secret weapon. They were an unsuspecting trio. Their penchant for drink was the perfect cover.

Don Gino flew home to San Francisco. He had a plan for the terrorists' demise. He also prepared for the Carnivolet cruise and the week in Barcelona. Don Gino was looking forward to some time in San Francisco before he solved the Salvador Dali murder. The notion of the terrorists murdering Dali's art was not only repugnant; it would bring the full force of swift justice to al Qaeda. No one disrespected the Don's Dali collection.

CHAPTER THREE

Salvadore Dali Connection

**"A painting is above all a product
Of the artist's imagination;
It must never be a copy." Edgar Degas**

San Francisco is foggy, most of the year. The mist sets in and Golden Gate Park looks like something out of a medieval castle. That is if a medieval castle was populated with dope smoking hippies. Trevor Blake's office in the Haight Ashbury is one that is always on the fringe of the fog. The Haight sits higher than the rest of San Francisco. There are Gucci and Prada stores, as well as other trendy designer shops by locals like Lucille Buell. Times have changed. The Haight Ashbury is a hot bed of traditional yuppie capitalism.

I climb the stairs, walk into my office and look at the Haight Ashbury sign. The two fat guys across the street smile at me. They are Ben and Jerry, and they make millions selling ice cream. I look at the gold plated nameplate on my desk: "Trevor Blake III: World's Greatest P.I." I love the sign. Don Gino Landry gave it to me for solving my first and only case. I was a famous private eye for about a week. Then I look up at my pictures of Janis Joplin and Van Morrison. I open the mail. Bills, bills, bills. Depressing. Not all the money I made is gone.

I put on Van Morrison's CD, **Magic Time**, and I pull out a checkbook. I can actually pay the bills. Since solving the murders of the Start Me Up drummers, I have had a steady income. I gaze at my new desk, my fancy computer and my pictures of Van Morrison and Janis Joplin hanging on the wall. I have arrived.

Guitar Jac, my trusty assistant, shows up to grab three auto repossessions and a court order to prevent a stalker from going after the blues singer Bonnie Raitt. Jac will have lunch with Raitt, they will talk music and then Jac will find the stalker and deliver the court order. He will then beat the hell out of the stalker. Despite his degrees from Stanford, Guitar Jac is a black belt, a blues singer and he comes from a wealthy family. He is also African American, a conservative Republican and a gun owner. He has a Rush Limbaugh sticker on his Ferrari 259 GTO. He claims he bought it for the GTO. There is a song "Little GTO" that Jac loves. The car is a tribute to the Ronnie and the Daytona's hit. The Ferrari is worth more than I will make in three lifetimes. What am I doing with this partner? I have no idea. He walks out onto the street and vanishes.

As I sit down at my desk, I hear a bevy of loud footsteps. The door opens and a midget in a purple suit walks in, followed by six three hundred pound Samoans in purple tuxedos. The midget is a nasty, reprehensible little toad. He sneers at me.

Then Don Gino Landry makes his grand entrance. Don Gino is the only gay Mafia figure in San Francisco. His outlandish suits, his purple and gold walking stick, his purple shoes and his purple limousine makes him a larger than life San Francisco character. Fortunately, he is not out of place. This is, after all, San Francisco.

He eats dinner with former San Francisco Mayor Gavin Newsom, Representative Barbara Boxer, Governor Jerry Brown is a frequent dinner companion, and author Danielle Steel and every major movie star and producer from Hollywood is his friend. Sharon Stone spent a week in Don Gino's guest bedroom when she divorced newspaper mogul Phil Bronstein. Sharon Stone credited Don Gino's friendship with her ability to recover from the rocky marriage to the newspaper tycoon. Stone had to convince Don Gino not to have a private discussion with Bronstein. The Don reluctantly agreed. One day he would straighten out the insipid publisher. I shutter every time I think how close Don Gino came to giving Bronstein an attitude adjustment.

Don Gino also counts me as a friend since I once saved his life. He smiles. I smile. He lights a small cigar. I frown.

"Greetings Trevor."

"Hello, Don Gino."

"I have a case for you."

"I was afraid of that."

"This is an assignment with wine, women and good times. I will also be paying for everything." Don Gino pulls out an envelope. He places $50,000 in one hundred dollars bills on my desk. I acted like the cool private eye.

"Do I get to accept or decline it?"

"You accept it," Don Gino said.

No one refuses the Don. No one refuses $50,000.

Don Gino lays out a first class airline voucher to Tampa Florida, a Carnivolet cruise line ticket to Barcelona and a pre-paid hotel in the legendary Ramblas area. I wonder what is going on. What kind of case could it be?

"Can I ask what this opulent treatment on your part is designed to do?"

Don Gino looked at Trevor quizzically: "Trevor, I need you to find out who is murdering Salvador Dali."

I was speechless. I think Dali died in 1989. That is if I can add it's twenty-five years ago.

"Don Gino, Dali is dead."

"No, Trevor you don't understand. I mean, that you are investigating who is murdering his art," Don Gino continued. "The fake Dali's are being merchandized to support a major terrorist attack. They are sold on a cruise ship using good looking women, liquor and fine food."

"This is my kind of case."

"You need to find out who is doing this and why."

"Good looking women, fine food, plentiful booze and dirty money. My specialties."

"Trevor, this case involves violent al Qaeda terrorists, you might want to forget the wine and women."

"The illicit money sounds good to me."

"Be careful you are dealing with sophisticated money oriented criminals."

"What do you mean by money oriented criminals?"

"There is an African American from the South who is the ringleader. He is elusive and smart. You will need to observe him."

"Don Gino I do need more information."

"In due time, Trevor."

"What is the plot that I am uncovering?"

"Be careful, the mystery surrounds a terrorist plot. One target is in Barcelona, the other in San Francisco. It will make 9-11 look like the work of amateurs. It is the major terrorist attack of the 21st century."

"What do you mean a major terrorist attack? What are the targets?"

Don Gino thought for a moment. He rubbed his chin. He said: "I don't know, this is why I need you. There is also the important question of why someone is murdering Salvador Dali's art."

"Murdering his art?"

'Forgeries are being used to replace his art. My Dali originals are declining in value." The Don did not sound happy.

The Don's Dali collection is one of the best in the world. He looked pissed. Don Gino said: "I have concerns other than the value of my art. I love my country. This case is a matter of national security. It is not just about art."

"I don't know anything about art. I do know something about national security. How can I help?"

"You didn't know anything about rock and roll and you solved the Stone Murder case."

I did and Hollywood bought the story for a movie. I solved the complex case of who was killing Rolling Stone style drummers in a multi-million dollar cover group the Start Me Up band. The cover band was making about ten million dollars a year. Unlike the Stones, they were young and didn't need Geritol. James Franco optioned a movie from the Start Me Up case. The script was still in a rewrite mode.

Tom Cruise will play me in the film version. He will have to put lifts in his shoes. I am six feet one. I am also not as handsome as

Cruise. I weight forty pounds more than Cruise. I'm not as articulate. I am taller. I don't speak well in person. Other than that, Tom and I could be twins. Guitar Jac's part is cast to Jamie Foxx. I want somebody taller to play me and Jac wants someone who sings better to play him. Guitar Jac also wants Brad Pitt to play the part of an African American detective. I am not sure how to break the news to Guitar Jac that this is a difficult task. Despite his Stanford education, there were still some things that Jac misses. I still had to consider Don Gino's request. I was thinking.

"Trevor! Are you on this planet? I need an answer." The Don looked unhappy.

"Can I decline, Don Gino? It sounds beyond my skills."

"No," Don Gino said. That cemented the argument. I was on the case.

I explained to Don Gino that I had a case in Memphis to solve. It was an Elvis Presley murder. Elvis had been dead since 1977, and I seemed to specialize in finding elusive killers. The Don listened and frowned. I could see that I wouldn't be going to Memphis. I sent the retainer for the Dead Elvis case back to the criminals who wanted to hire me. I was still trying to figure out who would want to investigate Presley's death almost forty years later. Don Gino asked me to refuse the case. I did. No one said no to Don Gino.

"Tell me Don Gino, what is my role?" The world's second greatest private eye was on the case. He didn't have a choice.

"No. In fact you leave in two weeks for Tampa. I have a room booked at Tampa's Hilton Garden Inn. You will receive a packet of key material. Here is the first informational envelope, there is more to follow."

"What do you mean key material?"

"I have identified the al Qaeda operatives. The targets for violent explosions remain a mystery."

He lit another small cigar and walked out of the room. I opened the large envelope and looked at the tickets. There was a second smaller envelope; it contained ten thousand Euros and a Platinum American Express card. It had an unlimited credit line. I could eat and drink well. I went home and my sometimes girl friend, Joyce Byers, was cleaning the bathroom and changing the bed linen. Maybe she wanted a roll in the hay with the world's greatest detective. Then I remembered that I wasn't Elvis Cole. Maybe a role in the hay with the world's second greatest detective would change her outlook. I told her that I needed to leave for a special case. When she asked why? I told her about the wine, women and terrorists. She was fine with the terrorists. The wine and women prompted her to walk out of my Chestnut Street apartment. I had two weeks before I left. I couldn't tell Joyce that I needed to educate myself on Salvador Dali.

Joyce hollered: "You are an asshole Trevor."

"Sorry," I shouted as she ran down the stairs. Bennie, my ex-brother in law and landlord, wouldn't fix the elevator. He said it wasn't cost effective.

Joyce and I were supposed to go to Carmel for a week. She is a San Francisco police officer, a detective at the moment, and her time off is rare. She was pissed. I understood. The bed was unmade as she left. I didn't imagine that things could get worse. They did.

Bennie and Bertie showed up. They are my ex-brother and sister in law. I rent their Chestnut Street apartment. Bennie is a major real estate investor, a retired scientist-entrepreneur, and he rents me the place cheap. It is to keep on eye on me. When Bennie gets upset his gray haired Afro stands on end and his eyes bug out. This happens a lot, as he can't stand me. It is a love-hate relationship predicated on family values.

I divorced his sister, Marilyn, two years ago. She got all our property and money. I got Bennie and Bertie. They felt sorry for my plight. Bennie also likes my girl friends. Not Joyce. The other ones. Those who are one of my girl friends for one night. The ones I meet at the Hi Fi Lounge near my house on Lombard Street. They are the love of my life. For at least one night. On rare occasions there is a two-night stand. Then it ends. They always want an expensive dinner. I like to go Dutch. I'm not cheap, just practical.

I was married to Bennie's sister, Marilyn, until she caught me in bed with her best friend. I couldn't explain it. I didn't try. Bennie felt sorry for me and rented the Chestnut Street apartment to me for $500 a month. I couldn't live in Oakland next to the brothers for that sum.

The only problem is that Bennie and Bertie act like they live in the apartment. Bennie never knocks. He simply walks in. He looks around the apartment with disdain. Bertie shakes her head. It isn't clean enough for her. She checks the refrigerator. I never buy anything from Whole Foods. She tells me that I will die young. I counter that I will die happy from Ben and Jerry's ice cream. She is disgusted by my eating habits. She walks into my bathroom and looks for the vitamins. There are none. Condoms for safety. Aspirin for hangovers. Viagra for sex. That is about it in my bathroom cabinet. The multivitamin for people over fifty is the only other staple. I am only forty-one, but I want to get an early start on the vitamins.

Bertie said: "You need to spend some time cleaning, you need to learn about vitamins, you need to get a physical and you need to put some food in the refrigerator. You also need to watch more Fox TV news. You know they are fair and impartial." I looked disparagingly at Bertie. She didn't catch my disapproving glance. For a $500 a month apartment, I said nothing.

Bennie said: "Trevor we need you to feed our cat. We are going on vacation. I have left a key for you under the front mat."

"I can't feed the cat. I am off to Europe to solve a major case in two weeks."

Bennie said: "We have a three day orientation tour with the Conservative Republican Cavalcade. You are around here at least a week."

"How do you know that?"

"I am a patriot, Trevor, I know everything." Bennie smiled. He had some secrets that he wouldn't share with Trevor.

Trevor said: "What is the Conservative Republican Cavalcade?" I shuttered at the answer.

"We're going to take America back," Bennie continued: "Mitt Romney is a real American, not like that socialist-Muslim in the White House. I still can't find his birth certificate. Osama has failed us all." Bennie smiled. He loved to call the president "Osama."

"I defer to the expertise of a patriot, Bennie." No sense ruining a $500 rent payment.

Bennie gave me a copy of the newspaper article that said that the CRC is the best and most expensive political tour group. They take seniors on political tours. It is indoctrination into the fair, balanced and impartial myth created by Fox TV News. Bennie and Bertie worship at the altar of Fox TV News. The members carry a Karl Rove Bible, a Bill O'Reilly quote book and a mandate to let the world know that Sarah Palin is America's future president. There are pictures of Glenn Beck in the front room. They are autographed.

Bennie said: "The best part of the tour is that we receive American flag pins for our lapels. We put them on and sing God Bless America. It doesn't get any better than that." Yuck!

Trevor looked at the CRC tour brochure. There were multiple pictures of Michelle Bachmann in a bathing sit. It was a full body covering bathing suit. There is a rumor of a right wing Republican calendar with Palin, Bachmann and ten other right wing female Nazi's making up the twelve months. At least Ann Coulter and Michelle Malkin looked good in bathing suits. That is until they start talking. Then they look like Godzilla. One wonders if there were any other picturesque Republican women. Probably not. Even Bennie couldn't imagine a Republican women's calendar. Bertie scolded him for being a sexist pig.

Bennie said: "We have our own chef, Robert McGrath, from Scottsdale. Rush Limbaugh has a dinner at his house before we fly to Paris, then we meet Ann Coulter in Paris and she shows us the city. We have a multi-cultural day with that lovely Filipina Michelle Malkin. You know I'm not racist. I just hate Osama-Obama." Bennie loved his jokes. Even the lame ones.

I said: "I hate to ask this question. Why do you need me for three days?"

"We have a real cat sitter coming in on Tuesday for a month."

I reluctantly agreed. "We do I need to do?"

"Nothing Trevor, we will leave food, money and specific instructions. Don't snoop, asshole. Don't plug up the toilet." I had accidentally dropped a paper cup in Bennie's toilet during our post-marriage dinner. The marriage failed, as did the toilet. He never let me forget either one. He is still mad about the toilet. Bennie is happy about the divorce.

My ex-wife Marilyn had the choice of becoming a partner in her law firm or going into counseling and saving our marriage. She selected the partner route. The marriage was done. I was done. All I had left were Bennie and Bertie. Not a pleasant thought.

"Does my ex-wife, you know your sister Marilyn, ever admit it was a mistake to leave me for the law firm?"

Bennie laughed: "She was nuts to marry you. She had a chance to hook up with a Stanford doctor, a University of Chicago scientist or a Harvard educated CEO. She chose you. Why? I don't know."

"It was about the sex Bennie." He looked like he had gas.

"I have forgiven you Trevor, as has Jesus." Bennie recently converted to the Church of Karl Rove.

"Who?" I asked.

"The good Lord, Trevor. You will be forgiven."

"Is the good Lord against Obamacare?"

"He is, Trevor, how did you know?"

I gave up. There was no besting Bennie at repartee. He is too bright.

It didn't sound like praise. Bennie earned a PhD in nuclear engineering. He always wanted his sister to marry a Stanford doctor. All he ever talked about was Stanford. He slept with a Stanford letter blanket on his bed. He earned it as the back up football mascot.

Trevor said: "What has Marilyn done that is acceptable?" There was nothing like putting Bennie on the spot.

"The second smartest thing she ever did was to go for a law firm partnership." Bennie smiled. He was proud of his verbal puns.

Trevor said: "What was the first smartest thing, I missed it? I am a slow learner."

"Getting rid of you asshole." He smiled. Bennie liked to laugh at his jokes. That was okay; I liked him despite the divorce. Marilyn? She is famous as a defense attorney, and now after all the publicity, she is famous as the ex-wife of the legendary Haight Ashbury detective Trevor Blake III. Bennie didn't like that. I had received an inordinate amount of publicity for solving the case of the drummers killed in the Start Me Up band. I was on the cover of **Rolling Stone** with a headline: "Hip, Cool, Rock and Roll Detective." I appeared on the Late Night With David Letterman Show and Saturday Night Live. I enjoyed my fifteen minutes of fame. I also made a lot of money. I could finally pay the bills. I was solvent. I still needed a $500 apartment.

I even had a few dates with beauty queens. When I got the ladies in my apartment, I had a secret sex weapon. It was designed to get them into bed. I read them my favorite book, **Beatle Poems**, and they all jumped into bed. I was getting laid. I was having fun.

When Bennie visited we had a standoff. I looked at Bennie. He was thinking. He always had something on his mind. He tried to be nice to me. It killed him. We were on opposite ends of the political, economic, cultural and social end of San Francisco life. Bennie is what I call a middle-white. That is he wants to take America back. I am not sure who has taken over. Bennie sees conspiracies everywhere. Fox TV News is the culprit for his political thoughts. I cringe. I also remember my rent is $500. That eases the criticism. We do have to talk. That is the problem.

Bennie said: "Trevor please don't talk politics with me. I can co-exist with you only on the most meaningless level of personal involvement. You are an asshole. That is my most positive thought about you." I could accept that.

"I can't wait to hear what is going on with your travels." I had to make Bennie and Bertie think I was interested.

Bennie said: "Do you really want to hear about my trip?" Bennie looked at me while I thought. I guess I had better hear about the trip.

"Give me the details." He would anyway no matter what I said.

"Bill O'Reilly is scheduled to feature our tour group on his show. Our group is called "The Real Americans.""

"I feel better already Bennie."

"When we return to the states, Trevor, we will tour colleges and tell the students the real story of America. Those fucking pinko

Communist professors don't have a God damned clue." He smiled like he had eaten a canary. I was trying not to get sick. I would be gone for a month and they would be gone for a month. This is a marriage made in heaven.

I got a key to their Mill Valley house. They lived in Plantation Acres, a million-dollar retirement community outside the quaint downtown Mill Valley area. There was a politically incorrect statue of Uncle Remus as one entered Plantation Acres. I wondered why the liberal rockers lived in this haven for moneyed white folks. Carlos Santana loved the area. He hated his neighbors. They were white, boring, racist, ignorant and rich. They thought that Mitt Romney was too liberal to be president. Then Carlos looked at his bank account, and he decided that Plantation Acres was his kind of place. No comment from Bonnie Raitt. She was too busy listening to her twenty-two year old boy friend giggle to socialize.

Bennie and Bertie's other neighbor, Eddie Money, proved that old rockers do make money. Money had two pools with stones inlaid to spell out "Two Tickets To Paradise." Not to be outdone, Carlos Santana had a Mexican style hacienda with a huge guitar shaped swimming pool while Raitt had a Frank Lloyd Wright knock off house. Her swimming pool was shaped to resemble the face of Muddy Waters. Eddie Money had the biggest and most impressive home at ten thousand square feet. He also had a cottage in the backyard. He couldn't stand looking at the wife. She couldn't stand hearing him sing "Two Tickets To Paradise." They had the perfect marriage. They never saw each other. All the houses were worth over ten million and they only had three bedrooms. So much for the rich and famous in Mill Valley's quaint setting in the scenic Muir Woods.

I took a nap. I would finish his duties at Bennie and Bertie's later. I had two days to unwind. As Trevor sprawled out on Bertie's couch, he noticed the Mustang Pool Table. Bennie loved to play pool. For $15,000 he had a pool table that looked like a Ford Mustang. The $3300 tufted ornate French Baroque couch was offset by two white chairs commissioned from Yves Saint Laurent. The eponymous YSL chairs cost more than $5000 each. They were made of white leather.

Trevor looked at the $30,000 worth of furniture and wondered if he should sit on one of the couches or worship the ensemble. Trevor fell asleep on the white couch.

He had a brief dream about his ex-wife, Marilyn, when Trevor awoke he was smiling. It was just a dream. Trevor remembered that Don Gino mentioned that Salvador Dali's secret life was hidden in Bennie and Bertie's palatial mansion. He was puzzled. The world's second greatest detective would investigate. But first he needed a sandwich.

CHAPTER FOUR

The Secret Life Of Salvador Dali
At Bennie And Bertie's

"Salvador Dali gave Mia Farrow a dead mouse in a bottle, hand painted, which her mother, Maureen O'Sullivan demanded be removed from her house, it was one of Dali's most outrageous and inventive pieces." Andy Warhol

As Trevor prepared for his latest case, he had some quiet downtime at Bennie and Bertie's. He used it wisely becoming a Dali expert. There was a great deal to Dali's life that was integral to solving the crime. He brought along every Dali biography. He rapidly became a Dali expert.

Salvador Dali was a surrealist. There is no doubt that he went out of his way to proclaim his surrealistic pedigree. A case in point is the dead mouse that he delivered to actress Mia Farrow's New York house during a party. Dali saw it as a moment of fun. It was an indication of extraordinary eccentricity. Dali saw it as simply his "artistic bent." He always said that he had a secret life. This life impacted Trevor Blake III.

At Bennie and Bertie's, he researched and reflected on Dali's life. Would it help solve the crime? Who knows! He was being paid well. He was on the case.

As he got up from his nap, Trevor looked at a note left by Bertie. There were a series of chores. He was to fed the cat, get the mail and leave everything alone. The note began: "Trevor we know how you like to snoop-the mail and cat that's it." I guess they didn't trust me.

Trevor Blake III opened Bennie and Bertie's mailbox. He took out a huge envelope. It was addressed to him. There was no return address. No mailing marks. No stamps. No fingerprints. Pros were at work. How did anyone know that he was at Bennie and Bertie's? He looked around there was no one in sight.

The envelope was thick with a set of printed papers and a book. Trevor looked around. There was nothing suspicious about Plantation Acres. Well maybe the Uncle Remus statue.

Bennie commissioned a statue of Br'er Rabbit for his front yard. Carlos Santana sent a letter of protest to the HOA. Bennie refused to apologize to Carlos. He pointed out that Br'er Rabbit was a trickster. Br'er Rabbit was a magician much like Bennie. He was also a symbol of the Old South. Bennie also had a statue of Speedy Gonzalez placed on his front lawn. In the hallway entrance to the house there was a picture of Pat Boone holding his gold record for his single "Speedy Gonzalez." Boone, like Bennie, was a patriot. Then Bennie had stationary made with a picture of Speedy Gonzalez playing a guitar. Santana gave up. When Bennie's front porch American flag was desecrated, Santana was suspected.

Trevor unlocked Bennie and Bertie's private study. There was a huge sign: "DO NOT ENTER." There were posters from Bertie's Birthers all over the wall. The **Marin Independent Journal** editorialized that "Bertie's Birthers were young women with DAR credentials."

Bertie was intent on proving that Barbra Streisand was not a citizen. Bertie believed that she was an Israeli agent who became a famous singer due to a Jewish media conspiracy. Bertie collected funds to deport Streisand. So far no one paid any attention to this lunatic campaign. She did have some friends working for the campaign. They had names like Trish, Barbie, Peg, Innocence, Cupcake, Lyn with one N and Peggy Sue. They all had axe handle asses, big mouths, bee hive hairdos, smoked cigarettes and spoke in awe of Fox TV News. It kept Bertie busy and out of Trevor's hair. Thank God!

The sign was Trevor's invitation to go into Bennie's working office. The lock was difficult to pick. The door was made of steel with a wood faux frame. Trevor had to pick the lock He looked around for any signs of entry. The small hair that Bennie left on the office door was intact. The hair that Bennie left was on the back door was in place. He checked the windows. There were no hairs moved. There was no sign of anyone entering. Trevor would have to put new hairs in place. Trevor wondered if he was being paranoid. Probably!

He opened the envelope. It contained a book, **The Secret Life of Salvador Dali**. Trevor shook the envelope. There was no note, no evidence of anything. Trevor opened the book. The Dial Press published it in 1942. What could this have to do with the case?

Before he left Bennie's sanctuary, he looked at his magic tricks. There were two that stood out. The one where you were beheaded and the one where you disappeared. Bennie practiced them daily. They were Bennie's favorites. Trevor thought that these were tricks Bennie practiced for him. Trevor left Bennie's office, fixed the lock and put the hairs back.

Trevor took the book into the guest bedroom. It was his bedroom. Bennie and Bertie treated him like family. It was hard on them but they did it. Then he went to the kitchen. He made a cup of low fat, hot chocolate. He also placed Robert Crais' latest novel, **Suspect,** next to his nightstand. Crais' P. I., Elvis Cole, would be proud of Trevor. As Trevor read **Suspect** there was inspiration from Elvis Cole. Elvis had Joe Pike a tough, no nonsense assistant. Trevor had Guitar Jac a trust fund kid from Stanford who was a musician. Jac was also African American and thought Rush Limbaugh should be president. Not a good combination. As Trevor read **Suspect** about a combat dog with post-traumatic stress disorder and a Los Angeles policeman with the same malady, he had an idea. Maybe he could smoke out the terrorist using Robert Crais' fictional detective. It was worth a try. But it was time to get back on the case. Maybe this case would give Trevor PTSD.

Trevor studied the case. With great care, he realized that there was more to the Salvador Dali angle than Don Gino believed. The Dali book did have some clues. There were references to Dali's life in the 1930s that provided reasons why terrorist activity centered on Dali.

What Trevor gleaned was that things with Dali didn't always appear what they seemed. He had a fantasy life that bordered on insanity. Then a small note fell out of the book. Weird! "The clues are in the wild jungle of fantasy in your hand." Trevor thought that he should read the book. He did so furtively.

As he scanned the pages of **The Secret Life of Salvador Dali**, Trevor noticed small, almost illegible notes. One notation read: "Flagrantly dishonest." This was a section on Dali's childhood. Trevor was puzzled. Then Trevor saw the clue and understood. Now he knew why Don Gino was outraged. It had as much to do with his personal life, as with his intellectual endeavors. Don Gino was in the process of resurrecting Dali's legacy. The Don made sure that no one libeled Salvador Dali. If they did, they experienced the Don's wrath.

There were notations all over the book about George Orwell. The English novelist, made famous by **1984**, was one of Dali's staunchest critics. He wondered what this had to do with al Qaeda terrorists? Trevor had no idea. Somehow it was all connected. The world's greatest detective didn't have a clue. It was time to finish the hot chocolate and go to bed. Alone! Not a pleasant thought.

But Trevor didn't go to sleep. He got caught up in the Dali autobiography. It was time to solve the case. The Dali autobiography was filled with clues to the art crime. Trevor noticed that Dali wanted to be a cook when he was a young boy. That explained the never before seen Dali paintings for sale on the ship. These unique and exquisite pieces were of people cooking and they had titles like **The Chef In The Kitchen**, **The Boulangerie** and **Soufflés From Heaven**. They were terrible Dali paintings and obviously fakes. Yet, as Trevor looked at a catalogue for these paintings, he saw more clues. Suddenly, he knew the artist that was reproducing the Dali fakes. Trevor wondered if he was part of the terrorist cell.

The 1500 paintings that Dali completed in his illustrious career were only a small part of his production. He also completed illustrations for books, lithographs, paintings, designs for theater and costumes, a large number of obscure drawings, dozens of sculptures, short films, feature films and movie scripts. There was also a Dali jewelry museum. There was a rumor that he produced greeting cards. These turned out to be pirated. It was difficult to separate the original Dali's from the fakes. Park Avenue Artists didn't have a sterling reputation. They were famous for plying passengers with champagne and pawning off mediocre and often pirated works. They were particularly notorious for faking Dali's work.

There were two new Dali's uncovered by Park Avenue Artists in a small Barcelona Museum. A brilliant drawing, A **Cook Who Wants To Be Napoleon**, which Park Avenue Artists dated from the period in which Dali drew **The Sacred Heart of Jesus Christ**. It was for sale by Park Avenue Artists' at auction with bids starting at one million dollars. There were 2061 passengers on the cruise ship and five hundred qualified with million dollar credit lines. Dr. Harold Weinstein called the drawing "one of a kind." Trevor was intrigued. Could this be fraud?

Dali said: "Drawing is the honesty of the art. There is no possibility of cheating. It is either good or bad." Park Avenue Artists had brochures printed featuring this quote. They advertised: "Dali's art is not one that anyone can reproduce." This deception worked magnificently.

When Park Avenue Artists hired Weinstein to study, authenticate and forge Dali's art, they assured everyone that he would prevent forgeries. He made his reputation studying the Italian masters Leonardo, Giotto, Botticelli and Giorgino among others. He provided a generation of American capitalists with low priced Dali's. He was a pioneering scholar and intellectual dilettante who helped give birth to a new and aggressive international Dali collector.

Dr. Harold Weinstein was a former professor of art history at Harvard. His real name was Dr. Harold Sussman. He was formerly Harvard's Walter Landfill Professor of Classical Art. He was fired for selling reproductions. He called his work "authentic fakes." It looked like Dr. Sussman was going to jail for twenty-five years. When the FBI Art Fraud Unit caught him, he made a deal. He turned in his partners, who were part of Whitey Bulger's Boston criminal activity, and five of Bulger's gang went away to long prison terms. He rolled over on Bulger for a place in the witness protection program.

After the feds left his life, he went to work for the Alabama al Qaeda terrorist cell. It was his way of getting even. He loved Salvador Dali's work. He had also written the definitive book on Gala, Dali's quirky wife. He believed that Gala was the window to Dali's creativity. He had five nude pictures of Gala in his New York apartment. They were all stolen.

Weinstein's lifestyle forced him into a career of crime. He had a home in St. Moritz. He maintained a New York penthouse apartment. His carefully attended reputation as a Dali authority afforded him a life of wealth and privilege. His problem was that he spent more than he earned and al Qaeda terrorists found him an easy mark. He needed the money. He didn't care where it originated. He was also a Gala authority.

It was Dali's life long companion, Gala, who inspired other previously unseen originals. When Dali met her in August 1929, he painted **A Life Long Romance**. He gave it to Gala who was married at the time. She was married to surrealist poet Paul Eluard. When Eluard contracted tuberculosis, Gala left him as quickly as she could. She also poisoned him. She had a gun. The irony is that Gala didn't know how to fire a gun. She had the safety on and couldn't figure out what to do with the weapon. When she shot Eluard he never died. Gala couldn't figure it out. He was immortal.

Dali's closest friends thought that she was intent on killing him. Dali talked her out of it. When Trevor discovered this information, he realized that one terrorist identified with Gala. Who? He wasn't sure. He had to find out. Trevor found Eluard's behavior strange.

The truth was more complex. The drugs that Gala administered to Dali late in life were anti-aging pills full of speed. He became a late in life speed freak. She thought that she was keeping him alive. She also mourned her first husband Paul Eluard. She still loved him. That was Gala. Too complicated. Too intellectual. Too unpredictable. Too weird. It was what attracted Dali.

Out of spite, Eluard sold the Dali painting in 1930 to a Montparnasse art dealer. This art dealer agreed to exhibit the painting as "the only real Dali original in Paris." This advertising was designed to sabotage one of Dali's early exhibitions. At the time Dali had a show in a Paris Montparnasse gallery. Eluard attended the Dali exhibit and called Dali's work: "the ravings of a lunatic." This singular statement made Dali's reputation.

Trevor traced the sale of **A Life Long Romance**. It had vanished. It was puzzling that it was sold to a party in Islamabad and then forwarded to an address at the University of Alabama. From Alabama it was shipped to Grand Cayman. This didn't make sense. This was an important clue. The al Qaeda terrorist had Alabama ties. Weird!

Then Trevor noticed a strange comment. In the Paris newspaper, **Le Soir**, Dali commented: "The revolution is coming." That phrase was in one of the files on al Qaeda. Was it possible that the revolutionaries envisioned Dali's art as the road to Allah's domination of the West? Maybe there was more to Gala. She might be a muse to al Qaeda revolutionaries. He decided to concentrate on her role.

Trevor looked for material on Gala. She was not only Dali's muse but also his wife and financial manger. She was a disaster as a money manager. Dali had to be productive, as she mismanaged their finances.

She also had a deep, dark secret. She was a closet Muslim. Trevor attempted to find Gala's old bank records. His computer skills were nil. He tried but found nothing. He did discover that Gala and Dali were broke most of their life. She gambled away most of Dali's money, slept with every young guy she could find, she read the Quran five times a day while offering a Muslim prayer. This was Gala's secret side. Now Trevor understood why Dali wrote about women in a peculiar way.

When Gala pointed toward Mecca five times each day, no one realized what she was doing. It was her way of being pure and worshipping God. She was nuts.

"Behind the party through the open kitchen door, I would hear the scurrying of those bestial women with red hands," Dali wrote. He was referring to Gala's penchant for evil. That line was another key to the mystery. The al Qaeda terrorist cell used the phrase "beasts with red hands will suffer." There was a picture of Gala in the U. S homes of key al Qaeda leaders.

James Smith had a secret prayer room devoted to Gala. The al Qaeda terrorists had a Gala statue next to a giant ceramic Quran. The pictures of Gala in the homes of converted female terrorists suggested the reverence of these recent converts.

As he pondered the mystery surrounding Dali and the terrorists, Trevor cast a glance at the Dali book. The critics were suspicious that Dali fabricated events. Trevor believed that the much-criticized auto-biography had a larger importance.

The Secret Life of Salvador Dali was the key to everything. Trevor spent another five hours taking notes. He had uncovered at least a portion of the plot. Dr. Harold Weinstein, the Park Avenue Artists authority, was undoubtedly an art forger. There was a small but complete CIA file on Dr. Weinstein. It was marked: "Sensitive Security." It also had a cryptic note from Homeland Security.

The good doctor was an art major at Stanford, he was a varsity wrestler and he had a secret. Then he had gone on to study and teach at Harvard. As a professor of art, no one suspected anything more than he was just another boring lecturer. He was balding and wore a double-breasted blue blazer with a tie. Once he changed his name from Harvey Sussman to Harold Weinstein, he began wearing conservative Muslim style clothes. Then he converted to the Muslim faith. He came from a traditional Jewish family. His father, Clarence, provided every-thing for his son, and he despised his son's Muslim conversion.

Harold told a friend: "You have a Jewish father named Clarence and you don't need to listen to him. I didn't want medical school, I didn't want engineering and I didn't want law."

The problem was the art history major. It convinced Harold that Allah was the real God and that the Quran was the real Holy Book. Like many converts, he was a fanatic. He was also the least suspected al Qaeda agent on the ship. Trevor realized that he had an insight into the way al Qaeda raised its money. Who would suspect a Jew of being a radical Muslim? No one!

As Trevor closed the book, he needed to become even more of a Dali expert. There was a great deal to the Dali legend that didn't make sense. The most significant part of the Dali story was his extensive symbolism. The al Qaeda terrorists viewed his use of symbolism as a road map to revolution.

The Secret Life of Salvador Dali provided Trevor Blake III a roadmap to solving the mystery. The art forgers were using Dali's life, his drawings, his paintings, his lithographs, his movie scripts, his books and his articles to code their actions. What looked like a reference to Dali's work was a code for selling art frauds, channeling the money to the Grand Cayman bank and pulling off the final crime? What the al Qaeda terrorists planned took attention away from their final target. Trevor had more than an inkling of what they were up to, but he had to follow the plot to the end. It was intricate. It wasn't fool proof. He would solve it.

Trevor took the Park Avenue Artists catalogue and perused it. They were selling fakes, as well as originals. The material listed included more than 100 Dali lithographs. They were all signed. A flag went up. Trevor knew that many Dali's lithographs were produced after his death. He had to find out how to verify this fraud. Trevor had to become a Dali expert.

On her deathbed Dali's crazy wife, Gala, who was poisoning him with drugs, had him sign thousands of blank pages. The drugs that she gave Dali were ones that she believed were anti-aging. In reality, they were speed and destroyed his central nervous system. Then she mysteriously died before Dali. The Alabama based al Qaeda terrorist cell saw this as divine intervention. James Smith found a painting, **Slave Market With The Disappearing Bust of Voltaire** from 1940, and he told his followers that it was a sign from the Dali that the slaves had to blow up the Mission Delores. The proof. The bust of Voltaire looked like Don Gino Landry.

The sale of Dali originals on cruise ships was a sophisticated crime. Trevor realized that he needed an intense education on the fake Dali's. He opened his computer to find out what he could about Dali. There was a great deal of material on his art, politics and his surrealist direction.

He e-mailed Zandra Filippi and asked for her help. Trevor met Zandra when he solved the murder of the Start Me Up drummers.

She worked for the Rolling Stones as a publicist. She also had a PHD in computer technology and opened a consulting business.

When he asked for her help, Zandra e-mailed Trevor: "Fuck Off!" He realized that he couldn't count on her computer skills. Trevor studied lawsuits against art forgers and the FBI investigations of Park Avenue Artists. He learned little that was useful.

What the Internet lacked was the in-depth data for analyzing why and how the Dali forgers were able to make so much money. So Trevor decided to head for the San Francisco Public Library.

Trevor vowed to quickly complete his study of the motives of the surrealistic master. There was a hidden message in Dali's art. Trevor had to find it.

Trevor stopped by a CVS and bought a big packet of napkins. It was time to take notes. The key to solving the Start Me Up murders came in the form of Trevor's meticulously researched napkins. He was ready to amass the napkins necessary to solve the Dali case.

Trevor spent too much time at Bennie and Bertie's. The time had come to find the al Qaeda scheme. They should be nervous. Trevor would solve the crime. The terrorists should be terrified Don Gino was coming to avenge Dali. Trevor decided to enhance his Dali education at the San Francisco Public Library.

CHAPTER FIVE

Trevor Becomes A Dali Expert

"Every morning when I wake up, I experience an exquisite joy - the joy of being Salvador Dali - and I ask myself in rapture: What wonderful things this Salvador Dali is going to accomplish today?" - Salvador Felipe Jacinto Dali

After spending the day taking care of Bennie and Bertie's cat, I filled the water and food tray and drove back into the city. I parked my car on Chestnut Street. I had a day to educate myself on Salvador Dali. I also had 200 napkins. This was my secret way of keeping the research straight.

As Trevor left his Chestnut Street apartment there was a pair of eyes following his every move. He walked down Chestnut Street and turned up Van Ness. The sun beat off the pavement. Trevor turned at the top of Van Ness to admire the bay and the Golden Gate Bridge. San Francisco was as close to heaven as possible.

Emilio continued to shadow Trevor. Then another figure emerged. Emilio didn't know why the Hispanic man was following Trevor. He pulled out his cell phone and called Don Gino. Emilio identified one of the locals assisting the terrorists. He was surprised. He spent twenty minutes walking and talking on his cell phone. Don Gino told Emilio to go back to his Haight donut shop. The first break in the case came thanks to Trevor.

Trevor stopped at Tommy's Joynt for a Buffalo stew. The Irish bartender was an old friend. Shamus O'Reilly came to San Francisco in 1960, and he was now pushing seventy. Like most Irish men, he wanted to work until he dropped. He would.

When his brother came to town there was a raucous celebration. He was a best selling Irish poet.

"Shamus, my man, can I get a Budweiser?"

"Well, well Trevor certainly." He pulled out a bottle of Guinness.

"How much do I pay extra for this Irish dribble?" I smiled. Always the clever P.I.

Shamus said: "It is the milkshake of beers, Trevor, a meal in a bottle, a roasted malt flavor with a hint of chocolate." I felt like I was living a television commercial.

"What do you know about Salvador Dali?"

He looked at me like I was nuts. "Nothing. Why would I want to know anything?" Shamus walked to the end of the bar. He hated being bothered by weirdoes. I guess I was a weirdo. I placed a five-dollar tip on the bar and left Tommy's Joynt as the regulars began singing Irish revolutionary songs. Van Morrison wouldn't touch a song like that. Too political! Then again Van Morrison was a jackass who wouldn't touch a song that he hadn't written. He was a sixty-five year old cranky drunken Irish midget. He was still screaming about lost royalties from "Brown Eyed Girl." I wondered who was a bigger asshole-Van Morrison or Salvador Dali? That question remains to be answered.

The two-mile walk cleared Trevor's head. He needed to find out about Dali fakes. His old friend, Marilyn Sowell, was the City Librarian. They had a two-year torrid relationship then she married a doctor. He was a PhD in history, not a real doctor. They had two kids and were happily married. The doctor taught labor studies at San Francisco State. Trevor realized that an out of work Private Investigator wasn't her thing.

"Trevor, good to see you." Marilyn gave him a big hug. The animal magnetism was still present.

She took me into the bowels of the SF Public Library and put in a reel of microfilm dated August 10, 1985. It was from the **Lewiston Daily Sun** and there was a story in which the 81-year-old Dali said that many of his "limited edition" art prints were fakes. His wife had him sign blank sheets of paper. Then she died. Since the 1960s Dali earned $40 for each piece of paper he signed. The blank sheets were sold to Park Avenue Artists and their attorney, a notorious Mafia lawyer, Rocky Montagne, prevented the FBI and IRS from convicting his client of art fraud.

Trevor went onto the Internet and found out that Park Avenue Artists flooded the market with fakes. If only Zandra Filippi would help. Things would be different. The FBI had not been successful in prosecuting the Las Vegas art sales firm headed by Vito Costello. The name alone should send him to jail. They sold most of their paintings on cruise ships outside of U. S. territorial waters. They plied you with liquor, assigned young women to help you select your art and then you were given a $200,000 line of credit. They also appealed to your ego as an art specialist while a young girl rubbed her breasts into your back. Not a bad sales pitch. Trevor knew that this assignment was ready made for him.

Trevor pulled out his cell phone and called Don Gino. He answered on the first ring. Not a good sign. The Don never answered his phone quickly. Something was up.

"Well Trevor to what do I owe this phone call?"

"I have good news and I have bad news." Try to keep it light with the Don.

"Speak Trevor."

"I need some computer help."

"Call Zandra Filippi."

"I did."

"And?"

"She told me to fuck off."

"Trevor when will you learn to stop mixing business with pleasure?"

"Maybe there was no pleasure in our one night stand."

"Don't worry Trevor, I have someone to help you."

"Who?"

"A good friend, she is right here."

"Hello Dickhead." It was none other than FBI agent Chastain Johnson. "What do you need Trevor? Maybe you need the directions to find your ass."

Chastain has a way of making me feel two inches tall. I ignored her comments.

"Chastain, if you can find the source of the Dali fakes, someone is loading them on the Carnivolet cruise line ship to Barcelona. It will help a great deal."

"What's in it for me?"

You have two choices, a night in bed with the world's greatest detective or a list of al Qaeda terrorists about to destroy a San Francisco landmark."

"I will take door number two, Dickhead."

Trevor said: "Many Dali lithographs and etchings are fakes. He signed blank papers for years." I stopped there.

Chastain said: "That is a problem I will remedy." I heard Don Gino light one of his small cigars. He came back on the phone. Don Gino told me about his art collection. He also congratulated me for learning something about Dali in one afternoon. I heard computers purring in the background. What in the hell was Don Gino doing with Chastain Johnson in his house? It wasn't hanky panky. What was it?

Don Gino said: "You will continue to educate yourself. I have sent fifty-two books. Read them." I don't' say a word. It took me a week to read a book. I didn't have a year. I did learn other things about Don Gino's Dali collection. It was valued at more than five hundred million dollars. That figure was for the legitimate Dali's. I didn't want to tell the Don that I had trouble with his math.

Don Gino's phone call was wasting my time. I couldn't tell the Don that. No one disrespects Don Gino.

"I have another two hours in the library, I'll call you back." Don Gino hung up. I was nervous. The Don purchased his art legitimately. He would be very unhappy if any of the pieces were not authentic. It was not good form to make the Don mad.

The Don is sensitive about his Dali collection. He is one of the foremost Dali collectors. He also has an affinity for Dali personally, as he met him at an early age. If anyone disparages Dali, the Don will come for retribution.

Don Gino mentioned that he had a floor full of Dali art. There were more than four hundred original Dali pieces in his Washington Street mansion. Trevor continued to read about the artist and soon realized that Dali was such a prolific artist that it was almost impossible to verify authenticity. Trevor hoped that Don Gino's collection was authentic. The etchings and lithographs were the easiest to forge. The Don would not be happy if any were not originals. He did not have a sense of humor when it came to art.

After spending another two hours in the San Francisco Public Library, Trevor had some ideas. Don Gino needed to have experts look at his collection. It was time to let the Don know where the investigation was headed.

Trevor called Don Gino, he asked him to have the Chicago Appraisers Association send out someone to authenticate his etchings and lithographs. The Don was not happy. He listened to Trevor's day of research. There was total silence. Not a good sign. Trevor found the reason for Don Gino's infatuation with Dali's work. It was an obscure, virtually unknown, painting, Dali's **Vision of Hell**.

Don Gino provided some other clues into Dali's life. He noted that the critics, notably George Orwell, weren't fans of Dali's surrealism. This was the shock art of the time that made Dali famous. Orwell hated surrealism. Orwell hated Dali. Don Gino took note of this and decided to put the English writer in his place. No one disrespects the Don's favorite artist.

As Trevor took notes on Dali's illustrious career, he was struck by the degree of political intrigue surrounding the surrealist artist. Dali was criticized for fleeing to New York. He was further roasted for his flirtation with fascism in Franco's Spain. What were Dali's politics? Did it matter? Trevor had to figure it out.

There were Dali drawings that showed him dressed in an Arabic style. There was evidence that Dali purchased Arabic clothing from Al Hannah Islamic Clothing in Islamabad. This further deepened the mystery. Then Trevor found a brief passage that stated Dali privately dressed in an Arabic style.

Then it dawned on Trevor where Dali fit into the mystery. The three partners who founded Park Avenue Artists lived next door to Dali in New York until 1948. The three partners in Park Avenue Artists were still alive. They were in their late eighties. One of them was a burglar. Another was a forger. The last one laundered money. Park Avenue Artists somehow escaped the clutches of the FBI Art Fraud Unit. They were known forgers who escaped prosecution.

They were all fledgling art students when Dali lived in New York. One of them was also a highly successful cat burglar who stole a number of Dali's works. He worked for years with a young, unidentified college student. They split the profits from selling the stolen art. Trevor had no idea where the cat burglar or the student fit into the plot. He had to find the culprit. None of the three were scheduled to be on the Carnivolet ship. Trevor e-mailed Guitar Jac. He was given the job of flying to New York and learning the identity of the Park Avenue Artist founder. He needed to know if they were working with al Qaeda.

Trevor e-mailed Zandra Filippi again. He begged for her help. She texted: "What part of 'Fuck Off' don't you understand?" Trevor had to depend upon Guitar Jac. His assistant was on the case.

When Guitar Jac returned the e-mail with an encrypted reply, there was more information than Trevor could assimilate. The terrorists were using a number of Dali paintings as code words for their actions. The early part of the al Qaeda plan was to divert attention away from San Francisco. Their activity centered on the unseen and unknown Dali work, **Vision of Hell**. Trevor had no idea where the painting hung. An anonymous private collector owned it. Some critics believe that it didn't exist. Others saw it as an overrated Dali piece. It was a matter of mystery. It was also one key to the mystery.

There were other keys to the puzzle. Guitar Jac sent along two movies that portrayed Dali. The first, **Little Ashes,** had Robert Pattinson portraying Dali as a non-conventional thinker. Guitar Jac concluded that the al Qaeda nut cases received a message from Dali in the movie. What neither Guitar Jac nor Trevor could figure out was the message. In the second movie, Adrien Brody in Woody Allen's

Midnight in Paris portrayed Dali. In the Allen movie, Salvador Dali is a bit of a buffoon, but this hides a serious side. The al Qaeda terrorists were convinced that Allen was out to destroy Dali. They vowed to bomb every theater in Paris showing a Woody Allen movie. There was a rumor that Mia Farrow sent money to the terrorists. It was just a rumor.

There was another side of Dali that appealed to the al Qaeda terrorist cell. They viewed Dali as a visionary intellectual. This resulted from his mid-1930s attack on what he termed "bourgeoisie intellectuals." The al Qaeda terrorists envisioned Dali as the critic who made fun of and destroyed popular western intellectual movements.

In 1934, Dali criticized the surrealist movement for lack of originality, trite works and a dearth of imagination. The surrealists held a brief trial and expelled Dali. The surrealists sent a letter to Dali stating: "You have repeatedly been guilty of counter-revolutionary activity involving the painting, writing and drawing of improper thoughts and ideas." That letter went on to conclude that he was not welcome among the surrealists. Dali laughed.

As Trevor wandered around the San Francisco Public Library, he found another important Dali book. Trevor pulled it from the dusty stacks; it was Sigmund Freud's **Moses And Monotheism**. Dali wrote the prologue. He also illustrated it. The illustrations had a mystical Middle Eastern quality and had drawings that indicated Islamic forces were in the mix. The al Qaeda terrorists often sent e-mails using **Moses And Monotheism** as a starting point. Did anyone see the symbolism?

The Dali-Freud meeting in London is historically important. The painting **Metamorphosis of Narcissus**, completed in 1937, is one of Dali's most brilliant works. The other painting described in the Dali story, **Freud On The Couch**, is a fictional work necessary to the terrorist plot. Once again this painting provided a hidden message.

There were some important clues. The critics talked of Dali's dirty little secrets. These clandestine deeds were never fully explained. But it made for great reading. What Dali intended was to answer the critics who suggested that he never addressed "true history." What in the hell is true history? It is whatever the critics perceive. As Dali said: "It contained all the obsessions of my entry into Surrealism." What Dali didn't mention was that this was the period in which he memorized the Quran. Dali had a secret Muslim archive. He regularly updated it. He also began studying with an Imam. Those around Dali kept his behavior a secret, as it was not good for sales. What Trevor saw was a contradiction. Dali was a Catholic, a Muslim and a creative artist. When he talked of his Arabic roots, no one suspected he had a dual faith.

As Trevor studied Spanish history and Barcelona architecture, he realized that there were only four other creative figures, other than Dali, in fifteen hundred years of Barcelona history. They were the cellist Pau Casals, the artist Joan Miro, the architect Antoni Gaudi and the co-founder of the cubist movement, Pablo Picasso. They were the premier Barcelona artists. They represented a cultural pattern of innovation, defiance and abject creativity. In the art book section of the SF Public Library, Trevor found a large picture of Sagrada Familia. He took out his cell phone. He shot a picture of it. There was a clue there. He wasn't sure where or how to find it.

He went back to his library desk. The librarian handed him a cryptic note. It read: "Look for Casa Mila." It took some time but he found a picture and brief history of Gaudi's Barcelona Stone Quarry house. There was a loose photo placed in the book. Trevor couldn't believe it. Someone was helping him. Perhaps even watching him. The picture revealed a clue that Trevor realized would help him solve the crime. There was a man in the background of the picture who would be helping Trevor and Don Gino. The picture clearly showed the man talking to a known terrorist. The man knew Don Gino. He was a hidden Muslim. Trevor would deal with him in due time. He continued looking at the Dali clues.

When Trevor viewed Dali's 1950 painting **Honey Is Sweeter Than Blood**, he saw another important clue. There was the sign of a Mosque in the paintings corner. It was a self-confession. Trevor was exhausted. It was time to leave the library. He knew what was going to happen. He also had a good idea how Dali was connected to the nefarious bombings. He also had another thirty-five napkins filled with Dali material.

Trevor walked downtown and thought a lot about Dali. It was F. Scott Fitzgerald who said that the biographical novel was a bastardized form. The collection of Dali's art, writings and miscellany that Don Gino possessed was more than a lot of masterpieces, it was a guide to solving the al Qaeda terrorist attacks. There was nothing that interested Muslim Dali collectors more than his **Vision of Hell**.

When Dali's **Vision of Hell** disappeared for forty years, it reappeared in 1997, eighty years after the Virgin Mary appeared in Fatima. The al Qaeda terrorists viewed this as a message from Allah. That is if Allah spoke through the **New York Times**.

Trevor thought a lot about terrorism. It never ends. It had to be attacked. Individual terrorist campaigns are impossible to penetrate. Then again maybe Don Gino can penetrate the single cells. He told Trevor that he could. No one contradicts the Don.

The **Vision of Hell** came at a time that Dali returned briefly to surrealism. His Muslim followers saw Dali's actions as leaving Christianity for the ways of the Middle East. Art, after all, was in the mind of the beholder. A painting could be interpreted in any manner. The Muslim fanatics saw Dali's **Vision of Hell** as a battle cry to destroy Western Civilization.

As he reviewed his notes on Salvador Dali, Trevor realized that the art historian and psychoanalyst, Ernst Kris, had it right. Artists like Dali were subject to interpretation by their work not their lives. In Dali's case, the al Qaeda terrorists found hidden clues in his life that may not have existed. The image of the artist is what drives people. Trevor realized how image made Dali a best selling artist. He had the talent but the image spurred sales. It also created the al Qaeda terrorist cell that misinterpreted his art.

Dali was a Catalan. That is he identified with Barcelona and the cities around it. He also loved to shock the surrealists. One of the earliest indications of Dali's ability to shock came when he produced **The Lugubrious Game**. This Dali piece was part oil painting and part collage on cardboard. It enraged Andre Breton. The stained shorts of a man holding a fish net in the background was not considered art. At least not according to Breton. Dali told critics that this strange piece was the Catalan way of looking at life. Dali was Catalan first and foremost.

Then Trevor picked up a book by Sacha Fourier **Salvador Dali: The Fake Surrealist**. In his book Fourier told a story of how Breton raged on about Dali's lack of talent. He argued that Dali was little more than a poster boy for commercialism. He wasn't a true surrealist, Fourier argued. A month after Fourier's book was published, he was found dead in the back of the Notre Dame cathedral. A purple garrote remained around his lifeless body. Paris police report that the case remains unsolved. Trevor looked at the file on Fourier. He realized that no one disrespected Dali. Don Gino saw to it.

Trevor looked at his notes. He filled a small book. Who was Dali? The outlandish behavior, the eccentric art, the over the top clothes and the quips that never fit into the mainstream defined Salvador Dali. His personal vision disgusted the establishment. He simply smiled.

Dali's penetrating eyes, his ever present gold plated cane, his dramatic clothes and his visionary ideas set him apart. When the surrealists banned Dali from the movement it was for excessive individual creativity. This appealed to Trevor. Dali was a true eccentric. The poseurs, the art frauds and the personal fakes were everywhere in the art world.

Every day for Dali was about artistic survival. He was only as good as his last work. He liked to poke fun at the supposedly normal world. The vain and the pompous felt his barbs. Trevor thought of Bennie. Dali perfectly described him. He had never met him. The Bennie's where everywhere and Dali made fun of them. Dali never followed the rules. Bennie not only followed the rules, he glorified in them. As Oscar Wilde said: "There are people who know the price of everything and the value of nothing." Trevor wondered if Wilde was writing about Bennie. Dali was the true definition of an eccentric. How and why the al Qaeda terrorists identified with him remained a mystery. But they did.

Trevor realized that in many ways Salvador Dali was his own biographer. He created many of the myths and hid the realities of his life. There was a mysterious interpretation of Dali's life connected to the Witches of Llers.

CHAPTER SIX

The Witches Of Llers

"Those who do not want to imitate anything, produce nothing."
Salvador Dali

In North East Spain the small Catalan town of Llers stands on a hill overlooking the plain of the Upper Emporda landscape. The town was destroyed during the Spanish Civil War. There are legends that the local witches continue to haunt the countryside.

The tall African American stood on the remains of this little Catalan town. He looked around.

"Can I help you sir?" a swarthy Spaniard asked.

The African American looked at the young man. He was stocky but harmless looking. He wanted to help. "Yes, I'm looking for some town records."

"Town records?"

"I need to find out about the Witches of Llers."

"I suggest that you purchase a copy of Carles Fages de Climent's book **The Witches of Llers**. Dali illustrated the book."

"Yes, I have it," the American said.

"What else do you want?"

"I need information on Dali's Muslim heritage."

"Muslim heritage?" The Spaniard looked puzzled.

"I am looking for Silvestre Dali Raguer."

"I can take you to the town journals." The Spaniard beckoned and the large African American walked to a small shed. The parish records revealed Silvestre Dali Raguer moved to Cadaques. It also noted that he was a devout Muslim. The African American had found his smoking gun. Salvador Dali's lineage was one tied to the Quran and Allah's wishes. The African American's al Qaeda cell would awaken the Spanish Muslims to their real history. The key to this revelation came from the Witches of Llers. The reason was a simple one.

The Witches of Llers were Muslims. When the Dali family moved some forty miles to Cadaques their Llers roots ended. Their Catholicism became the dominant religion. The truth was they were Muslims. Secret Muslims who hated Spain. Catholicism was a needed cover in the intolerant Spanish countryside.

The expensively dressed and elegant American drove from Cadaques to Figueres. It was only forty miles. Then the American began collecting biographical material on Salvador Dali. He discovered that his first teacher, known simply as Esteban Trayter-Colomer, had Dali secretly read the Quran. Dali's teacher was also a proclaimed atheist. This was a ruse to hide his devotion to the Muslim way of life.

It was Dali's Arabic roots that Trayter-Colomer emphasized. No one realized that Salvador Dali was a closet Muslim. The African American discovered that Dali was placed in the care of the Christian Brothers, a French teaching order, when he was only six years old. He showed signs of abnormal religious thoughts. It was at this point, the American reasoned, that Dali hid his religious orientation. He was not a good Catholic. His famous painting, **Vision of Hell**, was meant to chastise the church not praise it. It was an iconic Muslim art piece.

The tall African American left Figueres and drove back to Barcelona. He checked into the Hotel Condes de Barcelona and walked to the roof top bar. He was a good Muslim, but having a drink hid his true identify. The African American sat on the rooftop bar looking out at the famous Gaudi building La Pedrera. That monument was safe. He thought about his plan. He needed to arm his men. It would take money to blow up Sagrada Familia as well as the San Francisco landmark. He would bury Don Gino Landry in his self-righteous purple suit. He vowed to destroy the heretofore-unseen Dali painting **Vision of Hell**. It would be a fitting end to Don Gino Landry and his bastardized Catholic faith.

The tall African American disapproved of Don Gino's ostentatious life style, his larger than life dinners with Mayors, Senators, Governors, actors and President Barack Obama. Don Gino was a crime boss. This infuriated the elegantly dressed African American.

After he left the hotel, the quiet African American flew in his private jet to New York City. He was there to meet Donald Trump. Smith used his friendship with the Donald to obscure his fanatical Muslim roots. He hated liberals. He hated America. He hated affirmative action. He hated Obamacare. No one realized the extent of his Muslim fanaticism.

Smith anonymously sent money to the 1,200 U. S. Mosques. Since 9-11, 960 new Mosques were built in America and Smith quietly brought in Wahhabi clerics who preach the extreme brand of Islam practiced in Saudi Arabia. Muslim lawyers were in court attempting to impose Sharia law in the U. S. James Smith was in the forefront of the attack on America values.

As a respected businessman, philanthropist and member of President Barack Obama's re-election campaign, Smith had the perfect cover. He was frequently seen in the presence of Attorney General Eric Holder. The chief law enforcement officer had no idea that he had lunches with one of America's extreme terrorists. The Democrats were too politically correct to examine Smith's radicalism.

He didn't stand out. Despite his stylish Armani suit, his closely cropped hair and his smooth walk, he had the ability to blend into the crowd. Even in Barcelona he looked like just another tourist. He had good looks to go with his height. He talked in a soft ingratiating manner. He was no threat. He was after all African American.

It was time to prepare for his cruise on the Carnivolet Line from Tampa to Barcelona. He would set up the plan to destroy Gaudi's most prized architectural feat, Sagrada Familia. In 2010, the Pope consecrated it, and it opened as a church. It was the final blasphemy. The Catholic Church would pay. The San Francisco mafia figure, Don Gino Landry, would come to a quick end. The arrogant Italian in the gaudy purple clothing needed to be taught humility. Perhaps death was the ultimate humility.

Then the tall African American opened his cell phone and looked lovingly at Dali's **Vision of Hell**, it was a picture that he loved. The capitalistic west was ruining the world. Polluting it with infidel ideas. There was symbolism in Dali's work that prompted the African American to view the end of the decadent west.

The forks in **Vision of Hell** provided a sign that Christianity would soon be dealt a fatal blow. At least this was Dali's view. When Dali finished the painting, he said that it expressed his unique view that "a love of everything that is gilded and excessive; my passion for luxury and my love of Oriental clothes...." For the al Qaeda cell based on Dali's work, **Vision of Hell**, was a portent of things to come. The sharp forks would soon puncture the smug Catholic ideology that dominated the world.

Dali's **Vision of Hell** was a direct connection to his Muslim past. A connection that the young man from Alabama would soon present to the world.

The critics never realized the connection of **Vision of Hell** to Dali's political radicalism. The 1962, **Vision of Hell**, painting was obscure and hardly noticed. The image of melting clocks in **The Persistence of Memory** blinded the critics to Dali's Muslim sympathies. It was the perfect irony as no one suspected his religious following.

One critic spoke of Salvador Dali's "shameful life." That shame, this critic suggested, came from Dali's statement that he was neither a Spaniard nor a Catalan. Dali insisted on his Moorish heritage. He said that when the Moors invaded Spain in AD 711, the Dali family tree began with "Arab blood." The tall African American agreed with this conclusion. Dali was caught in the Catalan nationalistic web. He was more of an Arab than a Spaniard. The Witches of Llers proved that. By researching the Witches of Llers there was no question of Dali's Moorish connection.

The African American wasn't sure what Dali's **Vision of Hell** represented. The San Francisco Private Investigator, Trevor Blake III, was researching the work. Maybe he could provide a clue. The African American terrorist had Blake followed and he would monitor his activity.

CHAPTER SEVEN

Dali's Vision Of Hell

"Dali helped to initiate today's antiheroic mode of autobiography...the sex centered biographical interpretation of artists and art so prevalent since the 1960s." Charles Stuckey

Trevor Blake III left the San Francisco Public Library with a Xerox of the painting that put Don Gino on the trail of collecting Salvador Dali. That painting was **Vision of Hell**. The Don loved surrealistic art. He spent hours reading about the surrealists. Don Gino was also a good Catholic. So was Dali. When Padre Pio convinced Dali to paint his **Vision of Hell**, no one realized the furor that unfolded. Dali's work was a simple look at Sister Lucia's description of the third apparition of Our Lady Mary Magdalene.

In previous paintings of the Virgin Mary, Dali used his wife, Gala, as the model. His increasingly devout religious nature prevented him from employing his wife as a model. Don Gino told me that he had read everything he could on Dali's **Vision of Hell**. I remembered that Don Gino considered it a masterpiece. According to the Don, it was above criticism. Then he came across George Orwell's insensitive attack on Dali's painting and reputation. Don Gino took action. Trevor had been in Don Gino's house and witnessed his disgust with Orwell.

To get even with Orwell, Don Gino mounted a publicity campaign to get a sentence from Orwell's novel **1984** named the worst sentence to begin a book. The phrase from **1984** read: "It was a bright and cold day in April, and the clocks were striking thirteen." The **New York**

Times, with prodding from Don Gino, named this sentence the worst opening line in a novel. The Don wasn't through. He approached the American Grammar Association who named **1984** the worst punctuated best seller.

When the Orwell biographers began their work, Don Gino was the first person they encountered. In a series of letters, as well as informational files on Orwell, sent to Orwell's official biographer, Bernard Crick, Don Gino pointed out that Orwell's hatred for Spanish politics led him to unfairly criticize Dali. He didn't know Dali, and he had no idea about his work. Crick, a political scientist, wrote back with a note thanking the Don for his excellent information. He planned to use it in his book.

Don Gino had a series of dartboards in his house with the face of the **1984** novelist on it. He threw darts daily at Orwell for criticizing Dali. Orwell accused Dali of "scuttling off like a rat as soon as France was in danger." This criticism from Orwell came during World War II. It was Orwell's opinion that Dali made so much money in pre-World War II France that he should have been more supportive of the French underground. Orwell observed that Dali wanted to be close to a good cook, and he feared for his personal safety. So he moved to New York City. A coward's move, Orwell said. Don Gino was incensed with Orwell's writings and public statements. He would teach the crabby Englishman a lesson. This was a means of damaging his reputation posthumously causing his books to decline in sales.

Unlike others, Don Gino saw a serious side to surrealism. The puns, double entendres, the bizarre costumes, the fractured use of language, the absurd dress, the lack of gracious manners and Dali's morals of an alley cat had a serious side. It was Dali's way of criticizing which brought hostile reaction from the critics. Don Gino saw it differently. He envisioned Dali's unique art as a blueprint for criticizing society. The prime example of not understanding different forms of culture came when Don Gino talked with Bennie about art.

Don Gino said that he loved his friend Bennie, but his lack of culture doomed Bennie to being a "white bread American." That is a person who is bright, trite, predictable and without imagination. Bennie talked Stanford University football around Don Gino. Then much to Don Gino's surprise, he found out that Bennie had a master's degree in political science from Stanford. Bennie, the consummate businessman and multi-millionaire, was embarrassed to admit that he studied an academic subject. When Don Gino discovered the peculiarities of Bennie's life, he realized that Bennie had an extraordinary and well-developed intellect.

Bennie provided another service to Don Gino. He made a computer list of everyone who criticized or pilloried Dali's work. When people criticized Dali, it was Don Gino who got angry. He also got even. George Orwell paid for his criticism. As did every other critic.

Don Gino was so angry that every copy of an Orwell book was removed from the San Francisco Public Library. No one knew how he did this. The City Librarian, Marilyn Sowell, mysteriously came into a large sum of money. She purchased a penthouse with her husband on Nob Hill on an eighty thousand dollar a year salary. Rumor had it that Don Gino thanked her for removing Orwell's books. His generosity prompted others to denounce Orwell. Philip Kaufman, the American film director, said that Orwell's books weren't adapted for the movies. Kaufman said: "Orwell is the best mind never to leave grammar school." There were those who took exception to these comments.

In London, two homes that were once Orwell's were burned to the ground. When they were rebuilt they were burned again and only a purple rose was left at the fire. London police stated that the arson crimes remain unsolved.

When Don Gino found out that Orwell wrote in a review of Dali's autobiography that Dali was "a disgusting human being," he had Orwell's closest English relative, Dave Churchill Williams, exiled to a small island off the coast of Spain. Williams' blues collection was auctioned off, and the proceeds went to a Dali scholarship at Oxford University. Williams then had to write a book on Dali's redemptive qualities. It is still in progress and Williams is ninety-one years old. Fortunately, he is alive.

When Orwell wrote a critical essay on Dali, "Benefit of Clergy: Some Notes on Salvador Dali," published in 1944, Don Gino went on e-bay, other book auction sites, bookstores on line and purchased more than five thousand copies of this attack on Dali. Don Gino burnt every last copy. He was furious with George Orwell. He would have killed him, but Orwell was already dead.

Then Don Gino donated $200,000 to a brilliant, but maladjusted, Stanford University graduate student, Popkins Buddinsky, who completed a PhD dissertation questioning the political accuracy of Orwell's writings. The dissertation won the American Literary Guild prize for criticism. Buddinsky's next book, **The Pope Is A Liar**, was an attempt to historically disavow the importance of the Pope in Western Civilization. It didn't sell well. A year later, Buddinsky was found dead in San Francisco's Castro District. It was a hate crime. A purple handkerchief in his mouth caused him to suffocate to death. Buddinsky was found wearing a purple dress. His hair was dyed purple and he had purple fingernails. The case remains unsolved. Most people said good riddance. The guy was an academic nut.

Don Gino made notes over the years about George Orwell. The critics called Orwell a "great political journalist." To Don Gino, he was no more than a hack appealing to the masses. When Orwell wrote: "Dali's works are diseased and disgusting, and any investigation ought to start out from that fact," three well-known critics agreed with Orwell. Don Gino was enraged over this statement. He tracked down the three critics in the U. K., who had reviewed Orwell's work, and they were beaten to a pulp in a dark London alley. After that there was no more criticism about Dali in their reviews.

The protective side to Don Gino regarding Salvador Dali made sure there was no criticism of Dali. It was a matter of religion to the Don. He looked at his purple cane. This was just one of many influences that Dali had upon the stylish San Franciscan.

In the final act of revenge, Don Gino had George Orwell's grave painted with a purple rainbow. This was done each year on the anniversary of the publication of his 1944 article criticizing Dali.

Dali's work expressed the artistic subconscious nature of people. Don Gino believed that he had to unlock his subconscious inner-self. He envisioned Dali as the person who could help him accomplish this task. Dali's work looked at reality. This was another of Don Gino's passions. He was obsessed with reality.

From 1960 to 1962, when Dali painted **The Vision of Hell**, it showed arrows and demons pointing to hell. The eight carving forks piercing tormented flesh unnerved the clergy. The Catholic Church, who commissioned the work, never accepted it. The Catholic Clergy suggested that the demons plunged into fire and the arrow like lines pointing to hell were a pagan ritual. It was too graphic and too realistic. From time to time the Catholic hierarchy trotted out experts to say that the church was reevaluating Dali's work. Father Ludwig Isaac stated: "The church appreciates Dali, we are still revaluating some of his work." Another Catholic priest, Schwarcz Harven, a Polish Bishop, said: "**Vision of Hell** may not exist. We are not sure that Dali painted it." This was a code message that the church would not accept **The Vision of Hell**. The painting now sat in the private home of a Delaware collector. It was on the FBI's watch list for stolen art. This seemed strange as the Catholic Church acted like Dali's painting didn't exist. That is unless someone found it, auctioned it and donated the proceeds to the Catholic Church.

The truth is that **Vision of Hell** vanished and the painting didn't resurface until more than three decades after it was completed.

Don Gino had the rough sketch and a finished pencil drawing of **The Vision of Hell**. These two pieces had comments from the Pope on the back, and they were used to reconfigure the final painting. Don Gino was upset that the Catholic hierarchy wouldn't recognize Dali's worshipful tribute. He loved his church. He also loved Dali's art. It was a quandary.

Don Gino was intrigued that Dali believed that everyone had a personal flame related to creativity. He also liked the idea that **The Vision of Hell** was inspired by three Sheppard children, who told the story of Dali's tortured and troublesome Catholic beliefs. Don Gino experienced the same feelings. When Dali considered the afterlife a subject for his art, Don Gino agreed. The Don also spent an inordinate amount of time thinking about and analyzing death. This trait he had in common with Dali.

It wasn't just Dali's art that influenced Don Gino. He also affected his love for wearing a long cape, carrying a walking stick and grooming a waxed moustache. He was not an outrageous person like Dali. There were parts of Dali's personality that Don Gino abhorred. When Dali gave Mia Farrow an art piece that was a beautifully painted bottle with a dead mouse inside, Don Gino paid Farrow $100,000 for the bottle. He destroyed it. Mia Farrow took Liam Neeson to Paris for a week. She sent Don Gino a thank you note.

The **Vision of Hell** remained the catalyst to Don Gino's collector mania. Whoever stole it would have to reckon with a tragic fate. Don Gino had a very short fuse when it came to those who disrespected Dali.

After visits to Port Lligat, Barcelona, Figueres and other parts of Spain, Don Gino flew to San Francisco. His purple limousine whisked him home to Washington Street. He was tired but ready for the challenge of destroying Dali's enemies. As he entered his house, his neighbor Danielle Steel waved. Don Gino vowed to force her to read all her books. It would be punishment for the friendly waves. She really wanted to know about his private life. Good luck.

Don Gino's Washington Street home was modified to make his Dali collection stand out. He also had private rooms for the special Dali pieces. Some critics called these stolen or ill bought art objects. Don Gino laughed. If they only knew about his Dali collection, they would realize his fascination with the Spanish artist. He was also the protector of Dali's legacy.

Don Gino walked into a small, hidden room. He pressed a button on the wall. It opened a small door. It was a ten by ten room with one rough sketch and one painting. Dali's **Portrait Of A Pope** hung on the far wall. The sketch for the original was in a glass case with a special light. The room was temperature controlled. This was Don Gino's second favorite Dali piece.

Portrait Of A Pope, oil on canvas, 104 by 86 centimeters, was painted in Port Lligat during the later part of Dali's creative life. He attempted to make amends with the Catholic Church. His behavior was less than exemplary. The church was privately critical of Dali's work. But the Cardinals were mute on Dali. He attempted to ingratiate himself with the Catholic hierarchy with **Portrait Of A Pope**. When Dali presented the painting to Father Guido Sarducci, there was a gasp.

Sarducci said: "Is this a comedy piece?"

Dali responded: "Make of it what you may." Sarducci countered: "Why is Gala in the painting?"

"Why not?" Dali left in a huff.

The Catholic Church responded with disdain. Dali's use of the title **Portrait Of A Pope** was a misnomer. He was inherently critical of Catholicism. Dali's Muslim admirers silently approved. The Vatican hated it. There was another religious painting that Dali worked on during the same period from 1958 to 1960. He titled this painting, **The Ecumenical Council**, and he presented it to the Pope. There was some joy in the Vatican, as **The Ecumenical Council** painting was more representative of the Pope. It was also worth millions.

When Pope John XXIII was elected in 1958, Dali spent two years finishing the painting. Pope John XXIII described Dali's **The Ecumenical Council** as "an assemblage of too many religious scenes and symbols that did little to help the church's image." It was the artist Diego Velasquez that Dali was paying homage to in the painting.

Dali told friends that **Portrait Of A Pope** was for sale. It was designed to show that Velasquez blended art and religion. This was Dali's approach to art.

Portrait Of A Pope didn't cause a stir. No one knew that it existed. It was stolen upon completion. Dali was private about his work. No one knew about it. The painting wound up in a New York Mafia warehouse. When Dali's **Sistine Madonna** was exhibited at New York's 1960 International Surrealism Exhibition, the Mafia announced that **Portrait Of A Pope** was available. There was another Dali portrait from 1959, **The Discovery of America By Christopher Columbus** that took attention away from his other work. This painting commissioned for the billionaire Huntington Hartford for the opening of his Museum Gallery of Modern Art on Columbus Circle in New York had a sign for Smith and his al Qaeda terrorists. Smith interpreted

Gala's appearance in the painting twice, first as the Virgin Mary and secondly as a Saint, that violence was the next step. There was too much freedom in Dali's work. He would not be pleased that he was restricted artistically.

When a Barcelona art dealer purchased **Portrait Of A Pope** for a hefty sum, there was an immediate inquiry from a San Francisco collector. No one realized that the money was transferred to a Grand Cayman account controlled by James Smith.

When Don Gino bought it for a modest sum, he was unaware of its connection to terrorism. The Barcelona art dealer sold it quickly and inexpensively. The rumor was that the art dealer feared for his health.

Don Gino's will donated his art to the San Francisco Catholic Archdiocese. The stipulation was that any money raised be used to repair, refurbish and maintain the Mission Delores. This was the Franciscan Mission neighborhood where Don Gino's legitimate businesses operated.

The Mission District is home to Gino's Gourmet Dog Food, Gino's Organic Cleaners, Gino's Jazz Bar and Gino's Gluten Free Delicatessen. He launders his protection and gambling money through these businesses. The problem is that all his legitimate businesses made excessive profits. He was looking to establish a bank. It was the only way that he could launder money from his various criminal enterprises. Don Gino didn't consider himself a criminal. Prostitution, murder and drug dealing were not allowed in the Mission District. When Ed Juarez came in with his Columbian drugs, young Ed died in a car crash. The police investigated and found out that he had been shot twice. A purple rose was next to his lifeless body. The San Francisco Police Department closed the case. They found no evidence of foul play. The next night the police commissioner was seen having dinner with Don Gino. The Mission District wasn't safe for criminals. Don Gino saw to it. He protected the Mission Delores.

As a religious man, Don Gino was troubled by the controversies surrounding privacy. Since the Wiki Leaks, the release of sensitive government spying information, and the continual threat of violence on U. S. soil made Don Gino nervous. He had those who leaked sensitive government information exterminated. He needed to enter a confessional and let a priest wash away his sins. There were many sins and more to come. Don Gino had a conscience. No one knew the depth of his religious fervor. They would soon find out.

He had his driver take him down to the Saint Vincent De Paul Church at 2320 Green Street. When he entered the confessional, Don Gino smelled a cigarette. It was Father Burton who favored the French Gitano's. They were the cigarettes of the aristocrat.

Don Gino said: "Father I have sinned."

"Tell me, son and I will forgive you."

They had a long discussion and Don Gino apologized for those that he had killed, and those who would die at his hand in the next few weeks. They talked at length about evil and good. When Don Gino finished the priest had a parting comment.

"My son, the path to forgiveness is a strange journey. You are on it."

"What should I do, Father?"

"Nothing. You are serving God in a different manner. Say 25 hail Mary's for a week and provide new bingo tables for our parish."

"Thank you, Father." Don Gino realized that he needed another cleansing confession. He would have to go to the Mission District to have his soul rectified once again. He walked home. He needed time to think. Father Kenneth Westmont smiled. He watched Don Gino walk home to his palatial mansion. It was typical of Don Gino to have two confessions in a day. The Don never made it home as his purple limousine picked him up a block from the church.

The next morning twenty new bingo tables, a movie theater quality sound system, a set of one thousand bingo cards and fifty thousand specially designed bingo chips for the cards were delivered to Saint Vincent De Paul. An envelope with $100,000 in cash was handed to Father Westmont. He smiled. Don Gino was a good Catholic.

Don Gino had Catholic guilt. He reflected on Father Westmont's statement. Westmont said: "Confession brings reconciliation with your soul." Don Gino smiled. He would find absolution and reconciliation. Then he would kill the terrorists. Absolution was available 24-7.

CHAPTER EIGHT

Don Gino Confesses His Sins Again

"People love mystery, and that is why they love my paintings."
Salvador Dali

Don Gino Landry sits in the back seat of his purple limousine. He looks troubled. The driver turns into his driveway. He looks disgustingly next-door and waves to his neighbor, Danielle Steel, who is a best selling writer who lets her dog do his business on his lawn. He can't keep track of her husbands. They seem to change weekly. Don Gino did like the husband who was paroled from San Quentin. The tragedy is that Danielle Steel is his best neighbor. She told him that he would never be a character in her books. No one disrespects the Don.

On the other side of his palatial mansion, Sharon Stone lives without a husband. She is between significant others, as they say in Hollywood, and she appears unusually happy. When they divorced, Stone called her newspaper mogul husband, Phil Bronstein, a person who had only one thing in mind. Don Gino laughed. He recalled that Bronstein was nominated for a Pulitzer Prize for international reporting. Good thing he didn't win it. He didn't deserve it. Don Gino liked Stone. Everyone thought that she was the problem. If they only knew the truth about the marriage. Sharon Stone never said a word. Don Gino was not happy. He knew the truth.

Don Gino looks across the street. The neighbor had his home at 2090 Washington Avenue, the most exclusive Presidio Heights home, on the market for twenty-eight million. His neighbor, Bill Cunningham, is marrying a forty-year-old pole dancer. She has outgrown dancing half naked in front of young men. Now she would dance fully naked in front of an old man. A rich old man. An old man with a bad heart. She smiled. In a few years, she would be a wealthy widow.

You can't marry a forty-year old retired pole dancer and keep her happy. That is if you are in your seventies. Cunningham works out twice a day. He also takes Viagra, vitamin supplements and he has a doctor on a daily retainer. When he has his final heart attack, he will die happy. His bride to be is a beauty. Her name is Candy. Fitting! Appropriate! When the topless craze ended in San Francisco, she became a waitress at Enrico's. When Bill met her, he fell head over heels in love and proposed. She accepted. His neighbor was having a big party to celebrate the wedding. The odds in Las Vegas were three to one that he wouldn't live for another two years. The odds were also that he would be happy during the next two years. Don Gino got ready for his neighbor's party.

The neighbors often remark that Don Gino is reclusive. His music is never too loud. His lifestyle is quiet. His lack of critical comments worries the neighbors. Danielle Steel labeled him "the man who is invisible." San Francisco's Pacific Heights is snobbish, prickly and a group of self-indulgent people. But no one disrespects the Don.

When he surveys his neighborhood, Don Gino sees wealth, shortsighted attitudes, conservative Republican politics and legal business criminals. Bennie and Bertie would fit in fine. The problem is that they don't have enough money for Pacific Heights. They also don't have the proper education. They also don't have the requisite social skills. They dress more like Ma and Pa Kettle than Donald Trump. Bennie loves to mix striped pants with a plaid shirt.

They do have Bennie's magic show. Danielle Steel personally came over to Don Gino's house and asked him not to have Bennie drive his eighteen-year-old Lexus into the neighborhood. A Bank of America V. P. circulated a petition amongst Don Gino's neighbors requesting that he cease and desist from bringing large art items into his house after midnight. The effete corporate executive worried that his art might be stolen. It was. Surprise! A small Asian man was seen loading art into his car. The case remains unsolved.

The real problem is that the Pacific Heights crowd looks down on Don Gino. The loan sharking, the protection money and the support for legitimate businesses make him a more honest businessman than his friends at Bank of America. But he has business to take care of before Bill Cunningham's party.

After Don Gino returns home from a day of business in the Mission District, he is cranky. He is also concerned about the al Qaeda terrorists. No one realizes that he is working for the FBI, the Office of Homeland Security and the CIA. When Don Gino walks into his palatial home, the butler and maid greet him. They maintain a discreet distance. He is not happy. They know his moods.

He slowly walks up the stairs to the second floor. Don Gino takes a small key and unlocks a room. He quickly walks inside and looks at his art. Salvador Dali produced 1500 paintings. Don Gino has thirty and they fill two rooms. There is also a secret room for the special items. Dali's paintings are large and they are so magnificent that Don Gino feels lost in their fertile imagination. It isn't Dali's paintings that Don Gino covets. He collects Dali sketches and drawings produced in their roughest form.

He is the only person in the world who knows about the extensive sketches of Salvador Dali. After taking out a huge manila folder, Don Gino gazes at a rough drawing for Dali's masterpiece **A Vision of Hell**. He walks over and admires the sketch. The Dali drawing is unique, as it is a combination of pen and pencil. It was meant for Dali's eyes, no one else was to see it. There is no order and little cohesion in early Dali drawings. This is what Don Gino loves about his collection. It is unique. No one has these art pieces. Don Gino lights a small cigar. He blows the blue smoke toward the ceiling. He smiles. Dali was a genius. Someone was sullying his reputation. Don Gino decided to take action. No one disrespects Salvador Dali. Or for that matter Don Gino.

He hired Trevor Blake III to get next to the art forgers. In the San Francisco law enforcement community, Trevor was not well respected. Don Gino knew better as Trevor's research and detecting methods made him a skilled private investigator. His sidekick, Guitar Jac, was an even better investigator and surveillance person. The only problem was Blake's private life. He loved the San Francisco bars, and he was regularly seen with some of the most beautiful women in the city. How did he do it? No one knew.

Don Gino saw Trevor as the front man. He would provide the eyes and ears to finding the al Qaeda terrorist cell and its targets. No one suspected Trevor's skill. He didn't have the respect that he deserved. FBI agent Chastain Johnson at times made fun of him. No one knew that much of Don Gino's information about terrorists came directly from Guitar Jac and Trevor Blake III.

What infuriated Don Gino was that there were Muslim terrorists using the art world to funnel money into al Qaeda. Muslims were intent upon blaming Catholics for terrorist attacks. Don Gino would kill every one of the bastards. His conscience bothered him. It was time to go to confession. He would do it tomorrow. When he felt Catholic guilt, Don Gino turned to the confessional.

As Don Gino sat in his study-art room, he prepared a plan to get rid of the al Qaeda terrorists. He loved President Barack Obama, but he thought that the president was too centrist, too soft on the Muslims and too accommodating. He was a good man. That was his problem.

Don Gino took two folders from his desk. One was marked "CIA Confidential." The other had the notation: "FBI: al Qaeda Domestic Concerns." He tucked both files in a purple leather brief case. He had business to conduct. He would figure out his plan for the terrorists. He left the house and walked to his limousine.

While riding in the purple limousine, Don Gino made notes. He understood the problem. Salvador Dali's palatial Figueres home produced the art that was used to fund Muslim extremism. Since Dali died in 1989, he remained an elusive and maligned historical artist. Even though he had been dead for almost thirty years, new Dali paintings emerged, his books were reprinted and his lithographs stormed the market place. The business of counterfeits was a bustling criminal enterprise. How could Dali's legacy be connected to terrorists? Don Gino wasn't sure of the reason.

The rough sketches of Dali's finished products remain the basis of Don Gino's collection. He purchased many of these from Dali's butler. Don Gino bought the first one when he was twenty-one and now more than thirty years later he was the proud owner of three of Dali's sketches from **The Persistence of Memory**. These sketches were completed in 1931. When Dali displayed a soft melting pocket watch, he took the art world by storm. When the Julian Levy Gallery showed the piece in 1932, there were negative comments about the quality of the preliminary sketches. Don Gino owned those early sketches. There were three valued at one million dollars each. The melting pocket watches demonstrated Dali's disdain for time. As Dali completed the three preliminary sketches, he defined his limited sense of time.

What Don Gino loved about Dali was the artist's insistence that time is neither rigid nor deterministic. Unlike his Pacific Heights neighbors, who were rigid and deterministic, Don Gino had a sense of adventure.

Don Gino smiled when he thought about one preliminary sketch in pencil in his private gallery. This priceless sketch was for Dali's **The Crucifixion**. This 1954 work began as **Christ On the Cross**. Dali abandoned it, and his English butler; David Churchill Williams, sent it to his home in Guildford. In this London suburb, Williams stored Dali originals that he auctioned off privately after Dali's death. Don Gino paid one million dollars for it. It was a rough sketch for Dali's secret masterpiece **Vision of Hell**. This was the piece that the Catholic Church commissioned and rejected. The preliminary sketch was close to the finished product. It was a Dali original that escaped the critics. This was the genius of Don Gino's collection. He had Dali's that none of the critics had seen. These sketches differed vastly from the finished product.

One of the things that Don Gino loved to do was to open his Blackberry and admire Dali's rough sketches. Only a few of his friends have seen the collection. It is private. Don Gino is private. **The Vision**

of Hell stood out with its fierce Christian symbolism. The Catholic Church failed to recognize it. The Dali sketches gave Don Gino a purpose.

When Don Gino drove to the Mission Delores, he had to confess his sins. His Catholic guilt was overwhelming. He had plans for extraordinary sins. He hadn't committed these sins. The prospect of implementing them weighed heavily on his soul. He worshipped at the Catholic Church closest to the Mission Delores. Every time he drove by the Mission Delores, he celebrated the triumphs of Catholicism. Spaniards representing the Pope and the King of Spain settled what became the Golden State.

When the Spaniards founded Yerba Buena, it was a revelation for the Franciscan Order. The area was fertile in agriculture, abundant in fishing and the ready supply of timber provided building materials. The Franciscan Order made a pact with the Ohlone Indians. They began the process of creating the Catholic city soon to be known as Yerba Buena and then San Francisco. Don Gino loved the City. He also loved his country. He was going to end a terrorist threat. He had to confess his future sins time and time again.

The green light was on in the confessional. Don Gino walked in and talked for ten minutes. The Don liked to confess before he killed. When Dino Gino left the confessional, he felt like a new man. The priest explained forward forgiveness. The notion that when evil is present a person may act for just a moment apart from Catholic teachings. This is exactly what Don Gino needed. He felt at ease with a moment away from Catholic doctrine to protect America. He would kill for the Pope.

The Don had some other concerns. He was in the process of collecting newly discovered Dali's. He received a first edition of **Les Vins de Gala (Gala's Wines)** from a New York mafia boss. On the occasion of his fifty-seventh birthday on July 4, Don Gino was given the drawings that Dali made to illustrate Dante's **The Divine Comedy**. A Barcelona crime family shipped them to San Francisco and Don Gino added these illustrations to his private Dali room.

Don Gino spent hours examining and reorganizing his Salvador Dali collection. He would find out who was forging, who was selling, who was prospering and why they were making money from Dali. Then he would kill them. The Don smiled and lit a small cigar.

He decided to purchase a second home in the Mission District. He needed a place to get away from Washington Street. In the Mission, he could plan and carry out his various business plans. He would also have a place to plan to defeat the al Qaeda terrorists.

Don Gino called his realtor and described what he wanted. Cost was no object. The realtor assured him that he would be purchasing the highest priced home in the Mission, if not in San Francisco. Don Gino smiled. It would be good for his image. It would also be good to get rid of the excessive cash that was building up in his home safe, bank account and businesses.

Don Gino called Trevor. They talked about the plan to uncover the al Qaeda terrorist's money laundering plan on the Carnivolet line. Trevor informed Don Gino that he had a plan. He would implement it on the cruise to Barcelona.

He told Trevor to look for anything that Bennie and Bernie had in their house on al Qaeda. Trevor was puzzled. How did Don Gino know that Trevor was taking care of Bennie and Bertie's palatial mansion? Perhaps Bennie was the key to finding out what was going on with the al Qaeda terrorists. Who knows!

CHAPTER NINE

My Weekend Without Bennie And Bertie: Discovering Omar Abdul Hammadi

"There's only one difference between a madman and me. The madman thinks he is sane. I know I'm mad." Salvador Dali

Bennie and Bertie wanted me to take care of their home. They needed a house sitter. I needed to plan my part of the al Qaeda mystery. I needed to solve the crime. So I returned for a second visit. Their home is tranquil, located in a wooded enclave north of San Francisco. Where Bennie and Bertie live there is a block of old white people who hate minorities, CNN, Muslims, Democrats, legalized Marijuana shops, heavy metal music, Led Zeppelin and President Obama. They spend all day watching Fox TV New. Bennie established the Bill O'Reilly Fan Club in Mill Valley. Their slogan was "Fair and Balanced To Get Osama Out of the White House." When Bennie said "Osama," he got a big smile. They talked of taking America back. They thought that it had been stolen. Bennie and Bertie's street was appropriately named Reactionary Lane. It was in the heart of white Mill Valley conservative reaction.

For some unexplainable reason, Carlos Santana lives on Reactionary Lane, but rumor had it that he is the exception to the rule. Bonnie Raitt also lives on the street. She petitioned the Mill Valley Town Council to change the street name. They are considering it. Bennie threatened to sue. He is taking America back.

Bennie and Bertie told Trevor to enjoy Mill Valley. They also said "don't snoop." He would. It had everything. There was a Trader Joe's, a Penny's, Target, a Sam's Club and a Wal Mart. As Bennie said: "It doesn't' get any better than that." Rich white people with an attitude. They are Bennie's God's. Trevor realized that he would never be in the mix. But a $500 a month San Francisco apartment prevented any criticism.

Bennie said: "We have a great community, there are no Communists, Socialists, labor union members or Negroes." I had to tell Bennie that African American was the proper term. Bennie loved the fact that they didn't have a Whole Foods. "That store is for stupid white liberals, Socialists and neo-Communists." I wondered what was a neo-Communist?

When I left my Chestnut Street apartment to drive back to Mill Valley, a good-looking girl jogged by and flipped me the finger. It sure looked like Zandra Filippi. I suppose she is still upset over our drunken night in my bed. Or was it her bed? She said that it didn't matter. The night was a loss leader. I wasn't sure what that meant. Maybe the world's second greatest detective wasn't the world's greatest lover. Then again!

I drove over the Golden Gate Bridge. People no longer collected the tolls. I put money into a machine with a sexy, female voice. I talked to the machine. I asked her if we could get married. She didn't answer.

As I drove to Bennie and Bertie's, I remembered Don Gino making it clear that the case was one involving illegal money laundering and intrigue by al Qaeda. I wasn't sure what was going on, but I am a detective. I will figure it out. But first I was going to enjoy Mill Valley. It is a small boutique town next to Sausalito.

My car eased down to Mill Valley and I met John Goddard at Village Music. I needed to buy some CDs. Goddard's store closed down so he could retire. He has a garage with over a million CDs. We had coffee, talked music and I left with every Van Morrison bootleg concert CD that I didn't own. It turned out to be only ten CDs. John gave me a lock of hair that had once been Jerry Garcia's. I put it in a plastic bag. Who knows where it had been? I threw everything in the car's trunk.

Then I walked over to the Mill Valley Market and ordered a Stinson sandwich. This is albacore tuna Nicosia with a hard boiled egg, a pile of olives and enough garnish to feed an army. I bought a bottle of a 1998 Petrus Pomerol Merlot and gave the proprietor my Platinum American Express Card. The sandwich was $7.99 and the Merlot was $1459. Don Gino told me to go first class. I did.

Then it was over to Depot Books, where I asked Carlos Santana to move away from the spiritual books, so I could find Paul Perry's book on Jesus in Egypt. I wondered did the Egyptians know that Jesus was a Coptic? It's too late to worry about it now. Then I bought a book by Greil Marcus. It was a present for Bennie and Bertie. Marcus is a genius. His books are deep, dark and they make no sense. They are filled with pompous conclusions that bear no resemblance to reality. The perfect reading material for Bennie. Then I remembered Bennie doesn't read. Oh well! Bertie is an avid reader. Bennie doesn't read. He already knows everything. So why confuse the issue with another viewpoint. Besides books often have viewpoints that he despises. So why read them? He had purchased and burned copies of **Obama's Detractors: In The Right Wing Nut House**. It became a national best seller due to the large number of copies that Bennie burned.

I drove into Bennie and Bertie's gated community. I identified myself. The guard had a nametag, Fritz. He looked like a retired member of Hitler's Storm Troopers. He gave me a map. I thought I heard him mumble "liberal asshole." I guess that is better than just asshole.

Bennie and Bertie's house is one of Mill Valley's premier architectural marvels. It is a turn of the century home with vaulted wooden ceilings and a beautiful view of the Dipsea Trail. After spending over a million dollars remodeling it, **Architectural Digest** featured it in two issues. It is charming. That is an understatement. Too bad Bennie and Bertie aren't charming. Their home is known as the Castle Rock for its turn of the century look. The panoramic view is stupendous. The floor to ceiling windows look out on a lush valley, and the perpetually green Mill Valley countryside is beautiful.

My ex-brother and sister in law are what I term the "middle whites." That is everything they own is expensive, their friends are white Republic conservatives, their thoughts are upper middle class, they are deferential to me to the point of disdain as they talk about "taking America back." They bring new meaning to disdain for the working class. They are pompous and disingenuous. These are their good points. You wouldn't want to know the negatives.

They also tell me periodically that their family is better than mine. Of course, my brother McKenzie tells me the same thing. I have a little trouble with that comment. I don't have a family. I am divorced. Tony and Belinda, my parents are dead. They were alcoholics but had fun. Since my parents were AWOL when we were growing up there is a mixed bag of family achievement. McKenzie Dee is in an insane asylum where he calls himself Socrates or Nostradamus. He did an Ersel Hickey tribute show at Seattle bars before he crashed his city bus. The Seattle Municipal Bus District fired him. It didn't matter, he was famous for fifteen minutes. He made the Guinness Book of World Records when he drove off Seattle's Aurora Bridge into Lake Union. He was drunk, angry and talking about the time that the Highlighters didn't appear with Bobby Darin in a Seattle club. The passengers looked dumfounded, as he angrily went on about his brother. The Professor, as he called his brother, made mistakes so he was never going to talk to him.

McKenzie Dee drove the Seattle Transit Authority bus off the Aurora Bridge. Everyone survived. It was a miracle. When the police arrived, he told them an alien named Vince took over the wheel. Vince was talking about tank night, which McKenzie explained was a drunken party. When the police asked about the accident. He said the alien was dressed like Elvis. Then he went into a soft shoe dance step and sang like Elvis as the police looked on He was committed to the LaValley Reorientation Home. It is a behavior modification facility. This sounds better than an insane asylum.

James Franco optioned the story for a movie. A bus was brought in from Hollywood. McKenzie Dee was in the movie as a stunt driver, and he turned to make a point and the bus went off the Aurora Bridge.

They had to do the take six times and six busses were brought in from Hollywood.

His twin brother MacArthur Dee is the CEO of Kama Sutra Lotions. He doesn't talk to me. He also spends most of his time in Thailand. I don't want to know what was going on with either of them. My two brothers and my ex in laws all voted twice for George Bush. I call them middle whites. They are the last stand of conservative white Americans over sixty. The middle whites are intent on taking America back. I wonder who has it? Maybe aliens! Maybe Bennie. Maybe Bertie. Maybe Vince. Maybe Elvis.

Since Bennie and Bernie were on vacation, I had the run of the house. I usually sit in the front room. The kitchen or the dining room remains under Bertie's strict supervision. They watch me. I think that they worry that I will steal the throw rugs or the silverware. I had never been upstairs in their magnificent home. Why do I call it "magnificent?" That's what Bennie calls it. Who am I to disagree?

When I walk into Bennie and Bertie's kitchen, I am amazed at their affluence. Their Electrolux Grand Cuisine range is the same kitchen range used by Michelin chefs. Bertie is not only a gourmet cook, she is also a health food fanatic. She has a plastic bag filled with twenty-seven different pills that she takes at breakfast and lunch. She looks exactly like she did at twenty. She is now past fifty. So something is working right. Bennie is fit at fifty-four, and he looks like a twenty-five year old surfer. They are doing something right. I am envious.

Then I noticed that Bertie had written a book on kitchen stoves. Her book, **Bertie's Guide To The Historical Stove**, is in its sixth printing. She is also working on a cookbook. I was impressed.

Bertie was Miss Chicago some thirty years back and she is presently a perpetual contestant in the Mrs. America pageants. Bennie has spent $50,000 on face-lifts, $20,000 on breast enhancement, $5000 on finger and toe mail replacement and $10,000 on liposuction. She has weekly waxings, nails, hair service and her botox treatments are twice a month. I am afraid that she will soon look like Bruce Jenner. Then again Bruce Jenner doesn't look like himself. The plastic surgeon threw in a free lip job. Bertie is gorgeous. Her prematurely grey hair is also gone. So is Bennie's pocketbook.

As a scientist, Bennie had few peers. When Bertie began her hair transformation, Bennie invented a cream that modified gray hair. He sold this scientific discovery to No More Gray and Bennie opened a special "botox" account for Bertie. I had to admire them. They had the greatest marriage I have ever seen. It was based on money and good looks.

I put my sandwich down next to the $100,000 stove. How does one operate a $100,000 stove? Carefully. I was afraid to turn it on. I looked at Bennie and Bertie's Panasonic NE-328- Sonic Steamer Commercial Microwave Oven, at least that's what the brochure called it. They had just installed it. The three thousand dollar price tag was impressive. My forty-nine dollar microwave from Target paled in comparison. I couldn't figure out how to use the microwave. I decided to postpone dinner for an hour.

I put the sandwich back into the refrigerator. Nothing like an indecisive private eye. I fed the cat. Whiskers is a strange cat. He is violent. He is badly trained. He claws and scratches. He has a wretched personality. The odd thing is that he loves me. He cuddles up to me. Whiskers sleeps with me. He is a huge, nasty cat except when I am around. Bennie and Bertie are in awe of my cat prowess. I am confused by my cat prowess.

There was a small folder on Bertie's recipe box. It contained an article on the world's most expensive kitchen. The article described Claudio Celiberti's 1.6 million dollar kitchen that came with a Swarovski crystal chandelier costing $42,000 and a wine climate cabinet at the hefty price of $14,400. My car wasn't worth that much. I felt cheated. Celiberti's kitchen had $10,000 worth of stonework. I was still having trouble with the 1.6 million. A note from Bennie read: "Celiberti inspires me in the kitchen. I don't need Viagra." Sometimes there is too much information. There were detailed notes on how much less Bennie paid for his kitchen than a similar one installed for actor Brad Pitt. "Pitt's money is the Pitt's," Bennie wrote in a note. He probably laughed at his note.

Bennie and Bertie knew how to squeeze a nickel. He complained that the more than $200,000 he spent remodeling his kitchen was too much. When I looked at the $100,000 Electrolux Grand Cuisine, I admired Bennie for cutting a deal with the contractor. He had a Celiberti kitchen for a fifth of the price of Brad Pitt's.

I took the sandwich out of the refrigerator. It was a Sub-Zero PRO 48 and Bennie left the price tag on it. I looked and it was a $13,800 refrigerator made of 100% sculpted steel. I wondered what unsculpted steel was like? The sticker said that it featured dual refrigeration. I didn't understand the kitchen. I felt like I was in a foreign country. I was. It was Mill Valley California.

Carlos Santana and Bonnie Raitt were Bennie's neighbors. I saw Carlos in the backyard smoking a joint. Bonnie was in her house with her twenty-two year old boyfriend. The lights were low, the curtains were drawn and I heard giggling. It was probably the boy friend.

I wondered what Carlos's kitchen looked like. Bennie told me it wasn't as nice as his. Carlos' kitchen was too Mexican for Bennie. Every Mexican was too Mexican for Bennie. There was a note on the refrigerator asking Bertie not to borrow milk from Carlos. After reading the note my attention returned to the sandwich.

I thought about microwaving the sandwich. I love hot food. The kitchen was so sophisticated, I still couldn't figure out how to use what looked like a microwave. I ate the sandwich cold. I saved the wine for a date. After dinner I opened the folders that Don Gino had given me. I was on the trail of an art forger, a person trying to ruin Salvador Dali's reputation and some Muslim terrorists. No problem! I had to admit after looking at the files, I was confused. I knew nothing about terrorism. I knew less about art. This didn't sound like my kind of case. A dead artist, some smelly Muslims and people selling fake art. I couldn't wait to solve this case.

The files that Don Gino provided made for interesting reading. A series of art fakes sold by Park Avenue Artists on the Pearl of the Ocean raised money for terrorists. It sounds like a New York company, but it is located in Las Vegas. They provide Salvador Dali lithographs to sell on cruise ships. The forged Dali originals, and some "authentic fakes" were everywhere. I was trying to figure out what is an "authentic fake?"

Don Gino's file showed a Park Avenue Artists profit of over fifty million dollars a year. As a private company, there were no records of where Park Avenue Artists' money went. Zandra Filippi contacted Don Gino, and she documented that the funds were sent to a Dubai bank. Most of the wire transfers originated from the Carnivolet vessel Pearl of the Ocean.

I now know why Don Gino booked me on the Carnivolet Line from Tampa to Barcelona. I saw an order form that said I had a $100,000 credit line to purchase Dali lithographs. A note from Don Gino read: "Trevor be careful of the liquor, the young girls, the long drunken parties and the sales pitch when they try to sell you the art." I made a note to ignore the sales pitch. Why should I be careful? It was after all Don Gino's nickel.

The second folder was a detailed map and description of Dali's Cadaques residence. When it was built in the 1930s, the house was constructed from a series of smaller buildings. It was now a monument and museum to Dali's extraordinary genius. In the small, remote port town Port Lligat, it is an architectural marvel. It has turned a sleepy fishing village into a preferred tourist destination. Dali was inspired by the local countryside to such an extent that it dominated his paintings.

While in nearby Cadaques, Dali spent time with Pablo Picasso, Joan Miro and the actress Melina Mercouri. It was here that Dali was inspired to paint his tribute to Pablo Picasso. Dali's **Portrait of Picasso** demonstrated his humorous side. The painting showed Picasso on a pedestal with an elongated spoon coming out of his mouth. Dali completed the painting to demonstrate his affection for Picasso. After he saw the finished portrait, Picasso was angry. Dali attempted to challenge Picasso's imagination. What Picasso envisioned was disrespect. Dali said: "Picasso is an ignorant peasant."

When Dali discovered that Picasso disliked the painting, he labeled him "a destroyer of art." Don Gino loved the rivalry. The terrorists took Dali's side, and they threatened to destroy everything that was a Picasso. Don Gino also provided information to Trevor that the terrorists were lurking around the Cadaques fringes. They were intrigued with the small port town nearby that housed the Dali museum. Why? Don Gino didn't have a clue. It was up to Trevor to figure out what was going on.

The Port Lligat and Cadaques residences were a key. Port Lligat was Dali's summer home. He lived there with his wife Gala. Don Gino provided extensive architectural information and drawings highlighting some hiding spots. I was confused. What was I to find?

There was a third file marked: "Top Secret." It was an actual file copied from selected Homeland Security, FBI and CIA files. It linked Muslim terrorists to a series of art frauds. The sale of counterfeit Dali's were worth millions.

These files contained some strange documents. One was a photo where you could see a woman's breasts. Next to her breasts was a notebook. For the moment I ignored the notebook. I concentrated on the breasts. They gave me inspiration. Then I saw the small notation on the notebook 7-4501. The file title read: "Sagrada Familia File." I needed to find out more about the file. What the hell was going on?

I wondered if the key was in her breasts? Of course, this is always what I thought. This is when I encountered a beautiful young girl. That thought reminded me to make a phone call.

I called Zandra Filippi and gave her the information. I was hoping that 7-4501 was a computer file. She could hack into it. I was shocked at the e-mail that Zandra sent back. She agreed to search for the file. She didn't insult me. Maybe the world's second greatest private eye was making progress. In two hours, she came back with a download, which revealed the al Qaeda plan to blow up Gaudi's Sagrada Familia. I decided to keep this vital information to myself. I was Mr. Secrecy. Zandra didn't say "Fuck You." Maybe I still had a shot at her. Probably not!

I now had over sixty dense, note filled napkins on al Qaeda. The three napkins that I started on James Smith are now ten. There was almost too much information. The key to solving the crime, or should I say crimes, came in the preparation. I was Mr. Preparation. I was also Mr. Napkin.

I read every book I could on the architect, Antoni Gaudi, and his monumental church La Sagrada Familia. I took out three blank napkins. I marked them "Final Solution In Barcelona." I continued and made copious notes. I marked these "Smith-Hammadi." I was Mr. Detail. The napkins were numbered. I called these napkins-the keys to the highway.

I carefully arranged the napkins and numbered them. Now to begin deductive reasoning.

Napkin 1.) Find the art forgers. What was their relationship to Dali? Why did Don Gino want them found? I had no clue. I am the detective. I just couldn't tell Don Gino that I had no idea what I was doing. It wouldn't be good for my health. Park Avenue Artists was the key to finding the covert funds.

Napkin 2.) The Carnivolet Line was scheduled to sale from Tampa on a fifteen-day cruise to Barcelona. Don Gino gave me a ten-page list of things to look for on the ship. Someone was attempting to destroy Dali's reputation.

Napkin 3.) The terrorists placed a mole in Don Gino's entourage. Who? I didn't know. Don Gino worried about the attack on Dali's reputation. The flirtation with Dali's art was something that al Qaeda used to raise money. In time this would devalue his art. Don Gino was one of the largest, most influential and richest Dali collectors. He had a stake in maintaining Dali's reputation. I was a bit puzzled. Dali passed away in 1989. How could anyone besmirch his reputation? Or for that matter devalue his art?

I had to learn about art forgeries. There was another file on art forgeries. I felt like Professor Trevor Blake III, Art Historian. When I read the file, I didn't have a clue. Art forgery is a sophisticated crime. Park Avenue Artists had sued everyone who challenged their credibility. They were well-heeled criminals. They also had a bastion of lawyers that put competitors out of business. They had won every case against them. They also sued for libel three times. They won large settlements.

Napkin 4.) The last file was the most bizarre. Don Gino's material linked al Qaeda to Salvador Dali. When Dali died no one knew anything about Muslim terrorists. It wasn't until after 9-11 that James Smith emerged with his fiscal contributions to terrorism. After 9-11, he ramped up his monetary support, and he founded sleeper cells in the United States. A portion of the radical al Qaeda cells were hidden in a soul music business.

James Smith owned Motown Tribute. It was a cover for his nefarious al Qaeda activity. This was a company that sent fake Four Tops and Temptations to perform on cruise ships, Indian casinos and country clubs. It was where old white people loved nostalgia and paid big bucks to listen to authentic fakes. The tribute Four Tops and Temptations were young African Americans with links to al Qaeda. They were the perfect sleeper cell. No one suspected them. They were viewed as musicians not revolutionaries.

When the Motown Tribute performed in Dubai the U. S. Customs Department failed to search their luggage. President Barack Obama sent a directive. He ordered Customs officials to use discretion. They interpreted it as a pass for the African American singers. They used the Obama administration's obsession with political correctness to smuggle in al Qaeda instructions to Americans in Boston. Some blamed the Obama administration for the Boston Marathon bombings. It was in an apartment near the finish line for this ill-fated race that incendiary materials were delivered.

The various files showed that money flowed from Park Avenue Artists into al Qaeda training camps. The key figure was the mysterious Birmingham Alabama terrorist James Smith. This terrorist was a bizarre figure. He was once the starting center for the University of Alabama basketball team. Then he played for two years in the Iranian Professional Basketball league. He vanished into Pakistan to re-emerge as Omar Abdul Hammadi. He is the only al Qaeda terrorist who could dunk a basketball.

James Smith, aka Omar Abdul Hammadi, an African American attracted to Islam at the University of Alabama, was not in any law enforcement data bank. I had him on my personal radar. He also had impressive credentials. He was an A student who graduated Phi Beta Kappa in finance-business. Smith was praised for earning his degree with two majors. There were no signs of political radicalism. Smith was soft- spoken, low key, polite and gracious. He was also a respected businessman and a multi-millionaire. He was seen in the company of Donald Trump and at New York Knick games with Jay Z.

It was time to inform Don Gino of Smith-Hammadi's existence. But the Don was one step ahead of Trevor. Don Gino had discovered that Smith-Hammadi was involved in the illicit Salvador Dali art trade. When Don Gino realized that the African American business-man was not a collector, red flags went up. He quickly had an in-depth file, thanks to Zandra Filippi. As Don Gino perused the informa-tion, he was intrigued that Smith's money was retransferred to the Khushhali Bank Limited on Kinnah Avenue in Islamabad. Don Gino flew to Pakistan and talked quietly with the bank president. There was no evidence that Hammadi was a terrorist. The banker said that the account was set up to help Syrian refugees. Don Gino wasn't so sure. Hammadi's Pakistan address was in a remote, rural area. The bank president said that this was common. Another red flag went up when it was discovered that Smith-Hammadi was donating money to the Pakistan Institute of Space Technology. The scholarships were for engineers trained to build churches and other religious sites. Suddenly, Don Gino had an idea what Smith was targeting in Barcelona and San Francisco. He realized his evil intent. He also believed that there was a mole. This material was shared with Trevor.

Smith-Hammadi was a follower of the late Osama bin Laden. He read the works of Sayyid Qutb. The only person who realized this was Don Gino. American intelligence efforts failed. It was politically incorrect to have surveillance on a well-known African American.

President Barack Obama instructed the CIA and the FBI to take Smith off their radar. The President emphasized in his memo: "No terrorist profiling of African Americans." This memo was due to Smith's high-end friends.

Donald Trump was seen regularly with Smith. No one had a clue. Don Gino figured it all out from Smith's education. How could the Department of Homeland Security, FBI and CIA miss the Smith-Hammadi connection?

No one mentioned that Islamic Studies was James Smith's other area of concentration at the University of Alabama. Then Smith studied for one summer at the University of Tehran and his radicalism blossomed. It was in the Dehkhoda Dictionary Institute that Smith studied Muslim history and radicalism. He was schooled extensively in Persian Kings, literature and science from the Middle East. His professor told him that Salvador Dali was a Muslim and preached violence.

This was in the era of thawing relations with Iran. Smith was voted the outstanding foreign student at the University of Teheran for the decade of the 1980s. No one realized that he received terrorist training. It was the 1980s and America was not concerned with domestic terrorism. Smith, known to his radical Islamic compatriots as Omar Abdul Hammadi, was a quiet, studious thoughtful young man. He was gracious, he smiled a lot, and he uttered platitudes about politics. He was a trained al Qaeda killer.

The files exhausted me. I called Don Gino. He answered and didn't sound happy.

"Trevor, let me guess, you can't make heads or tails of the files?"

"I have a plan. I am also ready to catch our friend, Mr. Smith." I was expecting praise from Don Gino. It didn't work out that way.

"Do you have any idea who is financing the al Qaeda cell?"

Don Gino always asks the hard questions. I didn't have a clue.

Trevor said: "Tell me who is the financier?"

Don Gino said: "It is quite simple. Follow the money." There was a long pause. Follow the money sounded like a Woodward-Bernstein phrase.

"I'm on the case." There was a pause as a bic lighter flared up one of Don Gino's small cigars. I wanted to tell him smoking was bad for his health. I decided to wait. No one pisses off the Don.

"I want you to spend some time on the files and learn as much as you can." He hung up abruptly. I wanted to tell Don Gino that a day with the files was enough. I loved trivia. I loved nonsense. I didn't love the files. I couldn't wait for the Carnivolet cruise to Barcelona. I looked at the files and went over everything a dozen times. What was I missing?

It didn't pay to make Don Gino angry. I also was not a favorite of the six Samoan bodyguards and the midget valet. Every time I called him a midget, he corrected me. He was a dwarf.

Don Gino runs a highly profitable produce company and a dog food canning business. He is located in San Francisco's Mission District on Army Street. There is no crime in this warehouse area. There hasn't been a robbery or a break in for a decade. It is a place unsafe for criminals. Don Gino is the only criminal allowed to roam Army Street and the Mission District. He is a loan shark, he provides protection, he donates large sums to the Catholic Church, and his extensive funding makes the Mission schools San Francisco's best.

The rumor is that when a Mexican drug cartel came into his section of the Mission District, every member of the cartel vanished and wound up in his dog food cans. Cases of dog food were shipped to the homes of the Mexican criminals. There have been no further sightings of Mexican cartel members in San Francisco's Mission District.

Don Gino makes his money the old fashioned way, he provides loans and protection. During the last decade, he has increasingly become a successful, legitimate businessman. Word on the street is that his legitimate businesses have made Don Gino more money than his criminal enterprises. He confesses to being embarrassed by his legitimate business successes. He also regularly has dinner with former Mayor Gavin Newsom, Representative Barbara Boxer and Governor Jerry Brown. San Francisco's present Mayor, Edwin M. Lee, is not friendly to Don Gino or the Catholic Church. The Don has reached out to Mayor Lee and they patched up their differences. He now joins Don Gino at the IHOP for breakfast. Mayor Lee is seen running into the CVS on Lombard Street for Tums after eating at IHOP.

When the Secret Service came into town with President Obama, they consulted Don Gino on security. The most telling point about his influence came when Don Gino took President Obama to breakfast at the International House of Pancakes.

Don Gino loves the steak and eggs special. It is $4.99 and it is only offered from midnight to five in the morning. When President Obama and Don Gino met at ten in the morning, the manager waived the time period. There were fifty TV trucks more than five hundred reporters and every civic official as Don Gino walked in with a purple tuxedo, a long white cape and no security. If you looked closely six Samoans were in the crowd. The midget valet was nearby. They stood just behind the fifty secret service agents. No one knows what the president and Don Gino talked about.

In the crowd at this breakfast, James Smith watched as President Obama accorded Don Gino the ultimate respect. He was angry. Why would an African American president court the political favor of a San Francisco Mafia figure? Smith was perplexed. What was going on? He scanned the press for clues.

The press reported that President Obama and Don Gino discussed national security. Don Gino got into a limousine with the president and they left for a security briefing.

I spent the next day memorizing Don Gino's files. I looked at a picture of Omar Abdul Hammadi. I didn't think that it would be difficult to find a basketball-playing terrorist. There were other problems. I couldn't figure out who was trying to devalue the Salvador Dali works. My cell phone rang. I looked at the number. Once again it was the Don.

"Trevor," Don Gino said. "We need to talk. I have some new thoughts." When the Don has thoughts, you listen.

"I'm on the case. What can I do?" This is how Richard Prather's Shell Scott talked. He was my favorite fictional detective. He had a crew cut, blonde hair and he never aged beyond thirty. This was my goal. I wasn't making it as I had turned forty-one. I was a badly aging forty-one as my sometimes girl friend Joyce Byers observed. This is why she is my occasional girl friend. My other girl friends liked to do it with the lights off. Maybe that should tell me something.

Don Gino said: "Meet me at the International House of Pancakes tomorrow morning. Park off Lombard Street and come in the back door. This is a clandestine meeting."

"Ok." Should I mention to the Don that meeting a large Italian man in a purple suit was not clandestine. I decided to keep my opinions to myself. I would go back to being the tough P. I. Shell Scott.

I dressed like Shell Scott. I wore a long tan overcoat; I had an open necked shirt. My sneer was as good as Scott's. He was the mean street walking, alpha P. I. That part of my personality was a problem. I also didn't have his muscles. I was still working on the nasty strut that set Shell Scott apart. I had to remember that he was a fictional character. Then again I felt like a fictional character.

After I agreed to meet Don Gino the next morning, I had an attack of imaginary food poisoning. The International House of Pancakes was his favorite breakfast spot. Yuck! I couldn't tell the Don that I hated the place. It wasn't good for my health. Neither was the food nor the Don's fanciful attitude toward eating as many pancakes as possible.

My weekend at Bennie and Bertie's was a long one. Their house was so comfortable that I had spent the entire weekend analyzing the al Qaeda terrorist cell. I had spent so much time on the phone that I hadn't fully explored Bennie and Bertie's palatial residence. A sign on the door read: "The Snookums Hideaway." Yuck! It had seven magnificent rooms. Ones that I had never seen! It was time for the world's second greatest detective to solve the Bennie and Bertie mystery.

After I walked upstairs, I realized that I had never been in the second floor office. I was astonished. It had a full gym, two working desks, three computers, two of which were encrypted and a locked case full of weapons. Bennie collected Glocks. Paul M. Barrett's **Glock: The Rise of America's Gun** was on Bennie's desk. I opened it. Barrett had inscribed it: "To Bennie, a patriot who loves the Glock. Fuck Obama." I guess that put it in perspective for me.

There were select magic tricks, no signs of Fox TV and there were no right wing paranoid political books. It looked like a warriors den. Bennie was a middle white conservative. Maybe I had missed something. There were pictures of action heroes all over the walls. One of those action heroes, Dwayne Johnson, worked out with Bennie. I didn't think that Superman, Batman or the Lone Ranger worked out with Bennie. Tonto wouldn't be allowed in the complex. He was a Native American. Bennie called him an Indian. There is nothing like not being politically incorrect.

Bennie's workroom had three file cabinets. They were all locked. I used my trusted paper clip and bent it into the proper position. It took about five minutes. I opened all three-file cabinets. Why? Who knows! I am a curious person. I was floored by what I found.

Bennie fought in Operation Desert Storm in 1990-1991. He was a member of an elite Special Forces Commando unit that remained in Iraq after the war chasing radical Muslims. He never talked about it. The medals from his service for combat and leadership were hanging proudly on the wall.

The most intriguing file was one that had certificates for martial arts. This was a side of Bennie that he had hidden. He wore loose fitting t-shirts and he didn't talk about physical fitness. When I patted him on the shoulder it was like hitting a piece of steel. Another file dealt with his weight, body fat and agility. After reading this material, I decided I needed to be nicer to Bennie.

The last file cabinet contained CIA material. Bennie had a business selling orthopedic insoles for shoes around the world. It was a front. He was a God damned spy. He was also a trained killer. The orthopedic shoe company was a front for a murder for hire entity. He might do more than cut my head off or make me disappear with his magic tricks.

There was a "Kill File." I hoped that I wasn't in it. It detailed the people that Bennie eliminated. He was retired. No more killing. I redoubled my thoughts about being nice to him. He was off to Europe with some right wing Republican political horseshit that occupied his life. He often said that Fox TV News was sliding to a more liberal stance. His politics were beyond right wing.

As I left their house, I could imagine Bennie saying: "My family is better than yours." This is why l loved the guy. He was an asshole with a personality. Or maybe he was just an asshole. I heard Fox TV News blaring, "We are fair and balanced." Right!

Fair and balanced! Ho, ho, ho. A phrase that people accepted without question. It didn't bode well for the future. It did bode well for Bennie and Bertie. I looked over my notes. I copied a few things from Bennie's files. The Salvador Dali murder was not only a complex case, the mystery was compounded by intrigue in Barcelona and San Francisco. My sometimes girl friend, Joyce Byers, would be called on for favors. She wanted sexual favors. I guess I would have to comply. The world's second greatest detective needs to keep his mojo.

I looked out Bennie and Bertie's second floor window. Carlos Santana was mowing his back yard. Or rather he was sitting on a power driven lawnmower that cost more than my car. I had heard Carlos talking about doing yard work in interviews. A young girl stood to his side smiling at him. She looked like his daughter. That is until she took her clothes off and crawled on Carlos' lap. She smiled and ran in the house. Carlos followed. Now I knew why Carlos' wife left a few years ago.

After packing up my files, it was time to leave Bennie and Bertie's and head back to San Francisco. I had a lock on what al Qaeda was planning. Where and how was another problem?

I walked out into Bennie and Bertie's front yard. There was a small Asian man trimming the trees. I walked over.

"Emilio?"

"Hello Trevor."

"What are you doing here?"

"I'm trimming the trees."

"May I ask why?"

"They need trimming Trevor." He returned to pruning trees that looked perfect. Maybe Emilio was a Japanese gardener and not a donut shop owner who stole diamonds from rich people.

Trevor walked to his car and drove away. Emilio stopped. He looked down the street. Then six Samoans came out of Carlos Santana's yard. They held up two frightened African Americans.

Carlos Santana came screaming out of the house. "Stop, this racist action. These people are my friends."

Emilio walked over and talked quietly to Carlos. "The two gentleman are terrorists sent to exterminate Trevor Blake III."

"Why, isn't he that inept private eye?"

"He is, Carlos. He is also working on a case for Don Gino."

"I see, get those two Negroes out of my complex. Tell the Don hello and let him know that I am playing for his birthday party. I will try to bring Van Morrison along." There was a long period of silence. Emilio looked uncomfortable.

Emilio scowled: "Leave Mr. Morrison at home. He is no fun." The Samoans loaded the African American terrorists into a van. Santana waved. Good riddance. The bastards would ruin the neighborhood.

Emilio directed the Samoans to the Mill Valley landfill. It was in nearby San Rafael. After a brief interrogation, the African American terrorists told all they knew about James Smith. It wasn't much but it added to the already alarming material. Emilio prepared a file for Don Gino. Trevor was on his way to let Don Gino know what the terrorists had in mind. Little did Trevor know that the two African Americans were sent to kill him? Keeping Trevor safe was a full time job.

Don Gino made it clear. Trevor was to be watched. He was the key to solving the crime. When the al Qaeda terrorists were caught, killed and vanished, Trevor Blake III would once again be a national celebrity. Don Gino had recently entertained David Letterman and Trevor would guest on his show once the mystery was solved.

As Trevor prepared to meet Don Gino for breakfast, he had no idea how intricate and involved the Salvador Dali Murder plot was progressing. Yet, he was an integral part of the plan, and he knew much more than anyone realized.

CHAPTER TEN

Breakfast With Don Gino

"Behind every great fortune lies a great crime."
Honore de Balzac

The drive from Mill Valley across the Golden Gate Bridge was beautiful. The fog hanging over the Golden Gate Bridge cast an eerie shadow. The sun reflected off the steel girders and people walking across the bridge looked happy. No one wanted to jump. I placed a five-dollar bill in the toll machine and talked to the robot. She wished me a happy day. I asked her for a date. Maybe we could get together for coffee. The guy behind me honked his horn.

I found a parking place just off Lombard Street. The IHOP lot is always full. It has only six spaces. There is one reserved space with a large purple sign. I walked into IHOP and Don Gino was in the back sitting in his private booth. He waved as he puffed on a small cigar under a "No Smoking" sign.

"Trevor, thank you for coming."

Did I have a choice? "Don Gino it is my pleasure." I wonder could he tell that I was nervous? I looked over at a booth where two guys in dark suits, wing tips and bad ties were eating the $4.99 breakfast special. Businessmen or FBI agents? What else could they be in that get up?

I ordered the German pancakes and coffee. Don Gino was working on a big platter of French toast with coconut syrup. He spent an hour telling me about his Salvador Dali sketches. Somehow Don Gino purchased a Dali ink sketch "Tigre, Mao, Tigre" from 1961. Roger and Nicholas Descharnes in Paris authenticated this rare ink drawing. Then it was offered for sale. The sale offering quickly ended. Don Gino came in possession of the Dali sketch. No particulars on its purchase are available. The Don probably let someone live in exchange for this rare ink sketch.

To my surprise, Don Gino found some original Dali's at a San Francisco Mission District Goodwill store. He paid a dollar for the Goodwill find. He went to an auction in Las Vegas where Park Avenue Artists sold him an etching that Dali hastily drew at the Royal Academy of Art in Madrid in the mid-1920s. Don Gino paid $6,900 for Dali's "Etude De Couple Assisi." I looked at a photo of this unique piece of art. It was a pencil drawing that looked to me like two couples were leering at each other. Maybe it was a statement on marriage. I wasn't one to consult on the sanctity of marriage.

"You look confused, Trevor."

I was. A pencil drawing that was barely visible for almost seven thousand dollars. Not my idea of spending seven grand. "It's wonderful, Don Gino." I hoped I sounded convincing. I pulled out my Kindle Fire and I went online as Don Gino continued eating his French toast. The coconut syrup oozed over the side of the plate. I needed a Tums. I found out that Park Avenue Artists allowed you to bid on its art on line. I bid on a Dali drawing of Sigmund Freud. I was the winner. I sent them by American Express card. After all it was Don Gino's money. I wondered! Should I tell the Don what I paid? Probably not!

The sketch of Sigmund Freud resulted when Dali visited him at his London Primrose Hill house. It was meant as a tribute. Dali loved Freud's genius. When Dali traveled from Paris to met Freud at the 39 Elsworthy Road home, he brought along a set of charcoal pencils, ink pens and some pencils.

It was a warm London day on July 19, 1938 when Dali showed up at Freud's London home. They met and spoke in French.

Freud said: "To what do I owe this visit?"

Dali said: "I'm showing my admiration for you in my latest painting, I call it **Freud On The Couch**." Dali paused. "I also painted an oil canvas last year **Metamorphosis of Narcissus** that I believe reflects your genius." Dali smiled. Freud frowned.

Freud looked at it and said nothing. The men shook hands and Dali left. Freud wrote a letter critical of Dali in 1939 stating that Dali's painting **Metamorphosis of Narcissus** was demeaning to Freud's reputation. Freud sent this letter to Andre Breton and he showed it to Dali. Dali remarked: "Freud is showing signs of old age. He also doesn't understand surrealism."

Not only was Dali crestfallen, he had followed Freud's teachings since his student days. Dali was skeptical about Freud's understanding of surrealism. He had to respond to what he envisioned as Freud's slight of or misunderstanding of Dali's work.

Dali answered Freud in a blistering letter accusing the famed psychoanalyst of "excessive ego." Freud tore up the letter. Dali filed his copy. It vanished until it was discovered a decade after Dali's death.

The result was a private auction and Trevor purchased the unique Dali letter for $3799. It would be a gift to Don Gino.

"I have a gift for you, Don Gino." I smiled

He looked confused. "A gift?"

"Yes, something special."

"Hand me your computer, Trevor."

I did, he looked at my invoice and smiled. "You are smarter than I thought." He continued eating his French toast. I was getting sick looking at it. I looked at the waitress. She was old and ugly. The French toast looked better. There was an eerie silence. Don Gino was thinking.

I said: "I could use a little more information."

"You are on the right track." Don Gino lit a small cigar.

"What track?"

"When you get to Tampa you will join the Carnivolet Cruise Line 'Mystery And Art' tour. The waiters, the bar people, the entertainment and the crew are all dressed as historical mystery figures. One night Sherlock Holmes will wait on you and the next night it might be Jack Reacher. Or maybe Jack the Ripper."

I interrupted the Don. "Is there any chance Shell Scott will serve me a scotch and water?"

"Who the hell is Shell Scott?"

I explained in great detail about Richard Prather's books. Then I ran through the plots, the cool nature of Scott Shell and how the pulp writers were better than Hemingway, Don Gino looked at me like I had lost my mind. He was stunned. I decided to leave Shell Scott out of the equation.

"Trevor, the case is a simple one. Someone is trying to murder Salvador Dali's reputation. Considering his behavior before he passed on, it is easy to discredit him. The values of his drawings are declining. I need you to find out who is behind the Salvador Dali murder."

I didn't want to tell Don Gino that it had been almost thirty years since Dali passed away after surviving a fire in his bedroom. I said: "Is there more to his case?"

"You need to remember why I want your help." Don Gino continued. "Salvador Dali was a good Catholic. Late in his career, he celebrated his Catholic faith through paintings. He was never the atheist that others claimed. He has Arabic roots. Now we have a terrorist cell founded on Dali's ideas. I want them all dead."

Trevor said: "Am I missing anything?" When the Don wants them dead. They are dead.

Don Gino said: "There is much more to the case. It involves art fraud. The sale of Dali's provides monetary support to terrorists. Find out who is making my Dali originals decline. I will deal with that person." Don Gino smiled. I shivered.

When the Don talks of dealing with someone, it means it is the last deal. That person is dead. I graciously exited the International House of Pancakes. I walked across the street and bought a big bottle of Tums. IHOP does that to my stomach.

Like most of my cases, this one made no sense. Then I remembered that I had had only one other case. This one was tougher.

I was chasing someone who was making the Don unhappy. I was sure he could deal with it. I was paid well. I ignored my fears. This was a big mistake. The worst was yet to come.

The sixty plus napkins contained most of the clues. The hidden Muslim terrorist cells were in Barcelona and San Francisco. The al Qaeda cells appeared to be populated by amateurs. The leader, or whoever was funding the terrorist attacks, was brilliant. I had a choice of going after the morons or the brilliant planner. I was confident I would uncover the morons.

Maybe there was a hidden motive. Maybe there was an answer on the cruise ship or in Barcelona. I didn't have a clue. Don Gino was increasingly opaque. This was not a good sign. I was increasingly lost in the maze of information surrounding the case.

CHAPTER ELEVEN

Chastain Johnson Goes
After Al Qaeda

**"The only difference between me and the surrealists is that
I am a surrealist." Salvador Dali**

C hastain Johnson looked in the mirror. She saw lines around her eyes, wrinkles in her cheeks and lines on her forehead Her chin was sagging. Her breasts were still terrific. She knew that botox was an option. Chastain worried about her beauty. Trevor was coming to her apartment. Probably not a good idea. She liked him. He had trouble keeping his mouth shut. So an apartment briefing allowed her to tell him in no uncertain terms to keep his mouth shut. She doubted her request would register.

As Trevor walked into the Marina, he wondered how did an FBI agent afford an apartment in the same block where the late Joe DiMaggio lived? Maybe she was taking bribes. Maybe she was turning tricks. Chastain said that maybe I was an asshole. Probably an accurate statement.

I walked down to gaze at Chastain's 2148 Beach Street home in S. F.'s Marina. All the homes looked alike and they were stuck together. No side yard. No front yard. The cheapest one sold for a million and a half dollars. No wonder Joe DiMaggio had to sell coffee. Chastain even had a Mr. Coffee automatic drip machine and a signed DiMaggio ball on display in the front room. I had never been in the bedroom. I have tried. As soon as Mickey Rooney dies, I will be her next conquest.

She was the second smartest woman I knew. Zandra Filippi is the first. Joyce Byers comes in for honorable mention. Joyce was the only one I got regularly into bed. That is if no one else is available. Even the world's second greatest Private Eye needs to rate his women. Trevor decided to drop in at the Starbucks on Chestnut Street for a café mocha. He had to think abut how he would handle Chastain. She was smart, cunning, shrewd and calculating. There was no chance to get her in bed. She could provide leads. This is not what was on Trevor's mind.

Chastain was assigned the Salvador Dali Murder case because of her philosophy/art major at the University of California, Berkeley. She also had specialized in art fraud litigation at UC's Boalt Hall. It was during law school that she decided against practicing law and becoming an FBI agent. She loved the FBI.

Since 2009, when Barack Obama became president, Chastain was the FBI representative to the Insider Threat Program. This is a sweeping government unit that collects phone information to guard against government leaks. Chastain thought the program an excellent but not a successful one.

The Insider Threat Program gave Chastain access to a wide variety of personal materials. She identified James Smith as the American al Qaeda terrorist leader. What he planned wasn't clear. Chastain depended upon Zandra Filippi's private computer-security research company to find out what else she needed to know. Chastain spent hundred of hours educating herself on Salvador Dali.

Her bookshelf contained rows and rows of Dali books. She had read everything there was about Dali. She laughed when she told Joyce Byers that Trevor Blake III talked of his Dali expertise. He knew nothing. She wondered how Dali's art funded terrorists? The keys to the case were hidden clues in Dali's surrealism. The art contained the answer to the mystery. What appeared important wasn't and what was innocuous was significant. Chastain was puzzled by much of Dali's career. When he came to America in 1937, he worked in Hollywood with the Marx Brothers on a movie script. The file that Chastain had on Dali indicated that there was a Hollywood connection to the cruise and the planned terrorist attacks. What the hell could it be? Everyone was dead. Including Dali! The movie was never produced. The script entitled, "Giraffes On Horseback Salad" was re-titled "The Surrealist Woman." Chastain understood the clue. Now she needed more background material.

She grabbed the three files on her desk and walked into the kitchen. After pouring a cup of coffee, she continued studying the files. The CIA was looking for homegrown terrorists. They were college educated, they were closet Muslims, they were middle class and they were married with normal families. That nailed it down to one or two hundred million of the three hundred million Americans.

The first file was on Carnivolet Cruise potential terrorists. It was marked: "FOR YOUR EYES ONLY." It sounded like a title for a James Bond movie. This file contained information on other people on the Carnivolet Cruise Line and their connection to al Qaeda.

It was another file that concerned her. It contained dossiers on the large number of people that the Obama administration assigned to the Salvador Dali Murder. There were too many agents as the FBI, the CIA and President Obama's national security advisers tripped over each other attempting to find the terrorist. Everyone wanted to take credit for neutralizing the terrorists.

There was a file marked: "COMPLICATIONS." "Oh, God, Jesus," Chastain said out loud to no one. The file contained two names Trevor Blake III and Don Gino Landry. Someone was out to kill them. The file described Don Gino as a Salvador Dali collector who had a mammoth collection of original drawings, and signed lithographs. He had collected almost a thousand of Dali's personal letters. He also was concerned that the CIA didn't understand that Arab terrorists were using Dali art fakes to raise money to fight in Afghanistan and Iraq. The file detailed Don Gino's strong ties to the Catholic Church, his fervent patriotism and his cold blooded nature. Six Samoans accompanied him, a small valet in a purple tuxedo, and a San Francisco donut shop owner, Emilio, helped to dispose of people. The FBI had a detailed file on Emilio.

Emilio had a master's degree in English from San Francisco State. He was a former North Vietnam army officer. He was an expert in recognizing and defusing explosives. He was trained in the martial arts and the San Francisco police had chased him for years. He was a cat burglar who stole and fenced art. In the last few years he retired. He owned a donut shop in the Haight Ashbury near Trevor Blake III's office. Don Gino brought Emilio along for muscle, brains and appraisal.

As Chastain analyzed the crew around Don Gino, she wondered if they were as inept as Trevor Blake III. She decided that they were professionals and the Don would solve the case. Trevor would get the credit. Don Gino hated publicity, and he shied away from the limelight.

Chastain digested the material. She was puzzled. Why were all these people involved? She was missing something. Chastain made a note to look at three clues.

Why was Trevor Blake III part of this gang of private investigators? Trevor had neither brains nor skills. He was cute. He wasn't very good at being a private eye. He hit on every good-looking woman like it was the 1970s. He was born in that decade. Maybe it ruined his psyche.

Chastain sighed as she digested the more than one hundred pages of information. There was also a small attachment of just a few pages marked: "Trevor Blake III." The FBI described Blake as an inept, often comic, investigator who solved his first and only case by accident. Don Gino and Emilio helped him solve the case of who murdered the Start Me Up drummers. This was a multi-million dollar cover band that Blake helped remain in business by finding the chef poisoning their drummers. None of the bodies had ever been found. The FBI concluded that Don Gino and Emilio handed Trevor the clues, and he solved the case. As Detective Richard Sanchez of the San Francisco Police Department remarked to the press: "A monkey could have solved the case, Trevor Blake III couldn't find his ass if he was handed a road map to it." Chastain cringed. She had slept with the forty-year-old bachelor with the good looks. Fortunately, her liaison with Trevor was missing from the file. The FBI didn't have all the information.

Chastain thought a lot about Trevor. He was cute. He was mildly competent. He was also an inveterate womanizer. Oh well, two out of three wasn't bad.

The doorbell rang. She grabbed her Glock. She looked out the peephole. There stood Trevor Blake III. She had to admit, he was cute. Why did he call himself "the World's Greatest Detective?" Ego! Stupidity! Testosterone!

"Hello Chastain." Trevor smiled.

"Come in, Dickhead."

"The FBI taking bribes, how do you afford this beautiful house?"

"You really know how to flatter a girl."

"I'm not just the world's greatest detective, I'm an observant Shell Scott type."

"Who the hell is Shell Scott?"

"It's a long story. We need to get down to business."

"Does that mean we should go to bed?" Chastain smiled. She loved clever repartee.

"The files Chastain, we need to go over them."

"Ok, sit here in the kitchen. I'll make some coffee."

"Aren't you a feminist, they don't make coffee."

"How do you spell asshole, Trevor? Or should I say semi-literate dickhead."

"I surrender Chastain."

They spent an hour going over the various FBI, CIA and Homeland Security Files. Trevor shared what he had found. Chastain was mum on what she knew apart from the files. Trevor showed her his sixty plus napkins. She took notes. She got up and stretched. It was time to leave. He wanted to ask her to stretch again. What a set of breasts.

"Thanks Chastain, we actually can work together."

She smiled. "Yes, we can." Trevor left. He walked back to Chestnut Street for another Starbuck's. The world's second greatest detective needed caffeine. He also needed to think.

Chastain dressed, took her packed suitcase outside her apartment waiting for the cab. She was flying to Tampa to go undercover on the Carnivolet Cruise. She had a wardrobe of special clothes with a mystery evening theme. Every night for fifteen days she would dress up as a character, wear a mask and appear to be a Carnivolet guest. Her wardrobe allowed her to dress as Little Bo Peep, Cinderella, Jane

Fonda, Wonder Woman, Madonna, Cyndi Lauper, Gwen Stefani or Margaret Thatcher. Masks and the proper clothing accompanied the costumes. She wondered if a pervert was in charge of FBI costumes.

Trevor Blake III worried Chastain. He had a way of finding the clues, getting to the heart of the crime and solving it. When he caught the chef, the killer confessed. The San Francisco Police Department concluded that Don Gino got rid of the chef, Emilio helped kill him and they had taken him back to Don Gino's dog food canning plant. The word on the street was that the chef wound up in the dog food cans. Trevor was featured on 60 Minutes, he hosted Saturday Night Live, he was on the cover of **Rolling Stone** and he collected a substantial fee from the Start Me Up band. No one close to him believed that he solved the case. To add insult to injury, he wrote **Stone Murder** and his true crime memoir was number one of the **New York Times** best-seller list. Then Michael Douglas bought the screen rights to **Stone Murder** with Brad Pitt signed to play Trevor. Chastain couldn't believe his good luck. It wasn't detective skill that made famous. After the cab picked her up, she made a series of notes.

Chastain was not happy with Trevor's movie deal. Julia Roberts was cast as Chastain. She was upset. Julia wasn't young enough, her breasts were too small and she talked with a lisp. She did smoke. Roberts was also older than Chastain. When the movie director and Julia Roberts came to San Francisco to interview Chastain about Trevor, she told the producers that he was a warm and loveable person. She lied. She said that Trevor was a ladies man and great in bed. The truth was that Chastain faked an orgasm the night that she slept with Trevor. It was the only way to get him out of bed. She was still waiting for Mickey Rooney.

As Chastain rode to the airport, she realized that Trevor's presence on the Carnivolet cruise would impede her role. She was also uncertain about Don Gino, Emilio and the Don's entourage. They would complicate the case. She had no idea about her CIA contact. The FBI told her that her CIA contact was an agent brought out of retirement. He was one of the most decorated CIA agents. He would reveal himself on the cruise to Barcelona. This case was a mess. She wasn't happy. Trevor Blake III needed to be out of her life. Don Gino was also a worry and that little bastard from Vietnam was smart and cunning. Chasing the bad guys was no problem. It was keeping these fucking amateurs out of the way. She lit a cigarette.

The Indian taxi driver almost lost his turban screaming: "No smoking." She blew smoke up front flashed her FBI credential and then flashed her breasts. The Indian cab driver said: "Please smoke, beautiful lady." Chastain smiled. The fucking raghead was easily intimidated.

She walked outside the San Francisco International Airport smoking and thinking. Chastain had to have a plan. She did. It involved getting Trevor Blake III to sit back. She would give him key information to help solve the case. If he went straight ahead to solve the al Qaeda terrorist's actions, they would be warned. She had to neutralize Trevor.

Chastain walked into San Francisco International Airport. She noticed a tall, stately, handsome man in a purple suit twirling a purple cane as he smiled at people walking by him. This was obviously Don Gino Landry. She watched six Samoans walking well behind Don Gino Landry and a small Asian man carrying a boomerang. Maybe she should transfer to ATF. She walked by Don Gino. He tipped his bowler hat and cane. Chastain wondered does anyone wear a bowler hat?

As they boarded the Southwest flight to Tampa, the stewardess announced: "We are holding the plane for a celebrity." There was a burst of applause as Trevor Blake III entered the plane. He smiled. There was a seat saved in the first row. He took it. The stewardess handed him a drink with two napkins. One for the drink and the other had her phone number. Trevor might be slow in detecting. The women loved him. Chastain put a magazine up to hide her face and read about Brad Pitt as a father. What a waste. The waste is that Brad Pitt wasn't Chastain's main squeeze. She looked up at Trevor signing autographs.

"Folks, please buckle up for takeoff." The stewardess, whose nametag read: Buffy, continued: "Mr. Blake will sign all your napkins, books and anything else after we take off." Buffy giggled. Chastain looked out the window. She wanted a cigarette. She also wanted Trevor Blake III out of her life. She was stuck with him. Things could be worse. She didn't see how.

Maybe the cruise would provide a partial vacation. The ship was loaded with so many people looking to stop the al Qaeda terrorists that maybe she would have time for fun. Then again they were mostly amateurs. Trevor couldn't wipe his ass. Don Gino meant well, but he was a gangster with a Dali infatuation. Chastain would be in touch with Zandra Filippi. Her computer information, as well as the FBI files, would solve the case. The only unknown factor was the former CIA agent that they called Bennie the Beneficent. He was a trained agent. He knew what he was doing. Chastain hoped that he could help. No one else seemed up to the task. Bennie was well trained. She looked forward to meeting him.

CHAPTER TWELVE

Bennie Preparing To
Catch Terrorists

"The hero is often someone who has no idea that he is about to experience fifteen minutes of fame. I am still waiting for my fifteen minutes" Bennie Beratano

Bennie was ready to fly to Tampa. He was going to stay at the Marriott with an ocean view in a private suite. This is the strangest thing he had ever done. Bennie loved being a retired CIA agent. He loved performing his magic show at the world's best casinos. The "Magic Bennie Show" was a crowd pleaser. He had a week to reflect on his life. He was re-entering a dangerous world.

The CIA called Bennie back to the Farm. The Langley, Virginia training center was his former home. He agreed to take the case on a contract basis. There was only one problem. Bennie had to meet with President Obama. That was not acceptable. He hated Obama. "I call him Osama," Bennie often said to Bertie. He laughed. No one else did. Bertie ignored him. She was too busy trying to get Barbra Streisand deported because she didn't have a birth certificate. Bertie had failed in the campaign to prove President Obama didn't have a birth certificate.

Bennie's assignment was not only dangerous, he was working with liberal, socialist minded assholes. They all supported President Barack Obama. Bennie believed that the president was born in Indonesia. He also couldn't stand the way he dressed. President Obama was always in a white shirt and a dark suit. Yuck! Bennie was a patriot. He would endure. Bennie also dressed in stripped shirts and plaid pants.

He had a trunk filled with his magic tricks. He was rusty from not practicing. After performing at the Magic Castle in Beverly Hills, he completed a month long residency at the Las Vegas Wynn Hotel. Then Bennie retired from performing magic. The bubble in the housing market burst, and he had spent a year making back the millions he had lost in Scottsdale Arizona. He thought about his engineering-nuclear physics background. He had worked on nuclear explosive devices, small terrorist made bombs and IED's. There was no one with more knowledge of what Bennie called: "The raghead terrorist mentality." The call from the CIA Director brought Bennie to the Tampa hotel room.

Bennie's PhD in Nuclear Engineering made him an expert on nuclear devices. He also had a decade of experience as a covert CIA operative; his specialty was dismantling nuclear weapons. Then he went into a business engineering shoes. He was also a major real estate investor. He made hundreds of millions of dollars. Bennie's home in Malibu was next to Mel Gibson's palatial mansion. Bennie was unhappy with Gibson who put his house up for sale for $14.5 million dollars. The reason that Gibson was selling the house was to make his former girlfriend, Russian pianist Oksana Grigorieva, move out. The guy was a real shit. He hated Gibson, who he saw as a liberal Democratic asshole. The reality was that Gibson was a conservative Republican. Bennie never let the facts get in the way of his prejudices. Bennie sold the Malibu house and with Bertie in tow he moved to Mill Valley. He was still surrounded by liberals, socialists, and Democratic Party assholes. He was relieved that there was no more Mel Gibson. He couldn't seem to escape the assholes, they were everywhere.

After Bennie bought an apartment building on San Francisco's Chestnut Street, he rented an apartment to Trevor Blake III for a sum that was less than half the market value. Trevor couldn't wipe his ass financially. Bennie felt sorry for him. Bertie didn't say anything. She didn't like Trevor's family. His father Johnny was a drunk and his mother Betty Ann Shell was nuts. One brother was a binge drinker who had petty hatreds directed at Trevor. This is a guy who held a knife to his wife's throat while drunk. He calls Trevor regularly and lectures him on his behavior. "You know Trevor, Bobby Darin and the Highlighters never appeared together in Seattle." It was difficult to deal with him. Trevor ignored him.

Bertie had the perfect family. Her father was a Vice President at Mutual of Omaha and her mother was Miss Nebraska 1950. She was still a beauty queen looking forward to the Mrs. America pageants. She was a perennial runner up in the Mrs. America contest. She was also a nice and genuine person who worked for UNICEF. Bertie's parents lived their entire life in Omaha Nebraska next to Warren Buffet. They never got tired of saying "Warren said." Bertie's parents had dinner one night a month with Buffett at Gorat's Steak House. Warren ordered the ten-ounce Club Iron steak with Roquefort butter because it was only fifteen dollars. The billionaire investor was still concerned about his pocket book.

Bennie made so much money that Bertie didn't care about their finances. She was too busy with her cooking awards and her birther movement to deport that Israeli spy Barbra Streisand. Bertie liked Bennie's business associates. It was his business with a celebrity investor, Shaquille O'Neal that brought Bennie publicity and a second fortune.

He still owned Shaq's Orthopedic Shoe Company. They were making millions fitting people with orthopedic implants. Shaquille O'Neal was frequently on TV infomercials with Bennie. They won an EMMY for best infomercial. Bennie didn't need the money. He was a multi-millionaire. He was also a patriot. He couldn't stand al Qaeda terrorists. They ranked fifth behind liberal assholes like Trevor Blake III, members of the Democratic Party, college professors and anyone associated with President Barack Obama. Bennie liked to rank those that he hated. It made it easier to be spiteful.

It had been a decade since Bennie was a CIA Operative. He trained at the farm. Then he spent most of his time in the Middle East. He hated the camel jockeys. He thought that Iraq was better off with Saddam Hussein. He couldn't stand the Iranian Ayatollah and whatever puppet they put in charge. He had received a message from the CIA Director. The E-mail read: "Bennie, we need you to come out of retirement. It is a grave situation with al Qaeda planning another 9-11." Bennie was ready to kill with his magic tricks.

The horrific and brutal nature of the attacks on September 11, 2001 changed Bennie's world. He would do what he could to wipe out the al Qaeda. Their presence on American soil, the conversion of young Americans to Islam and the weak, waffling nature of President Obama's politics infuriated Bennie. Despite his hatred for the president, he would defend his country. To do that he had to work for President Obama. He would. It was not a pleasant choice.

The death of Osama bin Laden prompted Bennie to celebrate with a barbeque at his Mill Valley home. Carlos Santana turned down the invitation. Those who came agreed that bin Laden's death crippled al Qaeda. Bennie would do what he could to end the American al Qaeda threat.

When the CIA Director called Bennie; they talked at length on an encrypted phone. Someone delivered another encrypted phone to Bennie's house. Bertie wondered what was going on. The phone call contained a short message describing a well-organized plot to blow an undetermined site in Barcelona. The second part of the message identified a terrorist attack in San Francisco. When the CIA Director mentioned that Trevor Blake III was involved, Bennie was speechless. Trevor was a P. I. who couldn't find his ass. What the hell was he doing going after al Qaeda terrorists? No wonder Mitt Romney wanted to take back America. It was lost to a pinko, Communist, Socialist President who was a secret Muslim. Bennie still wanted to see Obama's birth certificate. That asshole Trevor was too liberal. He couldn't see Obama's danger to the Republic.

It was a week before the Carnivolet mystery cruise ship sailed for Barcelona. Bennie was the Carnivolet's featured magic act. He had costumes, masks, illusions, tricks and assorted paraphernalia to pack. To appear as a famous magician was not an easy task. Bennie was up to it.

There was one complication. His fucking ex-brother in law, Trevor Blake III, was on the ship. As were his buddies in solving crimes, Don

Gino Landry and some little Chinaman who called himself Emilio. It was love of his country that prompted Bennie to sign on as a CIA contract agent. He vowed to find the terrorists. He couldn't stand President Barack Obama, now he was working for this Goddamned Muslim president.

He called Bertie. "Hi, sweet pea." There was a long silence on Bertie's end. She hated the nickname.

"Be careful Bennie. I have bad news. That asshole Trevor the Turd is on the ship."

"I know and please call him Trevor The Third." Bennie laughed. He loved to laugh at his lame jokes.

Bertie said: "Be careful you are working for a president who isn't even a citizen. He is a Muslim born in Africa or somewhere in Asia. Who knows! He doesn't. We can't even find the god damned birth certificate. Trevor has a coffee cup with President Obama's birth certificate on it. Don't let any of this influence you Bennie."

"I know, I'm a patriot, I can overcome any prejudice, except those against Trevor."

"I am watching Bill O'Reilly, he's fair and balanced."

Bennie said: "I can't stand Trevor making fun of my magic shows, constantly berating me for watching Fox TV News and complaining about Marilyn. He has divorced her. She is a San Francisco lawyer making millions. He is a Private Eye who has solved one case. That faggot Don Gino helped him. When I get home we are divorcing Trevor. We will kick him out of the Chestnut Street apartment. He can fend for himself. Maybe he can live with Shell Scott."

"Bennie, remember Shell Scott is a fictional detective."

"So is Trevor, he couldn't find his ass with a road map."

Bertie said: "Trevor went upstairs and picked the locks on your three file cabinets. I would pay some attention to him. He is not as inept as you think. He may be in the middle of what you are doing as a CIA contract agent."

Bennie said: "Don't worry. I have convinced Trevor that I am just another old person watching Fox TV News. He would shit his pants if he knew I voted for my first Democrat in the last election."

"Bennie you voted for the Tucson Dog Catcher. He is a Democrat."

"How could I forget it?"

"I still love you Bennie despite your one liberal failing."

"Remember Bertie when Trevor told me that he voted for Bill Clinton. Not one time but twice. I told him that he has no common sense. Trevor is a Democrat and an asshole. Case closed. I may vote for the next Democratic presidential candidate. Who knows?"

Bertie said: "I am not sure we can stay married if you vote Democratic. My parent's fortune has a clause in the will. There is an investigation into anyone in our family who votes Democratic."

"So we disinherit Bennie Junior. He is a lawyer and rich as hell. He doesn't need the money,"

"He is our son."

"So you say, Bertie."

"What about President Obama? What can you do for him?"

"Don't worry Bertie that socialist in the White House is destroying the country. I will find the al Qaeda terrorists and expose Obama's friendly policies toward the Muslims. I am out there to protect American values. Maybe we can send Trevor to Guantanamo." Bennie laughed.

After they hung up, Bennie studied the file. Trevor would be a problem. He wondered about the FBI agent that he was meeting on the ship. Probably some macho guy with a crew cut who stood out like a sore thumb. FBI agents all looked alike. He wasn't looking forward to some FBI hillbilly messing up his work. The medals in Bennie's War Room spoke of his service to his country. He was Doctor Bennie, martial artist, magician and patriot. The god damned al Qaeda would be sorry that they messed with America. Or for that matter with Bennie.

Bennie opened a file from the FBI. There was a picture of the agent that would help him. He was glad Bertie was staying home. The agent known as Chastain Johnson might need protection. She also might need some amorous attention.

The Chastain Johnson photo was an official FBI photograph. Not even the FBI could hide her beauty. Or her breasts. Or her legs. Bennie drooled. He would have to be charming when he met her. Perhaps he could execute a magic trick that would make her clothes disappear.

CHAPTER THIRTEEN

Bennie Meets President Obama

"I call him Osama." Bennie talking with Bertie

Bennie woke up to a Tampa morning. The sun was shining, the weather was unusually warm and the flowers scented the air. Tampa glowed as the tourists spent like there was no tomorrow. Everything was perfect. He had a few days before the Carnivolet Cruise Line sailed to Barcelona. Bennie couldn't wait to explore the U. S. Army post Fort Brooke that established American rule. The Spanish briefly explored Tampa in the 16th century but they failed to permanently settle the area. In 1819, Americans moved in to establish a settlement.

Bennie told the bellhop that the Spanish didn't know how to settle and keep their, empire intact. The bellhops name tag read: Trinidad. He smiled. Trinidad looked at Bennie. He smiled and accepted a dollar tip. Trinidad would have thrown it on the floor. The hotel would fire him. He smiled. As he left Bennie's room, Trinidad mouthed: "Fuck you asshole." He said it in Spanish. Bennie had no clue.

He was going to do some sightseeing. Bennie couldn't wait to explore the Florida sunshine. Tampa was a white person's town. Bennie loved that. He was also going to do some shopping. He was taking the day off. He had a list of coin shops. He was looking for Indian head nickels. He liked to call them Native American nickels to poke fun at the politically correct crowd. He would also purchase some magic tricks. Suddenly, he heard the whir of a helicopter landing on the roof of the hotel. He looked out the window. It was a helicopter with U. S. Army in bright letters. Two Marines jumped off in full military dress. Bennie wondered if there was a military costume ball at nine in the morning. They looked like they were on a mission. It was time to get dressed.

Bennie quickly jumped into the shower. He stepped out of the shower as the door pounded. The noise distracted him. The pounding didn't stop. Bennie looked through the peephole. There stood two Marines in full dress. What the hell was going on? He opened the door.

"Sir, the president requests your company, Major." He was speechless. They knew his former military rank. "Please come to the heliport on the roof, we are ready to take off." They saluted. Bennie stood for a few minutes. Then he regained his composure. The Marines shifted nervously.

Bennie said: "I'll be right up." They saluted him again. Pretty weird. But Bennie could get used to it. The two Marines were both white. At least that was in Obama's favor. He dressed and wondered what the hell was going on? President Osama is what Bennie continually called the president. This was followed by an impish smile and a loud laugh. When President Barack Obama summoned him to the White House, it was a sobering moment. A patriot can't turn down the president. Even if he is a closet Muslim, the president deserved Bennie's support. He wondered if Obama would appreciate his skills. Bertie did.

The helicopter ride to Washington D. C. was smooth and quick. The Democrats knew how to waste the taxpayer's money. The military style helicopter was sleek and fast. Bennie loved looking at the countryside.

They landed on the lawn adjacent to the White House. Bennie didn't realize that the White House didn't have its own heliport. Probably the Democrats looking like they were saving taxpayer money. What assholes. Mitt Romney should have been allowed to save America.

As the trio of secret service agents with dark suits, sunglasses, a diffident look and bad haircuts greeted Bennie, they were nervous and imperious. They were feds no sense trying to hide it. The clothes, the glasses and the way that they carried themselves suggested that they took their cue from watching Men In Black. Bennie wondered which one was Will Smith. Then he got it. The black guy was Will Smith. Bennie smiled. He liked his private thoughts.

The tallest agent said: "Sir, this way." They walked Bennie into the Oval Office. There was a huge desk, two chairs side by side on a Persian rug. Bennie hoped that it wasn't a real Persian rug. It might have a bomb under it. Maybe he should share this joke with the president. He decided to maintain his silence.

When President Barack Obama summed Bennie to the Oval Office, he had a special message. This message was that his country needed the former Army officer and CIA agent to ferret out al Qaeda terrorists.

President Obama was good at public relations. He realized that Bennie was a conservative Republican. The file mentioned that Bennie was to the right of Karl Rove. That made President Obama nervous. He was prepared to flatter Bennie. It didn't take much to inflate his ego. He had an ego the size of Texas. The president had a file on Bennie's heroics in the Gulf War. The FBI also updated information on Bennie. The file detailed his business interests, his politics and there were transcripts of his phone conversations. He was a right wing Republican who was kind to his three kids and his brother in law. His sister, Marilyn, was a Democrat. Bennie attributed her politics to her short marriage to "that asshole Trevor Blake III." Or Trevor the Turd, as Bennie christened him. Bennie also called Trevor "weird." It was his way of maintaining the upper hand. Control was important to Bennie. He wanted to let Trevor know that he was in charge. He never forgave Trevor for marrying his sister. He never forgave his sister. Their dad, Bernard, had even paid for Marilyn's college. Bennie never forgave his dad for that slight.

Bennie was happy that Marilyn came to her senses and divorced Trevor. He could still harass him, as he rented Trevor an apartment at a low rate to give him crap. It was money well lost. Trevor was an asshole. He still loved him. Family was always family. No matter what! Even an asshole was family.

When President Obama opened a file on Bennie's twin brother, Bruce, he was intrigued. Finally, there was an interesting family member. Bruce was a natural healer in Naperville, Illinois. He had eight different medical degrees, three were from China, one from Castro's Cuba, he was a Tibetan faith healer, a Hindu medicine man, and he had certificates in treating sexual malfunction from the University of Mumbai, the University of New Delhi and the Maharajah Institute of Creative Medicine. Bruce was unmarried. Bennie thought that perhaps he should treat himself. Sexual dysfunction was a growth industry, and Bruce was a star in the field. Bennie wondered if he got laid. President Obama found Bruce's file interesting. Bennie's was boring.

There was nothing else that caused alarm in Bennie's file. There were some concerns for the Obama administration. President Obama realized that Bennie represented the reactionary right wing. He could deal with that, as Congress was full of those assholes.

As President Obama searched Bennie's file, it revealed that he watched too much Fox TV news. He did have some positives. Bennie still worked out daily; he still had martial arts skills. He still had as much knowledge of terrorists as anyone and Bennie could blend into any crowd. Bennie was also a one-handicap golfer. President Obama was a fifteen handicap. Rufus Romulus was President Obama's appointment secretary. The forty-eight year old Romulus grew up in Florence, Alabama. His dad owned every cotton plantation in the area. After the Civil War, the Romulus family had to hire sharecroppers. Rufus liked to say that his great grandfather made more money with the slaves.

The Romulus fortune was made in recent years through the production of fertilizer. His dad said: "The chickens shit and we make millions." Rufus was a C student in high school and he was admitted to Harvard. He graduated in sociology with a C average from Harvard. He was active in extracurricular activities. Rufus was a cheerleader and he was the only white member of the Harvard's secret African American fraternity named for the Rapper Fifty Cent. In the last few years Fifty Cent sued and the name was abandoned. Rufus helped them find a new fraternity name. They called themselves the Leahcim Noskcaj fraternity. They told the school that it was a Greek name. It actually was Michael Jackson spelled backwards.

Rufus' dad donated ten million to each of Obama's election campaigns. The president had to endure this fool because of the political contributions. Rufus wrote a memo to President Obama warning that Don Gino, Bennie, Trevor, Emilio and the FBI agent with the big boobs were targeting an African American terrorist. He saw it as politically incorrect. President Obama reviewed the memo. He approved it. He asked Rufus to take out two words "Big Boobs." After this encounter, President summarily promoted Romulus. He was named the Secretary of Agriculture. He left that Cabinet position after one year to accept a million dollar private industry position. Rufus Romulus now heads the "Americans For Sheep Protection." He is also the first person in America to demand a federal law to protect sheep from Mutton Poachers. President Obama has distanced himself from Romulus.

Rufus' last official task in the White House was to announce Bennie. Rufus told President Obama "Bennie was America's last living patriot." Now that Pat Tillman was dead, Bennie was the poster boy for American strength abroad.

Bennie had spent a decade in the CIA; he retired on a medical disability. A terrorist had shot him in the ass. The bullet couldn't be removed. He had to stand for long periods. Bennie was perfect for the undercover job. He was ushered into the Oval Office. President Barack Obama was playing a game of hopscotch with his youngest daughter. No one would believe this as President Obama hopped around the room. He dismissed his daughter. He was taller than Bennie remembered. He was also thinner. He had more grey hair than the media showed. This was evidence that the media continued to support the president. He also had a handshake that would break your knuckles. He had a warm smile. Bennie was impressed. The president did have charisma. He had to get away from President Obama. He could come to like the guy. Bertie would divorce him. He couldn't let her know. Bennie wondered what was wrong. The President was a cool guy.

He wondered if he should tell the president that he voted for John McCain. Probably not a good idea! Bennie was a patriot. He would listen. The thought of al Qaeda terrorists doing damage in San Francisco angered Bennie.

President Obama sat down. He had aged dramatically since his second election. He looked for a long time at Bennie. The Oval Office was eerily silent. Bennie took out a stick of gum. He smiled. The President also had ten wads of paper. He began throwing them like basketballs into a wastebasket. Maybe the president was organizing a wastebasket league. Bennie looked bored.

"I need your help," President Obama said.

Bennie said: "Mr. President, I am at your disposal." Bennie felt strange. He couldn't stand Obama. His neighbor, Carlos Santana, wouldn't talk to him. He called Bennie a white supremacist This was due to Bennie lecturing Carlos on the indisputable fact that the President was a socialist, a communist, a community organizer and a follower of Saul Alinsky.

Bennie's book **Obama's Deception: Rules For Radicals** argued that Obamacare resulted from the President's training as a Chicago community organizer. Bennie was featured on Fox TV News for his statement: "No politician can sit on a hot issue if you make it hot enough." The numerous appearances on the O'Reilly Factor made Bennie a **New York Times** best selling author. Bennie was also working on other aspects of Obama's life.

He was also a tricky politician. That was Bennie's definition of a Democrat. Maybe President Obama was one of those Indian tricksters. Like a witch, a medicine man, a Shaman. Then Bennie thought of Trevor. That asshole loved President Obama. He campaigned for him. He voted for him. He genuflected in front of a framed Obama portrait. Maybe there was something Bennie was missing.

The President rocked back in his chair and placed his finger on his cheek. He was thinking. Bennie didn't say a word. "Bennie I need to send you undercover. You have talent as a magician. I am placing you on board the Carnivolet as the resident entertainment. You will be known as "The Hidden Magician." You will wear masks and present a few shows from behind a screen. There are Muslim terrorists hidden on the Carnivolet and in Barcelona. They are using Salvador Dali prints and art fakes to raise money to attack America. Your country needs your help."

"I'm ready Mr. President." Bennie felt strange. He had never voted for a Democratic President and now he was serving one. Bertie would not be happy. She hated Obama. Bennie would have to get into a damage control mode at home. Even Barbra Streisand had a higher rating in Bertie's political lexicon.

"I need more information Mr. President."

"I will have the Secretary of State brief you, Bennie."

"Thank you, Mr. President."

"You are a credit to your country." The President stood. The meeting was over.

Bennie was ready to return to Tampa to join the Carnivolet Cruise and figure out what the terrorists had in mind. The President told him that Trevor Blake III was in the mix. Bennie thought that his trick to make a person vanish, or the illusion of cutting of someone's head would work well on Trevor. He would give anything to make that smug prick disappear into the San Francisco sunset. Or for that matter into the dust or perhaps eaten by rapid dogs. Bennie the Beneficent would not disappoint his president. The terrorists were history. Bennie would see to it.

Bennie left the White House. He was taken to the Secretary of State's office. Hillary Clinton was smaller than she looked on television. She was also healthier looking. No wonder she couldn't handle the Benghazi controversy. She was too busy working out and eating right. She wanted to be the next president. Over Bennie's dead body. Hillary was wearing a pantsuit. She looked like a dyke. Bennie reminded himself not to share these opinions. No wonder Bill cheated.

She shook Bennie's hand. He felt strange. He hadn't voted for her husband. He liked him. Boy, did he get along with the babes. Bennie remembered that he had to be serious. He wondered what it would be like to hang out with Bill Clinton. It would beat hanging out with that asshole, his ex-brother in law, Trevor Blake III.

He was led out to a garden. Two seats, a pile of folders and a coffee pot and assorted pastries sat on the table.

"Welcome Bennie," Hillary Clinton said. He took a second look. She looked great in her stylish pantsuit. Her hair was colored and perfectly coiffed. She extended her hand. Bennie was impressed. She had style and presence. She also had a crunching hand shake. Maybe he had judged her too harshly. Too much influence from Bill O'Reilly and the other patriot newscasters at Fox TV News. Fair and balanced. What a trite thought.

"Madame Secretary, thank you for your help."

"We need to thank you, Bennie for your help." Bennie thought he misunderstood her. Didn't she say "yo?" Maybe she was hanging out with President Obama who said "yo." Probably not. After all neither Hillary of Obama were from the ghetto. Bennie reminded himself to control his racism. He often said to Trevor: "I'm not racist." He was.

"What do I need to know?"

Hillary thought for a moment. "We are killing al Qaeda members with drones. That is not enough. We need more information. Leon Panetta, the director of the CIA, is at a breaking point."

Bennie said: "What do you mean breaking point?"

"We can't find or identify neither the casual terrorists, nor the newly formed al Qaeda radical cells. It appears that a Carnivolet line ship sailing from Tampa to Barcelona is populated with terrorists. Your job is to find them."

"I am already working on the intelligence."

"Your credentials, Bennie, are superb, we need you to quickly rid the Carnivolet of the suspected terrorists."

"Madame Secretary, is this a direct kill order?"

Hillary smiled: "Just find them, we have people who will terminate the targets."

"Terminate!" Bennie said.

"Yes, terminate or you might say assassinate. I prefer terminate."

"Whom am I working with?" Bennie looked confused.

"You don't need to know that. I can say that the good-looking womanizer, Trevor Blake III, is on the cruise. He can't find his ass. He has been set up to think that he is investigating the al Qaeda terrorists. He is a pawn in our game. If we are successful, he gets the credit. If he fails, he goes to jail. Any questions?"

"I hope that he fails." Bennie thought it would be fun to bring Trevor cookies in San Quentin.

Bennie hoped that the mission wasn't successful. That way that loud mouthed jackass, Trevor Blake III, would be in prison. He could become someone's surfer boyfriend. Or maybe husband or wife to a Mexican gangbanger. After all it would be a maximum-security prison. Maybe Bennie could screw up the investigation. That would help Trevor on his way to prison. Bennie smiled.

"I need more information," Bennie said.

"I can tell you that the lead terrorist is an African American. One man leads them. We are interrogating key terrorists. The plot is to blow up something in Barcelona. I could care less about what they blow up in Barcelona. It is America that I am concerned with as we can't have another 9-11."

"Can you tell me the San Francisco target?"

Hillary thought for a moment. "We are not sure, it is a religious site. That makes it probable that Grace Cathedral, the Temple Emanu-El, Glide Memorial, Mission Delores or the Brahma Kumaris World Spiritual Center will be attacked."

Bennie said: "I think we are looking at Grace Cathedral, it is the most important San Francisco religious artifact."

Hillary said: "You need to use your persuasive powers to find out the target."

When Bennie met with President Obama, he gave him instructions not to torture any suspects. He relayed the conversation to Secretary Clinton: "The President said that we don't torture. How are you finding out the key information?"

Hillary said: "We are torturing the terrorists."

"What is President Obama's position?"

Hillary continued: "My husband has pointed out continually what is wrong with the President, he is a wuss."

"A wuss, I am not sure what that means." Bennie smiled. He knew what it meant. He was putting Hillary on the spot. She looked daggers at him. She loved the challenge. She remembered that Bennie's CIA file had a psychological section concentrated on his delusional behavior and grandiose thoughts. She would appeal to his hatred of President Obama.

"President Obama sits on his couch watching Fox TV News," Hillary continued. "I find Fox TV News Fair and Balanced."

"You do," Bennie said.

"I do."

"Then define a wuss for me." Bennie smiled. He was putting Hillary on the spot.

"A person who has a middle ground in politics, and life." Hilary paused. "That is a wuss."

"What does the president think of your plans?"

"He doesn't have an idea what we are doing. We killed Osama bin Laden. If we failed, President Obama could have disavowed our actions. If we succeed he gets the credit. It's the same with this operation.

"That doesn't sound fair."

"Don't be naïve, Bennie, it's politics."

"Do you approve of the use of torture?"

Hillary looked at Bennie with disdain. She said: "We received good intelligence. You are a right wing conservative, you seldom read anything on politics, you have no interest in the Democratic Party, you call the president "Osama," and you watch Fox TV News from morning to night. So you obviously approve of torture. Did I get everything right Bennie." She glared at him.

Bennie said: "How can those conclusions be qualifications? You seem to have disdain for me." Bennie thought she had it right. There was no doubt he was all of the above.

"You are exactly what we want, Bennie." Hillary continued: "Your cover is perfect. Anyone who investigates you would think you are more at home with Karl Rove than Karl Marx." Hillary smiled. Bennie frowned. He wondered who was Karl Marx?

"Tell me, Mrs. Clinton, what could I do? I am a retired CIA contract agent. No one in my family, except for Bertie, knows my past. Bennie Jr. thinks I am selling medical equipment or orthopedic shoe implants."

"We have a plan Bennie and you are integral to it."

What's the plan?"

"At the moment we can't say. In due time you will be brought up to speed on the mission."

"Sounds like Democratic double speak," Bennie smiled.

"We need you Bennie. The country needs you. The President needs you."

"Well, two out of three is not bad. I am aboard."

"Remember Bennie the president will explain our policy." Mrs. Clinton hurriedly left the room.

A tall, good-looking Marine enters and announces: "President Barack Obama." Bennie almost laughed. He was meeting with the president for a second time. It must be important. Mrs. Clinton had made a point. The president would explain his terrorist policy. Bennie knew it was one designed for votes. Bennie wondered did the president forget something? Good old President Obama, he doesn't have a policy. He can't make up his mind.

The President enters the room. President Barack Obama comes around the table. Trevor is sitting in a comfortable chair. He looks even taller than Bennie imagined an hour ago. He looks Bennie in the eye. He doesn't look like a Muslim. He doesn't look like a Socialist. He does look like a community organizer who is president.

The president sat down with Bennie. Obama said: "Do you know what I have missed?" This confused Bennie.

"What did you miss Mr. President?"

"Bennie, despite your illusions about my leadership, you have skills that will allow us to defeat a carefully planned al Qaeda attack. You are exactly what America needs. Here is an extended file that explains everything." Bennie smiled. He was about to try to one up the president. He couldn't. President Obama needed Bennie. It was a great feeling.

"I am at our service, Mr. President." Bennie felt like a hypocrite. He had said that an hour ago. He didn't believe it then, and he almost choked on the words. Oh well. It was better than being a Communist. Or for that matter a Socialist. Bennie left the White House feeling important. He couldn't wait to tell that turd, Trevor Blake III, how important he was to national security. Even if it was in service to a left wing Socialist-Communist-Muslim President without a birth certificate. After all Bennie was patriotic. That was more than he could say about Trevor. Or for that matter President Obama.

President Obama made it clear that the threat was as great as 9-11. Bennie was impressed. Not only did the Democratic president appear in charge, he was knowledgeable and charismatic. He better not let Bertie know that he was in service to what she called "the most radical and un-American president in our history." Bennie wasn't so sure. He liked what he heard from President Obama. Bennie was a patriot and he would make sure that the terrorists didn't survive. Maybe he could accidentally eliminate Trevor Blake III. That was a sweet thought.

Bennie was bothered by his admiration for President Obama. He sat down and wrote Bertie a letter: "Sweetums' I just spend some time with President Obama. He is a terrific person. I was wrong about him. He is the guide to a hidden instrument of power, the Presidency, and he will change the course of history. Don't worry I will vote for all the Republicans." Your husband Snookers. Bennie quickly sealed and mailed the letter. Sweetums and Snookers! Yuck!

Bennie left the President's office. He was conflicted. He didn't like working for a socialist-Muslim-community organizer, but he was quite impressed by President Obama. It was time for Bennie to pull out his best magic tricks and make the Muslims disappear. Bennie was ready for murder on the high seas.

PART II:
MURDER ON THE HIGH SEAS

"We will make no distinction between the terrorists who committed these acts and those who harbor them."
President George W. Bush

CHAPTER FOURTEEN

The Carnivolet Line Leaves Tampa

"I myself am surrealism." Salvador Dali

As I got off the Southwest Airlines flight from San Francisco, a swarthy Hispanic held a sign: "Trevor Blake III." He walked me over to a purple limousine. In twenty minutes, I was at my hotel and I had two glasses of Mumm's champagne.

Tampa is a town dominated by tourism. I checked into the Marriott Waterside and went to my room for a nap. The diligent private eye needs sleep. I also had Don Gino's Platinum American Express card. It was time to spend some of his money. After about two hours of peaceful slumber the phone rang.

"Trevor," a voice I didn't recognize continued. It was a sweet, sexy, syrupy female voice. "Meet in the lobby." The phone went dead. I dressed in a Tommy Bahama shirt and headed for the lobby. The female waiting for me in the lobby sounded sexy. I hoped it was someone special. I walked off the elevator and spotted her. My anticipation level sank to a new low. It was none other than my favorite FBI agent Chastain Johnson. She walked over with a big smile. I frowned. When I solved the Start Me Up murders, Chastain was the FBI agent in charge. We had a brief fling. It was one night and five minutes. She held a grudge against me for being bad in bed. I was tired. I was drunk. I was horny. I was ready. I thought five minutes was a long time in bed. She didn't.

"Hello Dickhead."

"Chastain, as I live and breathe, you are gorgeous."

She said: "Save it asshole for the Molly Ringwald types."

"To what do I owe this honor?"

"Shut the fuck up and listen." She lit a cigarette. Chastain went on to explain in great detail the problem. It seemed that someone working with the art company on board, the Pearl of the Ocean, was raising illicit funds to help al Qaeda terrorists. They were using fake Salvador Dali lithographs and original paintings to fund their nefarious terrorism.

Chastain said: "We know that they blend in and don't have beards. They have not only an education but money." She went on to describe them as probably looking like wealthy sophisticates on a cruise. This was an obvious oxymoron. She showed me a file with advanced weaponry.

Chastain had no idea that she was dealing with an African American. The ship held 6,200 passengers and more than 600 were African American. Not exactly great odds in identifying a terrorist on a fifteen day cruise. There were more than 100 African-American entertainers on board. This further complicated things.

Trevor said: "Well Chastain what do we do? Perhaps we could meet in my room for a private tutoring session on terrorism." I smiled. She frowned.

"Listen asshole, be serious for a moment."

She went on in great detail and suggested that unidentified terrorists possessed money, weapons and intelligence. There was another serious problem. She pointed out that Don Gino Landry, Emilio and my ex-brother in law, Bennie, were on the cruise in disguise. They were working for President Barack Obama under a special appointment by the State Department. I was still the point man for securing intelligence.

After she explained all this, I wanted to run to the airport and fly back to San Francisco. This wasn't a case. It was a Three Stooges movie with a modern twist. It was a fricking nightmare. The terrorists I could handle. Don Gino, Bennie, Emilio and Chastain were another story.

Chastain said: "You need to relax tonight and look over your files. We will talk on board the ship." She blew smoke in my face and walked out of the hotel. I needed to have a great dinner.

I took a cab to Bern's Steak House. I ordered the chateaubriand with all the trimmings. Brad Dixon, the sommelier, walked over and he recommended a bottle of the 2007 Sassicaia from Tuscany. This Italian red was a mix of Bordeaux varieties that made the French envious. At $250 a bottle it was a bargain. It was also the Don's money. I was enjoying a brandy and a cappuccino when I heard a familiar voice.

"Trevor, I hope you are eating and drinking well." It was Don Gino. He had on a white suit with a purple shirt, white tie, purple shoes and no cape. The gangster in vacation dress.

"I'm on the case, Don Gino." Fortunately I had brought my brief case along. I had all the key documents.

"I can see that Trevor."

"I was just about ready to pull out the files and go over them one more time."

"There is no need." Don Gino lit a small cigar. No one said a word. The Don could smoke anywhere. The rest of us were subject to the law.

"Is there anything else I need to know?"

"I think you have it."

"Good, I'll see you tomorrow on board the Pearl of the Ocean." Don Gino smiled and left. I had put out my own money for the bill. When he left, I put it back in my pocket and took out the Don's credit card. No sense wasting my good money. It was early. I went home and got to bed at ten o'clock. The next day my assignment began.

At noon, I settled into my cabin on the Presidential deck. The Pearl of the Ocean is a cruise ship specializing in mystery cruises. The best selling mystery authors Michael Connelly, Robert Crais and Jeffrey Deaver were featured speakers. There was also an up and coming author, Mark Gimenez. As a licensed private eye, I had trouble solving cases. I was famous for solving a case that is one case, my only case. To this day I don't know how I did it. Maybe the fiction writers could help me. They always solved their cases.

My luggage was inside the Blue Presidential Suite 106, the Purple Presidential Suite 101 was obviously Don Gino's, the Pink Suite 102 belonged to Chastain Johnson and the Orange Suite 103 belonged to Bennie, Suites 104 and 105 housed the six Samoans and the little bastard in the purple tuxedo. At least I was safe. I had six Samoans within easy reach. I forgot they hated me. They would rather see me dead. Don Gino gave them orders to protect me. They didn't look happy. We had fifteen days at sea and I had to find the al Qaeda terrorists. I had to find out who was raising funds for Muslim terrorists from art sales and what they intended to blow up. My plate was full. I also didn't have a clue when or where the crime was taking place. I did have a lot of material. The files and my rapidly growing collection of clue napkins helped.

I settled into my cabin and once again looked over my files. I had literally memorized the files. I also looked over the files that I had lifted from Bennie's house. After an hour I headed for the bar. Scott Shell would be at the bar if he was on the boat. Shell Scott would have three blondes around him. I was lucky if I met Chastain Johnson. If Elvis Cole was on board, Joe Pike would attract the women. Then I remembered that they were fictional characters. At times I felt like a fictional character.

As I entered the bar, I saw Army Elvis and Las Vegas Elvis enjoying a glass of champagne. I walked down to the Captain's Wine Bar. The Three Amigos were sitting there drinking a Chilean Merlot arguing whether or not it was better than the California Merlot.

The Three Amigos were Juan, Carlos and Jorge. They lived and worked in San Francisco's Haight Ashbury. They looked like they were illegal's. In fact, they all graduated from Stanford University and the University of California, Berkeley. Juan was a prosecuting attorney, Carlos was a defense attorney and Jorge was a judge. They had all gone to Stanford as undergraduates and then on to UC's Boalt Law School. They were affirmative action admissions to Stanford and the Boalt Law School. There were two books on their athletic and academic feats.

They were close friends of my investigator Guitar Jac. Then something happened. Jac could never figure it out. They weren't as friendly to him after law school. He was puzzled.

The Three Amigos played football at Stanford with Guitar Jac. They were all millionaires. They were also Catholics, divorced and wealthy. Nothing made sense with the Three Amigos. Hispanic and divorced ladies' men! Even worse rumor on the street was that their millions dwindled due to the divorces. They had married blondes from Scottsdale Arizona. Their friends noted that their wives had so much cosmetic surgery that they looked like new people. This soured the Three Amigos on marriage. They were legends in the San Francisco dating community. They were legends whose pocketbook diminished daily. Hispanic lovers with little control over their finances did not make for a happy ending.

The Three Amigos were good-looking men who couldn't keep their pants on around a breathing female. San Francisco was filled with good times for the Three Amigos. They were having fun as their finances drained.

They also met every morning at Emilio's donut shop in the Haight. Emilio had appeared twice before Judge Jorge Castillo and each time the case was dismissed due to a technicality. The San Francisco Police Department gave up on prosecuting Emilio for his cat burglar crimes. He stole art from the rich and sold the paintings in China. Juan had prosecuted Emilio with little enthusiasm and Carlos had defended him with zeal. Emilio had never been convicted of a crime. They were all bachelors and when they met every morning for coffee and donuts they talked about the young ladies at Perry's on Union Street. Trevor recalled that the young ladies at Perry's were all over forty. Too old for Trevor.

What were the Three Amigos doing on this cruise? That was more of a question than finding the terrorists. It puzzled Trevor. He snuck into a corner table and ordered a bottle of Jordan Merlot. He used his Platinum American Express card. The wait staff informed Trevor that he signed for everything. They looked at him like he was a hillbilly. He was.

He remembered that Don Gino said that everyone was going first class. Then Trevor recalled Don Gino's comment. Treat everyone nicely. So Trevor sent the Three Amigos a bottle of Jordan Merlot. He requested anonymity. Each person had a mask and the crew changed into a different mask each day. It was a nice touch to the mystery cruise. It also allowed the tourists and art forgers a free run for their crimes. I heard the Three Amigos holler: "Here, Here," as I exited the lounge for my room.

On the way to my presidential suite a beautiful young woman with a black wig, a long black dress, pointed high heels and a huge black headdress glided into the elevator. She was beautiful in a strange way.

Time for the Trevor Blake III charm: "Hello."

She said: "Hello."

I said: "It is a nice day."

"I can't tell we are in an elevator." The door opened at floor 2. "I am in room 2229, call me, and ask for Gala." She walked down the large hallway. The elevator door almost closed on my head. She was gorgeous. Gala. It was the same name as Dali's wife. She looked and dressed like Gala. The swept up hairdo and the crazy dresses identified Gala. Maybe I should grow a moustache and dress up as Salvador Dali. It was this fruitcake woman who had screwed all of Dali's friends and then poisoned him slowly in his later years. I decided to forget about Gala. She was too dangerous.

I also had a fifteen-day trip to find Muslim terrorists and art criminals funding al Qaeda. I had to steer clear of the Gala's and find the killers. Don Gino hired me with the stipulation that he would stay out of the way. I didn't think so. He seemed to be everywhere. I got off the elevator and the little midget in the purple tuxedo walked over. He smiled and kicked me in the shins. "Asshole," he murmured as he went into his room. Well that was better than dickhead. I had met a crazy woman, bought three Mexicans a hundred dollar bottle of wine and a deranged midget kicked me. Things were not going well.

CHAPTER FIFTEEN

The Welcome Dinner And The Captain's Feast

"I'm crazy about Lavin chocolate." Salvador Dali, a 1969 advertisement in which he bites into a piece of chocolate as his moustache swivels upward.

The Captain's welcome dinner was casual. The theme was chocolate. Everyone was requested to come dressed appropriately for the chocolate themed dinner. The 1969 television ad with Dali biting into a piece of chocolate as his moustache turns to the sky was played over and over on a dozen large television screens. It was funny. It was also tedious and tiresome. It also suggested that Dali was a strange person. The dinner was sumptuous. It was a five course feast highlighted by steak tartar, followed by a Caesar salad, a lobster in black bean sauce, a medley of vegetables, freshly baked breads and a medley of deserts. The Carnivolet line was big on a medley of beef, pork, chicken, lamb sausage and duck followed by an assortment of veggies and a desert cart that took up two tables. The Mayo Clinic was expecting the passengers to check in at the end of the cruise. There were four high-end wines and Dionne Warwick entertained the guests. Her career must be in the toilet. She was living in Brazil and recovering from bankruptcy and gangster management. I looked out from my table. I was dressed as a chocolate ice cream salesman replete with a white suit with a little white hat and a purple handkerchief. Just in case Don Gino didn't recognize me, the handkerchief would give me away.

"Hello Dickhead."

I looked up. It was none other than Chastain Johnson. She was dressed as Willy Wonka. That is if Willy had big breasts, cigarette breath and a nasty attitude. She didn't realize that Willy Wonka wasn't a woman.

I said: "Well, well the lovely FBI Agent undercover."

"Call me that again and I will cut off your testicles. Notice I didn't say balls because you have no balls." She smiled. She was always the clever FBI agent.

"To what do I owe this honor? Does the white suit remind you of my virginity or perhaps my wholesome nature?"

She said: "It reminds me that you don't have enough brains to solve a case."

"Have you forgotten I was on the cover of **Rolling Stone**? I did solve the Start Me Up drummers case."

"Don't remind me. Don Gino must have helped you." She lit a cigarette.

"Sleep with me and I will reveal all my secrets."

"I did that once and I am still in counseling." She walked over to another table. Good riddance. Then I noticed that Willy Wonka had marvelous breasts.

Then a handsome man with a brown cane, a brown hat, brown shoes, a brown shirt and tie and a light brown suit walked over with a mask of Johnny Depp. It was none other than Don Gino. I wanted to tell the Don that Johnny Depp wasn't in the movie. I didn't. There was no sense riling the Don. There were also six Samoan waiters hovering nearby. The asshole valet stepped on my foot. I had to ignore the little bastard.

He smiled: "Fuck you." He walked away.

Don Gino didn't care for cruises. He looked bored. I looked bored. It didn't pay to look bored around the Don.

"Trevor, we need to talk."

This was Don Gino's way of telling me what to do. He talked. I listened.

I said: "Talk away."

"We have a problem. Our terrorists look like you and I." I don't know what to say.

"You mean they are young, intelligent, handsome and well dressed."

Don Gino didn't laugh. I didn't laugh. We sat in silence. The Don was thinking.

"There is a woman, Gala is her name, and she is on one of the floors below you."

"She is in one of the cheaper cabins." Don Gino looked at me.

"What do you mean?"

Don Gino continued: "I mean this fake Gala is just like Dali's wife. She is pompous and an ass."

Trevor said:" I have spotted her."

Don Gino scowled. Not a good sign. Then he smiled. That was a good sign. "Thanks Trevor that tells me all I need to know."

"And that is, Don Gino?" He didn't answer. He looked at me for a long time. It is the Don's way of making me uncomfortable.

I said: "I met her, she's nuts."

"I need you to romance her." I didn't look happy. "She is the key?"

"The key to what?"

Don Gino said: "The key to everything."

I was confused. "Do you mean the terrorists, the illegal funds or the art fraud?"

"They are all connected, Trevor. Work on one and the others will fall in place." I always liked riddles I didn't understand. Don Gino turned and walked toward the elevator. Don Gino retired for the evening. I looked around and the six Samoan waiters vanished. The midget valet closed the elevator giving me the finger.

I had work ahead of me. I looked around the ship. Everyone looked the same-old, fat, white, boring and uninspiring. Was this my future? The terrorists and criminals had to be somewhere in the mix. Trevor Blake III was on the case. I would find them.

After a good nights sleep, I woke and went to the gym. I warmed up with fifteen minutes of light lifting; I did an hour on the recumbent bike and I finished with fifteen minutes of heavy lifting. If I was to look like Shell Scott, I had to work on it. My hair was too long to be Shell Scott. I would work on a Hollywood hairstyle. Maybe I could get Vidal Sassoon in for a quick styling. Then I remembered that Sassoon died.

The day went by quickly with bingo games populated by old, fat people. The casino was filled with smokers. Chastain Johnson sat at a dollar slot machine methodically pulling the handle. She was also methodically smoking. Did the FBI have an entertainment fund? What was the FBI doing in international waters? I had more questions than answers. Chastain looked my way and sneered.

It was the second day of the cruise. I was already bored. My ADD was kicking in. Maybe it was just the cruise! I walked into the casino and charged $5000 worth of chips. I wondered if Don Gino was really paying for it? If not, I was in trouble. The casino was filled with Bennie and Bertie look a likes. They were talking Fox TV, Sarah Palin and the Republican who had turned into President Obama's friend. That would be John McCain. It was time to go to my cabin. Everyone looked like a slice of wonder bread gone to seed.

I spent an hour in my palatial cabin suite putting on a newly purchased tuxedo. I looked in the mirror. I looked great. That is if you liked forty one year old penguins. It has been a year since I solved the Start Me Up band killings. My fame had faded. I was no longer on the cover of **Rolling Stone**. Late Night With David Letterman had me on for a half an hour. Now they wouldn't return my phone calls.

I was invited to the Captain's Table for a formal dinner. I arrived dressed in a Sherlock Holmes costume. I had brought along a mask to look like Shell Scott. I spent the evening explaining to anyone who asked that Richard Prather's detective novels featured Shell Scott. Everyone yawned and ran away. Philip Marlowe, Sam Spade, Sherlock Holmes, Watson, Inspector Maigret, Elvis Cole and Harry Bosch masks were most prominent. I asked the guy wearing the Ricky Ricardo mask. "Was Ricky Ricardo a detective?" There was a dead silence.

He looked at me like I was nuts. "You would have to be to get rid of Lucille Ball." The guy continued: "Besides Ricky had to figure out those English scripts." He laughed. Pure racism. Is there any other kind?

The dinner was a masterpiece. Not only was it the highest level of gourmet sophistication, but the old and young alike looked regal in their tuxedos, fancy evening gowns and sophisticated costumes. Everyone wore a mask. There were also some costumes from the fairy tale world. I looked at the most beautiful Cinderella I had ever seen. She walked regally through the dining room. She stood at my table smiling. Her beautiful blonde hair, her makeup and her Cinderella mask couldn't hide a body that made Jayne Mansfield look flat chested.

"Hello Dickhead." The mask smiled. I didn't. It was none other than the lovely Chastain Johnson. She didn't light a cigarette.

"Giving up smoking for lent, Chastain?"

She smiled. Then she dug her spiked toe into my shoe. I hopped around like I was dancing an Irish jig. I stopped. My toe hurt. She left. I felt a hand on my shoulder. Little Red Riding Hood was smiling at me. She also had a great body. I never noticed any of this when I was a kid.

"How's the big bad wolf?"

"Ready to eat you my dear."

Little Red Riding Hood said: "Your place or mine?"

I said: "Yours." We almost ran to her room. I hadn't finished my desert. Oh well, there was a more appropriate desert awaiting me. I spent the night with Little Red Riding Hood. She wouldn't take off her mask. I got through the night without ever seeing her face. She had fake blonde hair. I didn't care and I hobbled back to my room at five in the morning. I took a vow not to eat and drink so much. Sex was another matter. I couldn't swear that off, I was only forty-one. I fell asleep with a smile. The Captain's Feast had been memorable. I had to find out. Who was Little Red Riding Hood?

I woke up the next morning. My tuxedo was on a chair. There was only one problem. There were no pants. I checked. The silk jacket with silk lapels was laid over the back of the chair. The cummerbund was neatly folded. I couldn't have done that. I have never neatly folded anything. The studs for the shirt were on top of the cummerbund. The pleated white shirt had red wine stains all over it. The trousers with the satin ribbons going down the side of the leg were nowhere in sight. The black patent leather shoes were scuffed but on the floor. The mystery of the trousers bothered me. How could I come back to the room without my pants? A good question! I didn't have an answer. The mystery of my missing pants needed to be solved. I wasn't doing well with the crime. Maybe I would have more luck with my tuxedo pants.

CHAPTER SIXTEEN
Trevor's Pants Land Him In Jail

"You know the worst thing is freedom. Freedom of any kind is the worst for creativity." Salvador Dali

Trevor woke up with a splitting headache. He looked at the clock beside his bed. It was five thirty in the morning. He had been asleep for two hours. His head ached. His body felt like someone had hit him in every conceivable place. One place did feel good. He felt miserable. He got up and splashed some water on his face. He looked in the mirror. His eyes were bloodshot. Someone began beating on the door.

He put the cabin robe on and opened the door. The Captain stood stiffly at attention with two armed officers. This was strange.

Trevor said: "Yes."

"We have come to arrest you. Please step out of your suite."

"What? Step out of my suite. Are you nuts?"

Trevor stepped out and he was handcuffed.

"As the Captain of the Pearl of the Ocean, I am arresting you for murder." The two-armed officers led Trevor to the elevator. He stopped.

"Who did I murder?"

"Don't be coy."

"Coy! What the hell is going on?"

"You know as well as I do." The Captain continued: "Strangulation is a crime."

This guy is a bit over the top. Trevor said: "I need to know the victim."

"You do. You slept with her last night." The Captain smiled.

"You mean Gala?"

"Yes. Her name isn't Gala, her real name is Bar Markowitz."

"Bar!" Trevor stuttered.

"Yes, Bar." The Captain continued: "She is one of Israel's most famous actresses. Now she is dead. She is also a Mossad agent. Or should I say was?"

"A Mossad agent?"

"Yes, Mr. Blake, you are in serious trouble."

"What do you do next Captain?"

"We call in Interpol." The Captain looked confident. He had Trevor taken to a cell in level one of the Pearl of the Ocean.

Trevor walked into a ten by ten cell with a cot, a sink, a bucket and a blanket. He wondered if he could use his Platinum American Express card for room service.

Trevor said: "Do I get a special menu?" There was no laughter. The guards ignored him.

The Captain reappeared: "We have a request for two sets of people to see you. Until we hear from Interpol, who we just radioed, we have to grant you some rights. It is the American way." This was an Italian Captain talking. That was strange, the American way. I was in the middle of the Caribbean. What in the hell was the American way out on the international seaway? I would soon find out.

"Mr. Blake, you have three visitors." The guard turned and left. Through the door the Three Amigos walked in looking solemn. Juan, Carlos and Jorge were a Judge, a defense attorney and a prosecutor. The sat down on hard small stools.

Juan said: "Trevor, how could your pants have strangled a female Mossad agent?"

Trevor looked perplexed. "Maybe she had such a good time with me that she had to kill herself. The sex was so good she could never duplicate it. I understand why she killed herself."

Jorge said: "Not only is that not funny, we now have an international incident. How are we going to explain the Mossad agents death?"

"You could say she was screwed to death." I smiled. They frowned.

Carlos said: "We are leaving you in the brig for your own protection."

"You mean I am Trevor Blake III prisoner."

Jorge said: "The Israelis have put a contract out on you."

"Oh shit!"

Juan said: "We will be back. Stay here."

Trevor laughed. "I could escape to the buffet." The Three Amigos left looking disgusted.

Trevor lay down in his cold cell and he fell asleep. It was only ten in the morning. He was emotionally exhausted. When Trevor awoke it was dark. He looked at the cell door. There was a tray of food. A ham and cheese sandwich, a bag of barbecue potato chips, an apple and a diet coke. Well at least he wouldn't get fat.

He picked up the tray and started to eat the sandwich. Trevor looked up. Don Gino stood outside the cell smiling. Why in the hell was he smiling?

"Trevor, you have served the investigation well."

"You mean by killing a female Mossad agent?"

"Exactly."

Trevor was confused. Don Gino lit a small cigar. Trevor hoped that he wouldn't blow up the ship.

Don Gino said: "It will take me another day to contact the Justice Department. Sit back and enjoy the food." The Don left. Enjoy the food. I wondered if he was nuts?

Trevor looked around and fell asleep. He felt something on his shoulder. He opened his eyes and a hood was put over his head. He was dragged from the cell and taken to an elevator.

He was pulled and pushed into an elevator. Maybe they were going to throw me overboard. He would go bravely. He was also scared to death. With his hands cuffed behind his back, he had difficulty moving. They shoved Trevor into a room. He regained his composure. He looked around.

There wasn't a sound. What in the hell is going on? Hours passed. Trevor heard voices. They were talking. He recognized the language as Modern Hebrew. Oh, shit. They were Mossad. They talked quietly and without passion. Maybe before they kill someone, they have a quiet discussion. I would miss dinner. That was ok. The jail food wasn't a buffet.

"Boss wonder what you do here?" So much for the Modern Hebrew. Or for that matter the King's English. I scrunched up into a ball. There were no blows struck. "You coward?" I decided not to answer the question or to criticize his use of the King's English. I stood up. The fearless detective returns.

I was dragged from a chair and forced to stand in the middle of the room. I told myself to pay attention. If I didn't die, I needed to remember everything.

I realized that I had to live for the moment. I thought of clever things to say. I couldn't come up with one smart comment. I was too scared. I stood in the center of the room for twenty minutes. I needed to go the bathroom. Best to leave that need to myself. If they wanted to kill me, I would be thrown overboard. The guy with the bad language smelled, and I wondered if he knew another sentence. It was time to turn on the Trevor Blake III charm.

"Will somebody talk?" I shouted. There was silence. I fell to the floor and curled up in a ball. Someone pulled me up.

"We need to know what you are doing here?" The voice was commanding and in a clipped English accent. It sounded like James Bond meets the Mossad. Then the two men began talking in Modern Hebrew. One of the men hosted me up to a chair. He tied me tightly to it. I knew this was not good.

`"One more time. What are you doing here?" I decided to answer honestly. My last words.

"I am a San Francisco Private Eye, I'm on a case."

There was derisive laughter. Not exactly respect for the world's second greatest Private Eye. Elvis Cole would send Joe Pike to take these guys down. Shell Scott would simply beat them up. Unfortunately, these fictional characters weren't available.

I told myself to be strong. Grace under pressure and other clichés came to mind. Where was Guitar Jac when I needed him? They took my wallet and passport. That was not a good sign.

"We need to know one thing?"

"Yes." It was a weak frantic answer. I was nervous. Why? Who knows! I wasn't guilty. Maybe I was guilty of being excessively heterosexual.

"Did you kill Gala?"

"Gala wasn't Gala. She was some sort of secret agent."

"You don't say." The clipped British accent just got more clipped.

"I didn't kill her. My pants did." I realized how stupid this sounded. But it was the truth. "I don't control my pants." No one laughed. Humor was dead. So was the young lady.

'We know you didn't kill her."

"Then why am I tied up, preparing to be thrown into the sea?"

"We want to find out what you know." Someone lit a cigarette. Yuck, it smelled. It was French. "It is obvious that you know very little."

Not exactly respect for the famous San Francisco P. I. They left the room. I was alone. This was not going well.

Then another person came into the room. Whoever it was took the hood off me. He was standing behind me. Then I felt some well developed breasts. He was a she. She was strong. She stood me up. I wasn't going to die. Hallelujah! I was still tied up.

"I want to know one thing?" The feminine voice intrigued me.

"Anything, my phone number, my sexual resume. Whatever you want." She began twisting my arm and it felt like it would break. She eased up.

"All I can say is find the al Qaeda cell."

"We know that. Do you have a name?"

"No."

She wasn't sure. I needed to tell her something. She said: "Ask Matt Luman. He knows everything." She turned me to the wall. She left the room. I was still tied up, but I could see the sunlight coming in from the door. I quickly untied my restraints. I picked up my wallet and passport. All the money was still in it. I guess that they weren't robbers. I walked out and looked at the number. It wasn't a suite. It was a cleaning closet.

I walked toward the elevator. I got on. I asked the people to press my floor. They looked at me in horror and got out of the elevator.

A young lady entered the elevator. "Hello Dickhead." The beautiful Chastain Johnson came to the rescue.

"Cat got your tongue."

I sneered, got off the elevator and walked to my room.

CHAPTER SEVENTEEN
Don Gino Inspects His Product

"I am painting pictures which make me die for joy, I am creating with an absolute naturalness, without the slightest aesthetic concern, I am making things that inspire me with a profound emotion and I am trying to paint them honestly."
Salvador Dali

Don Gino finished his exercises. There was a section of the ship's gym cordoned off for the Don. He had a demanding daily workout. He had to stay trim for all those breakfasts at IHOP.

He drank a cup of coffee. He called the six Samoans. He alerted the ship's Captain. They all went down to the cargo area. Don Gino inspected the two-dog food canning machines that he was transporting to Barcelona. He was opening a branch of his dog food canning business and donating the proceeds to the completion of La Sagrada Familia.

"I want the dog food canning machines hooked up," Don Gino remarked to the Captain.

"Don Gino, no problem, it will take a day." The Captain snapped his fingers. A group of burly longshoremen unpacked and began assembling the machines.

"Thank you Captain, I will remember your cooperation." The Captain smiled. Anything to please Don Gino. The Don was looking forward to spending some tourist time in Barcelona. It brought him fond memories of his childhood.

When he was a young boy, Don Gino's father talked about Antoni Gaudi who befriended his family when they moved from Barcelona to San Francisco. Although Don Gino's dad was Italian, he had lived for some time in Barcelona. Don Guido was an architect. He made millions in San Francisco and Barcelona. Don Gino's father was known as Don Guido the businessman who helps Italians. He was a silent partner with A. P. Giannini who founded the Bank of Italy. It was Don Guido's money, his expertise in locating commercial property for branch banks and his skill in convincing people to invest with the Bank of Italy that made the bank profitable.

Then Don Guido met a small Los Angeles banker, Orra E. Monnette. They talked at length about his small bank. Monnette's Bank of America was small and not very successful. Don Guido convinced Monnette to join forces with Giannini and a new Bank of America was born. Don Guido was given preferential banking loans, and his son followed along the same lines developing businesses and real estate.

Don Guido made a fortune building key San Francisco buildings. As an architect, Don Guido was trained in Italy. He became a multifaceted American businessman and took his son Gino to Europe each summer. Then Don Guido told his son that he had a visit from the Virgin Mary. He needed to help finish La Sagrada Familia.

When Don Guido arrived in Barcelona, he vowed to help the Gaudi Foundation with the completion of La Sagrada Familia. The famed architect had been dead for thirty years. As his young son, Gino, came with his father to Barcelona in the 1960s, he was fascinated with Gaudi's magnificent religious edifice.

When Sagrada Familia began construction in 1882, Antoni Gaudi was intrigued. He took over the architectural design and construction the following year and worked until his untimely death in 1926. Don Guido always called Gaudi's incomplete church, the Temple of the Holy Family. Don Gino's dad was twenty-five and a recent graduate of Italy's most famous architectural school in 1928 when he came on a one year internship to Barcelona to help the Gaudi Foundation complete the church. Gaudi died before Don Guido arrived. He was visibly upset. A distraught father took his wife to San Francisco. It was twenty years before Don Gino's mother got pregnant. She did so after his father and mother took a vacation to Spain and toured the still uncompleted La Sagrada Familia.

As Don Gino's father was dying, he made his son promise to support Gaudi's historic church. It was now sixty-seven years later and the multi-millionaire Don Gino Landry was in the process of establishing a dog food canning business in Barcelona. His Barcelona dog food canning business was located near Sagrada Familia and every penny of profit would go into refurbishing the famed church

There were other concerns for Don Gino. He remembered the day that he met Dali in La Perpignan. The famous artist was not only nice to him; there was a twinkle in Dali's eye. He suggested the Don collect his art. He did. He never forgot meeting Dali. He thought of him a lot. He was now on a ship, the Pearl of the Ocean, where Dali's art was for sale. He wondered how much of it was original and how much counterfeited. He would find out.

As Don Gino descended into the cargo area, he was troubled by the attacks on Dali's reputation. He was also concerned that Dali's artistic endeavors were being sullied. The last Dali, **Portrait Of A Pope**, had never seen the light of day. There was a simple reason. Don Gino owned it. It hung in his house. It was a rare, private painting. He also had enough Dali's to open his own museum. Those who attacked Dali and America would experience Don Gino's wrath. He lit a small cigar. Retribution was coming.

He walked over to the crates. The dog food processing machines were in good condition. No one inspected the other crates. They contained millions of dollars of Dali's work. Don Gino had kept that a secret. He was getting ready to donate the obscure and completely unseen, **Portrait Of A Pope**, to the Dali Foundation. He would unveil the preliminary sketch and the finished product at a press conference outside Sagrada Familia. This rare painting had never been seen in public. Some doubted its authenticity. The picture of Dali finishing it with Gala standing by his side was the authentication. There were others who came forth. The imprint of Dali's personal photographer of forty years validated the work. Don Gino also had documents signed by a wide variety of Dali's friends.

As Don Gino gazed at Gala's harsh image, he was filled with hatred. Her hair was swept up like a cleaning lady. She was a Russian. Obviously, one who was without nobility? He had to go to confession. When he thought nasty notions, he needed to confess. It was the burden of being a good Catholic that caused Don Gino to be repulsed by Gala's behavior. She had a peasant's mentality. She was also a nymphomaniac. Don Gino had a strong moral sense. When he was outraged by immorality, he had to find a confessional. Hate was a sin that bothered him. Fortunately, there wasn't a Catholic priest on the Pearl of the Ocean. He could hate for fifteen days. Gala had not only poisoned Dali, she spent his money precariously. She had taken lovers. What was wrong with her? Her legacy would remain an obscure one. The Don would see to it. She was a vile woman.

Then Don Gino walked over to the crate containing **Portrait Of A Pope**. He took out a small drill, carefully drilling a hole in the wood. He placed a miniature transistor in the hole and sealed it with putty. This was a precaution against theft. He could track the crate.

Don Gino was a careful art collector. Theft, fraud and manipulation were traits that dominated the art world. Dali included extensive symbolism in his work. This symbolism allowed the identification and authentication of his paintings. In **The Persistence of Memory**, Dali suggested that Einstein's theories needed to be tested. Dali did this by including the symbolism of "melting watches" to challenge Einstein's ideas. **Portrait Of A Pope** included four Holy Fathers of different ethnicity. What was Dali suggesting? Don Gino believed that the Catholic Church had to embrace a wider cultural message. Dali's work heralded that change in Catholic doctrine. Dali believed that clocks were a symbol for a changing civilization. That is they ticked their way to ultimate destruction.

Dali's **Portrait Of A Pope** was inspired by Diego Velazquez' work. In 1650, when Velazquez completed the **Portrait of Pope Innocent X**, the Spanish artist unwittingly provided Dali with the model for his papal portrait. The difference is that soldiers were in the bottom right corner of Dali's painting. There were also four Popes. It was a protest to purify the Catholic Church. Muslim radicals envisioned it as a call to arms. James Smith saw it as divine providence.

The idea that Dali had Arabesque roots irritated Don Gino. Because Dali talked about his Middle Eastern heritage, it didn't make it a fact. The Don would get rid of those who would cast blasphemy on Dali. He had a large notebook with all the facts. He would act.

After Don Gino put his notebook away, he pulled out his kindle and powered up his pictures. He looked at **The Great Masturbator** and **The Metamorphosis of Narcissus** to admire the Daliesque use of the egg in his work. Dali had a way of interpreting death that intrigued Don Gino. The images that Don Gino kept in his computer were a constant source of pleasure. He walked up from the Pearl of the Ocean's lower depths ready for another wonderful dinner. He could relax on the Carnivolet. For Don Gino, it was a rare moment.

The dinner on the Carnivolet caused Don Gino to pause and think. There was something that he was missing. The 5 Star dining was replete with black leather chairs and purple pillows. The chestnut and porcini mushroom soup was outstanding, the caviar was lavish, the clay pot caramelized chicken was succulent and the baked Alaska ended a sumptuous meal. The wine was perfect. Suddenly, Don Gino remembered what he had overlooked. He would find the answer in the casino.

He recognized one of Dali's detractors. The man was quiet, unobtrusive and handsome. He was also African American. He was one of Donald Trump's close friends. James Smith was beyond suspicion. He dressed well. He was educated, classy and sophisticated. This was the perfect cover for an al Qaeda terrorist. Don Gino walked over and watched him gamble. He made small bets. He was gracious to everyone, and he moved from blackjack, to craps to the baccarat table with ease. He belonged in this wealthy environment. If this man was a Muslim sympathizer, he had a brilliant cover. Don Gino wondered if Trevor had discovered this unlikely terrorist.

Don Gino left the casino for a moment. He pulled out his encrypted phone. He sent a long voice mail. It was time to call in the cavalry. He went to a ship phone. He called Emilio. The instructions were clear. Emilio told the Don that the requested task would be accomplished within the hour.

The walk back into the casino, where he would gamble into the night, calmed Don Gino. He would reestablish Dali's reputation with the church and in the process rehabilitate the great artist. He would also eliminate Dali's detractors. They were using Muslim ideology to smear a great artist. The Don was not happy.

As Don Gino walked into the casino, he didn't notice the terrorist eyes trained on him. They squinted and look intently at him. They also noticed the six Samoans hovering nearby. What they didn't see was the small Vietnamese man in the room service uniform. He had a small broom and a dustbin. He swept up. Then he put the broom away. He had a smile on his face.

"Excuse me, Sir," Emilio said.

"Get away, you fucking Chinaman."

Emilio brushed up against the men. "Sorry Gentlemen, I didn't mean to bump into you, I am old and my balance is not so good." Emilio bowed. He left the area where the men were watching Don Gino.

The two men observing Don Gino didn't notice when Emilio attached a small listening device to their clothing. It was no bigger than a toothpick. He smiled. He bowed. He walked to the elevator. The listening device was activated. The next time they called him an old Chinaman, they would die. No one disrespected Emilio.

Trevor Blake III did notice. He watched the small Asian man wearing a service uniform. The small man was older, perhaps past sixty, his muscles rippled and he moved quickly and silently. Trevor lost him in the crowd. Emilio was shadowing Don Gino and despite the six Samoan bodyguards; Emilio provided tight security. Emilio was a contract agent hired by the CIA to help find the terrorists. He knew that Chastain Johnson, Bennie and Matt were also in the hunt. Few people realized that Emilio was on the Pearl of the Ocean. He was the CIA's inside security man. He would only act in a dire emergency. Until then, he was making $5000 a week thanks to the CIA.

The CIA also gave him clearance to perform any cat burglary act that he desired, and to hack into anyone's computer. This was a verbal, not a written, agreement.

After Emilio returned to his cabin, he emptied his pockets. There were two passports. The first one was in the name of Dan Fesperman. Emilio looked perplexed. Fesperman was a foreign correspondent with the **Baltimore Sun**. The real Fesperman had written eight spy novels. The other passport was for John Fullerton. It was also an obvious fake. Fullerton, a Reuter's reporter in London, had written a number of British thrillers. What the hell was going on? Maybe somebody didn't like mystery writers.

The ruse was one that Emilio couldn't figure out. He took out his encrypted cell phone and read off the biometric number from the passports. The real names came up. The two senior Mossad agents, Herbie Mizells and Arnie Weinstein, were art fraud experts. Could they be going after Park Avenue Artists?

Emilio pulled out his confidential files. There were no signs of the terrorists. The people engaged in art fraud were an easy target. They hired good-looking young ladies, served extensive flutes of champagne, and they auctioned off high priced goods of the most dubious quality. The only problem was tracing the money. Emilio couldn't figure out where it was deposited.

Emilio believed that Park Avenue Artists out of Las Vegas couldn't possibly be engaged in any form of terrorism. The owners were Jewish, they were religious and despite U. S. Justice Department attempts to convict them, they were clean. He was missing something.

Who then was behind the terrorist schemes? Emilio would find out. Emilio was upset with the terrorists. He recently received American citizenship, and he told Don Gino that the threat to America was once Communism. Now it was a Socialist President. There were also threats from al Qaeda. Emilio couldn't do anything about the socialist president, the al Qaeda were another matter. They would soon be eliminated. Perhaps on the high seas, perhaps in Barcelona, perhaps in San Francisco.

CHAPTER EIGHTEEN

After Stops In Nassau And Bermuda Four Days At Sea: Art Fraud On The High Seas

"Surrealism will at least have served to give experimental proof that total sterility and attempts at automatizations have gone too far and have led to a totalitarian system.... Today's laziness and the total lack of technique have reached their paroxysm...." Salvador Dali writing in a 1943 catalog advertising his work in a New York exhibit.

The Atlantic Ocean crossing was calm and boring. The Carnivolet line was first class with a chef from Italy, a pastry specialist from France and a sommelier who was knowledgeable about French, California, South African, Australian and Italian wines. Don Gino personally selected a portion of the wine list.

The casino was full of gamblers as Park Avenue Artists prepared for its initial auction. The multi-colored brochure delivered to every stateroom headlined: "Free Gift." Trevor looked at the brilliantly colored brochure that also read: "Free Champagne." A beautiful blonde model held up an art piece. It was common for Park Avenue Artists to ply a prospective buyer with champagne, the touch of a beautiful woman and the opportunity to purchase an art piece at a bargain price. You didn't have to pay cash. Your credit card would do. It was an offer too good to be true. It was an offer Trevor couldn't refuse. He would investigate.

Trevor left his suite and wandered down to deck three to peruse the art pieces. He couldn't help but notice the young girls in halter-tops. That is if young girls are just beyond thirty. Everyone else on the ship looked one step from the grave. Just past thirty would do just fine.

Trevor stood in front of a huge display of Dali lithographs. The third deck had an art row and the long procession of Dali lithographs drew a large crowd. There were three prominent Dali etching lithographs: **Casanova**, **Alice In Wonderland** and **Holy Bible**. Trevor stared at the last one. It seemed blasphemous. **Holy Bible** is not exactly a lithograph one associates with Dali.

There was also a Dali Historical Gallery. This was a means for Park Avenue Artists to charge twice what the Dali's were worth. Trevor walked up and looked closely at the Dali marked "Retrospective Signed Suite of 4." The price was $30,000. Don Gino purchased the same set on eBay for $8,000. Something was terribly wrong.

Park Avenue Artists advertised that they were selling priceless originals. There was one Dali set of watercolors that collectors considered priceless. The fourteen rare botanical artworks sold for over a million dollars. The watercolors painted in the 1960s brought out a new side of Dali. The description of the watercolors left little to the imagination. People purchasing art on the Pearl of the Ocean weren't exactly rocket scientists.

The Park Avenue Artists catalogue stated: "Titles like **Hasty Plum** and **Penitent Peach** present some of the world's most expensive, slightly erotic depictions of fruit in the history of art." Trevor looked at the description and laughed. Fruit as erotic! Not really.

"Getting an education, Dickhead. Or is it an erection?" Trevor knew the voice. He turned and there in full costume stood Gala. Chastain's depiction of Gala was a nice improvement. The lovely Chastain Johnson was in drag just like Gala. The black dress, the black hair, the black shoes, the black eyebrows, the black lips. Unfortunately, Chastain Johnson's breasts made Gala look like she was in grade school.

"Does the FBI have a costume budget?" Trevor laughed.

"You might pay attention to who is in the room." She turned and left.

Trevor looked around the auction site and saw nothing. The art interested him. But not at Park Avenue Artists' price.

There were a number of other Dali originals up for auction. The bidding started at $500,000. Some were originals. Some weren't. Where was the FBI when you needed their detailed expertise? Chastain Johnson probably was smoking a cigarette, putting her make-up on and swearing at the men that she disliked. Maybe she was still disguised as Gala. Sigmund Freud would have fun analyzing Chastain. The Gala costume was in character for her. He noticed a sign for another special Dali room. How many special Dali rooms were on the third deck?

Trevor walked around to the next special room. It was filled with champagne and good-looking young ladies. He couldn't wait for the sales pitch. He had Don Gino's Platinum American Express card. Then he decided it was time for a little drinking. Trevor wandered down to the Billie Holiday Lounge. There was a small jazz combo playing and a good-looking blonde was singing "Strange Fruit." Somewhere Billy Holiday was turning over in her grave. Trevor nursed his drink. What was it that attracted the terrorists to Dali? Then he recalled while Dali was in school in Barcelona, he wanted to put a bomb in the reception room for a member of the royal family. When King Alfonso XIII arrived in an old fashioned horse drawn carriage to visit the Special School of Painting, Sculpture and Engraving in 1920 a diary kept by Joseph Rigol noted: "Dali was very anti-monarchist, said to me quite seriously. 'We're going to put a bomb under him.'" James Smith purchased Rigol's diary at Sotheby's. He realized it was a sign.

Although the bombing didn't take place, the al Qaeda terrorists were aware of this apocryphal tale. Maybe the Park Avenue Artists auction would provide a clue? Then a husky voice interrupted his thoughts.

"Hoping to get lucky again, Dickhead?"

Trevor looked at the lovely Chastain Johnson dressed as Little Bo Peep.

Chastain said: "Can you come and blow my horn,"

Trevor said. "You weren't a very good Gala. Little Bo Peep suits you."

"Your horn is a half inch long." Chastain continued. "It's probably longer than your pee-pee."

"Let me guess, you are an art connoisseur."

"No, Dickhead, I am going to educate you on art. Or should I say art fraud."

"What do you know about art?" I asked.

"As much as you know about being a private eye." She smiled. She had a point.

"Have you forgotten my fame from the Start Me Up drummers deaths?"

"That was an accidental discovery on your part of a crime that others solved. You have had good fortune to go along with no brains."

"Did you forget that you slept with me?"

"I am still beating up myself over that mistake."

"The women tell me I'm great in bed."

"You mean the ugly fat ones that are so desperate they sleep with you? Or they sleep with any breathing male."

"Let's cut the crap and talk about the case."

"I'm an FBI agent, Trevor, what do you mean, cut the crap, I listen you talk."

"I thought the FBI didn't operate outside the U. S."

"How stupid are you, Trevor?"

I wasn't sure this was a question I wanted to answer. "Let's call a truce and concentrate upon the art."

Trevor and Chastain walked around the special Dali room and everyone was looking at Little Bo Peep. She was gorgeous. She had a staff with a listening device. She also had a small listening device in her ear. She could hear everything.

'I'm listening Chastain, enlighten me on art."

"If you quit staring at my breasts." I did. She enlightened me.

Chastain explained that in the art world the principle of Provenance ruled. This is the written record of the painting's ownership chain. Generally, dealers did not sell paintings without a clear record of Provenance.

Trevor said: "It's a French term, it means 'to come from."

"I am impressed, Trevor, where did you learn this little fact?"

"I spent six weeks studying French at the Sorbonne when I was twenty five."

"You are mentally twenty, so in five years you will be at the Sorbonne." Chastain lit a cigarette and laughed at her joke. I hated that.

As Chastain explained that Park Avenue Artists did more than $300 million dollars of business annually, she also described various methods of art fraud. She explained that a trilogy of Salvador Dali prints valued at $35,000 a set sold on the Pearl of the Ocean. When these prints sold for a discount of $24,000 the buyer found out that Sotheby's sold the same Dali set for less than $10,000. There was nothing illegal. It was simply Park Avenue Artists taking advantage of the situation.

Chastain said: "They sell so many paintings and lithographs at sea that Park Avenue Artists bills themselves as the world's largest art dealer. They are also crooks. They don't take any criticism. They will sue you in a minute."

"How does this impact the investigation, Chastain?"

"It's simple. The money raised on the Pearl of the Ocean is placed in an offshore bank. It funds al Qaeda."

"When did you learn all this, Chastain?"

"James Venible."

"Isn't Venible a Georgia lawyer who heads the Ku Klux Klan?"

"He is, Trevor, so what?"

"Is the FBI paying racists for information?"

Chastain lit a cigarette. Lung cancer was in her future. "He is a confidential informant. We don't do background checks dickhead."

"Now for the leading question. Did Venible provide any leads? Wasn't Venible the guy who kept a file he labeled the radical Negro file? He is also the guy who said: 'the only good Negro is one who works for low wages for the white man.'"

"He is the guy, so what?" Chastain looked like she wanted to shoot me.

"I heard Mr. Venible say that the only thing worse than a Negro is a Jew."

"Trevor please no inane comments. What was in the file?"

"The only person in the file was the comedian Dick Gregory. There was a lot of information on him."

Chastain looked surprised. "Who the hell is Dick Gregory? Is he on twitter or Facebook? I have never heard of him."

Trevor explained Gregory's political activism in the 1960s.

"Once again Trevor you miss the whole point."

"And that point is Chastain?"

She looked at Trevor like he was nuts. "We are solving a crime that has to do with al Qaeda terrorists and fake Salvador Dali art. Excuse me if I have never heard of this Dick what's his name." She laughed. "I need to show you some things that will help solve the case."

"What do you want to show me, Chastain? Maybe your breasts."

"I want to show you the original Dali pieces that Venible alerted us to on Carnivolet." She put a certificate of authenticity for a print from Dali's **Divine Comedy** in front of Trevor. He looked at it in awe.

"I guess you can trust a KKK guy." Trevor laughed.

"He is no longer a KKK guy." Chastain paused. "He was found dead in a pile of cow manure."

"Who killed him Chastain?"

They suspect Ernie Feinstein."

"Who the hell is Ernie Feinstein?"

"He is the head of the Irish-Scottish Society in Atlanta."

"A Jew heading an Irish-Scottish organization."

"He's not a Jew, Trevor. You need to lighten up on the judgments."

"Did Feinstein get convicted?

"No, the case remains unsolved."

"What about the art. How does one go about proving its authenticity?"

Chastain continued: "Park Avenue Artists had a fire two years ago and many of their Provenance records were destroyed."

Convenient. She said that the records were miraculously found. Then Chastain pointed to the corner of the room. She picked out a small man with round eyeglasses, a comb over and ill-fitting pants held up by suspenders. He wore a shirt speckled with paint. Chastain smiled.

"Look in the corner, Trevor."

"So!"

"It's Harold Weinstein. He's the world's foremost art restorer."

I felt stupid. I asked. "What is an art restorer?"

Chastain looked at me like I was the dumbest man in the world. I felt that way.

"He is a person who takes an old master and restores it to its original form."

"Why is that important?" I didn't get it.

"Let me spell it out for you, Trevor."

"Art restorer or art forger. It's all the same."

I really felt stupid. I don't get the simple facts. Maybe this is why I needed help solving my cases. Then I remembered I had solved only one case. I was famous. If everyone knew that Don Gino pointed me to the solution, I would be the laughing stock of the P. I. world. I wouldn't mention it.

Chastain said: "You might want to look into where and when Salvador Dali sketched and then painted **Portrait Of A Pope**. Does the painting even exist?"

"Of course it does, Don Gino has it hanging in his special Dali room at his San Francisco home." I wondered if Danielle Steel had ever seen it?

"You might want to tell the Don to check its authenticity."

"Not me, Chastain, the Don doesn't take kindly to criticism of authenticity. If it's not authentic, I don't want to be around the Don."

"Trevor, you are afraid of some god-damned queer Mafia type? I can't believe it."

"Believe it."

"Just between you and me, Trevor, the Don does a good job looking me over. I can't stand it when some old Queen does that."

"No need for homophobia." I frowned. The Don was sensitive to slurs. They made him violent. The six Samoans were even more sensitive. The midget valet would stomp on both your shoes. It didn't make for a good combination. Mild violence and excessive violence added up to mayhem.

"Thanks for everything Chastain. I am off to do some research."

"Let me guess, you are going to see which of the young ladies you can bed. Try the ones over sixty, they're your type." Chastain walked away.

The ship had a computer room. It was time to learn a bit more about art fraud. Harold Weinstein was a little guy who looked like a small rodent. He was anonymous on the Pearl of the Ocean. On the Internet, Harold Weinstein had four hundred twenty seven sites. He was a rock star in the art-forging world.

The computer had a great deal of information on Weinstein. It was Weinstein's appalling biography that alerted Trevor to the problems of finding not only the art fraud, but also the source of funds raised by al Qaeda terrorists. Born into an upper class Jewish banking family in San Francisco, Weinstein attended Stanford University. His three brothers were doctors and he majored in art history. His father was livid and insisted that his son study for an MBA. He was admitted to the Wharton School of Finance at the University of Pennsylvania. Rumor was that the Wharton School received a sizeable donation. Young Weinstein took to finance and received the MBA with highest honors.

After graduation Harold became a Vice President for the Equitable Insurance Company. Then his father died and young Weinstein retired. He left Harold fifteen million dollars. There was no need to work. His father had no idea that he had converted from Judaism to become a Muslim. Weinstein was a secret Muslim. He grew to hate Jews. He also became one of America's most acclaimed art restorers.

Trevor spent hours on the computer. There was no doubt that Weinstein was involved in the plot. Where? How? When? Trevor had no clue. He would find out.

Trevor wondered why a person with fifteen million dollars would fleece Madge and Bill from Des Moines. Probably made him feel superior.

Passengers came on board with a credit line, drank champagne, looked at art held by young girls with big breasts and left the ship with a Weinstein fake. The irony was that Park Avenue Artists had been sued numerous times and never lost. Something was amiss.

After Trevor returned to his room, he concentrated on figuring out who the enemy was and why they were on the ship. He had no idea. They were more sophisticated than the rock and roll criminals that he encountered in his earlier case. This case required education. It was time for Trevor to learn about the worlds of art and terrorism.

Trevor's first stop was the Park Avenue Artists auction. He went back to the third deck and walked into the auction room. He was given a card. Trevor had a hundred thousand dollar line of credit. Don Gino had spared no expense. The brightly flashing strobe lights almost blinded Trevor. He was handed a champagne flute. It was awful. Probably Andre. After three glasses it tasted better. By the fifth glass the young ladies handing out the champagne looked like movie stars. The Andre also tasted pretty good.

Someone bumped him. An envelope was handed to Trevor. Inside was a Certificate of Authenticity for an Emile Bellet Seri lithograph in color on paper. The certificate stated that it was signed on the plate and then reproduced in only one hundred copies. It was free. Who was hell is Emile Bellet? Trevor wasn't sure. It was probably worth very little.

Trevor was a Dali expert not a Bellet expert. Maybe he wasn't an expert. Before he boarded the Pearl of the Ocean, Trevor flew to Santé Fe to talk with the Dali Detective. His name was Bernard Ewell and the motto on his letterhead read: "If a person has integrity, nothing else matters. If a person does not have integrity nothing else matters." Exactly. I agreed. After spending a day in Santé Fe with Ewell, Trevor was ready to catch the art frauds.

As the auction was about to commence, there was a frivolous atmosphere. Half the people in attendance came in costume. There was a Ho Chi Minh! There was a Jack Nicholson. There was a Jimmy Carter. He was African American. There was a short, ugly white guy dressed as Kobe Bryant. My favorite was the black guy dressed as

Abraham Lincoln. Then a woman with a beautiful body walked in dressed as Cleopatra. She was smoking a cigarette. Ho Chi Minh left. I guess he didn't like cigarette smoke. A midget walked in dressed as Michael Dukakis. Someone asked me. "Who is Michael Dukakis?" I told them. "He's the little guy in the small tank." I laughed. The person walked away.

Then Little Bo Peep, Eleanor Roosevelt and Cyndi Lauper entered the room. I wanted to tell Cyndi Lauper that she was sixty years old. I also wanted to tell Eleanor Roosevelt that she was out of her element. Someone tapped me on the shoulder. The same guy was back. He asked me. "Who is Cyndi Lauper?" I told him "girls just wanna have fun." He walked away indignant. No sense of humor.

Then every eye in the room looked as a young Elizabeth Taylor dressed as Cleopatra entered, carried on a bed by four guys who looked like they played for the San Francisco 49ers. Except they were all Samoans. Thank goodness. The old Elizabeth Taylor was pretty nasty. One of the women was Chastain Johnson. Which one? Who cared! They all looked good.

Harold Weinstein walked out onto a small stage to thunderous applause. He smiled. He began the auction. Even Andre Champagne produces thunderous applause. The auction ran smoothly for two hours. I was into my seventh glass of champagne. Andre is not bad. I almost bid on a Thomas Kinkade. He was dead. He was famous. He was overpriced. I asked the waiter for a coffee. He ignored me. I asked for a second coffee. It came as a coffee royal. The liquor tasted pretty good. I had a nice buzz. Even a few of the sixty-year-old women looked good. Andre will do that to you. I was keeping track of the sales. In two hours Park Avenue Artists sold more than three million dollars of common art. The net cost was somewhere in the neighborhood of $20,000. Not a bad profit.

Then Harold Weinstein said: "Wine, cheese, canopies, olives, champagne and petit fours are being served." I guessed the suckers had spent enough money. I had wine and cheese. I also had my eighth glass of Andre. Not a bad champagne.

The FBI Art Fraud Unit with its newest member, Chastain Johnson, was on board the Pearl of the Ocean. The problem was that the American court system was one that had trouble ruling on art fraud. Park Avenue Artists won the majority of its cases. They had one lawyer, Isaac Louis, who knew the art world inside out.

The walk back to his room exhausted Trevor. Andre will do that to you. He walked in and took of his shoes, took off his clothes and put on the ship's robe. He looked around for his paper work.

Trevor found the file that he needed. He paid ten dollars for a membership to the Fine Art Registry. He looked at his material. The Dali's were often not signed. They might be originals. They might be duplicates. No one knew. The courts were still dealing with this delicate problem. He was about to meet evil in many forms.

Then Trevor discovered that Park Avenue West sued the Fine Art Registry for alleging that they were selling fake Dali prints. What did this have to do with the al Qaeda terrorists? Trevor was about to find out. He was about to discover evil in many forms.

In an interview with Mike Wallace in 1958 on American television, Dali talked about incarnate evil. Zandra Filippi sent Trevor a clip from the Dali interview: "Life is erotic and therefore ugly. Death is not erotic but sublime, therefore beautiful." Zandra's note read: "Find the person who knows this Dali comment and you have found a terrorist." She told Trevor to look for evil in many forms.

Trevor went onto You Tube and watched Salvador Dali wandering around the Crazy Horse Saloon looking bewildered. It was 1966. Everyone looked bewildered. Dali was the only person in the video who looked normal. He watched as the crazy dancers wore football helmets and numbered shirts. Dali knew he was normal. As Trevor watched the You Tube video he wondered what it meant? Then Trevor noticed a clue. It was on Dali's lapel. There was a large button that he wore. It gave the terrorists an excuse for the newly formed al Qaeda cell. Dali's button read: "Evil in many forms is the way to Allah." That was all Trevor needed to know, he now had more than one suspect. He was about to discover evil in many forms.

CHAPTER NINETEEN

Discovering Evil In Many Forms

"I split with Luis Bunuel because he was a Communist and an atheist....He was evil in many forms." Salvador Dali

Don Gino lent Trevor a series of private letters between Luis Bunuel and Salvador Dali. The Don purchased these from a Barcelona Mafia Don. The rumor was that it was a fair price. The Barcelona mafia Don probably wanted to live.

The letters began in 1929 when Bunuel and Dali made a silent surrealist short film. It was Bunuel's first cinema effort. Dali plays a confused priest. As Don Gino's notes suggested, al Qaeda terrorists saw this as another sign that Dali wanted Allah to triumph. Trevor wondered: Are these people nuts?

The file that Trevor read on the Luis Bunuel and Salvador Dali relationship was puzzling. What was it doing in the middle of this case? This was another historical clue. When Bunuel settled in America, he was the director of the New York Museum of Modern Art. He was an atheist critical of all religions. He was fired when Cardinal Francis Spellman objected to an atheist running MOMA. The clue in the file said that the al Qaeda terrorists labeled their San Francisco target "Bunuel." They were going to blow up the symbol of Bunuel's resistance to American religious belief. There were too many Christian denominations in San Francisco. Trevor Blake III needed more information. Once again he pulled out his I Pad and sent a message to Guitar Jac.

"I need information on evil in many forms. Find out who, what, why, when and where the al Qaeda terrorists will strike. Look at the Luis Bunuel-Salvador Dali correspondence during World War II." Guitar Jac texted back: "Done in a day, boss."

Blake realized that Salvador Dali had some notions of evil. To ward off evil spirits, Dali carried a piece of lucky driftwood. Although he was a staunch Catholic, Dali's lithograph, **The Doctor (The Fight Against Evil)**, was hanging in Don Gino's study. The lithograph suggested that evil took on strange forms. The Don loved the signed and numbered lithograph, number 2, and the $3000 price tag was a bargain. The seller probably wanted to stay alive. Trevor took a picture of it before he went on the cruise. In that picture at the bottom a man on a horse was fighting evil. Now Trevor knew "The Doctor" was a code word for al Qaeda terrorists.

Trevor Blake III confronted evil in only a few forms. He stopped the Chef from poisoning the Start Me Up band drummers. The new case was a complicated one. He was dealing with art forgers, counterfeiters, drug dealers, terrorists and he had gotten wind of the political right being involved. Maybe Bennie was helping the bad guys. Trevor had no idea who was who and what was going on. It was time to call in the Calvary. Trevor went to the computer. He e-mailed his encrypted computer in the Haight Ashbury office.

"Jac, tell me what you have found."

"I got it boss, I have only been on the request for a few minutes give me another hour."

Guitar Jac answered in exactly one hour. The extensive background checks on all the employees of Park Avenue Artist and a complete dossier on Harold Weinstein was on Trevor's encrypted phone. He walked over to his printer. He plugged the phone in and more than sixty pages streamed out.

Trevor instructed Guitar Jac to send it in an encrypted file to Chastain Johnson's personal computer. Jac said that it would take a few minutes. It took less than sixty seconds.

Chastain was watching what passed for television on the Pearl of the Ocean. Her printer began pouring out pages. That god damned

Trevor has information that no one else possessed. Maybe he isn't a moron. Then again, he is a fool. He is also awful in bed.

Trevor called Chastain Johnson and asked her to meet him in his room. She refused. "I have the files you sent. What else is there?"

He explained. "I need you to meet me in the sky bar in five minutes."

"I will be there, Trevor."

They sat for almost two hours with gin fizzes and put together three files on the various al Qaeda clandestine activities. Trevor now had sixty plus napkins to help him solve the al Qaeda terrorist plots. Chastain returned to her cabin twice for folders and shared her information with Trevor. She also walked unsteadily. Chastain didn't light one cigarette. She was interested in the case.

"Well Dickhead, you surprise me. You are not a stupid as I thought."

"Sleeping with me would improve your mood."

"I will sleep with you when Mickey Rooney is no longer available. I'm saving myself for him." She smiled. Chastain was always the clever FBI agent. Trevor thought Mickey Rooney was dead. He wasn't.

Trevor said: "We need more help, I just don't get it. I have the general idea. Now I need to find the targets."

"I have a confession, Trevor."

"A confession!"

"Yes."

"I can't wait."

"I have two people on board."

Chastain explained that a singer who performed in the lounges and main show room was on board as a contract agent. He was also a former CIA and military figure. I wondered what the hell was going on? Carnivolet spared no expense and the fifteen-day cruise included concert and lounge performances by Frankie Avalon, Fabian, Bobby Rydell, Chubby Checker and Matt Luman. They were all from Philadelphia except for Luman. I didn't know his music. He sounded like a black guy. Maybe he was brought in to balance all the white musicians. I hoped that Frankie Avalon wasn't the hidden ex-CIA agent. I was hoping that Geritol sponsored the shows.

"Tell you what Dickhead," Chastain said. "You figure out on your own who the famous entertainer is that is working with us."

"Thanks for your confidence in me Chastain."

"The other operative Trevor is an Asian."

"You are a big help, Chastain. Most of the crew and staff are from Indonesia, China, the Philippines, Thailand, Vietnam, Laos and Cambodia. There are about eight hundred employees with Asian roots."

"Good, Trevor. It will take you time to figure it out. You can't screw up the investigation."

"I think there are more agents than terrorists on the Pearl of the Ocean, maybe I should call it the Peril of the Ocean."

"Ah, Trevor always the clever P. I."

Then it dawned on me. I saw the good-looking piano playing legend, Matt Luman. I remember when he ruled the San Francisco club circuit.

Chastain said: "Figured out which entertainer is helping us, Dickhead?"

"Matt Luman. I used to see Luman at the Fillmore when he had some rock and roll hits. It will be good to catch up with him." I failed to mention that Matt was a jazz guy who re-invented his act when rock and roll arrived.

Chastain said: "Is he on twitter?"

"No!" I smiled. Her stupidity was incredulous.

"How about Facebook?"

"No."

"When's the last time he had a hit record?"

"It was 1963."

She got in the elevator. Trevor stood in the elevator door. Smiling.

Chastain said: "I pushed the up button, I wonder if you could still get it up?" She laughed. She probably learned that from Bennie. She smiled lasciviously at Trevor. He got in the elevator.

"Going up Dickhead." Chastain closed the elevator and pushed the up bottom. She said: "Tell me about Matt Luman." Trevor couldn't stop looking at Chastain. She was beautiful.

"You will love him Chastain." There was a part of Luman's life that neither Chastain nor Trevor knew about. They would soon find out.

Matt Luman made James Bond look tame. He was also a better singer than James Bond.

CHAPTER TWENTY

Matt Luman Is On The Case
At President Obama's Request

"A true artist is not one who is inspired, but one who inspires."
Salvador Dali

Matt Luman got up in his stateroom. The separate sitting room was filled with FBI, CIA and Homeland Security files. Luman was pissed. He wasn't in one of the presidential suites. Oh well, he was a piano player in the jazz lounge. He also performed in the glitzy main showroom. He brought in Elvis Presley's guitarist James Burton to play with him in the Carnivolet Theater. Luman had a mega top ten hit "I'm Movin' On," and regional hits with "Ooby Dolby," "Maybellene" and "Turn On Your Love Light." Then Luman's career crashed. He reinvented his music in Canada with Ronnie Hawkins. Luman was Canada's top club draw for three decades while working as a CIA contract agent. He invested his money wisely. He retired to his Beverly Hills home. He and Peter Ford were seen daily in coffee shops. Luman, a life long bachelor, told Ford that he would never get married. The permanent move to Beverly Hills reinforced that resolve.

Luman was seen around town with Sandra Bullock, Beyonce and Julia Roberts. He had dates with Jane Fonda and Nancy Sinatra. He told Ford that it was like going out with his mother when he hung out with Sinatra or Fonda. Nearing seventy, Luman was physically fit and looked like George Clooney's brother. He missed the action. Not with the ladies. He missed the CIA thrills.

Luman worked for the CIA as a special agent and then as a contract operative for forty years. His cover was that he was a musician. He almost screwed up his CIA cover by having a Top 40 hit and a number of regional hits. It was a different CIA. Prior to 9-11, the CIA was an information-gathering agency. While working as a CIA operative, Luman was questioned about the apparent theft of a Rembrandt painting. The Rembrandt was never found. When Luman retired he had over a million dollars in a Grand Cayman account. He sold the Rembrandt.

When 9-11 transformed the CIA into a killing machine, Luman rethought his life goals. One of his goals was to stay alive. After personally carrying out four assassinations, Luman retired. It was time. He had the money. He would make music and keep the ladies happy. It didn't work out. He became restive. He was still making the ladies happy. He worried about America's future. The god damned Muslims were taking over. He was tired of it.

Luman had a conscience, but he was a trained agent who recognized the realities of the spy game. He was not concerned about the CIA's abuse of power. He loved the CIA's abuse of power. When he reported to CIA headquarters in Langley, he was told of the CIA's new powers. He didn't like what he heard. The CIA contracted killers. If caught, the agency disavowed its involvement.

When Luman entered the Counterterrorism Center, he was greeted with loud applause. Then he was told that killing operations in Pakistan, Yemen and Syria no longer were allowed. The CIA Director, John O. Brennan, briefed Luman on his role on the Pearl of the Ocean. Luman could kill as a contract agent. Welcome to the new and improved CIA. President Obama continued to blow smoke at news conferences about "the responsible CIA." It was laughable.

When Matt was on the ground after the armed drone strikes for the George W. Bush Administration, he was able to take art, gold, silver and expensive furniture from the Middle East. He shipped everything back as "art relics." He rented a warehouse and began selling off key art items. This is how he met Don Gino Landry who bought all of the stolen Dali's. Then Matt retired. He was independently wealthy.

The Bush administration investigated and found that Luman was not guilty. This reopened the door for his return to the CIA. The Obama administration persuaded him to come back to work. He burnt out after one year. Then he retired again. He was brought back as a contract agent. They were hiring associates to carry out the assassinations. It was too dangerous to use CIA agents. Luman couldn't believe it.

For a time, Luman was semi-retired writing music for the movies. He worked on a Clint Eastwood movie about a woman boxer, and he wrote the music for a television show, **Family Guy**. It didn't take much time and he worked out with his old martial arts buddies. The six feet two inch Luman was a rock solid one hundred and eighty pounds. He also missed the killing.

After a year of retirement, Luman was conflicted about going back to work. Then lightning struck. He accepted a weeklong engagement at London's Jazz Café. Luman was happy about the gig, as Jimmy Smith was his opening act. Smith was in the process of saving Blue Note Records from financial ruin. When Luman allowed Blue Note to record his shows, he didn't read the contract carefully. Blue Note issued **Matt Luman: Live At the Jazz Café**. The CD included vocal duets with Amy Winehouse, Van Morrison and Tony Bennett. The vocal duets were released as singles and they went platinum. Luman received his second Grammy for the Blue Note album. The first Grammy was for best jazz vocal on "I'm Movin' On." It went platinum and Luman moved to London. He purchased a small flat on Oval Road in Camden Town.

Then Van Morrison sued for copyright infringement and the suit included Blue Note Records. Morrison was increasingly agitated and spewed venom about Luman to the London press. The irony is that Luman's record sales soared. He received the largest royalty checks of his lengthy career.

This lawsuit cost Luman more than a million dollars in royalties. His royalties after the Morrison lawsuit increased to more than two million dollars a year. Luman liked to say that he made money when Van sued him. He still had plenty of money. The lawsuit soured his interest in performing and recording. Luman also told anyone who would listen that Van Morrison was an asshole. No one disagreed.

When he wasn't performing, Luman hung out at Camden Town's Spread Eagle Pub with Jessie Hector, the former lead singer of the Hammersmith Gorillas. Rob, Mike, Roger and Bob came in to talk music. They all worked for the retro reissue label Ace. The Spread Eagle was a gathering spot for musicians and rock music writers. Jeff Beck, Keith Richards and Eric Clapton came in regularly to talk with Luman.

Every morning Luman walked out of his Camden Town flat. He had a deep, dark secret. No one knew this side of Matt Luman. He ran in his jogging outfit from Camden Town to Portobello Market. It was a five-mile run down to where he worked out vigorously. The gym at Portobello's Green Fitness Club was filled with friends. Luman liked to have a breakfast at Mike's Café on Blenheim Crescent. Before his breakfast of beans, sausage, eggs, fried tomato and a cup of Earl Grey tea, Luman spent two hours in a rigorous cross training fitness program. He had another secret. Luman worked as an assassin for the CIA. He retired when he decided to take his tinkling piano sound into the record business. Everyone told him he was nuts. He had a pension if he remained in the CIA for another eighteen years. Luman laughed. He had another secret. He wasn't much of a piano player. He was a drummer. It was not commercial to play the drums. His drop-dead good looks and smooth vocal styling caused Europeans to nickname him "The Vanilla Nat King Cole." Luman was uneasy with this nickname. Then he received a check for half a million dollars. On European TV shows, he referred to himself as "the Vanilla Nat King Cole." The money was too good not to become a well-paid vanilla star.

After five years in London, Luman sold the Oval Road flat, he returned to Beverly Hills. He was now richer than ever and determined to retire. Then Barack Obama was elected to a second term. Luman donated ten million dollars to Obama's Election Campaign. Now Luman was sitting in the Oval Office with the president. The CIA had chauffeured Matt from Langley to the Oval Office.

President Obama walked into the Oval Office. Matt noticed he was taller and had more grey hair than five years ago. He was also in his second term. Matt didn't know what to say. He remained silent.

President Obama: "Matt it's good to see you. I was singing 'I'm Moving On' for my wife this morning. I call myself the best Matt Luman impersonator in the world."

"Mr. President if I may interrupt you. You are the only Matt Luman impersonator in the world. You know what? I love that."

They both laughed. Then President Obama got a serious look on his face. "Matt your country needs you."

"Matt you are the best assassin in Washington. We need your skills in other areas." The President smiled and continued. "Of course, we don't recognize assassins. There are other areas where you skills are needed."

"What do you mean?"

"Your government needs you to eliminate some people."

The President told Luman he would have to deny the CIA's black bag program and illegal assassinations. "Do you understand, Matt? Can you carry out the assignment?"

"I can. Mr. President. I understand the need for secrecy."

President Obama said: "President Bush signed an order restoring CIA assassination powers. I can't praise Bush, I would love to. He was even a better president than Bill Clinton. Don't quote me Matt." The president smiled.

Luman said: "Mr. President where do I fit into this scenario?"

"You need to find al Qaeda terrorists and quietly terminate them."

"I'm at your disposal Mr. President. They are toast." Matt wondered. How is someone quietly terminated?

"There is another problem Mr. Luman. President Clinton took an absurd view of the terrorist challenge. He would kill with a Tomahawk cruise missile but not with a CIA bullet. That type of thinking is antiquated. You will kill with a CIA bullet."

"I understand."

"I have booked you on a cruise ship as a piano player. When you reach Barcelona you will seek out the al Qaeda terrorists and find out what they are planning to attack. This is a difficult, complicated mission."

"I already have three intelligence files, Mr. President."

"Good." President Obama smiled. He had picked the right person.

The President explained the shadowy Muslim terrorists. He described the art dealers raising money for al Qaeda, and how and why the FBI was operating outside the U. S. This was all done with President Obama's approval.

President Obama said: "You must not reveal your cover. There is a Mafia Don on board, you can trust him."

Luman said: "Wait a minute Mr. President. What in the hell is a Mafia Don doing working for the government?"

Obama said: "You ever hear of President John F. Kennedy. He used the Mafia more than he used the FBI or CIA."

Luman said: "What!"

"Don't worry Matt, there is also a former North Vietnamese General working for me."

"Oh shit! You mean I have a Mafia Don that will kill on spot and a Vietnamese General trained as an assassin. I think I know both of them. Don Gino Landry and Emilio."

President Obama smiled. He twirled a pen in his hands. There was an awkward silence. After some time the president explained everything in great detail.

"There's more Matt." The President looked uneasy. He continued. "The Mafia Don is a gay man from San Francisco. I would advise you never to use homophobic slurs. The last person who did this wound up in a can of Don Gino's dog food and is considered missing. You see Don Gino also has legitimate business interests in San Francisco. He is a staunch Catholic and a very moral man. He has just one flaw. He kills other criminals and those who threaten the U. S. He is perfect as a contract CIA agent. He is also accompanied by six Samoans and a midget valet."

Luman said: "Mr. President, this sounds like a fictional exercise in espionage. Just my kind of case."

"Make no mistake, Matt, this is real. The terrorists are targeting an American monument that will make 9-11 look like a small operation."

"Mr. President! What do the terrorists have in mind?"

President Obama looked nervous. He paused. He put a stick of gum in his mouth. "They're going to blow up one of San Francisco's prestigious landmarks."

"Which one?"

"We don't know. That is the reason we are bringing you into the picture."

Matt looked nervous. This is too much information. "Is there anything else I need to know Mr. President?"

"Yes, Matt there is a minor concern. There is a Private Investigator on board who is inexperienced. His name is Trevor Blake III. He has skills and we have a bodyguard hired to watch his every move. The bodyguard is hired on as a magician. He works on the ship. His entertainment name is Bennie the Beneficent."

"A bodyguard for a private eye." Luman paused. "How inept is this guy?"

"Very." President Obama looked nervous.

"What am I missing?"

"Nothing. Matt."

"Mr. President with all due respect, what is my role?"

"Matt you will be the person who disposes of the bodies much the way that you did in Desert Storm."

"No problem, Mr. President."

Barack Obama shook Matt's hand. He left the room. The head of the CIA walked in for a second visit with briefing papers, a suitcase full of cash, another suitcase with entertainer's clothes and a new passport. He said only four words.

"Good luck, Agent Luman." Then the director left the office.

Matt stood alone in the Oval Office and in less than a minute two Marines came in. They saluted and took him out a side door. A limousine was waiting. He was taken to Dulles International and a private plane flew him to the Azores. Matt Luman was no longer retired. He was a CIA agent. If only a contract operative. He was going on board the Pearl of the Ocean as a featured entertainer. After he landed at Ponta Delgada in the Azores, Matt spent a day relaxing.

Then the Carnivolet sailed into this small, quaint port. Rumor has it that Ponta Delgada was once a part of the sunken kingdom of Atlantis. Ponta Delgada was the only part that didn't sink. Luman loved that thought. The girls with big breasts walking around the beach would have drowned. Maybe God did exist. How else could you explain the survival of Ponta Delgada?

There was a negative to Ponta Delgada. There was bird shit everywhere. The Portuguese who named the island did so for the birds. Ponta Delgada was probably a better name than Bird Shit Island. Maybe not!

As Luman boarded the Carnivolet Pearl of the Ocean, gusts of freezing wind made him eager to get on board. As he entered the ship lobby, the music director, the legendary Solly Lukowitz who played bass with Jimi Hendrix, met him. "Mr. Luman, we are so happy to have you on board. I couldn't believe it when you signed a contract for a thousand dollars a week. I checked your finances. You are worth more than Van Morrison. You are also a nicer guy."

Luman said: "I am also a better piano player, I have a better voice and I'm not an asshole." Morrison once snubbed Luman. He hated him. Morrison once snubbed Solly Lukowitz. He was found beaten up in an alley after one of his concerts. Van always said nice things about Solly. Then again Van snubbed everyone. That is except for Solly Lukowitz. It was nothing personal. It was just Van. He was an asshole. That was part of his charm.

As Luman walked into his cabin, he wasn't sure what his role was in the Salvador Dali murder. What the hell was the government doing with a Dali case? Then he opened the files that President Obama had given him and he found out about the Salvador Dali angle. The case would be a difficult one.

He relished the idea of going undercover. He had hit records for twenty years, he was wealthy, he was bored, and he was looking for a challenge. He also had an itch to kill. Old habits die-hard.

While in his cabin, Luman went through his exercise routine. He did three hundred setups, he did his five-pound weights for half an hour, he did his yoga exercises and he finished with an hour of meditation. He was ready to find the al Qaeda operatives. They would vanish. He was still well trained. Then he took a nap.

Before he left Hollywood, Luman visited Glenn Ford's grave. He talked to the dead iconic actor. This was Luman's ritual. He would talk out his plans to help catch the terrorists. It was strange to sit at Ford's grave talking about catching terrorists. Ford had no idea about terrorists. He was dead. But it helped Luman focus. Once on the ship and in his cabin he pulled out notes he had taken while talking to Glenn Ford.

The copious notes defined Luman's role in catching the al Qaeda terrorists. When Luman turned on the movie channel in his cabin the ship was showing Glenn Ford's 1955 movie "The Violent Men." As Luman looked at the screen Edward G. Robinson said to Ford: "You never know the bad guy, he is the least likely person." Luman got it. He suddenly identified one of the two al Qaeda perpetrators. Glenn Ford was helpful.

CHAPTER TWENTY-ONE
An Old Crook On Carnivolet

"The best liar is he who makes the smallest amount of lying go the longest way." Samuel Butler

Bob Burton is an old crook. He is a smart crook. He pays people for inside information. The Muslim terrorists hired him to use his company, Park Avenue Artists, to launder al Qaeda money. Burton has no idea about the attacks planned for either Barcelona or San Francisco. He doesn't care. A huge ego and a bank account that needs constant replenishing suggests the portly, wispy haired Burton's greed. He isn't stupid. He is unaware. He is consumed by money. He has no idea that he is working with people intent upon destroying America. He was told that he was laundering drug money through his art company that sold dubious fakes to the unsuspecting tourists. The purpose of this money, his Muslim benefactors said, was to educate young Muslims. It was a charity. Burton's greed blinded him to the truth.

When he talked to his al Qaeda benefactors, Burton described how he would sell Dali's fake art. Bob never met a hillbilly that he couldn't sell a bogus piece of art. Don Gino found out about Burton. He would be taken care of in due time. There was one man even more dangerous. That was Dr. Harold Weinstein. Don Gino had a special place in hell for Weinstein. Greed blinded both men.

Weinstein was on the payroll of Park Avenue Artists as a consultant. The truth is that he is not an art restorer, as the company brochures suggests. He produced "authentic fakes" as well as pirated copies of rare Dali's. He had only a vague idea of how to counterfeit some of the Dali's. The lithographs were no problem. But Dali's **Vision of Hell** and **Portrait Of A Pope** were not publicly perused paintings. There wasn't one image on the Internet. Weinstein would have to improvise. This was not one of his strong talents. He was a copyist. There wasn't an original bone in Weinstein's creative spirit.

Don Gino was aware that Weinstein was a copyist. He took out a magnifying glass and looked at Weinstein's lines. They were good but it wasn't close to Dali's brilliance. The idea of Park Avenue Artists advertising original Dali's did not sit well with the Don.

When Park Avenue Artists advertised the proposed auction of Dali originals, **Vision of Hell** and **Portrait Of A Pope**, the company received a puppet. It was a life size likeness of Weinstein. It had a purple garrote around the puppet's neck. Someone had made Don Gino angry.

Burton had information that an old gangster was on board looking at the Dali's. He alerted Weinstein. The San Francisco Mafia figure, known as Don Gino, was a Dali collector. He was dangerous. Burton's sources also pointed to a San Francisco Private Eye who was famous as a rock and roll detective. He was also on board. His name was Trevor Blake III. Burton mentioned that Trevor knew nothing about being a private investigator. There were others on board that couldn't be identified. Burton and Weinstein were aware that they were targeted. By whom? For what? They didn't know. They weren't nervous. They should have been.

Burton had plenty of money. He also had numerous sources of information. For a cash payment placed with a mole in the CIA, he had files on various people. When one of his informants told him to be careful, Burton was not worried. There was no file on Don Gino Landry. That was a mistake.

When Burton asked his San Francisco investigator to put together a file, he refused. The investigator sent a telegram. It read: "No one investigates the Don. No one disrespects the Don. I resign." This put a crimp in Burton's plans. He wasn't smart enough to visualize Don Gino's power. Or his level of vengeance.

Burton didn't have all the intelligence. There were too many agents and too many unanswered questions. Burton was used to knowing everything. He was in the dark. It was not a good feeling. The FBI and CIA were on board, a gangster who collected Dali paintings lurked in the shadows and there were rumors of a deadly Chinaman with ties to the U.S. government. As Burton looked around, the entire crew looked like Chinamen from the Philippines, Thailand, Vietnam, Laos, Cambodia and Myanmar. They were from everywhere but China. The wages were too high in China. Why did the source say Chinaman? No one was from China. They wanted high wages. Burton was worried about his source of intelligence. It was time to take action.

Bob knew that the CIA and FBI were lurking in the shadows. He had to quickly launder the al Qaeda money. He didn't have a good feeling about his Muslim friends. They were up to something. They thought that he was stupid. He realized that they had a plan to dispose of Don Gino Landry. He approved. The Don was a loose cannon. The gay San Francisco Mafioso could cause problems. Don Gino would have to disappear. He would be eliminated before they reached Barcelona. Burton realized that the Don was too dangerous to ignore. He hoped that his Muslim benefactors took the Don seriously. If they didn't, they were dead.

It was time to seek a solution. Burton went to his closet, and he pulled out a suitcase of one hundred dollar bills. He stuffed the one hundred thousand dollars into a laundry bag. He tied a laundry tag to it requesting cleaning and pressing. The tag also had a place to request immediate service. Burton checked the four-hour service. He walked to the first deck of the ship and knocked on the door marked: "LAUNDRY." Humberto Diaz answered. Bob Burton walked inside. Humberto locked the door. He placed a sign: "Closed For Lunch" on the door. They went into a private room. It was nine in the morning.

Burton provided photos, a cabin number and an itinerary of the comings and goings of Don Gino. The six Samoans needed to be neutralized. The midget valet was to be exterminated. Humberto could ignore Trevor Blake III. He was harmless. Humberto took the money and placed it in a safe hidden under his bunk. It was $100,000 to make Don Gino vanish. No problem. Humberto wondered. Who is this Don Gino? He looks like some old queer in a purple suit. Ridiculous! Then Humberto did his due diligence on Don Gino. He realized that the mysterious purple Don was a formidable foe. Diaz believed that he was an invisible assassin.

Humberto remained in his mind an unknown assassin. He was careful. He was professional. He was working with amateurs. Don Gino knew his every move. There was a bug in Diaz' room. Bob Burton was an art dealer with a penchant for greed and mistakes. This could get you killed. Humberto realized that he needed to be careful. Don Gino Landry was a formidable adversary. He also had hidden resources. The public picture of Don Gino obscured the fact that he was a deadly foe who could kill you at any moment. Humberto needed to be cautious.

He began following Don Gino. That was a mistake. In the shadows a small, muscular Vietnamese man swept up the ship. He swept everywhere that Humberto Diaz walked. Humberto would soon meet this small man. It would not be a pleasant meeting. Emilio smiled. He was ready to take action. Don Gino had persuaded him to turn a blind eye to the terrorists. At least for the moment. They would be very sorry that they called him a "little Chinaman." Emilio smiled. They should remember he was a dangerous little Chinaman.

Emilio walked down to deck one. He used a small wire to enter Humberto's room. He searched under the bed and found the $100,000 payment for what he was about to do. Humberto was like most other criminals. They were predictable. So was Emilio. He would dispose of Humberto. Tout suite.

CHAPTER TWENTY-TWO

Omar Abdul Hammadi Emerges:
Terrorism On The High Seas

**"I practice the paranoiac-critical method, a mental exercise
of accessing the subconscious to enhance artistic creativity."**
Salvador Dali

Omar Abdul Hammadi sat on his balcony reading the Quran. He also has a copy of **Basketball Today**. He is the only al Qaeda terrorist who can talk NBA basketball. It helps him release the tension from his al Qaeda planning. He is a forty-five year old Birmingham Alabama terrorist whose name is James Smith. As a terrorist, he is undercover. In his previous life, he was the starting center for the University of Alabama basketball team that won the NIT in the 1980s. Then he played for two years in the Iranian Professional Basketball league. Then he vanished into Pakistan to re-emerge as Omar Abdul Hammadi. He converted to Islam while playing in Teheran.

When Smith found out that al Qaeda meant "the Base" in English, he began long religious conversations with radical Sunni Muslims. Soon he was not only a convert, he was a field operative. While in Iran, Smith met and was taught by Dr. Abdullah Azzam, a Palestinian, who was one of the founders of the anti-Soviet jihad in Afghanistan. He convinced Smith that African Americans were not advancing socially or economically due to inherent racism. Azzam's notion of a "defensive jihad" appealed to Smith. He saw it as a means of leveling the playing field in business for African Americans.

Smith had written articles for **Sports Illustrated** charging that the NBA was the new slavery. Lebron James was furious. James replied: "It is the new slavery with millions of dollars." Smith ignored him. On his trips to Tehran, Smith watched as the Iranian capital went from the Paris of the Middle East to a reactionary, fundamentalist enclave. He approved. The bright clothes, the gaudy make up and the high heels were gone from the harlots who walked Tehran's Golestand shopping mall. The short skirts, the low cut blouses and the booty shaking Americans were not allowed in Tehran. The Muslim way of life, Smith wrote in his diary, led to purity in mind and body.

It was not long after religious fundamentalists took over the Iranian government that Omar Abdul Hammadi became a member of al Qaeda. Iran funded his plan to destroy major monuments in America and Spain. He gladly donated a portion of his wealth. Al Qaeda also approved of his plan to blow up a section of Barcelona's Sagrada Familia. The CIA, England's MI 6 and the Israeli Mossad had not been able to find out any of Hammadi's targets. They were clueless.

The two encrypted telephones that Smith-Hammadi carried had the latest technology. One phone was silent only accepting incoming messages while the other had a flashing green light to signal a number that needed to be called. The Silent Circle model 3G/4G/WiFi allowed Hammadi to take pictures and videos and send them anywhere in the world. For his al Qaeda brothers, it was a highly useful piece of technology. But there were intelligence agencies monitoring Smith-Hammadi. He had no idea that he was being monitored.

Zandra Filippi sat in her central control room watching Smith's every move. She had a picture of Smith in his basketball uniform. She threw darts at it daily. Zandra wondered why the British and Americans were so inept. Even that fool, Trevor Blake III, knew more than the intelligence agencies.

The British intelligence agency MI5 had Hammadi's name displayed prominently in information on the planning and execution behind the terrorist blast in the London Underground system. When the July 7, 2005 bombs ignited in the London Underground,

MI5 found a basketball with a University of Alabama logo. There was no evidence linking Smith-Hammadi, but MI5 knew that he was involved. MI5 was in charge on British domestic intelligence. They shared their file with MI6, which tracked Hammadi's international travels. When he was in London, a seasoned female agent Farah Asad followed Hammadi closely. She was young, beautiful and a remarkable field agent. Asad was given the assignment of proving Smith's membership and activity for al Qaeda. There was no concrete proof. He was laughing in the face of British Intelligence agencies.

MI6 also reported that he had met with Osama bin Laden's top aide Ayman al-Zawahiri. But again they found no evidence to prosecute Smith-Hammadi. The large file on Smith-Hammadi contained detailed files of the homemade organic peroxide based devices placed in backpacks used to kill fifty-two Londoners and injure more than seven hundred. He was responsible. There was no proof.

MI6 also noted that Hammadi was looking for soft targets in the U. S. Unbeknownst to U. S. intelligence agencies, Hammadi had a plan to target a well-known San Francisco monument. One Don Gino would not suspect terrorists would attack. It was a monument associated with what Hammadi called "the nefarious deeds of Don Gino Landry."

As an African American businessman, James Smith, donated millions to President Barack Obama's re-election campaign. He would have his revenge when his al Qaeda brothers destroyed a well-known San Francisco landmark. By then James Smith would be in Northern Pakistan on television as Omar Abdul Hammadi. He couldn't wait to lecture America on the coming Muslim triumph. The will of Allah was about to strike America. Hammadi was prepared for the ultimate victory. He thought of his life in America. It would soon end. He would be in Pakistan as a newly proclaimed al Qaeda leader. The first African American to establish roots in the radical Middle East.

In his New York Park Avenue apartment, James Smith had a wall of Salvador Dali lithographs and original paintings. He seethed. Don Gino had a much larger collection. The old faggot had everything. Soon he would be dead. His Catholic Church would be destroyed and his reputation in shreds. Smith couldn't wait to see Don Gino's face. Then he looked around at his Dali collection.

The Dali room, as Smith labeled it, was air-conditioned and dust free. There was also a small section with pictures of Dali's wife, Gala, and some memorabilia. Smith had the original 1958 marriage certificate that the Angels Chapel, near the small town of Girona, issued to Dali and Gala. He also had a previously unseen sketch of Gradiva. This was the name Dali gave to Gala that he took from a novel by Wilhelm Jensen. This novel featured Sigmund Freud and the Gradiva character who was evil, manipulative, corrupt, and beautiful. She was also great in bed. She was also the book's heroine. This 1902 novel was the basis of Sigmund Freud's 1907 study **Delusion and Dream in Jensen's Gradiva**. As Smith read Jensen and Freud, he received a secret message. Freud's writing argued that the quest for monetary rewards eroded life's pleasures.

Freud argued and Smith agreed that the western capitalistic way of life was an anachronism. Dali's Gala discovered the purity of the Muslim way; she needed to end her life of sex, slavery, nudity and sadomasochism. Smith decided his terrorist's acts were a means to purify Gala. They were also on the road to Dali's redemption. The surrealistic notion of an al Qaeda cell dedicated to Dali and Gala made Smith happy. It seemed unrealistic. That is why it would succeed.

Smith smiled as he looked at his Dali-Gala collection. Dali's secret Muslim life led Smith to form an al Qaeda cell that would destroy some of America and Spain's most coveted historical sites. But the final blow to American Imperialism would take place in an unlikely San Francisco historical site.

San Francisco prided itself as "The City." What a pompous bunch of horseshit, Smith thought. Don Gino would experience the ultimate comeuppance. It would take a large cache of money to pull off this grandiose plot.

The problem was to raise enough money for the final coup. The Pearl of the Ocean would not only provide the funds through the art sales to bring a violent attack upon America, but Omar Abdul Hammadi had a plan to sink the Pearl of the Ocean. He had a helicopter coming to the ship an hour before the explosion that would destroy the Carnivolet Line's billion-dollar luxury liner.

Smith looked at the dossier that he had on Don Gino Landry. This was the one person who would die. He was Allah's enemy. There would be no future for the Mafia Don. He defiled the Muslim faith with his Catholicism. His plan to restore San Francisco's Mission Delores was an affront to Islam. He would be dealt with in due time.

Hammadi opened his Quran. He read. He prayed. He took his time to collect his thoughts. The large number of people on board the Pearl of the Ocean had no chance to stop the coming apocalypse. The sinking of the Carnivolet would be just the first act in a string of attacks upon the American way of life.

After pulling out the blueprints for the Pearl of the Ocean, Hammadi began taking copious notes on the soft spots in the ships security. He quickly found a dozen such places.

The dynamite was to be placed in the weak spots. There was no chance of detection as the Department of Homeland Security didn't operate on the High Seas. The Pearl of the Ocean, like most cruise ships, had a tremendous weight, and its displacement hull was designed to push water out of the way. It was the most vulnerable spot on a ship. Hammadi prepared to dynamite the displacement hull.

What escaped Hammadi was the full extent of Don Gino Landry's criminal enterprise. Don Gino was the Robin Hood of San Francisco criminals. He protected the poor. He found jobs for young Italians and Catholics. So what if he had to charge a local police neighborhood fee. He also lent money at a thirty plus-per-cent interest to recent immigrants. It wasn't really a crime. It was Visa and Master Card with higher interest rates. To complicate matters, Don Gino was making more money from his legitimate businesses. This bothered him.

Hammadi had no idea that Don Gino was much more than a Salvador Dali collector or for that matter a top level San Francisco criminal. Hammadi didn't realize the extent of Don Gino's connection to President Barack Obama. When Obama came to California, Don Gino was seen in the background. At least once a month the President and Don Gino were photographed playing basketball on the White

House court. Don Gino had been a shooting guard at the University of California, Berkeley. After the Golden State Warriors drafted him in the second round, he opted for a business career.

The president frequently called Don Gino for advice on policy matters. To the general public Don Gino was one of President Obama's unofficial advisers. This puzzled many people. It also made other criminals wary of Don Gino.

Those who underestimated the Don didn't live to tell about it. He appeared to be a dandified dresser, a warm personality and a shrewd businessman. The truth is that he was ruthless. Many people didn't understand the six Samoans. It was simple. Protection.

Smith-Hammadi also didn't have information on the six Samoans. He didn't think that they mattered in the scheme of things. He viewed Trevor Blake III as inept. He had no idea where anyone fit into the plan. He also didn't care. There was an arrogance born of success. He had risen from James Smith to become a multi-millionaire, and a well respected Muslim radical.

Hammadi circled the week after April 15, Patriot's Day in Boston Massachusetts, as the target date to sink the Pearl of the Ocean. Then Hammadi would finish the job by exploding a device in Barcelona at a place where the Spanish officials never suspected. Then it was on to San Francisco to blow up a revered local monument. Homeland Security could protect the White House, the Pentagon, State Government offices, the Statue of Liberty and airports. The attack that Hammadi had in mind would come in a San Francisco neighborhood protected by Don Gino. It would ruin his reputation. The terrorist bombing would not only target something near and dear to Don Gino Landry, it would ruin his protectoral image.

The **San Francisco Chronicle** went out of its way to praise Don Gino. The San Francisco Mafia figure thwarted two terrorist attacks in the last ten years. His criminal informants had more success tracking down native grown terrorists than Janet Napolitano's Homeland Security office. Don Gino Landry would pay for his defense of the Catholic Church, his reconstruction of San Francisco's Mission

Delores and his fund raising activity to help the victims of terrorism. He would also pay for his hostile attitude toward Islam.

Hammadi told his followers that Don Gino Landry was a greater danger to the Muslim faith than President Barack Obama. Hammadi believed that the president was a secret Muslim. While watching Fox TV News, Smith-Hammadi wrote down Sean Hannity's comment about President Obama. Hannity said: "President Obama studied the Quran." Then Smith-Hammadi listened to the brilliant psychiatrist, Charles Krauthammer remark: "President Obama had a Muslim upbringing." This was enough for Smith-Hammadi to give the president a pass. He would one day come back to his Muslim roots.

Since the American president was sympathetic to Islam, Smith believed that he would help them. At least this is what he continually told his dimwitted followers in the small American cells. The enemy was Don Gino Landry. He would be eliminated. Don Gino's evil intrusions into the Muslim world guaranteed his demise. The others would be killed because they were Don Gino's associates. The tightly wound midget who stomped on toes would be the first to die, then the six Samoans and finally Don Gino. Their deaths would take place accidentally on the Pearl of the Ocean. Good riddance to the scum.

Security on the Pearl of the Ocean was lax. Hammadi had less than a week to put everything into place. Not only would Don Gino Landry die, Dali's art would be destroyed in front of him. Hammadi defined this as the double death. First it was the destruction of Dali's art, then of Don Gino's collection. The Don would die slowly and with great pain.

While sitting in his elegant stateroom, Smith-Hammadi walked out onto his balcony. He took his Quran. He opened to a section that he had underlined. The Quran's explanation of Islamic art pointed to Illumination and pottery pieces. Dali pottery was so successful that there was a Facebook page, a part of e-bay that sold only Dali pottery and select pieces sold at Dali's Pottery Barn in Barcelona. Most of the Dali's were fakes. Hammadi vowed to blow up Barcelona's Dali Pottery Barn. This would cause Don Gino the ultimate pain. The Don was the world's largest Dali pottery collector. He would make sure that there was little Dali pottery to purchase. The Don would wonder what happened to the scores of Dali pottery? It would drive him crazy.

As Hammadi prepared for bed, he turned in the direction of Mecca for a prayer. He was the Muslim's avenging angel. He would not be denied. Then Hammadi took out his blue contract lenses, he cut his Afro and styled his hair like President Obama. Americans were anything if not politically correct. He shaved so close no one could tell that he once had a beard. He was a proud Muslim. For the next few weeks, he would look like a conservative Republican. Although he was African American, the tendency toward political correctness made him less than suspect. His plan was to spell the end of Don Gino Landry. That vile bastard would meet a violent end. He smiled.

After he turned on his computer, Hammadi went on the Internet. He looked at The Salvador Dali Gallery's website. The gallery located in New York's St. Regis Hotel was the world's most excusive Dali dealer. He sent a cable purchasing a three piece Dali trilogy **Eternity of Love**, **Prince of Love** and **Love's Promise**. He cabled the sixteen thousand dollars and had the pieces delivered to his Park Avenue New York Penthouse. He might not survive. The magnificent Dali pieces would endure. They remained an inspiration for future jihads.

Hammadi had no idea that he was being watched. A small pair of eyes attached to a small body looked through his balcony window. He was dressed in weather clothes. He had a small camera. He shot pictures of Hammadi's room. He was a midget who moved quietly in the shadows.

He had been inside the suite. He had used his computer skills to copy a small number of documents. It was his friend, Don Gino Landry, who needed to take care of this vile terrorist as quickly as possible. The Don's valet used his gymnastic skills to scale down to the next level and walk to his room. Hammadi had no idea who he was dealing with, but he would soon find out.

Then Hammadi went into the bathroom, he began the laborious process of maintaining his false look. He continued to work on his appearance while listening to Van Morrison's **Astral Weeks**. The mystical quality of Morrison's voice soothed Hammadi. He would soon re-emerge as his alter ego James Smith.

For Smith there was a hidden message in Morrison's lyrics. When Van crooned: "If I ventured into the slipstream,

Between the viaducts of your dreams

Could you find me?"

There was no doubt in Smith's mind that no one could or would find him. He was on a mission to preserve the Muslim way of life. He would be successful.

The midget valet smiled. Did Smith know that Van Morrison was as big an asshole as all his Muslim friends? Probably not!

CHAPTER TWENTY-THREE
Murder On The High Seas

"I do not believe in my death." Salvador Dali commenting to a startled Mike Wallace on the American TV program 60 Minutes.

S alvador Dali wrote and produced an interactive mystery to be presented during dinner. The show, known as Murder on the High Seas, was an audience participating form of entertainment to find an imaginary killer. The plot evolved around blowing up the ship's hull. One passenger on the ship, James Smith from Alabama, suggested that the Dali play be produced on the Pearl of the Ocean. The Carnivolet Line agreed. Don Gino intercepted the e-mails between Smith and the Carnivolet management. The problem was that he could not read who signed the message. He had no idea that it came from Smith. But Don Gino smiled. The play would serve his purposes. He told Trevor Blake III to monitor the play.

Don Gino told Trevor that he had facial recognition software in the dining room. As the Dali play took place it would discover and analyze terrorists who were quite different in Dali's day. The Pearl of the Ocean captain updated the play using al Qaeda references.

It would smoke out the terrorists. After consulting with the entertainment director and the dining room maitre'd, Trevor was ready to discover the terrorists during a four-course dinner. Everyone is a suspect the Captain announced when he informed the ship that this new brand of entertainment would provide laughs and thrills.

Don Gino approved of the plan. He told Trevor that the Samoans would circulate and be ready when the terrorists were discovered. Don Gino had a file on Omar Abdul Hammadi. He didn't have a picture. He couldn't identify him. He would.

The morning of the dinner play, Chastain Johnson, Don Gino and Trevor met for breakfast. They sat at the buffet on the top deck of the Pearl of the Ocean. Don Gino ate French toast with coconut syrup, Trevor dug into a ham and cheese omelet and Chastain smoked.

Don Gino said: "Trevor, we need to see who reacts to the terrorist plot. The Dali play will help us identify the terrorists. It is a surprise. We have dressed Emilio as Ho Chi Minh and he will talk terrorism. I think someone will have nervous tendencies."

"It's a long shot, Don Gino, we have no other options."

Chastain blew smoke toward the ceiling. "How about solving this the old fashioned way guys, you know clues, deduction, smoking out the bad guys."

"Ah, Chastain, we are in the midst of smart criminals with plans that are abstract." Don Gino finished his French toast. He had no comment. He did have a plan.

Trevor said: "This is a diversion. I have asked Zandra Filippi to send us a list of reactions. She has three cameras feeding images from the dining room. Her software recognition will identify the thoughts of everyone. I have hired a mentalist. She will be dressed as a waitress and pouring water at each table. She can tell in a minute who is nervous."

Chastain laughed. "Let me guess Trevor, she is recently graduated from college with an M. A. in psychology, she is maybe twenty-three, she is gorgeous and you want to get her in bed. Did I miss anything?"

"Yes you did, Chastain, she is twenty four. I have already slept with her."

"Case closed." Chastain snubbed out her cigarette and left.

"Trevor, you have a way with women. What can I say?"

"You can praise me, Don Gino." The Don laughed. He left a twenty-dollar bill on the table and walked to the elevator. A large Samoan opened a private elevator. The Don vanished.

Trevor sat and thought. He was having trouble figuring out the case.

The diversion was set. Murder on the High Seas would cause the real plot to unravel. Then all hell broke loose. The ship was locked down for an inspection. A senseless bombing at the Boston Marathon prompted the Pearl of the Ocean captain to make an announcement.

The Captain's booming voice over the ship's address system said: "Ladies and Gentleman, there has been a terrorist attack at the conclusion of the Boston Marathon. We will be slowing our cruising speed for a full ship inspection. I am sorry for the delay. We will arrive in Barcelona at Noon rather than eight in the morning. Please go to your cabins for the lock down inspection."

There was a scurrying of frantic people. The weather was cold outside and a slight frost tinted the ship's windows. It was unusually warm inside the Pearl Of The Ocean. The lock down complicated the plan for Omar Abdul Hammadi to murder Don Gino Landry. Hammadi would leave the ship. He would terminate Don Gino Landry in Barcelona. The final attacks would remain in place. The Pearl of the Ocean was safe. Like the unsuspected bombings at the conclusion of the Boston Marathon, the bombings in Barcelona and San Francisco would be the final nails in the coffin of American exploitation. It is too bad that Don Gino would not be around to view San Francisco's unsuspected destruction.

After the inspection, which revealed no ship irregularities, Hammadi called Bob Burton. The American businessman was the perfect greedy partner. When Burton walked into Hammadi's suite, he was dressed in a Louis Vuitton suit, he wore a diamond studded Rolex and his Dries Van Noutin shoes made for the perfect dress ensemble. His hair was cut finely. He had an air of elegance. His personal refinement did little to hide his abject greed. This was the personality that fleeced unsuspecting tourists.

"Excuse me while I make a phone call." Burton stood by quietly. He looked at the elegantly dressed African American. He was impressed. There was a refinement and a sense of civility to Hammadi. Burton did his best to control his racism.

Hammadi hung up. He made another call to the best counterfeiter in the art world. Dr. Harold Weinstein, who was also the auctioneer, counterfeited Burton's more expensive art pieces. Hammadi called him the most accomplished counterfeiter in the art world. He also hated the guy. But he needed him.

Hammadi said: "Hello Dr. Weinstein." He hated to call the little weasel doctor. It was necessary to inflate Weinstein's already out of control ego.

Weinstein said: "What do I do to help you get rid of Don Gino?"

"We have a problem. The ship security makes it difficult to do away with Don Gino Landry. I have thought long and hard. We will spare him."

"Perhaps I can copy a key to his suite."

"Thank you." Hammadi hung up. The little weasel was helpful if you played to his ego. Then Hammadi turned to Burton.

"Bob, I need to spend some time with the extensive blueprints for the presidential suite deck."

"I am at your disposal Mr. Smith." He couldn't figure out why Smith wanted the architectural plans. That was his business. Burton had no idea that he was talking to a Muslim terrorist. Smith never used the name Hammadi. He told Burton that he was part of the African American business community. Burton, like most white liberals, took Hammadi at this word. A big mistake! Burton would die. Hammadi couldn't wait for the greedy, little arrogant bastard to die. "I am leaving the ship in Malaga."

"Why?" Burton was wary.

Hammadi said: "I want to educate myself at the Picasso Museum. I know little of the art world. I am a pious and humble man who desires the truth." Hammadi knew that he had fooled the pompous white liberal. Burton didn't have a clue.

"There is one more thing, Mr. Burton. Picasso said that Dali was 'an outboard motor that's always running.' I purchase Picasso's and burn them. Does that tell you the depth of my feeling?"

Burton couldn't believe this guy. He was an entitled Negro. He thought that he was a real art dealer. He was a non-talented poseur.

This was worst kind of art snob. Burning Picasso's. Now Burton realized that he was dealing with an amateur. There was no need to worry about his criminal activity. He was dealing with a fool. Burton believed that Hammadi was as unaware of what was and what wasn't legal in the art world. He was disgusted with this Negro who believed that he could infiltrate the art world.

Hammadi smiled. He had fooled this dimwitted businessman. The rest would be easy. It was time to bait the trap. Hammadi left his stateroom and walked down to the champagne bar. There was one of his cohorts drinking a diet coke.

Hammadi said: "I need to bring in your assassin."

"I will call him." The Muslim radical walked away. He was Hammadi's twin brother. He was from Los Angeles, and he had played basketball for the L. A. Clippers before converting to Islam. Hammadi was proud of his twin brother. His name was Johnson Smith. He had played for Rick Patino at the University of Louisville. He was the fourth pick in the 1990 NBA draft. After playing two years in the NBA, he invested in a Dubai bank. He was a multi-millionaire. He was also a superbly, well-educated radical Muslim and a theoretical terrorist preparing to become an active assassin. Everyone kidded him that he had two last names.

They also kidded him about his Johnson. He didn't care. They were infidels. He was ready to destroy America's racial and capitalistic inequality

It was time for Hammadi to tie up some loose ends. He took his files, and he haphazardly tore them up. Then he walked down to the ships hold and placed the papers into an incinerator. Hammadi didn't notice the small Asian man following him. The small man looked at his purple watch, he took out a purple handkerchief and wiped his forehead. It was hot in the bottom of the ship.

The small Asian man had turned off the incinerator. He retrieved Hammadi's papers. Emilio took them to his room to reassemble Hammadi's file.

When Hammadi returned to his cabin the phone rang: "Mr. Smith we are ready." It was his brother who had the assassin in tow. They agreed to meet in the Billie Holliday lounge. It was a stainless steel cocktail lounge that looked modern. Billie Holliday would have been embarrassed to play in such a place. She would also have been embarrassed to be around African Americans who had a grudge against their country. Somewhere in heaven Billie Holliday wondered what the hell was going on? A blonde white girl performing "Strange Fruit." Weird!

After listening to the music they talked at length. The plan was complicated and dangerous. It was also not foolproof.

Hammadi said: "My brother, we are going to make history."

"I know."

"Are you ready for 300 Virgins." Johnson Smith looked around. He thought how could anyone be ready for death? He wasn't like the brother who called himself Hammadi. He wasn't sure that Allah and the Quran guaranteed immortality.

"I will do what you desire my brother, you saved my life." They continued to talk and left to return for evening prayer. They had no idea that they were being watched. A small Asian man swept up the corner areas of the Billie Holliday lounge. He had an earpiece. He didn't look happy.

CHAPTER TWENTY-FOUR

Hammadi And Chastain
Johnson Shadow Each Other

"My love of everything that is gilded and excessive, my passion for luxury and my love of oriental clothes is due to an Arab lineage." Salvador Dali

Chastain Johnson obscured herself. She was standing behind a pole near Hammadi's room. She pulled her breasts in as they stuck out beyond the hiding place. She considered breast reduction but didn't have time. As Hammadi left his room, he was carrying a bulky bag. She waited. He looked around. He turned the corner. She watched him enter the elevator.

She moved toward his door. Suddenly a small person in a purple jogging suit came around the corner. He stopped. He smiled. He turned toward Hammadi's door. Chastain pulled her Glock out of her back holster and released the safety. The small man bowed. She moved away. She might need a quick shot. He walked to Hammadi's door, took out a small pick and opened it. He bowed He smiled. He turned and walked to the elevator. Chastain Johnson, FBI agent, didn't have to break into Hammadi's room. It was wide open, and she saw a batch of papers on his desk.

She held her gun to her side. Chastain checked the bathroom. She checked the large walk in closet. This was a hell of a ship. She looked on the balcony. No one was around. She took out a small camera and quickly photographed the papers on Hammadi's desk. She was careful not to move anything. Then she saw the clue that was most important. It was a small piece of California history. Chastain knew the al Qaeda terrorist target in San Francisco.

As Chastain left the room, she was watched. Humberto Diaz was in the shadows. He didn't like what he saw. The young American FBI agent was smart, she moved like a cat burglar. She would have to be dealt with and quickly. He followed Chastain to her room. She looked around and unlocked it. He waited until he heard the shower and then he moved into her cabin with his pick opening her door in seconds. When she came out of the bathroom, he raised his Glock to hit her on the head. It was the last thing she remembered.

Chastain awoke tied to a chair. Humberto smiled. "Hello my dear, welcome to hell."

"Fuck you, you raghead bastard." Chastain struggled with the tight ropes.

"Fuck me!"

"You stupid asshole, don't you understand English?" Humberto took out a small silver knife and began cleaning his fingernails. Chastain looked at him in disgust.

"You will answer my questions."

"Go fuck a goat." Chastain wanted a cigarette.

"I will cut you up?" He waved a smile knife. He also smiled lecherously.

"You stupid, ignorant bastard, do you really think that will scare me? You must have left your rag at home."

"If you die, I scare you." Chastain laughed in his face.

Suddenly there was a slight sound followed by billowing smoke. The cabin door burst open. Humberto trained his gun on the door. He moved to the side of Chastain's suite. Whoever was coming through the door would be killed instantly.

A man dressed as a magician, wearing a Houdini mask, stood in front of Humberto. He was carrying a bird in one hand and a cane in the other. He wasn't armed.

"You asshole, you are that crazy magician." Bennie the Beneficent bowed. His graying hair seemed to stand on end. He wore plaid red pants and a pink-stripped shirt. He smiled. He waved the cane. Humberto awoke ten-minutes later tied to Chastain's chair.

There was no sign of Chastain Johnson. She had left for her suite.

Bennie the Beneficent, the world's greatest illusionist, was going to make Humberto Diaz disappear. He had to find some answers before Diaz was bodily disassembled. But that would take time. There was a slight knock on the door. It opened. A man in a purple suit, with a purple cane and a large white cape set off in purple walked into the room smoking a small cigar. The man smiled. There was a much smaller man with a purple suit who was followed by six Samoans dressed as waiters in the Carnivolet's new purple uniforms.

Bennie said: "Is there room for all of us? Perhaps I could make a few of you disappear." There was no laughter. Only glaring. The Don and his henchmen didn't have a sense of humor.

"Allow me to introduce myself." The man paused. "I am an emissary from Allah."

"You are an emissary from the devil. At least my friend Mick Jagger would think so." The Don smiled

"I will broker a deal with you," Humberto said.

"No deal my friend. Would you like some persuasion?" Humberto was frightened.

"There is no need, Don Gino." Humberto perspired and looked scared. The Don didn't look happy. Don Gino took out another small cigar. He didn't light it. It simply stuck out from the corner of his sneering mouth. He looked agitated.

Don Gino said: "I saw the plan to kill me. That doesn't dismay me. What bothers me is the scheme to blow up a sacred San Francisco shrine. I need all of your information."

Now it was Humberto Diaz' turn to smile. He was a member of al Qaeda. He would happily go to his grave without uttering a word. His defiant smile prompted Don Gino to look dismayed.

"Mr. Humberto, I am a patient man. You don't want to test me."

Humberto said: "I will go to my grave quietly." Don Gino smiled. He thought, we shall see. After three hours of various techniques, it was obvious that Humberto would not talk. Don Gino thought. There was one way to force him to talk.

He took out his cell phone. He called Chastain Johnson. She showed up within two minutes.

"Greetings, Miss Johnson."

"Don Gino, as always a pleasure."

"We have a problem. A hidden Muslim who won't talk. It seems he will go to his grave to please Allah. Do you have any thoughts?"

Chastain smiled. "I have more than thoughts." She took off her sweater. She took off her blouse. She took off her bra. Humberto's eyes almost jumped out of his head. There was nothing more disgusting to a Muslim than a bare breasted woman. Even a magnificent woman who looked like a stallion with breasts could attract a Muslim. He would guess her bra size 36DD. He felt guilty for knowing such insignificant information. Chastain walked over to Humberto. He looked horrified.

She began rubbing her breasts on his face. Then she lit a cigarette and blew smoke in his face. She burned his ears, his neck and his chest. She grabbed Mr. Winkey and he began screaming. It took Chastain an hour for Humberto to confess the al Qaeda plan. At least the part that Humberto played in the intricate plot.

Humberto pointed out that in 1949 Dali began his work stressing religious themes. He did this while drawing, painting and writing about the scientific advances of the Muslim world. Dali secretly read Sayyid Qutb's **Milestones**. This book had a strong influence on Islamic insurgent/terrorist groups. In the decade after 9-11, al Qaeda used Qutb's writings and philosophy to promote Islamic jihad. Dali quietly agreed.

Milestones is the book that gave birth to the Muslim Brotherhood and al Qaeda. Its popularity obscured Qutb's influence on artists. Salvador Dali read Qutb's books. He had almost a hundred sketches that he completed in a few minutes that he sold to members of Egypt's Muslim Brotherhood. When Hassan al-Banna, the Muslim Brotherhood founder, died in 1949, his followers sent a note to Salvador Dali. "You are the inspiration for our future." Dali never saw it. Gala threw the note away. When Gala looked into Dali's drawings file, there were three magnificent drawings of the Muslim Brotherhood founder. She tore them up. This was typical Dali. It was also typical Gala. She threw away what she detested. Dali was secretive.

James Smith found this out before he invented the Hammadi persona. It further reinforced his belief that Dali was a Muslim savior.

Humberto informed them that Dali completed a number of secret drawings that he sold to a rich Arab sheik. Those drawings influenced the philosophy and direction of al Qaeda terrorists. When Osama bin Laden joined the Mujahideen to fight the Russians in Afghanistan, he carried a copy of Dali's painting **The Persistence of Memory**. This 1931 work with the melted clocks was the symbol bin Laden needed for his attack upon decadent western imperialism. There were other paintings that bin Laden admired, and he was a secret Dali collector.

The most significant was **Christ In Mecca**. When this painting surfaced in the Muslim art world, it was the subject of intense debate. Did Dali paint it? It was sold twice. Then it vanished from the Middle East. The rumor was that a Catholic monk stole it and brought it to Rome. The Pope carefully examined it and had a fit. He demanded that the painting be stored for posterity. It was a blasphemous critique of Catholicism. Then this painting somehow was transported to San Francisco. It was there that Don Gino Landry destroyed it. At least this was the rumor. No one was sure. The truth was that it was in Don Gino's private room.

Humberto confessed that the al Qaeda cell in San Francisco put out a contract on Don Gino. They planned to blow up the Mission Delores. Don Gino spent more than a million dollars on an artistic cross in the chapel and improvements throughout the Mission. The terrorist attack on the Mission Delores was al Qaeda's way of punishing the Catholic Church and Don Gino.

Since learning of the terrorist plots, directed at Barcelona and San Francisco, Don Gino had enlisted specialized agents. He went to the FBI and CIA for help. He began quietly working with Chastain Johnson. For almost a year, Don Gino and Chastain took notes on the al Qaeda cell. They had a good part of the plan down. There was still the question of where Dali's home near Cadaques fit into the scheme. They had some information but not all of it. Humberto Diaz provided all of the remaining information. He was no longer an asset. He was a liability.

Bennie the Beneficent took Humberto into the bathroom. He came out in small pieces. "You raghead piece of shit," Bennie smiled. "You will find out that I am Magic Bennie." There was a great deal of noise. Bennie spent a half an hour with the noise. He came out of the bathroom with a Cheshire cat smile.

"I always knew that the vanishing person trick would work." Bennie chuckled. He dropped a small pill, smoke pillowed up and there were six bags and a very small container.

"These are for you." Bennie pointed to the six Samoans. "My friend." Bennie looked toward the midget. He glowered. He picked up the small bag.

As six Samoans disposed of the body, Don Gino hurried to prevent the next step in the terrorist plot.

The Samoans were wearing their maintenance uniforms. They weren't looked at twice. They emptied the trash. Good riddance. Humberto Diaz was history.

Don Gino took some time. He needed to make sure that he hadn't missed a key point. How could someone as inept as Humberto Diaz become involved in an intricate plot? Something didn't seem right. Humberto sounded more American than foreign. Who hired him? Was it the Hammadi-Smith fellow? Or was someone else in the mix? Something bothered him. There were too many unanswered questions. There was also too much knowledge in the terrorist camp. Someone close to him was leaking information.

CHAPTER TWENTY-FIVE
In The Azores And The Art Auction

"Sometimes, I spit for fun on my mother's grave." Salvador Dali

It was a blustery, cold day when the Pearl of the Ocean landed in the Azores. There was excitement as passengers prepared to disembark. The public address system announced that Matt Luman was boarding the ship as the featured entertainer. The anticipation of a day on shore and a major recording artist entertaining made for a euphoric time.

Luman's long list of hit records and drop-dead good looks made him a favorite of the sixtyish, big-butted women from Des Moines and Fargo. No one noticed that Luman brought in a suitcase full of surveillance equipment. He also had a suitcase full of guns, explosive devices and hundreds of rounds of ammunition. Luman's flowing blonde hair, his lithe, muscular body and his ability to talk smoothly to the ladies made him a hidden CIA operative. Everyone was too busy looking at Ponta Delgada's beauty to notice that Luman had more than music, alcohol and women on his mind. He was a patriot. He hated terrorists. He would end their nefarious schemes.

Ponta Delgada was sunny, but cold, as the Azores prepared for a holiday celebration. Portugal was going broke and the Azores was caught in the European Union crisis that threatened to bankrupt the world. Still they partied like there was no tomorrow.

Trevor Blake III got off the ship and looked around. Yuck! There wasn't much to do. He wanted to tell the locals that China would come in and buy their money. Then Trevor remembered that they didn't have money. They had Euros. Everyone knew that this was a rapidly diminishing currency.

Trevor walked around downtown Ponta Delgado. Chastain Johnson walked by and wandered into Zara. She was in the lingerie department. He could only imagine what she was trying on. He continued peeking into the window. She went into the dressing room. Trevor noticed a small man with a cane and a purple suit. He walked by planting his cane on Trevor's shoe. Trevor howled and moved around the street. Did Don Gino have the little bastard doing surveillance? Or was he having his flunky shadow the lovely FBI agent Chastain Johnson? Who knows! Who cares! As Trevor stumbled over to an out door café, he ordered a cappuccino. When Trevor looked over at the ship, he saw a strange procession leaving the Pearl of the Ocean.

As six Samoans came off the ship carrying six separate suitcases, they struggled to carry the heavy bags. What the hell was going on? The world's second greatest detective didn't have a clue. Then he remembered Robert Crais was on the ship. He was a featured speaker. His detective, Elvis Cole, was billed as the world's greatest detective. Joe Pike might differ. Trevor did differ. Well! Trevor could be number two. He could call himself: "almost the world's greatest detective." He wondered what was going on? Don Gino said nothing. The Samoans sat outside a coffee shop in the blustery, but sunny, Azores. They were joined by a group of six female tourists. They were big beautiful blonde ladies wearing lederhosen. They talked for an hour. The Samoans were laughing, joking, and speaking German. They acted like they hadn't seen the girls in years. When the Samoans left, the beautiful German ladies picked up the suitcases and walked back to the Terminal Maritime. They walked over to a private boat of about 65 feet and threw the suitcases aboard. What was in the suitcases? Another mystery. Where were they going? What was going on? Trevor didn't have a clue. Samoans speaking German?

As Trevor walked back onto the Pearl of the Ocean, he needed to rethink the case. He was missing something. What was it? It seemed that he was always missing a key clue. He walked into his cabin and pulled out the files. He had read them three times. What was in the key file that wasn't registering?

After two hours of reading through the material, Trevor came up with a key fact. One that he had missed. Harry Bosch would be proud of him. Michael Connelly was on board, and he probably thought Trevor was inept. Or perhaps Connelly thought at the least mildly incompetent.

It was time for a drink. Trevor walked into the Billie Holliday lounge. Matt Luman was sitting at the piano entertaining a small group of fans. He was signing Memphis songs by Jerry Lee Lewis, Elvis Presley, Roy Orbison, Narvel Felts, Warren Smith, Matt Lucas and Johnny Cash. When he saw Trevor, Luman said: "Ladies and Gentleman, the man who caught the Start Me Up drummers murders." Everyone looked at Trevor. Nervously, Trevor smiled.

"Hello." It was weak. It was lame. The Three Amigos raised their glasses at the bar and hollered: "Here, Here." A fan requested "Ooby Dooby." Trevor was forgotten as Matt played to his rapt audience. Trevor sat in the corner drinking a glass of Chilean Merlot. Trevor sent a round over for the Three Amigos. He heard them chant: "Here Here." They also shouted: "all for one, one for all." The Three Amigos were party animals. It was time to get away from them. Trevor needed the quiet to figure things out. It didn't last.

As he watched, Trevor noticed that one of the Three Amigos was using a calculator. What in the hell was he doing? This was a pleasure cruise. Was he figuring his income tax? Something was amiss with the Three Amigos. At times they were friendly. In other settings, they were aloof. They didn't look twice at Chastain Johnson. I thought of her a lot. Then I heard a voice.

"Hello Dickhead." The lovely Chastain Johnson stood in front of him. She had on a jogging suit with a low cut top. She looked anxious. Trevor looked anxious. It was a different anxious.

"Well Chastain, you either need a cigarette or sex. Which is it?"

"Remember Dickhead, when Mickey Rooney is no longer available, you will get your chance." She smiled. Always the clever FBI agent.

Trevor said: "Sit down, we can talk." He was surprised. She sat. She smiled. She was civil. She wanted something. She also took out a stick of nicorette and started chewing two pieces. Trevor vowed never to go to bed with another smoker. He would make an exception for Chastain.

Trevor showed her his file on Bob Burton. She spent a long time studying it. Chastain took out a small notebook. She made copious notes. Trevor said nothing.

She said: "I have to hand it to you. This is good stuff."

"Always the compliant private eye."

She smiled: "Now let me share with you what you have missed." I didn't like being corrected. Or for that matter lectured on what I missed.

"Missed!" I said. "I don't think so."

"Bob Burton will suffer an unfortunate accident."

"Unfortunate?" I was baffled. Was it Nietzsche who said: "Unfortunate is fortunate when it came to an accident." The P. I. had too many philosophy courses in college.

"Is there such a thing as a fortunate accident?" The clever P. I. strikes verbally.

"Trevor, the money will be raised for the al Qaeda project at tonight's art auction.

"What is so special about tonight?"

Chastain said: "Ah, Trevor, always the observant P. I. Tonight Park Avenue Artists will unveil the original operatic score of **Jo, Dali (I Dali)** that the Catalan composer Xavier Benguerel wrote about the tenuous relationship between Dali and Gala." Trevor had no idea what she was talking about or why it was important. He acted like he did.

"So!" Trevor didn't see the connection to the al Qaeda coming act of terrorism. He sat quietly.

"Trevor, Gala was nuts. She poisoned Dali at the end of his life. He couldn't draw, paint or write." She put another stick of nicorette into her mouth.

"You sound like a male chauvinist."

"Would you like me to explain things to you, dim one?" Put that way Trevor listened. He was not happy.

"Enlighten me." Trevor scowled.

"Listen Trevor, there is more. Gala and Dali showed up at a New York debutante costume party dressed as the Lindberg kidnapper and the baby. The press roasted him. The newspaper clippings for this event were found in al Qaeda files and copied by that horrible little pervert who works for Don Gino."

"I still don't see the connection. What does this have to do with our case?"

"Our case. Are you nuts? Why you are here enrages me?" Chastain lit a cigarette.

"I'm the world's greatest detective. Have you forgotten?"

"Asshole."

"That too." Trevor smiled. The repartee was going his way. Chastain looked flustered.

"It is simple Trevor. The al Qaeda operatives use these events as code words. We are still figuring out what they mean."

"This sounds surrealistic."

"We know the 'Lindberg baby' is a code name for violence."

"Do you know when and where al Qaeda will use the code words?"

"Not really," Chastain paused.

"But Dali was never political."

"That's the beauty of coding his words for political purposes. No one suspects. He was inordinately apolitical, you moron."

"I like your explanation, except for the use of the word moron, try deductive detective."

"I prefer Dickhead."

Chastain has a way of putting things in perspective. It did make sense. The problem was to figure out the coded words or phrases. While Dali always maintained an apolitical stance, Dali's **Vision of Hell** was a warning sign. Why? Trevor realized that Dali's **Vision of Hell** revealed a secret about the artist. He was trapped between his feelings for reforming Communist atheism and embracing traditional Catholicism. This contradiction continually surfaced in his drawings and paintings.

Then Trevor explained everything to Chastain. She sat transfixed. She was interested. He told her that Dali was fifty-five years old and feared burning in hell. "Heaven is to be found exactly in the center of the bosom of the man who has faith," Dali wrote. In 1959 Dali was asked to paint **Vision of Hell** to celebrate the children who saw the Virgin Mary at Fatima. When Dali finished the painting, it vanished for more than three and a half decades before critics figured out where it was, what it was and why the provenance was so clouded.

The genesis of al Qaeda's infatuation with **Vision of Hell** resulted from its dangled historical past. James Smith, aka Hammadi, told his followers that the painting was a repudiation of Dali's Catholicism. He told his followers to ignore comments by Don Gino Landry and Trevor Blake III. One follower asked: "Who are these gentleman?" Hammadi vowed to find smarter followers.

When Trevor talked about the lost painting, there was a sense of mystery. No one knew where it was warehoused. Then a San Francisco collector, Don Gino Landry, found it. **Vision of Hell** surfaced in 1997. Don Gino said: "I wanted to purchase this painting eighty years after the Virgin Mary appeared at Fatima." He bought it. The word on the street was that a European Mafia family owned it. They donated it to Don Gino. They probably wanted to stay alive. No one questioned the Don. He did bring the painting to San Francisco. There was a report of two Arab Sheiks who died after hoarding a number of Dali paintings. They were found in a remote area near Islamabad strangled by a purple garrote. The crime remains unsolved. Don Gino felt redemption. He skipped the usual confession. He knew God understood.

For unexplainable reasons, al Qaeda terrorists interpreted **Vision of Hell** as an omen for the triumph of the Muslim faith. Irrational! Yes! Explainable! No! Why was **Vision of Hell** so important to the terrorists? Trevor needed to find out.

Chastain said: "I need to apologize to you. You have done your homework. I knew very little of what you have told me and now I will get into action."

"Does that mean we are going to bed?"

"Yes, Trevor, you in your bed and me in mine waiting for Mickey Rooney." Chastain smiled and left.

"Mickey Rooney has standards, Chastain."

Trevor realized that the answer to many of his questions was on deck three. He walked down to examine the art pieces. The Dali work would ignite the terrorist attack. After he walked down to deck three and the Park Avenue Artists office, a statuesque blonde stood by a Dali lithograph. It was signed. It was one of 5,000. She smiled. Trevor smiled. There was a long list of available Dali's. There were all signed lithographs. There were ceramics figures. There were a large number of paintings, unpublished magazine articles and movie scripts to be auctioned. The treasure of the evening's auction was one magnificent piece that wasn't for sale. It was the 1978 Dali hyper stereoscopic painting **Dali Lifting The Skin of the Mediterranean To Show Gala The Birth of Venus**. When he completed this painting in 1977 it attracted interest from the Middle East. The absence of the bottom portion of the right leg in the painting convinced James Smith that here was a victim of a land mine. Smith further speculated that Americans planted it. This further intensified his resolve to terrorize the capitalistic and democratic world. Trevor was looking at the painting at the same time Smith admired it. They smiled at each other.

The young lady approached Trevor.

"Hello." She smiled.

"I am interested n the authentic fakes." She looked disappointed.

"Mr. Blake you have a one hundred thousand dollar line of credit. Why do you want to spend a thousand dollars on authentic fakes?"

Trevor looked at her in amazement. This was getting strange. She didn't have a clue what Trevor wanted. He was trying to find out who was responsible for the authentic fakes.

She said: "Well!"

"Well what?" Trevor looked perplexed. He felt like he was talking to Paris Hilton. Pretty but stupid.

Trevor continued: "I need to know who produces the authentic fakes?"

"Mr. Blake you need to talk to Bob Burton or Dr. Weinstein."

"Ok." She turned and left. Trevor picked up a Guggenheim Museum of Art catalogue.

The Solomon R. Guggenheim Museum of Art in New York was selling a portion of the Dali originals to pay for an addition to its surrealism wing. The bidding for these pieces began at five million dollars. Park Avenue Artists also offered authentic fakes for a thousand dollars. Case closed. Bob Burton come over and introduced himself. He was told that Trevor wanted an explanation of authentic fakes. Burton spent over an hour explaining the subject of authentic fakes. He talked of their collectible nature. Trevor pretended to be interested. This guy loved to talk. Who would collect authentic fakes? These people were beyond stupid. Trevor elicited interest from Burton and Weinstein. They were uneasy around him. They realized that they were missing something in his demeanor.

"Can I ask you a question, Mr. Burton?" Trevor realized that Burton had an ego the size of Texas.

"Yes, of course." Burton looked at Trevor with disdain.

"Who allows you to market authentic fakes?" Nothing like the world's second greatest private eye putting the tough questions forward.

"Mr. Blake, we have a licensing agreement with the Guggenheim to sell authentic fakes. They come with a certificate of authenticity." Trevor couldn't believe it, fakes with a provenance sticker. Weird! Burton left.

"Hello! May I help you?" The voice was soft and feminine.

Trevor looked her up and down. She had on a blue business suit. The white truffle shirt was open to reveal just enough cleavage to make her interesting. Trevor noticed the Jimmy Choo shoes. She reeked of money. The dark horn rimmed glasses were an attempt to hide her natural beauty. They didn't work. She was gorgeous.

Trevor said: "What time is the Dali auction?" The always-clever P. I. asks the right questions.

"It's private. Are you on the list?"

I wasn't sure. "I'm Trevor Blake III." She looked at one sheet of paper.

"Oh, yes, Mr. Blake, you have a one hundred thousand dollar line of credit. It is attached to your Platinum American Express card." It was time to rethink the clues.

Trevor was nervous.

"What time is the auction?"

She smiled. "We will see you at eleven. There is an hour cocktail party before the auction and once the Midnight Chime sounds we will commence the auction."

I loved the way that she talked, dressed and looked. She said: "Commence, let the auction begin." I was looking at her breasts when a sharp finger poked into my side. It was none other than the lovely Chastain Johnson. She stood smiling in a form fitting light blue work out outfit. Nike was emblazoned on the front of the blue top. A nice touch! Or maybe another way of deceiving. Maybe the FBI charged for advertising.

"Is this your wife?"

"She's my sister."

"Then she may also attend the auction."

Chastain said: "Well thank you, I wasn't planning to attend, but I have to keep my older brother from spending his money." If the truth were told Chastain was three years older than me. If she kept smoking she would look ten years older. She would still look better.

We left and walked back toward my cabin. Chastain stopped.

"Thanks Trevor. This is a rare opportunity. You can pick me up at five minutes to eleven."

"What?" I said. "It sounds like a date."

"In your wildest dreams, Dickhead." She walked down a flight of stairs to her cabin. I had six hours to kill. It was time to do some investigating. I walked down to the Pearl of the Ocean computer room. I googled Park Avenue Artists. This company sold art on cruise ships. I also found that it was sued for selling Dali fakes. They had beaten the rap using the Los Angeles based law firm of Isaacs-Schwartz-Page. There was a red flag. In fact, there were two red flags. Park Avenue Artists had headquarters in Las Vegas at the Wynn Hotel and in Pakistan. The Pakistan address was a post office box. Did Pakistan have post office boxes? What the hell was going on? Did Pakistan have Dali art?

Then it became clear how the money was being laundered. It wasn't through the Las Vegas or Islamabad connections, it was another, virtually unseen, but simple money laundering scheme. Park Avenue Artists placed the funds from their sales in a special account that was untraceable. They had set up the Friends of Salvador Dali, a nonprofit corporation, in the Cayman Islands to help starving artists. The starving artists were apparently terrorists. They were starving for IED's and other explosive devices. Salvador Dali's art was funding these nefarious enterprises. Don Gino would not be happy. After the Pope, Don Gino considered Dali the most important man in the world.

The auction might provide some missing clues. The auction began after an hour cocktail party. Nothing like bringing out flutes of champagne with art consultants who looked like models serving as many glasses as you could drink. It doesn't get any better than that. The auction began when Bob Burton stood up. He smiled. The designer suit and the smooth delivery reeked of a snake oil salesman. His hair had enough grease to block up the Panama Canal.

"Greetings, my fellow art enthusiasts." Burton looked directly at Chastain and smiled. She smiled. I could tell that she wanted to cut his balls off. Then again she wanted to cut my balls off. Chastain wanted to cut every man's balls off. So it was nothing personal.

"We will start the bidding." It took an hour and a half for the minor items to be auctioned off. The minor items raised a little more than two million dollars. Now it was time for the big show.

Dali Lifting The Skin of the Mediterranean To Show Gala The Birth of Venus was auctioned as an authentic fake. No one seemed to know why. They had the beautiful salesperson-model tell the unsuspecting buyer that it was an authentic fake. It was. What was I missing? When it was brought out there was a loud chorus of 'oohs" and "aahs" that quickly turned into angry screams. When the hostile voices calmed down the auctioneer said that the authentic fake was a rare collectible. The fake was for auction purposes to the serious collector. The auctioneer held up an art provenance in the fake category. He explained that this was a new and highly collectible field. The provenances for the fakes indicated that there was only one such fake. As such, the auctioneer emphasized, those who bought authentic fakes early made money. There was a stunned silence. The auctioneer emphasized that the authentic fake looked nothing like the original. Trevor watched in stunned silence. These people didn't know an authentic fake from the real thing. Sad!

The auctioneer announced that this authentic fake was available to private collectors. Trevor looked around the room and the watches on the wrists of those attending cost more than his car. He watched in awe as the little signs went up. Time and time again the bidding increased. A million dollar bid from an anonymous collector won the coveted authentic fake. The anonymous buyer went to the foyer and pulled out his cell phone. Trevor finally got it. The anonymous buyer was elsewhere. Trevor felt like a hillbilly at an auction. He was. Now Trevor had to figure out who bought the Dali work and why. He looked at the cell phone. Maybe he could steal it.

Then it dawned on Trevor. The authentic fake sold for one million dollars to raise money for al Qaeda. He had to find the anonymous buyer. He was the person funding al Qaeda.

As Trevor left the auction room, a young woman approached him. She said: "Hello."

Trevor said: "Please allow me introduce myself, I'm a man of wealth and taste, I've been around a long, long time. Stole many a man's soul and faith."

"That lame line from the Rolling Stones' 'Sympathy For The Devil,' does little to enhance your private eye credentials. You even get the line wrong." He wondered who was this woman?

"Then you know I'm Trevor Blake III."

"Take this envelope and read the material carefully. Gala is the key."

"What do you mean the key?"

"Don't ask questions, Trevor, read and analyze."

"You sound like my mother." She walked away. She didn't look my mother. Thank goodness! The envelope was weighty. So I returned to my suite.

In my luxurious stateroom, I opened the envelope and there were more than three hundred pages. Gala had written a novel. I read through it. Gala was determined not to be like Hemingway's wife Hadley. She kept Dali interested. She was also jealous of Dali's success. The novel showed that she would make him pay. She talked of poisoning Dali. She did exactly that in his later years. The novel's conclusion had two acts of violence. Trevor now had a clue to what was going to happen in Barcelona and later in San Francisco.

He took the novel and dropped it off at Don Gino's room. One of the Samoans took it and placed it on the Don's desk. He would read it. Trevor was happy that he could present Don Gino with yet another Dali rarity. Then the big Samoan slammed the door in Trevor's face. He didn't allow Trevor in the stateroom. The midget looked out the window. He gave Trevor the finger. He mouthed: "Fuck you." Trevor had enough of the Samoans and the wretched midget.

Now it was time for some fun. Trevor went to the Pearl of the Ocean jazz bar for a nightcap. Matt Luman was at the piano singing "I'm Movin' On" and talking to two young girls who couldn't have been more than twenty-five. Matt still had the touch.

Luman said: "Ladies and Gentleman, Trevor Blake III, the world's greatest private eye is in the room."

"Hello, Matt, remember Elvis Cole is the world's greatest P. I."

Matt said: "Maybe you can be Shell Scott." I forgot Matt reads a lot of mystery novels. He collects Richard Prather. I was overmatched. I listened to Matt until two in the morning, and then they kicked me out of the jazz club. I went to my room alone. Matt was escorting the two young ladies to his room. Maybe Chastain Johnson was naked in my bed. I walked into my suite and there was a duck made out of a towel and a chocolate mint on my pillowcase. Ah, the life of a famous detective!

I was ready to find out what the al Qaeda terrorists were up to. The best way was to follow the money. That meant drinking more Andre Champagne with the beautiful young ladies at the Park Avenue Artists gallery. It was a tough job. Trevor Blake III was on the case.

CHAPTER TWENTY-SIX

Friar Berardi: Christ On The Cross

"Don't bother about being modern. Unfortunately, it is the one thing that, whatever you do, you cannot avoid." Salvador Dali

The number of missing, unaccounted for, and never seen Salvador Dali originals could fill a warehouse. These works probably could fill a football stadium. There were some works that were esoteric and special. Myth and reality were difficult to separate. This helped to popularize Dali's art.

In 1983, a young San Francisco businessman, Don Gino Landry, began his collection in Ballina, Ecuador when he purchased a sail for a ship that Dali painted to support locals who were trying to navigate three rafts to Australia. Don Gino paid a large sum of money for an "authentic Dali sail." For thirty years the San Francisco collector quietly became the world's chief authority on collecting Dali. What Don Gino came to realize is that the large number of fakes created anxiety. When he discovered that a Ballina company forged Dali sails, he sent them a note to cease and desist. They didn't. The company founders died in a fire and all the fake Dali's were destroyed. The only thing to survive in the fire was a small purple handkerchief. The case remains unsolved. Don Gino hated people who took advantage of Dali.

There were two Dali's works that confused Dali collectors. One was **Christ of St. John Of The Cross**, which he completed in 1951, and the other was a sculpture **Christ On The Cross**. The problem was that only the Catholic clergy had viewed the sculpture. Confusion ensued. The sculpture's whereabouts intrigued collectors, as well as al Qaeda terrorists. It was the last lost Dali. Why and how it came about was not well known. The art world loves mysteries.

When the press reported that Dali created the sculpture to rid himself of the Devil, James Smith took out ads in every major Muslim newspaper. He attempted to draw in unsuspecting young men to the terrorist cause. Most young Muslims had one question. Who is Salvador Dali?

In Italy, Friar Gabriele Maria Berardi performed an exorcism on Salvador Dali. There is no firm date for verifying the exorcism. It did take place. What is known is that Dali created a sculpture, **Christ On The Cross** as a thank you to Friar Berardi. After two Spanish art experts confirmed that it was a Dali, the matter ended. The criminals who collected Dali attempted to purchase it. After two gangsters died strangled with purple garrotes, the Catholic Church warehoused the painting. Italian law enforcement suspected Don Gino. They had no proof. The case remains unsolved. The Pope awarded Don Gino a special medal for service to the faith. The Italian legal officials ended their investigation.

When Friar Berardi contacted Don Gino, the Friar wanted an authenticity appraisal from a collector. That led to Dr. Harold Weinstein authenticating **Christ On The Cross**. The academics and art critics commented that the sculpture demonstrated "sufficient stylistic reasons" to conclude that it was a Dali.

James Smith was aware of the sculpture and the exorcism. To Smith-Hammadi, Dali's relationship with the Catholic Church was simply another indication that his Islamic beliefs were in the way of his Catholicism. Hammadi traveled to Rome to see Father Berardi. He was too late. Father Berardi died.

Then Smith-Hammadi investigated the headquarters of the Associaione Fra I Volontari della Carita, an organization Berardi founded to sell the Dali to provide money for Catholic charities. The only problem is that the organization founded for raising money from the sale of Dali art couldn't find the art that it intended to sell. Fraud was written all over the operation. The Catholic charities were criminals. Hammadi-Smith saw this as another sign that a Muslim uprising in Dali's name was essential to an Islamic triumph. As Hammadi looked at a picture of the sculpture, he noticed that Jesus was bent over on the cross in supplication to a deity. He envisioned the deity as Mohammad.

Christ On The Cross vanished to the relief of the Catholic Church. The Pope and the Vatican Hierarchy hated the sculpture. They were overjoyed when it disappeared. Everyone suspected that it had been taken to San Francisco. It had. It was in a home on Washington Street. Danielle Steel told Don Gino that it was ugly. The next morning her Mercedes had four flat tires, a window broken and her gas cap was missing. A purple handkerchief was in her gas tank. Don Gino called it unfortunate. The police investigated. The case remains unsolved.

When the San Francisco Archdiocese announced that it was in financially trouble, an anonymous donor donated the rare Dali sculpture for auction. The proceeds were to benefit the Mission Delores for restoration purposes.

Then **Christ On The Cross** showed up at an art auction in Dubai. It sold to an anonymous buyer. There was no mention of price. The Provenance, the tracing of the sculpture's origin, was a perfect record of the sculpture's past. There was no doubt that **Christ On The Cross** was real. Then the sculpture took a strange path. It vanished from sight. Whoever bought it remained anonymous. The owner was located in Iraq. Then American military forces marched into Baghdad and found the sculpture in an al Qaeda safe house. No one thought much about the find. It was sold to a Connecticut collector. He paid two million dollars for it. Then he sold it to a Middle Eastern buyer for four million dollars. The sculpture was considered unavailable. The problem with **Christ On The Cross** was that very few people had seen the sculpture. It was virtually impossible to authenticate. Dali collectors scoffed at its existence. The Catholic Church was quiet. They did everything possible to minimize publicity.

There was a continual rumor in the art world that the sculpture existed. The next phase came when New York's top public relations firm, Edelman, held a press conference and announced the imminent sale of **Christ On The Cross**.

Park Avenue Artists was selected to auction the sculpture on the Pearl of the Ocean. There was a buzz in the art world. The starting bid was ten million dollars. The date for the **Christ On The Cross** auction was in two days. What was going on? The Pearl of the Ocean seemed like the last place to auction off a valued Dali original. There was no question that **Christ On The Cross** was not only a Dali original, it was a coveted item. It was time for Matt Luman to get involved in the case.

The CIA picked up an e-mail transmission from a cell phone in Alabama some months ago. The text was in Urdu. There weren't many Alabamans fluent in Urdu. The text read: "Sagrada Familia." That was it.

When the e-mail was delivered to Don Gino Landry, he spent hours analyzing it. He understood why President Barack Obama brought in retired CIA agent Matt Luman. He also appreciated having Bennie the Beneficent on board. Bennie's specialty was getting rid of bodies, and he was also an explosives specialist. Matt and Bennie were important to ending the al Qaeda menace. President Obama was a brilliant man. How he could persuade a conservative Republican like Bennie and a full time ladies man like Matt Luman to get rid of the terrorists attests to the president's eloquence and powers of persuasion.

CHAPTER TWENTY-SEVEN
Matt Luman: Cia Agent

"Matt Luman is the best undercover agent in the history of the CIA. Why? I don't know. He spends too much time with the women, he drinks too much, and he plays too much music. What makes him so good? It's simple, brains and attention to detail."
Former President Bill Clinton

When Matt Luman left the CIA, he was young, physically fit, well educated and cunning. President Bill Clinton presented Luman with America's Medal of Honor on his retirement. It was done in secrecy. None of Luman' friends believed that he had any medals except for womanizing, drinking and playing music. Luman had the last laugh. He had a high six-figure income, royalties from music, money flowing from his real estate and a stock portfolio that would choke a horse. He had also anonymously written most of the songs recorded by Billy Joel. Luman was fond of telling close friends. "I wrote all that dog shit for Billy Joel as a joke. Then when 'Piano Man' went gold, I realized that I could write more hits."

Then Luman went to a party in New York and he and his old friend Liza Minnelli talked at length.

"Matt, I want to have my boyfriend record some of your songs," Minnelli continued. "Do you think that he could have some hits?"

Matt: "How would I know?"

Liza: "Could you talk to him?"

Luman: "Sure."

Luman went over and sat down next to Peter Allen. He was a good-looking Australian kid with a slightly effeminate manner. When Allen talked he had a booming voice. Luman wondered if Allen was man or woman. It didn't matter at all; it was Liza Minnelli who was going to marry Peter Allen. Not Matt Luman. He didn't care. During the course of the evening, Luman taught Allen some dance moves. He left Allen with a cache of songs that Luman had written that afternoon. Matt hadn't copyrighted the new tunes. The little bastard changed the songs a bit and copyrighted them under his name. Luman found out about it later. When Allen died, everyone suspected Matt Luman. There was no criminal investigation. When Luman was asked about Peter Allen. He smiled. He never said a word. The rumor was that Allen's estate left Luman and an unnamed San Francisco businessman the lion's share of his estate. The will was handwritten on purple paper with white ink. A San Francisco Court upheld its legality. Allen was living in San Francisco's Castro District when he passed away. His boyfriend Popkins Buddinsky was killed in a hate crime. Luman had plenty of money and great stories. He couldn't wait to get back in action as a musician and secret agent.

As Luman walked up to the Pearl of the Ocean's ninth level presidential suites, he was happy that the Pearl Of the Ocean upgraded him to the Presidential suites. He entered his suite with an L shaped balcony. The luxury was fitting. He deserved it. He noticed his telephone message light blinking. Matt needed a moment to think. No one knew his room number. What was going on? He turned on his 55-inch Samsung flat screen TV and put the documentary **Searching For Sugar Man** in to watch the Academy Award documentary. He liked Rodriguez' music. They had gotten drunk one night at the Old Miami Bar in Detroit. They gave an impromptu concert that sells on e-bay for a hundred dollars a CD. The room was perfect. Matt looked again at the telephone.

The message button was pressed and Matt listened to the CIA director. He was told to go to the dressing room behind the main stage. He forgot about the documentary. He walked down to his dressing room. The previous act, Jennifer Flowers, was cleaning her stuff out the dressing room.

Luman said: "Jennifer we both know Bill Clinton." He smiled.

She said: "Asshole."

"No sense of humor, Jennifer."

"Fuck off," she tore out of the room. Luman thought about her. Matt guessed he wouldn't be going bed with her. That's all right everyone else was. Luman found an envelope on top of his piano suitcase. He opened it. The message read: "Look for the least likely suspect." It was seven hours before show time. It was two hours before the boat left port.

Matt went down to meet the band. He was told that there was a change of plans. He would be in the Liberace Showroom, as well as the George W. Bush Ballroom. The Carnivolet Line was a big time right wing Republican hangout. They would have trouble believing that Muslim extremists used their ships for terrorist fund raising.

The Pearl of the Ocean's twelve-piece orchestra came complete with horns. A few moments after he started talking to the musicians, a four-piece string section walked into the show room.

The bandleader, Harold Kudlets, asked: "How do you want the charts arranged?"

Matt said: "You can arrange the charts on the floor, and then you can piss on them. We are going to improvise."

The musicians stood and applauded in unison. The hated the charts, they hated Kudlets and they hated the music they played.

Luman said: "We're not going to do this show sitting down, I want the band up and moving. There will be no country or pop hits. If I find anyone even saying the name Barry Manilow, they will be fired." The band cheered and applauded.

There was another round of applause. Luman then spent over an hour going through a set that included songs by Elvis Presley, Roy Orbison, Jerry Lee Lewis, Fats Domino, Chuck Berry, Matt Lucas and Narvel Felts. He liked the Lucas songs the best.

Luman said: "This guy Matt Lucas covers all my songs. He is talented but I'm going to have to talk to Don Gino about having him quit singing my hits. He never sends me royalties. He is married and boring. I can't hang out with him. He sometimes tells people he is me." Matt scowled and cracked his knuckles.

Even though Luman said that he wanted to jam, he led the musicians through a loose set of classic rock standards. Then he spent half an hour practicing a Matt Luman greatest hits medley. The musicians loved it.

Then Luman picked up the phone. He asked for the bar manager. He went to each musician and requested that they select a quart of whiskey of their choice.

"Mr. Luman," two musicians said. "We don't drink."

Matt smiled: "Then order two bottles of scotch for me. I like the sixteen year single malt."

"Yes sir," they smiled in unison.

It was time for Matt Luman CIA agent to begin his investigation. He sauntered down to the Park Avenue Artists office. He walked up to the sales desk. He introduced himself to Dagmar Marichiski. The six foot tall Croatian had a body that made Chastain Johnson look like a nun. Matt reminded himself that he would tell Chastain that she had small breasts. Nothing like Dagmar's magnificent cantaloupe's to bring one's psyche to full attention. Mr. Winkey also responded to her.

They talked for an hour about art. She kept stumbling and knocking her breasts into Luman. He smiled. Dagmar thought that Luman was an art aficionado. He did have a million dollar purchasing credit. Thanks to the CIA.

Dagmar had no idea that the CIA funded the line of credit. Luman had trouble keeping his eyes off Dagmar's breasts. She noticed.

Dagmar said: "You seem uncomfortable."

"It's all part of the fame game." Matt smiled.

"Perhaps we could talk somewhere private."

"I would like that." Dagmar smiled.

Two hours later Matt and Dagmar were still in his bed talking. There hadn't been much talking the first hour. Dagmar informed Matt what was really up with Park Avenue Artists. He found out how and where they laundered the money.

Dagmar made a joke when she said: "What is really up?"

"Me." They both laughed. Dagmar's English wasn't good enough to understand the joke. She did after another hour in bed. When Dagmar left. Luman took a shower. He did twenty minutes of weights to recover from Dagmar. He dressed. It was time to get into action. James Bond playing the piano with hit records.

He pulled out his notebook. He wrote his notes in an obscure Eskimo dialect. If anyone found the notebook, they would have no idea what was in it.

Matt had the al Qaeda plan. He would personally eliminate one of the Park Avenue Artist employees. Dagmar was safe. At least until the next time they went to bed.

When Matt returned to his room, he found an encrypted phone message with a down loaded file. The message read: "Intercepted cell phone call from Alabama, the number 3." Matt downloaded two words: "Sagrada Familia." He had the target for the Barcelona al Qaeda cell. Now to find the reprehensible bastards. Who were the al Qaeda terrorists and what did they did want?

Turning on a small lamp, Matt took out his magnifying glass. He had some examples of Dali's work that the al Qaeda terrorists used to justify their plots. The photos of Dali's paintings, his lithographs and some personal correspondence provided clues. Matt realized that Dali's playful, complex mind continued to provide clues from the grave. It was as if Dali was directing the investigation.

He studied the pictures for hours. Then he saw the two sites clearly targeted for bombing. They were two churches and the Dali paintings clearly pointed to Barcelona and San Francisco. There were too many people searching for clues. Matt would let them continue to hunt for the terrorist plot. He had it down and he would quietly help Don Gino get rid of the terrorists.

CHAPTER TWENTY-EIGHT
The Dali Al Qaeda Terrorists

"Salvador Dali supported the Spanish dictator, General Francisco Franco, and in the process he honored the Muslim faith. We have organized a branch of al Qaeda to honor Dali and destroy his detractors." Omar Abdul Hammadi in a speech to his followers on You Tube.

Omar Abdul Hammadi remembered years ago when he sat in his college dorm. He was taking an Islamic art history course. He wasn't particularly interested. He had recently converted to Islam. It was a secret conversion. He was looking for a sign. He was looking for a direction. He opened a book on Salvador Dali's art. It stood out at him like a personal message from Allah. He saw a drawing. Then a painting. Then a lithograph. He read some magazine articles. Dali set it out for him clearly. In Dali's world, he saw the roadmap to the destruction of the capitalist west.

Dali proclaimed his Arabic roots. His blasphemous behavior toward the Catholic Church was forgiven for the art he donated. Dali hated Catholicism. He was private about his hatred. The Catholic Church conflicted his thinking. He feared finding a real vision of hell. So Dali did his best to pay lip serve to the church while privately hating Catholicism. The dogma was too much for Dali's creativity. The only people who realized this were the few very recent al Qaeda converts. James Smith became Omar Abdul Hammadi to continue Dali's attack on decadent western culture, as well as the Catholic faith.

Hammadi took Dali's writings, his art and his public persona, and he put together a Dali book. That is a primer of Dali's ideas as they related to terrorism. After Hammadi had books printed, he used a photograph of Islamabad on the cover. Muslims consider drawing pictures of people a form of idolatry and he quoted a former Professor at al-Imam University in Riyadh who said that pictures of people and animals are unlawful. Then Hammadi wrote that the Prophet banned graven images. In this way Muslims had a superior moral tone.

It had been more than twenty years since Hammadi, then known as James Smith, began to study Salvador Dali. Smith was also aware of an Italian San Francisco businessman that he grew to hate. Hammadi was happy to provide the millions of dollars to blow up the two artistic sights that would bring triumph to the Muslim way of life. Don Gino Landry would pay for collecting Dali.

Hammadi's obsession with the rise of the San Francisco businessman, Don Gino Landry, prompted his plan to eliminate him. After putting together a file on the Don, Hammadi digested the material.

When Hammadi found out that Don Gino was America's premier Dali collector, he vowed to kill him. Don Gino was Allah's enemy. Don Gino supported the invasions of Afghanistan and Iraq, which Hammadi considered even more blasphemous than being gay. Don Gino advised President George W. Bush to place Hamid Karzai in charge of Afghanistan. The true meaning of Islam was lost in this puppet government. Hammadi told his followers that the infidel Americans would experience terrorism from within. Hammadi's cell would continue the attacks upon unsuspecting American targets. The explosions and resulting public panic at the conclusion of the Boston Marathon was an indication of the problems that America had created for itself.

Hammadi sat in his cabin on the Pearl of the Ocean. He looked at his youthful basketball picture. It had been more than twenty-five years since he left college as a basketball player, and African American who was never treated properly. He was an honor's finance graduate. He received an affirmative action slot at the University of Pennsylvania's Wharton School. He graduated with top honors. A Wall Street finance firm hired him.

When Hammadi appeared as James Smith on the Apprentice with Donald Trump, he was an instant celebrity. He not only won the show by putting together the best new company, he was hired by Warren Buffet to oversee a portion of the Omaha icon's business empire. When the tragic events of 9-11 took place, Hammadi took a vacation to New York. He smiled as he viewed the destruction brought in New York at the World Trade Center.

He had visited it for a dozen years to celebrate the attack upon decadent American capitalism. Each year since 2001, Hammadi killed a New York policeman near the World Trade Center. He made it look like a random crime. The truth was that Hammadi was a serial killer. "I am a phantom," Hammadi wrote to his twin brother, "who is Allah's avenging Angel."

There was no one who realized that he intended to bring the force of Muslim destruction to America's shore. It would be in San Francisco. This was the one place that Homeland Security believed was impregnable. The Golden Gate Bridge was guarded 24-7. The San Francisco Bay Bridge had security cameras and twenty-four hour patrols. The major downtown San Francisco buildings had so much security that they were never in danger. The San Francisco port was protected by land and sea. Hammadi smiled. He saw the one symbol of American religious decadence that he would destroy. It would take millions of dollars, strategic planning and some degree of luck. The money that Hammadi was raising was the key to his nefarious terrorist plot. The Americans would be sorry that they killed Osama bin Laden. They would be sorry that they attacked Sharia law. Revenge was on its way.

For more than two decades, Hammadi was a major figure in American finance. Along the way he became a multi-millionaire, a respected art collector and a major voice in the African American community.

Smith supported Barack Obama's bid for the presidency. He did so because he believed that Obama's Muslim roots made him a potential ally. Smith watched Fox TV News daily. They had the right take on the new president. He didn't have a birth certificate. He was a Muslim.

He was a socialist. Every week Smith sent a check to Fox TV News in support of whatever charity Roger Ailes deemed appropriate. This led to Smith appearing with Bill O'Reilly numerous times. Not only was O'Reilly a real American, he was friendly to African Americans. Smith's actions hid his terrorism.

Hammadi cringed when he saw how America had co-opted its African American roots. He was further incensed that Muslims were in a position beneath the black man. In the South, Hammadi believed that nothing had changed. He would have his revenge. He would then vanish to Islamabad and live out his life as a Muslim hero. James Smith would be forgotten. Omar Abdul Hammadi would go down in the history books as a modern Muslim hero.

It was the Salvador Dali connection that brought Hammadi peace. He had spent almost three decades collecting and interpreting Dali's work. He saw hidden messages, obscure symbolism and hints for future action in the lithographs, the paintings, the sculpture and most of all Dali's writing. There were these hidden keys in the Dali work that give birth to the most radical form of Islamic terror in America. There was one thing that the major Dali interpreters missed, that is his interest in San Francisco. Dali hated San Francisco. Hammadi had proof. He would rub Don Gino's nose in this well kept secret.

Dali never painted anything about San Francisco. He wasn't interested in the city. He had New York, Paris, London and Barcelona based homes. In Dali's writing there was an unpublished article that Hammadi found on the Internet. This obscure Dali piece concentrated upon Catholicism and Italians in San Francisco. It was a sign from Dali to support jihad. This article had hints of what Dali wanted destroyed and why he had these thoughts.

The Dali article pointed out that San Francisco's Mission Delores had a beautiful garden. Hammadi believed that this garden was a link between Catholic and Muslim cultures, as Dali described the lush plants that had a Middle East touch. Hammadi read this article with care. There was water everywhere in San Francisco. In the Middle East water is a paramount factor in determining the distribution of plants. For a small part of the Mission Delores garden to have plants that didn't need water was an indication of the Muslim influence. It was a sign to Hammadi to continue to destroy the blasphemous Catholic landmark.

Dali speculated that the Catholic Church had an early alliance with Muslim's. The Pope ended this alliance. His theory was that there was a religious peace settled over Europe in the early twentieth century brought about by the Pope. That peace came with the exclusion of Muslim influences and the systematic removal of Muslim settlers.

Then, as he studied Dali, Hammadi realized that in his paintings there was a clear message. Dali proclaimed over the years that San Francisco's Mission Delores had to be destroyed, or it would end Muslim influences in the City by the Bay. Dali was conflicted about the Mission Delores. Hammadi deduced that blowing up the Catholic historical site was what Dali wanted. He did have to preserve the garden. He just didn't know it. These conclusions were in Hammadi's notebooks. He also planned another book on Dali's political philosophy.

As an observer of European life, Dali was conflicted about the afterlife. Did the afterlife rest with the Catholic Church? There was no answer that Dali accepted.

What Hammadi realized was that the article comparing Catholicism with the Muslim faith was another insight into Dali's mind. Hammadi believed that Dali concluded that the Muslim afterlife was better than anything Catholicism offered. Salvador Dali provided a beacon for radical jihad. He not only condoned violence, Dali provided a blueprint for it.

When Smith established his terrorist cell, he based his highly defined ideology on this obscure Dali article, his autobiographical writings, and the belief that Dali's wishes could only be implemented with excessive violence.

Then Hammadi found out that this article was in the hands of a San Francisco collector. It was that horrid homosexual Don Gino Landry. He was infuriated. His American al Qaeda compatriots sent a detailed file about the person that they knew as Don Gino Landry. Hammadi was shocked that the Don knew about this obscure article.

Perhaps he had underestimated him. The Don was not only a good Catholic; he was an American patriot who vowed to exterminate al Qaeda.

Hammadi looked at his file on Don Gino. He pulled it out. He carefully read it. Don Gino wore purple clothing. He was a San Francisco businessman who was known to be gay and a devout Catholic. There seemed to be a contradiction. He was also philanthropic. There was a civic side to Don Gino that intrigued Hammadi. It wouldn't matter. The Don soon would be dead.

Don Gino was seen in the company of powerful politicians, business people and movie stars. George Clooney regularly flew into the city for lunch at Gary Danko's with Don Gino. From his Skywalker ranch, George Lucas drove to San Francisco for cultural consultation. When Lucas received the National Medal of Arts, Don Gino was at his side. Herb Alpert received the same medal and they went out for a raucous celebration. Herb Alpert and the Tijuana Brass recorded a tribute CD, "A Don's Serenade." It was number one on **Billboard** for six weeks.

Now that the American al Qaeda terrorist cell had identified Don Gino, they would make him pay for his infidel ways. Smith looked at his notes on a trip that he had made two months earlier to Barcelona. It was a journey in which he intended to scout out Sagrada Familia, and he would make sure a part of the famed Barcelona landscape would be destroyed. It was Allah's will.

During an earlier trip to Barcelona, when Omar Abdul Hammadi went to the two Barcelona Mosques, he discovered no terrorists. Barcelona Muslims were on the whole reverent. There was little notion of terrorism. As Hammadi left the Barcelona Mosque at Carrer de la Mare de Deu de Nuria, he noticed that he was being followed by two clean-shaven young men. They looked like police. Hammadi walked into a McDonald's and ordered a cup of coffee. The men came over and sat with him.

They looked at him without saying a word. He had to remember that he was James Smith, American millionaire, friend of Donald Trump and supporter of President Barack Obama. He needed to organize Barcelona Muslims. They were among the least radical in the world.

"We need you to come back and help us," the bigger of the two men said.

"What?" Hammadi couldn't believe they weren't police. They didn't look or act like police. But then what did police look or act like? They were Muslim sympathizers.

Smith said: "I am going back to New York, then I will sail on the Carnivolet Pearl of the Ocean to return to Barcelona."

"We know that."

Smith paused. Could he trust them? "What do you want me to do?"

"Mr. Smith when you land in Barcelona, watch yourself, we will be with you." They got up and left. Smith-Hammadi was puzzled. Then it dawned on him. These two men were the first two al Qaeda terrorists that he met in Barcelona. He felt better. Someone had warned Smith about the dearth of Barcelona Muslim radicalism. He would solve that lack of local commitment to Allah's will. He recalled this meeting while he finished the Carnivolet trip. Allah would triumph. Smith-Hammadi was put on earth for that purpose.

When the Barcelona police busted the first radical Muslim political organization, they were astonished that it was little more than a group of pickpockets. They had no clue about al Qaeda. There was no al Qaeda ring in Barcelona. Smith would not only bring glory to Barcelona Muslims, he would use images of Salvador Dali to reawaken Muslim radicalism. His terrorist faction would emerge in Figueres where everything was Dali oriented. He knew a great deal about Barcelona from his previous visits.

A month later, he would be in place in Barcelona to make the most of his opportunity to radicalize the docile local Muslim population. This trip to Barcelona prior to the Carnivolet cruise made a lasting impression. He was ready for the cruise. He was also ready to implement his nefarious plan. The cruise reinforced the decadence of western culture.

As he prepared to leave the Pearl of the Ocean, Smith noticed Don Gino Landry in the forefront of a group of people leaving the ship.

The San Francisco Mafia Don would soon find his fate. It would not be with 300 virgins, it would be in a Christian hell. It was the worst form of punishment for a heathen.

The ramp to get off the Pearl of the Ocean was crowded as six large Samoans hauled off six purple suitcases. Smith walked around them. He looked back to see Trevor Blake III coming off the ship with a beautiful blonde with large breasts smoking a cigarette. Allah had to be redeemed. The infidels were destroying the world. The blasphemy was constant.

Trevor Blake III looked around the port. He spotted a limousine driver. His sign read: "Mr. Trevor." A smile on Blake's face indicated his happiness. The woman smoking the cigarette shook her head. They walked to the car. It sped away.

Chastain said: "How did you pull this off?"

"Pull what off?"

"Forget it."

"We are off to the Palacette Continental Hotel. Famous San Francisco Private Eye comes to Barcelona to give a series of talks on detecting. Shell Scott would be impressed. So would Elvis Cole."

"Who the hell is Shell Scott?"

"He's my mentor."

Chastain couldn't believe the conversation. She said: "I am shutting my eyes and taking a short nap." It was short as twenty minutes later they checked into the hotel.

CHAPTER TWENTY-NINE

On To Barcelona

"Intelligence without ambition is a bird without wings."
Salvador Dali

The Barcelona Ramblas bustled with taxis. Trevor pulled his suitcase from the limousine trunk. The tree-lined Ramblas was full of tourists; as well as pickpockets, boring Brits, gypsies and the curious.

The Trevor Blake III nametag was gone from his suitcase. Maybe he had a fan. They stole it as a souvenir. The Palacette Continental Hotel was on the second floor of the cleanest looking building in downtown Barcelona. Don Gino had a private room. When Trevor checked in, he was told all the rooms were pink. There was one purple room. Everyone felt safe with Don Gino nearby.

The hotel manager's nametag read: Peter. He said: "May I ask about the young lady?"

Trevor said: "Yes, she is with me. We would like one small bed."

Chastain said: "Make it two beds far apart in two rooms. Perhaps Trevor's bed could be in Madrid."

Peter smiled: "May I presume this is not a honeymoon?"

The check in was quick. Chastain looked at the no smoking sign in the room. She frowned. She left the room. It was time to do some detecting.

"Chastain, I will see you in the lounge."

"Lounge!" She looked confused.

"Just come to the pink room with the food." I walked down past Peter.

I grabbed a cappuccino from their machine.

Peter shook my hand. I had never met him. He seemed to know me.

Peter said: "Don Gino asked me to extend you every courtesy." When the Don asks people respond.

"Thanks, the Don is a good man. I take him with me everywhere." There was a dead silence. No one made jokes about Don Gino.

Peter said: "Well, old chap, we placed you and the voluptuous young lady in two special rooms."

"I wanted one room for us, Peter."

"Sir that would not be good for my health. Don Gino's orders." Peter smiled. The insidious little bastard knew I couldn't overrule Don Gino.

"Let me guess, Peter, you are English."

"Actually, South African, I left the Isle of Wight at age seven for Cape Town."

I thanked him for my room. It was replete with pink walls, pink sheets and bedspreads, pink towels. I thought I was in San Francisco's Castro District. I won't mention that to Don Gino.

Chastain was still in her room. I walked down and knocked on her door.

"What are you doing?" She was in the bathroom.

"My makeup, the eyeliner ran."

"Take the falsies out of you bra."

I laughed as a middle finger came out of the bathroom door. "Do something, Trevor, I will be out in a moment."

Chastain came out of the bathroom looking gorgeous.

"You look good enough to eat for lunch."

"When Mickey Rooney is no longer available you will share my bed along with Curly, Larry and Moe."

"I think this is not good for my ego."

She laughed: "What ego?"

We walked out to the Ramblas for coffee. Or should I say a cappuccino. As I was sitting going through his terrorism file, Gala showed up. At least she told me that she was Gala. Not to be confused with Salvador Dali's wife. She said that she was Gala Epstein, a literary agent from New York. This was the third Gala to come into my life. What did this portend? My pants strangled one and the other vanished. Being Gala was dangerous. Hanging out with Trevor Blake III was even more dangerous.

Chastain and Gala talked about books. She was in Barcelona to negotiate a manuscript on Spanish terrorism. Trevor wondered whatever happened to cook books? Since Paula Deen used the "N" word, cookbooks didn't sell. They had a pleasant chat about nothing, and Gala left with her black hair showing signs of blonde underneath. I guessed you couldn't look like Dali's wife with blonde hair. Chastain walked into a scarf shop. I left.

The food in Barcelona is second to none. As I walked down to Cinco Jotas, I heard the refrain: "Here, Here."

I stopped and looked into an outdoor café and the Three Amigos were drinking a huge pitcher of sangria. They were singing Mexican Revolution songs. Weird!

There were two men with the Three Amigos. I stood obscured in an entryway to an office building. I watched as the two men passed a bulging envelope to one of the Three Amigos. Juan opened the envelope. He smiled. They all looked in the envelope. In unison they chanted: "Here, Here." I wrapped a scarf around my neck and walked out of the hidden alcove. The chilly Barcelona wind reminded me that there is danger. I looked around and the Three Amigos vanished into a tapas bar. What the hell is going on? I was beginning to get an inkling of the problem. I was cold. I stopped for a coffee at a sidewalk café. The beautiful women who walked by warmed me.

As I sat at the sidewalk café, I remembered when I was a kid and came to Barcelona. My parents brought me on a Christmas trip. The lights, the sweet smell of the meats and the happy people made Barcelona a place that I have never forgotten. The only signs of dissent were independent minded Catalonians and those who thought General Franco deserved the death squad. There were few outside political forces.

How times have changed in Barcelona. A Muslim cleric walks down the Ramblas leading a group of schoolboys talking religion. Then two women dressed out of **Vogue** walked by talking fashion. Everyone had an air of sophistication. I looked around and there were more nondescript looking people. If anyone followed me, it would be hard to pick out the tail. The trees on the Ramblas splashed varied colors of brown, yellow and red as the overcast weather made a top coat essential. I love Barcelona. It is San Francisco in Europe.

Barcelona is windy in March. It is not unlike San Francisco. I continued to read my files while drinking a cappuccino. I noted that Gala Epstein left. She walked toward her hotel. My brief moment of calm ended. My coffee cup was empty.

"Hello Dickhead." Chastain returned too quickly. I needed time to think.

Trevor said: "It is none other than the irascible Chastain Johnson." She was smoking a cigarette and wearing her new scarf. "Getting a little exercise, I could recommend the Trevor Blake III love cure. It is spending a night with me in bed."

She said: "I'm still waiting for Mickey Rooney."

"Where do I fail?"

"He has standards."

"Ah, once again upstaged by a midget." She looked serious. Not a good sign.

"Trevor, I have another file for you. I will bring it tonight when you buy me dinner. See you at Meson Cinco Jotas at nine o'clock."

"I'm usually in bed by that time, for you I will make an exception." She laughed and ran away.

I walked into the hotel. Then after an hour doing heavy exercise and lifting some weights, I e-mailed Guitar Jac for information on Barcelona's al Qaeda cell. In an hour, he sent a three-page memo. The Barcelona al Qaeda cell was small or almost non-existent. "I think you are dealing with amateurs," Guitar Jac wrote. He included a list of restaurants where potential al-Qaeda recruits met with Smith-Hammadi. Nothing else. I needed to find out more from my favorite FBI agent. I invited Chastain Johnson to dinner. She would be waiting for me. The suave private eye needed to turn on the charm. It was essential to the flow of key information.

Chastain stood in front of Cinco Jotas dressed in a short pink skirt, a skimpy pink and white top and pink high heels. I wondered if her underwear was pink. I would never find out. Oh well, better to use my imagination.

Barcelona was freezing. She didn't seem to notice. The men who walked toward her, bumped into trees and cars as well as other people. One man crossing the street looked back at Chastain. He was almost hit by an onrushing car as he gave the driver the finger. He didn't mind. He got a good look at Chastain. She looked gorgeous.

As Trevor walked down to Cinco Jotas, he didn't notice the small man following him. He was a small Asian man in a raincoat. Don Gino told Emilio that Trevor might be in danger. When he saw Chastain Johnson, Emilio realized that Trevor might be screwed to death. He went back to the hotel. She was capable. Trevor? Probably not.

Trevor gave her a hug. He squeezed her a little too long. She stabbed him gently in the ribs. Chastain smiled. Maybe Mickey Rooney wouldn't have to die. It was time for a Barcelona feast. He did it up right with four kinds of meat, a trio of salads, vegetables and two bottles of fine red Spanish wine. The suave private eye working on the FBI agent. It didn't work. She was pleasant. Trevor received nothing in the way of new information. Oh well, the dinner was great. He paid with Don Gino's Platinum American Express card. The Don could afford it. Chastain ate quietly and said very little. She also drank too much wine. Something was up.

After dinner Trevor and Chastain walked back toward the Palacette Continental Hotel as Barcelona's beautiful, chilly climate and exciting nightlife made this slow leisurely walk a pleasant one. Trevor spoke passable Spanish, and he knew more about local wines than anyone in the city. It didn't help that most people spoke Catalan. Trevor had trouble with this language, but he began studying it. The fact that everyone spoke English made it easy.

The Catalan influence remained strong in Barcelona. The locals used the term "Seny" to signify common sense. To Catalans "Seny" also means that there is a natural wisdom. Trevor realized that this gave Barcelona residents a calm quiet demeanor. The locals were in direct contrast to the frequent visitors. Nothing was simple in Barcelona. There were contradictions.

There was another side to the Catalan personality. It was known as" Rauxa," which means "uncontrollable emotion." This explains the dual nature of Barcelona society. A calm exterior often punctuated by obscene humor defining the Catalan. Salvador Dali was the perfect example of Seny and Rauxa. He was reserved but flamboyant.

With its streets teeming with tourists, Barcelona was a playground. Trevor remembered that he was on assignment. He looked up and saw a sky that turned into a picture postcard blue. The weather, while neither warm nor cold, held the locals in a captive state. They drank coffee at small kiosks, they smoked cigarettes and the repressive days of Generalissimo Franco were past. Barcelona is as close to paradise as possible.

The streets were filled with tourists. Trevor walked down to Vincon and looked in the window. It was a knick-knack store. Did Spaniards know about knick knacks? Maybe Chastain Johnson liked playthings. "Can I help you sir?" Trevor looked at the beautiful girl.

"I am looking in the window. Does it look like I need help?"

"You do. You just don't know it." She handed him an envelope. He opened it. There were notes on Figueres. More clues. It was time to find these clues in Dali's Figueres. The woman quickly left.

The mysterious woman looked like Gala. She had ravenous black hair. Her black dress was offset with white pearls and high-heeled Jimmy Choo shoes. I wondered was there a Jimmy Choo when Gala was rubbing the back and other parts of Dali's male friends? She started walking away, and I noticed that she took off her black wig. She was a blonde. Strange!

Trevor walked for a few blocks. He noticed that Chastain hailed a cab and left for the hotel. As Trevor walked down the Ramblas he admired many beautiful women. One caught his eye.

She smiled.

He smiled. Maybe he would get lucky. She wore a Custo Barcelona Psychedelic Floral print top with a pair of $10,000 Escada luxury designer jeans. Trevor looked at her with envy. She also looked like Gala. I looked for black roots. Maybe everybody in Barcelona looked like Gala. She smiled.

She said: "Do you like what you see?"

"Sorry Miss, I was looking in the window of El Cortes Ingles."

"Then there is something you need to know."

And what do I need to know?"

"I have some information for you."

"And you are?"

"I am a friend of Chastain Johnson."

"I hope that she isn't involved."

"Oh, she is. She made it clear I had to explain everything twice to you. You have spent our entire conversation looking at my breasts. Yes, they are real."

"Great. I feel better already." Trevor was getting an uneasy feeling.

"Here is some information on Salvador Dali, Figueres and the al Qaeda cell."

"Why are you giving it to me?"

"Chastain doesn't want to be seen with you."

"She just had dinner with me."

"I am still trying to figure that out."

"This does wonders for my confidence."

"Don't take it personally, Trevor, she is being watched."

"You are not."

"No. I am safe. I wonder if that is a plus?"

"Quit asking questions. Listen. Read. Pay attention."

She handed over the bulging package. He now had another envelope of new clues as well as a bulging clue folder. Too much reading! Too much information! Too many unanswered questions. Not enough detective work. Where were the bad guys?

The file held more than fifty pages. The front page read: "Beware, the enemy is not what you think. Look into every nook and cranny. Also, remember that there is safety in numbers. That is the key to solving the crime." This is another crazy series of sentence that meant nothing. He would have to decode the clues.

Trevor needed to walk and think. He started along the 1.2 kilometers that make up Las Ramblas. He walked down to Port Vell and looked toward Cataluña. Dali said that he was "a Catalonian." The prostitutes were out at the Southern end of the Ramblas. Trevor walked back from the seedy end into the tourist mecca. What were the al Qaeda terrorists up to? He thought of the magnificent and tourist packed Sagrada Familia. How could they blow it up? Security was tight. Who was James Smith? Who was Hammadi? Trevor had this information on Hammadi's life and career. He didn't know what to do with it. He also had no idea where to find him.

When Trevor walked up to La Rambla 96, he stood in awe. It was the Erotica Museum. No sense going in, he preferred the real thing. He stood and watched a human statue dressed as Galileo. Across the street there was a statue of a white painter. The statue picked up the tip jar and walked into a pita place. Trevor stood around and watched. He realized that he was standing on a mural created by Joan Miro.

It was time to drink with the people. Trevor walked into La Boqueria. This open-air market was filled with fresh fruits and vegetables. Everywhere there were people drinking great Spanish wine. As Trevor sat down at a small open-air counter, Gala Epstein joined him.

"Still trying to find the Barcelona Ernest Hemingway?"

"No, I am trying to sign a good mystery writer."

"How about Shell Scott?" I smiled. Always the clever P. I.

"Does he have a Facebook page?"

"He's dead!"

"What are you a smart guy?"

"Ever hear of Richard Prather?"

"Is he on twitter or is he dead?"

"He's a hard boiled writer. He created Shell Scott. He is dead."

"Oh! Why are you talking about an obscure writer? Can't you think of something more interesting?" She smiled and left.

I was about to say no and lecture her on the importance of mystery authors. I couldn't do it as she walked rapidly down the street. I decided to enjoy the Ramblas.

Barcelona lived up to its name. The designer shops along the Ramblas drew a sophisticated, high end, moneyed tourist. The imposing urban skyline made Barcelona an urban jewel. The Salvador Dali Museum in Figueres was one of the main tourist draws.

My calm and reverie ended when I saw a midget in a purple tuxedo coming down the street. He saw me. He waved his middle finger. The six Samoans walked quickly behind an elegantly dressed man. He had on a Savile Row suit. It wasn't purple. He wasn't smoking a small cigar. He also had an angry look on his face. It was Don Gino. Not the Don that I knew but the one intent on rooting out al Qaeda.

"Hello Trevor." He sounded like the old, happy Don Gino. I wasn't fooled. He was planning his revenge. Al Qaeda was toast.

I knew that Don Gino Landry looked forward to visiting the citadel to Salvador Dali's greatness. That would be the magnificent town of Figueres. Don Gino had a pet phrase: "On to Figueres."

Don Gino considered Pablo Picasso an ignorant peasant. Yet, he always visited the Passeig de Picasso. It was a Barcelona street that was calm, tranquil and beautiful. It was the one place in Barcelona where Don Gino could walk and think. The air of quiet majesty that goes along with this monument built to Picasso in 1983 was the result of a large donation by an anonymous San Francisco businessman. The trees surrounding the Passeig de Picasso were kept trimmed by a yearly donation from Don Gino. Before he traveled to Figueres, Don Gino spent the better part of the day thinking and taking notes on his plan to end the al Qaeda threat.

After he talked with Trevor, Don Gino gave him three more folders. The information on al Qaeda never ceased.

CHAPTER THIRTY

On To Figueres

"At the age of six I wanted to be a cook. At seven I wanted to be Napoleon. And my ambition has been growing steadily ever since." Salvador Dali

D on Gino checked the train schedule. He would take the early morning train to the sleepy city of Figueres. He was eager to find new Dali's for his collection. He also had a good idea what the terrorists had in mind. The entire town of Figueres stood as a monument to Dali. The Museum Dali is the focal point of that interest. The tourists dominated the central city; they also obscured the beauty that inspired Dali. There were so many architectural gems that enthralled artists like Dali.

Don Gino had another destination. He was going to have coffee with Manuel Cantino, who was a freelance painter. He was also one of Don Gino's primary sources for unofficial Dali's. That is a Dali original not available for sale to the general public. The FBI called it fraud. Collectors labeled it "authentic fakes." Private collectors bought them in droves. Don Gino had an "unofficial Dali room" complete with climate control. He also had sensor cameras attached to his computer. The Don had a few minutes so he went onto his computer and checked his house. Not surprisingly, his wonderful neighbor, Danielle Steel, was making sure everything was fine. He told her to check on the house periodically.

Danielle Steel persuaded the maid to take a look at Dali's collection. She was constantly in Don Gino's house. He smiled as he watched her on surveillance tapes. She was a wonderful neighbor. He just couldn't read her books. When Manuel Cantino came to San Francisco, Steel took him out to dinner. He was nicer than all her previous husbands. Personally, Don Gino liked the husband from San Quentin. He was the most honest one of the bunch.

Manuel Cantino's cover story was that he produced "historical significant, genuine Dali fakes." This sounded much better than bootlegging, copying, reproducing or pirating original Dali's. Cantino spent hours helping Don Gino display his Dali's. But the San Franciscan had a new collector mania. He was pursuing heretofore unknown Gala prints and portraits. That is legitimate ones. Don Gino quietly became the world's largest Gala collector. Trevor often told Guitar Jac that there was nothing that the Don took more seriously than his Dali collection. The terrorists were toast.

There was a small room being redone in Don Gino's home for his Gala portraits. She was not only Dali's wife, but his muse, partner and financial adviser. The sultry seductress was nuts. She once told a close friend: "Why marry and make one man unhappy when you can stay single and make so many happy?" That thought was at the heart of her intellect. Dali loved it. When Dali constructed his infamous **Homage To Mae West** it was a love letter to Gala.

The thousands of blank pages that Dali signed prior to his death created a market for fake Dali's. In a Hawaii trial an art appraiser, Dena Hall, testified that Dali fakes were as common as "pancakes at the pancake house." Don Gino showed that he had a sense of humor when he purchased six fake Dali's for permanent display at the Lombard Street International House of Pancakes. The **New York Times** did a front-page story and IHOP did wonderful business. Unfortunately, the food still was awful.

After Don Gino arrived in Figueres, he walked to Vila's Café. The small coffee shop at Carrer Rutlla 7 is a reminder of times past. After a cappuccino and checking his notes, Don Gino caught a cab to Manuel Cantino's studio. There were more than five hundred Dali copies, fakes, reproductions, pirated editions of one sort or another in Cantino's possession. There were also originals. He also had over a thousand authentic reproductions for sale on cruise ships. It was a growth industry.

Unbeknownst to Don Gino, Omar Abdul Hammadi arrived in Figueres. He was determined to make Don Gino pay for his infidel ways. Not only was Don Gino a Mafia Don, he was a gay man. Hammadi couldn't decide which was worse. He would kill Don Gino in time, and he would empty his Washington Street mansion of his precious Dali's.

Hammadi was the only terrorist in the world who saw the encrypted hidden meaning in Dali's paintings. Don Gino simply collected these magnificent pieces; he didn't understand Dali's greatness.

It was time to implement the Barcelona terrorist plan. La Sagrada Familia would be destroyed by Hammadi's two terrorist followers.

Hammadi watched as local citizens greeted Don Gino with affection. He didn't notice a small Asian man standing behind a tree. Emilio watched as Hammadi shadowed Don Gino. As Hammadi walked back to the center of Figueres no one gave him a second glance. He reveled in anonymity. Emilio watched and waited. He couldn't wait to teach the arrogant American millionaire humility. The bastard was an African American al Qaeda terrorist. Emilio would end his life. Hammadi wasn't going to meet 300 virgins; there is no doubt that he was going to hell. A personal hell dictated by Don Gino.

As Dali's birthplace, Figueres occupied a special place in Hammadi and Don Gino's heart. Emilio continued to watch Hammadi. He was acting like a tourist but there was something else. He seemed to be targeting something. What? Emilio didn't have a clue. Was it Don Gino? Or what was it?

Then it dawned on Emilio, that rat Hammadi was searching for a Mosque in Figueres. He had to know there wasn't one. When Hammadi entered the home of a local Muslim with a large suitcase, Emilio figured it out.

It was Hammadi's goal to build the first Mosque in Figueres. This wasn't going to happen as Emilio watched Hammadi leaving the home of a local Muslim with the suitcase thrown after him. It opened and one hundred dollar bills littered the street. It was time for Hammadi to return to Barcelona.

Emilio walked over to the house that Hammadi exited. The small cottage had flowers planted in the front. There was music coming from the house, the chatter of small children and the aroma of spicy food wafted from the house. This was the house where Hammadi had found a Muslim who was not a Catalan. This Muslim was a loyal Spaniard. Emilio knew the target in Barcelona. He would foil the plot.

When Emilio knocked on the door, Assad Ayah answered. Emilio was invited in for a cup of tea. After an hour of conversation, Emilio felt better. Assad was not a terrorist. Hammadi or James Smith was fighting a losing battle. An al Qaeda cell in Figueres was not feasible.

CHAPTER THIRTY-ONE
Hammadi In Barcelona

"Surrealism is destructive, but it destroys only what it considers to be shackles limiting our vision." Salvador Dali

After going to two of the Barcelona Mosques, Hammadi rented a storefront on Las Ramblas. He opened a sunglasses business and converted the back room into the third Barcelona Mosque. It was here that he would prey on the youth who were susceptible to the radical al Qaeda message. He also had the money to attract the forty-seven per cent of the Muslim population who were among Barcelona's unemployed. Perfect for al Qaeda's organizational skills.

The Muslim presence in Barcelona had a storied history as Muslims ruled southern Spain from 711 to 1492. These ancient roots continued to attract working class Muslims. Those who couldn't find employment were the perfect recruits. He would teach them the cold, hard facts of Muslim repression.

By the time that Muslims were expelled from Spain in 1500 they had stamped the Iberian Peninsula with their faith and culture.

The remains of Muslim influences were seen in Moorish architecture and in Barcelona's oldest church, Sant Pau del Camp. It was built in the ninth century as a monastery. It was the center of a vibrant Muslim community. Not surprisingly, it was known as "Saint Paul of the Countryside." The monastery documented the first Muslims who came into the Catholic fold. They were fierce warriors and conquerors. They were also fooled by the irreverent Catholic message.

Sant Pau del Camp is a small church. There is a statue of Saint Mark as a lion and a sculpture of the hand of God, and it gives the church a sense of strength. Early Muslims flocked to it. Hammadi saw a message in the architecture. The message was to destroy Gaudi's Sagrada Familia. He began proselytizing for al Qaeda.

As Barcelona grew, the church was located in the Raval quarter. This is where radical Muslims clustered to view the Moorish architecture. The décor was of Arabic origins. It was at the site of this ancient church that Hammadi met with a group of young Muslims. He would make them see the need for al Qaeda. Hammadi told everyone that the Muslim path was desecrated in Barcelona. Hammadi would make its young Muslim population realize the need for violence. The half million Barcelona Muslims didn't have a voice. Hammadi would solve that problem.

Hammadi told the young men that Muslim rule lasted eight hundred years in Barcelona. The 300,000 Barcelona Muslims were primarily from North Africa. They were the most susceptible to Hammadi's radical message. Hammadi's book on Salvador Dali's Muslim roots was a primer for al Qaeda radicalism. He argued that Muslims first set foot in Figueres and Port Lligat to make Spain an Islamic paradise. Then he demonstrated how various Dali paintings, drawings and writings demanded Muslim violence.

When Hammadi rented a conference room at the Cinco Jotas, he held a meeting with thirty young Muslim men of education and prominence. His message was a simple one. The al Qaeda cell needed to blow up a Barcelona landmark. It would send a message that Muslims had to be treated fairly. The right symbol, Hammadi told his eager listeners, would send more than a warning. The meeting was not fruitful. No one was interested in half-baked Muslim radicalism. They had prestigious legal educations. This still didn't guarantee brains.

Much like in Figueres, Hammadi realized that radical Muslims didn't exist. Spain had provided too well for them. There were half a million Muslims in Barcelona, and the sense of equality, the presence of opportunity and the lack of racism made it difficult to become a radical. There was great difficulty in recruiting new al Qaeda members. Hammadi was determined to find some al Qaeda converts. He would appeal to their obsessive Catalan nationalism. The independent Spanish area that called itself Catalonia had eleven mosques and more than thirty major Muslim meeting places. There were also more than 1.5 million Muslims in Spain. Hammadi hoped that he could find a base for his hate filled message.

When Hammadi entered the Catalan Islamic Cultural Center, he was thrown out. His ranting on capitalism, democracy and Catholic corruption fell on deaf ears. They were Muslims second and Spaniards first. Hammadi couldn't believe it. When Salim Benarama, a thirty three year old Imam from Algeria, complained that most Mosques were in garages or apartments, Hammadi called for Muslims to join his radical message. They ignored him.

The role of Saudi money in Barcelona is important to the rise of Muslim worshippers. Saudi philanthropists were building Mosques throughout Spain. Barcelona is the main focus of Saudi money. Hammadi liked this. He knew that he could find some converts.

He would lead his new followers to blow up La Sagrada Familia. He needed to show local Muslims their history. Hammadi continued a number of al Qaeda meetings, and he always offered a sumptuous lunch. The vegetarian feast followed by a hateful sermon was an invitation to al Qaeda. He built up their hopes for the future. He talked to them about a specific plan to guarantee Muslim equality. He needed to show local Muslims a forgotten part of their history. He took them to the Sant Pau del Camp church, a former monastery, that how stands in the El Ravel section in central Barcelona.

Hammadi also took his followers to the tomb of Wilfred II. He was the founder of Sant Pau del Camp. Then Hammadi showed potential recruits historical documents that proved Wilfred II was a Muslim. The documents were forged. His new followers weren't sophisticated enough to detect this duplicity.

He told them of his dual identity. He was an American, James Smith, who was rechristened as the Muslim Omar Abdul Hammadi. They would also learn of his wealth and his devotion to Islam.

As Hammadi took the dozen Muslims to El Ravel he said: "This is a former slum. What do you think is Arabic?"

"We don't know Mr. Hammadi."

Hammadi said: "Let me explain. Sant Pau del Camp was taken over by Muslim soldiers in 985. Then the Monks abandoned it. It was an early center of Muslim faith. The soldiers built a cloister dedicated to the Quran and Allah."

Hammadi walked them behind the church. In a left corner wall there were Arabic symbols. Then Hammadi removed his backpack. He pulled out a book written about the Muslim Tariq who in 711 landed at Gibraltar. He used the name Gibraltar, which meant Tariq's Mountain. By 732, Hammadi pointed out that Muslim forces ruled with kindness and intelligence. It wasn't until Louis the Pious took Barcelona in 801 that Muslim influences declined. As Hammadi explained, the early forces of Muslim history, his listeners were spellbound.

His rhetorical brilliance allowed Hammadi to argue that there was eight hundred years of Muslim influences in Barcelona. For centuries there was a concentrated Muslim influence. There were eleven Mosques and thirty official Islamic organizations recently founded by Muslim Catalans.

After a half dozen lunch's and informal meetings, Hammadi had only two followers. When he trained as an al Qaeda organizer, he didn't realize that the message was difficult to sell. He had an easier time making money in the American stock market.

One stunned listener said: "You mean there is a Muslim presence in El Ravel?"

"There was and there still is," Hammadi continued. "You see that some 50,000 people presently live here of the Muslim faith. You have no opportunity. You are treated like second class citizens." Hammadi smiled. He didn't want to say too much. Boredom. This wasn't something he wanted in his message.

His followers were uneducated, naïve young men who dreamed of 300 virgins. They believed in Hammadi's stilted message. Many of the Barcelona Muslims were Pakistani's. They should have been aroused by his message. They weren't. There were too many government subsidies. Too much social welfare! Barcelona was a paradise for immigrants and ethnics. Diversity and tolerance were celebrated daily.

He continued trying to lure locals with fancy meals. Hammadi had an air of unrealistic expectations. At these meetings there was often a small, quiet Asian man in the corner. But no one cared. He also didn't eat the food. Emilio was furious. Hammadi would meet his wrath.

Then Hammadi had an idea. He would go into the heart of Barcelona's Muslim ghetto. When he walked into the Raval area, he saw the need for Muslim radicalism. There was poverty in Barcelona. There was dissatisfaction with the government. The Raval was home to forty-five percent of Barcelona's Muslim population. Hammadi noticed a sign: "Muslim Outreach: A Talk By Ambassador Alan Solomont." Hammadi couldn't believe it. The U. S. was apologizing for its actions against Muslims. He wondered if anyone believed that lying shit who called himself the ambassador.

Hammadi quickly exploited the U. S apology for its foreign policy mistakes. He held numerous luncheons demanding retaliation for American misdeeds. He was frustrated there weren't many Barcelona Muslims listening to him. Recruitment was difficult. But Hammadi persevered.

Hammadi walked his guests down the Carrer del Peu de la Creu to the Centro Riojano de Barcelona restaurant where he planned to update his message. The food was also top notch. This fact led to more than thirty potential recruits filling Restaurant La Riojano. The restaurant served the best home cooking from Spain's La Rioja wine country. Restaurante La Rioja opened in 1892 and Hammadi guided his Muslim cohorts through a vegetarian meal. The Muslim religion designates that certain foods are not allowed. Those foods that are allowed are called Halal. They are not made of animal products. The menu had enough variety to support a Halal meal. His guests basked in the sumptuous meal. He stood up to give a speech.

Hammadi said: "We look forward to sharing our inspirational message with you. Allah has a secret. He has plans for Barcelona." Hammadi bowed, smiled and clapped his hands. A group of young ladies in berkas walked into the room with their eyes on the ground and handed out cards for another meeting. Most people threw the cards in the waste can. Hammadi's message wasn't resonating.

When it was over, Hammadi said: "Those who want to join me in political discussions can come tomorrow night to the Pita House on La Ramblas." Everyone thanked Hammadi for the lesson in Islamic history. They weren't sure what to make of him.

The next night Hammadi walked through the tourist laden La Ramblas and discovered that there were three Pita restaurants. Fortunately, there was only one at La Ramblas 54. Hammadi walked in and two swarthy Muslims sat at a table. The Pita House is the worst Halal restaurant in Barcelona. Hammadi had a plan. After the best food last night, the worst food would convince his followers of his piety.

He sat down and once again the two men introduced themselves. "I am Sayyid named for the Egyptian revolutionary." He bowed. "I am Aashif. I am named for my grandfather."

"Ah," Hammadi said: "Aashif meaning bold and courageous."

"Thank you patron."

"I remember you well, my friend."

Aashif smiled: "I am quiet but principled. The infidels have not altered my religious beliefs. Allah will triumph. I have read Sayyid Qutb's books, the writings of the Muslim Brotherhood and the Quran." He bowed. 'I'm ready to work for Allah's triumph.'

Sayyid said: "We need guidance. We have no idea how to bring victory for Allah."

Hammadi said: "Do you subscribe to his message? Are you willing to experience 300 virgins?"

"We are," they said in unison.

Hammadi thought for a moment. Sayyid Qutb wrote **Milestones**, while in an Egyptian prison. It is the centerpiece of radical Muslim political philosophy. Perhaps Sayyid could be the philosopher of Spanish al Qaeda. Hammadi made a note to import his books.

Hammadi said: "And you Sayyid are you familiar with Sayyid Qutb's book **Milestones**?"

"I am." Sayyid had no idea who Sayyid Qutb was or why he was important. Hammadi could read the level of ignorance on Sayyid's face. It didn't matter. He would still serve his purpose

Everyone looked up as a small Asian man nosily swept out a corner of the room. He smiled. He bowed. He exited the room. The interruption gave Hammadi time to think.

He reflected: "The book advocated a revolutionary vanguard to free Muslims from western oppression." Hammadi looked at his potential followers. Did they get it?

It was a message that Hammadi took to his followers. They left the Pita House after only a few bites of their food. It was awful. They walked down the street and talked.

Sayyid said: "Mr. Hammadi I have memorized the **Quran**."

Hammadi smiled: "I will see you tomorrow night. Meet me at the Liceu Metro station." This was a small and seemingly insignificant stop on the subway.

The next night Hammadi waited as Aashif and Sayyid showed up. He took them to a small, dark restaurant near the Metro station where he outlined the plans for organizing his al Qaeda cell.

Surprisingly, they agreed. It was time to make Allah's presence felt in Barcelona. Before he left for the evening, Hammadi spent some time questioning Sayyid and Aashif on the basic tenets of the Muslim faith. They knew next to nothing. Both had read the Quran. Neither understood it. They had no idea that Spain in general and Barcelona in particular had a Muslim heritage. They were ready for immediate radical conversion. They were always ready for lunch or dinner. Hammadi spent a great deal of time weaving a picture of Christian atrocities. He detailed the storied Barcelona Muslim history. He also vividly described how the Catholic Church erased Muslim contributions. He painted a picture of Muslim persecution in Spanish history. The Muslims were expelled from Spain between 1609 and 1614 and they never recovered.

Sayyid said: "Hammadi, the only Muslims we know are thieves and pick pockets."

Smith-Hammadi said: "That is the perception we will change."

The Spanish government and enlightened Barcelona citizens were attempting to meet the needs of the growing Muslim population. There were a number of Imam's who had positions of respect and authority. Hammadi did his best to minimize these advances.

The difficulty Hammadi had in convincing Barcelona Muslims that they were ill treated came from the election of Mohammed Chaib to the Catalan Parliament. He was a Muslim of Moroccan birth. Hammadi countered that argument by preparing a file, which claimed that Chaib was neither a Muslim nor a Moroccan.

Hammadi made notes about the Catalonia roots in Barcelona. These historical roots made the city independent. Barcelonans didn't think of themselves as Spaniards but as Catalonians. In the Cuitat Vella, where most Muslims lived, Hammadi concentrated his recruiting.

It was time for Hammadi to become James Smith. He had done his best to recruit the ill-educated and unappreciative Barcelona Muslims. He would have a tough time garnering a following. He would persevere.

He needed to set the stage for the final terrorist triumph. As James Smith he was above suspicion. At night he would turn once again into Hammadi and implement his plan to destroy Sagrada Familia. He was in the midst of Don Gino, Chastain Johnson and that bumbling fool Trevor Blake III. No one realized his role. He was the prophet of Muslim destruction.

CHAPTER THIRTY-TWO
Setting The Stage For Terrorism

"Surrealism is destructive, but it destroys only what it considers to be shackles limiting our vision." Salvador Dali

James Smith returned to the Palacette Continental Hotel. He hated the pink rooms. He complained. He found out all the rooms were pink. That is except for the one purple room. While it was purple, it was also double the size of the other hotel rooms. It was for a very special guest who visited often.

It was reserved permanently for this special San Francisco guest. The desk clerk, Peter, was a typical liberal, naive South African. Smith couldn't stand him. He was so God damned polite. It was nauseating. He pulled out his al Qaeda file. It was time to organize the Barcelona Muslims. After putting together a series of lessons, Smith prepared to teach his fledgling al Qaeda cell, if you could call two followers a cell.

He was careful to feed those who followed him. He set up his third restaurant meeting. He would cajole, convince and connive to form an al Qaeda cell. It was one that lacked the fierce nature of the Iraq and Afghanistan cells. But it was a beginning. He hoped that it would attract artists with a political persuasion.

After renting the back room at the 4GATS restaurant on Carrer de Montsio, 3, Smith had food catered into a private room. The 4GATS began in 1897 when a Paris waiter, Pere Romeu, opened a Barcelona restaurant much like the famed Paris Cabaret Le Chat Noir. When someone told him that it would be himself and four Black Cats in a restaurant that was open all night, he laughed. Over the years among Catalans, the 4GATS was renowned for its political activism.

The 4GATS was a restaurant where the environment promoted inexpensive food, good music and a radical political atmosphere. When seventeen year old Pablo Picasso began frequenting the place, it established the link between art and politics. The streets around the 4GATS remain impregnated with Bohemia and the aroma of dissent prompted Hammadi to promote his radial political agenda.

Once Antoni Gaudi became a regular at the 4GATS, it became the center of Barcelona's architectural community, as well as an artistic enclave. Smith smiled. Terrorism was born in the midst of artistic endeavor. It was sweet revenge. Barcelonans believed that Muslim radicalism was tempered by middle class success. He would show them the folly of their ways. Culture with a western tinge did not subdue the Muslim way.

Smith loved the bohemian setting around the 4GATS. Musicians, street artists, pamphleteers and political lunatics roamed the streets. It was fertile ground for dissent. Once Aashif and Sayyid finished their meal, Smith began the training. They had no idea that al Qaeda was Arabic for "the base." It made sense; al Qaeda was the center of the imminent Muslim triumph. Hammadi worried about his two ill-trained recruits. They were slow learners. They were also inept about weaponry.

There was no time to fly two terrorists in training to Pakistan. Sayyid and Aashif had little knowledge of the Muslim way of life and less training in matters of explosives and terrorist tactics. There was no one in Barcelona who al Qaeda used to train its Spanish cell.

Smith would have to be the trainer. The renowned terrorist, Ayman al–Zawahiri, trained Smith christening him Hammadi. To convince him of Muslim superiority, al Zawahiri lectured on Middle Eastern history. Hammadi was like a parrot that echoed Zawahiri's words.

Hammadi spent hours listening to Zawahiri talking aobut the Muslim world's scientific advances. The invention of magnifying lenses was an Arab triumph as were the elephant clock and the camera. Zawahiri was the person who made Hammadi aware of the long and glorious traditions of Muslim history. Glory to Allah!

As Ayman al-Zawahiri trained Smith-Hammadi, he went through the inventions from the medieval Islamic world. He told Smith that citric acid, as well as nitric acid, were Arab inventions. It was Zawahiri's belief that modern science dated from medieval Muslim times. The West was a decadent civilization usurping Muslim science.

Zawahiri said: "The British, Germans and Americans take credit for our chemistry finds. They can't take credit for our Minaret's and architecture. We also built the first bridge mills in Cordoba Spain in the 12th century. The attacks on Spain and the U. S. will make the world aware how they have slighted us."

Smith said: "I will personally guarantee that the Islamic Golden Age of Invention will be appreciated." He bowed to Ayman al-Zawahiri. The Imam smiled.

When Hammadi left Zawahiri's teaching, he had a plan to implement Allah's full glory. What had Zawahiri taught Hammadi?

The sixty-two year old Egyptian physician turned terrorist taught Smith to blend in and to take advantage of Americans turning a blind eye to an African American who might be a terrorist. Smith's cover as a millionaire businessman, a supporter of Democratic president Barack Obama and a well-known philanthropist was perfect. Once Smith accomplished his two acts of terrorism, he would retire to a remote Pakistan village with his five wives. It was nirvana on earth and in time 300 virgins would be waiting for him in Paradise. Why was Zawahiri so important to Hammadi? Why did he worship the Imam? The answer was a simple one. Hammadi viewed this clerical wizard as the George Washington of terrorists.

Ayman al-Zawahiri orchestrated the 1998 bombing of the U. S. Embassies in two East African cities. He was instrumental in the 2000 attack on the U. S. Cole. By 2001, President George W. Bush named al-Zawahiri as one of the most wanted terrorists. By 2009, the year that James Smith met with him, al-Zawahiri was al Qaeda's chief commander. Smith was trained well. Smith's goal was to get even with the American military and government after the death of Osama bin Laden. This notion was reinforced by al-Zawahiri's teachings.

Since Osama bin Laden's death, Zawahiri led al Qaeda. The U. S. State Department offered a twenty-five million dollar reward for information leading to his capture. He remains an elusive figure. He is also a dedicated teacher. His pupils are all over the world teaching an end to democracy and capitalism.

For a decade, James Smith taught al-Zawahiri's views to a host of Americans, and two inept Spanish terrorists. Zawahiri's teachings included the notion that Muslims had to be at all times loyal to Islam. They also had to be loyal to each other while hating and destroying the West. Smith was ready to give his life. If it meant killing Don Gino Landry, it would make Islam's victory even sweeter.

As he formulated his plans for a Muslim victory, Smith reminded himself that surrealists believed that Dali's brand of surrealism was destructive enough to bring about positive change. The al Qaeda terrorists attracted to Dali's teachings misunderstood his concept of surrealism.

Smith taught his followers that it was necessary to destroy the forces that impeded ones inevitable path toward paradise. The Salvador Dali al Qaeda cell would bring Barcelona to its knees and the plot to blow up La Sagrada Familia would end the fame of the architect Antoni Gaudi. Then it was on to San Francisco where Don Gino Landry would be put in his place for his Catholic proselytizing. If James Smith died, in the pursuit of Muslim dream, it was for al-Zawahiri's teachings.

In Barcelona there had to be a terrorist attack on something that the Spanish revered. Hammadi had a plan. No one was more respected than the architect Antoni Gaudi and his La Sagrada Familia. When Gaudi began the project in 1883, he continued working on it until his death. When a tram in the middle of Barcelona hit Gaudi, he died instantly. The Barcelona tram driver thought that he had killed a vagrant. Gaudi dressed like a poor man. In 2010 an emissary from Rome consecrated Sagrada Familia. It held Mass and as many as 50,000 people a month attended church services. It was now an official Catholic Church. That singular event prompted Hammadi to act.

The consecration of Sagrada Familia infuriated radical Muslims. It was a symbol that Hammadi detested. He would make sure that Gaudi's eighteen towers were never completed. He would also leave a sign that Salvador Dali disapproved of the colossal church dedicated to the birth of Christ. Smith took a cab to Sagrada Familia. He walked around the magnificent architectural marvel. He carefully examined the spires dedicated to the Twelve Apostles. The spire, that was a part of the tribute to the Virgin Mary, was magnificent in design and execution. The tallest spire of all was for Jesus Christ. He would smile when they exploded. Allah would triumph.

"Sir, can I give you a private tour." The voice was there. But where was the person? Smith looked down. There was a small man dressed elegantly. He smiled.

"You are," Smith said. He looked the little man over. He was dressed like an English gentleman. He wore a bowler and spats. Not a single person in Barcelona wore a bowler or spats. The pin stripped pants and elegant dress coat reeked of money.

"I am Pip at your service."

Smith almost laughed out loud. Pip was one of Smith's favorite characters from Charles Dickens' **Great Expectations**. "And Pip what might you offer?"

The small man smiled: "I can show you the corners and the crevices of Sagrada Familia for the paltry sum of twenty Euros."

"Let us proceed." Smith handed the small man twenty-five Euros. "The tip is for an excellent tour."

"Sir, we haven't started the tour."

Smith-Hammadi smiled: "I know a quality human being and a closet Muslim."

Pip smiled: "Yes, sir."

As they walked inside Sagrada Familia, Smith noticed the Passion Facade. Pip explained its significance. He was mesmerized by it. The Passion Façade was a skin and bones skeleton that symbolized Christ's passion. Smith saw it as a sign that Catholicism was declining. Gaudi had been dead for two decades when work on the Passion Façade began in 1947. Using Gaudi's drawings, the Façade was designed to strike fear in the hearts of local Catholics.

Hammadi said: "Pip do you see the manner in which Catholicism strikes fear into the heart of common people?"

"I do," Pip replied. He was a man of few words.

Pip's tour was surprisingly thorough. The small, agreeable man had great knowledge of architecture and the Sagrada Familia. Smith took copious notes. After two hours they shook hands and Smith walked across the street for a cappuccino.

Then Smith stopped and turned. He watched Pip walk over to a hidden corner. He pointed to Mecca and began a Muslim prayer. The man was judged correctly. There were devout Muslims in and around Barcelona. He would find them and organize a terrorist cell second to none.

Mecca was twenty five hundred miles nautical miles away. Smith watched realizing for the folks with the rugs it was closer. Smith stood and watched two devoted Muslims pray near the Sagrada Familia. It was surrealistic. Maybe Dali watched a Muslim prayer and drew a sketch or painted a picture. Who knows!

Once he was seated in a small café, Smith took out a notebook. He sketched where and how the Passion Façade would explode. The C4 explosives would be placed near the bronze figure representing the Ascension of Jesus. Smith smiled. He was ready to surprise the Catholic hierarchy, as well as the people of Barcelona with a terrorist triumph. There would be no warning. Then Smith walked back to the Sagrada Familia.

He stopped at the great doors of the Passion Façade. It would be sweet revenge for a church that ignores the downtrodden, the poor and those who think differently. The Gaudi inspired Sagrada Familia was little more than an ugly monstrosity dedicated to religious filth. Allah showed the way to religious purity. Smith would make sure that the Muslim message rang true. The excesses of the Catholic faith were everywhere. The new church organ was a paean to that excess.

There was one more surprise that Smith planned, as he walked back inside Sagrada Familia. He admired the organ installed in 2010.

He had plans to place the C4 explosives in this musical instrument. It would be another reminder of how the 1492 organ pipes could be silenced. Blasphemy in sound! Silenced!

Smith walked over to the Pizza Emporia for a glass of wine, a Caesar salad and a capriccioso pizza. He sat looking at Sagrada Familia. Then two shadowy figures loomed over the table. They were well dressed. They didn't look tough. A perfect Italian pizza dinner in Spain was about to end. Smith looked up.

He said: "Can I help you?" There was no hiding his irritation. One man was tall and thin and the other was short and fat.

The tall one said: "It is I who can help you." There was a long silence. The two men looked at each other. The short man fidgeted. The tall man was cool. The short man had sweat running down his forehead.

Smith said "Sit down!"

"Let me introduce myself, I'm a close friend of al Zawahiri." The tall one smiled. Smith looked at his stylish slicked back hair, his pin stripped Armani suit and his Python Loafers from Salvatore Ferragamo. The mystery man was not only well-dressed, he had an aura of sophistication. He didn't look like the friend of an international terrorist. Then again James Smith didn't look like someone who organized an al Qaeda cell. The small, portly man left.

"What can I do for you?" Smith said.

"Plenty."

"I'm listening."

The mystery man looked around. "I need to help you with bombing Sagrada Familia."

Smith was suspicious. "What bombing?"

"The one you have planned."

"When did I plan this?" Smith said with a chuckle.

"In your dormitory room at the University of Alabama."

"Let's see, twenty five years ago you were hiding in my dorm room as I outlined this fantasy."

"Yes, my friend, your twin brother corroborated the plan."

"My twin brother?"

"Yes, we are business partners."

"What?" Smith had talked only to his twin brother about his plan.

"Yes, I know what you are thinking. You only discussed this with your brother. Your brother is also close mouthed. He had some difficulty telling us. I persuaded him." The mystery man smiled.

Smith looked angry: "Did you torture him?" He felt for the Glock in his armpit holster. It was still there. The tall man stood over Smith looking menacing.

"And my brother," Smith said.

"He is well and alive." The mysterious stranger paused. "We are business partners. No violence was necessary. He is now a man of wealth and means. He has seen the light."

"And that light is?"

"The greater good of Allah." Smith didn't like the way that the tall stranger talked.

Smith didn't like those last words. It sounded like Mick Jagger uttered them after lunch with the Devil.

"Excuse me a moment, I need to go onto my computer." Smith was nervous and confused. He went to his e-mail and there was an anonymous message. That was never a good sign.

The message read: "The woman has the final clue." Smith wasn't sure what this meant. There was another message. "Look for the Chinese lady in a plaid Burberry skirt." None of this made sense. He hadn't seen one Chinese lady in Barcelona. Let alone one with a Burberry skirt. Maybe he wasn't looking closely.

The mysterious stranger smiled. "I am offering dinner. Go to the roof of the Hotel Condes, take a seat at the bar, I will be there at seven this evening." The mysterious stranger left.

After Smith paid his lunch bill, he walked outside to gaze at the spires of Sagrada Familia. It was an amazing sight. Then he noticed something. The Nativity façade celebrating the birth of Jesus, the Messiah, had a small dab of green paint on the bottom. For Muslim's green is used to decorate Mosques. There was also a small Crescent and star virtually invisible to the naked eye next to the statue. In pre-Islamic times, the Crescent was the symbol of the ruler. For Smith the message was clear. He needed to destroy the parts of Sagrada Familia that were blasphemous to Islam.

Sagrada Familia was magnificent. It was testimony to the infidel Catholic faith. Smith heard a squeaky, high-pitched voice.

"Sir!"

He looked behind a small kiosk. There stood an old lady with a shopping bag. He looked her up and down. She didn't seem threatening. She was Chinese. She wore a plaid Burberry skirt. She smiled.

Smith said: "Can I help you?"

"I think it is the other way. I can help you."

The little lady looked homeless. "Help me." Smith laughed.

She handed him a note and left. The note read: "Go to the Picasso Museum coffee shop. You will be contacted today." Smith looked down to ask the lady a question. She was gone. He walked to the corner and hailed a cab. In twenty-five minutes he was at the entrance to Museu Picasso. Smith stood in line behind Blanche and Barney from Des Moines. Blanche's beehive hairdo and ever-present cigarette gave her away. He heard Blanche whisper: "I didn't know Negros came to art museums." It was this ignorance that turned Smith into a Muslim terrorist. He purchased his ticket and walked into the museum. He accidentally tripped Blanche. He didn't say sorry Madame as he stepped on her foot. Stupid bitch.

The Museu Picasso has more than 3,500 Picasso works. Smith would enjoy the art. Even if the visit was wasted. Smith didn't like the Museu Picasso. It was an indication of the peasant artist's favor with the Spanish government. Dali never had the same relationship with the Barcelona politicos. Smith resented those who ignored Dali. He was prepared to find help for his plot in the Museu Picasso.

CHAPTER THIRTY-THREE

Museu Picasso And Help From Al Qaeda

"Happy is he who causes a scandal." Salvador Dali

After checking his brief case in a secure locker, Smith wandered around for an hour at the Museu Picasso. There was a special Picasso exhibit. It was a retrospective of his early work. It was stunning. Then Smith walked down to the coffee shop. He wanted to eat in the sit down gourmet restaurant. This was not a possibility. Every table was taken. At the counter, he ordered a ham and cheese Panini and a cappuccino. He walked outside and took a seat near the rear wall. He could see all parts of the restaurant and coffee shop. His food came. He ate it. He ordered another cappuccino. An hour passed. No one was coming.

Smith stood. He stretched. He noticed a napkin with writing. A message read: "Get on any bus in front of the Picasso Museum. You will be contacted." This was getting absurd. Smith went out front. He stood at the bus stop. Once the bus arrived, he stepped on and paid two Euros. He sat in the back. After four stops a rabbi got on board. The bus was virtually empty. The rabbi could sit anywhere. He came back and asked.

"Sir, may I take this seat?" Smith said nothing. He looked out the window. The rabbi sat down. He reached into a brief case. He took out an envelope. He pulled the chord to get off the bus. Thank God, Smith thought. He almost blurted it out. The rabbi stood up. He smiled. He dropped the envelope in Smith's lap and quickly exited the back door.

The envelope read: "A rabbi is not always a rabbi, Mr. Smith."
Strange! Smith opened the envelope. He couldn't believe its contents.
There was a schematic map of Sagrada Familia. The questions were:
Who had given him the schematic? Why? What was he to do? Why
did the schematic have places where Smith-Hammadi could place
explosives? Who was helping him? There were too many questions.
There were too few answers. Someone was watching over him. Was
it Allah?

Now Smith had his own mystery. He got off the bus on the
Ramblas. It was time for a beer. No one knew he drank beer. He wasn't
a perfect Muslim. He was more of a closet devotee. He walked over
to El Cortes Ingles and took the escalator to the rooftop. He bought a
beer at the counter and walked to a remote seat that looked out over
the Barcelona skyline. He opened the envelope. The schematic was
perfect. He studied it for an hour. Someone was helping. He looked
for the spots to place the C4 explosives. There were some suggestions. All good ones. The plan was coming together.

"Hello!" Smith looked up. The young woman standing in front of
him was beautiful. He was a Muslim, but he still had an attraction to
beautiful young ladies. He felt guilty. Most of the Muslim ladies were
dowdy, overweight and stupid. He realized that he was being politically incorrect. It felt good.

Smith said: "Hello! What can I do for you?"

"It is what I can do for you."

"Tell me." Smith couldn't keep his eyes off her. She had big breasts,
dark piercing eyes and a lithe figure.

"Can you buy me a drink?" She didn't look like a Muslim. Then
again what did a Muslim look like in a trendy bar in downtown
Barcelona? Who knows!

They looked at each other as she ordered a Brandy Alexander.
Smith wondered. What in the hell was a Brandy Alexander? It arrived.
She took a small sip.

Smith said: "I'm waiting."

She pulled an envelope out of her purse. Smith opened it. He
was silent. The material provided another way to destroy Sagrada

Familia. The large envelope contained an all-access construction pass. It included an architectural drawing of the eight completed Sagrada Familia towers. Smith studied it. He was amazed. There was a detailed drawing of where to place C4 explosives. Someone was helping to blow up the apostles. He now had two plans. One would work. There was a one-page memorandum deftly explaining how to avoid detection while blowing up Sagrada Familia. He hurriedly put it in his back pocket.

"I see that you are happy, Mr. Smith."

He wondered how she knew his name. "You are!" Smith said.

"Who I am is unimportant. It is what I can do for you."

"Shall we continue to play verbal games?" Smith smiled.

"I will get to the point." She paused and took a single sheet of paper out of her purse.

Smith watched intently. She handed the paper to him. He looked in amazement. It was a list of people working inside Sagrada Familia. The ones who would help with its destruction. Smith went back to the large folder. The towers symbolizing the apostles intrigued him. There were the two towers dedicated to Mary and Joseph. The eight towers already constructed were not connected. They have independent entrances. It was in these towers that Smith saw his chance for destruction. Now he understood why the Nativity Tower had to be blown up. This tower celebrated the birth and the life of Jesus. The Nativity Tower is a celebration of Jesus' childhood. For that fact alone, it needed to be destroyed.

"I'm leaving now." The mysterious woman got up and walked away. Smith didn't say a word. He smiled. He had all that he needed. It was time to go to work. He left El Cortes Ingles and took a taxi back to the hotel. He had his architectural drawings, his details on Sagrada Familia, his al Qaeda allies and his plan. There was no sense waiting. He didn't need anything else. He was ready to strike.

What Smith didn't see was the small man in a purple raincoat following him. He also didn't see the six Samoans. As he jumped into the cab, Smith didn't have a clue that retired CIA agent, Matt Luman, was back on the job. Matt said: "Where to Buddy?"

Smith said: "Down to the Ramblas. Drop me at La Boqueria." Luman took off with a smile. This guy couldn't blow up his tires. When Smith exited the cab, he walked into the open-air market. A gentleman in a purple suit, with a dark cape smoking a small cigar watched as Smith walked casually through the market. He wandered down to the stalls filled with cheeses, fruits, meats and vegetables and just about any delicacy for the gastronomic. Smith bought a fresh fruit cup for a euro. Big spender. A small Asian man brushed by Smith apologizing for rudely bumping into the American. The one page memo that was in Smith's pocket was missing. The small Asian man walked out of the market smiling.

Smith sat down at an open-air counter selling fresh fish. Two people joined him. Don Gino followed and looked at the two men. It was Aashif and Sayyid. Don Gino had a folder on each man. Neither was educated. Neither was smart. Neither was cunning. Don Gino knew what they were doing with Smith. They talked for over an hour. The waiter was wired. Don Gino walked out of the Mercat de La Boqueria. He hailed a cab and returned to the Palacette Continental Hotel. He would shower and change his clothes. It was time to deal with Smith.

No one disrespects the Don. If they do they don't live to talk about it.

CHAPTER THIRTY-FOUR

Preparing To Destroy
Sagrada Familia

"Let my enemies devour each other." Salvador Dali

S mith left the Mercat de La Boqueria with his two friends. They took a cab to a non-descript building. It was time to assemble the explosives. As Aashif and Sayyid left the taxi, they were nervous. The small warehouse where Smith stored his explosives was cold and damp. They were out of their element. Smith was out of his element.

As they entered the dank warehouse, six Samoans surrounded the building. The terrorists went inside. Smith announced that they would pray. Don Gino had the building bugged. He laughed. Pray! For what? They were about to vanish. Maybe they should pray for brains. Don Gino put the power in his cell phone on. "Get ready." He watched. Then the unexpected happened. A dozen police vehicles pulled up. What the hell was going on?

The police battered down the door. Smith and his two associates came out handcuffed. The policeman in charge was confidently smoking a cigar and smiling. Don Gino walked over. The smile on the Barcelona policeman's face revealed his mirthful joy. He was just over six feet tall with a lithe frame that reeked of strenuous workouts. His hair was cut short. He had a confident air. He reeked of being in charge.

"Well Don Gino, allow me to introduce myself. I am Hector Alfonso Domingo-Mercedes, head of the Guardia Urbana de Barcelona. I have apprehended the al Qaeda terrorists. They will be dealt with in the Spanish courts. Any questions?" His steely blue eyes suggested that he was not used to explaining his actions.

"Good to meet you Inspector Domingo-Mercedes." Don Gino took a small drag on his cigar. "I will be discussing this matter shortly with your superiors. Or we night have a brief conversation. I am here, as you know in a semi-official capacity."

For a brief moment, Domingo-Mercedes paused. He was thinking. He realized that there was more to the case than he originally expected. Domingo-Mercedes did not get this far in the Barcelona police establishment without knowing the facts. It was time for a strategic retreat. He was aware of Don Gino's connections. They went deeper than even he knew.

Domingo-Mercedes said: "A brief conversation over a glass of wine would be good." He walked over to the vehicles and instructed two police cars and the van carrying the prisoners to follow them.

Don Gino said: "I would prefer someplace quiet to talk."

"I know just the place."

Don Gino wasn't sure what to make of this situation. They drove to the El Raval neighborhood and Domingo-Mercedes entered The Quiet Man bar. Don Gino wondered if something wasn't lost in translation. When Don Gino walked into the Quiet Man, he realized it was an Irish bar. There was a big picture of John Wayne on the wall. Guess what movie the picture was from? The 1952 Quiet Man. Hubris and history meet. There was an area roped off for Inspector Domingo-Mercedes. His assistant sat drinking a Guinness.

It was the Calle Arco del Teatro that intrigued Don Gino. It was the entrance to the Raval Quarter. It was here that a scene from Alexandre Dumas' romances could be reenacted. The Raval was like entering a vault of blue haze. It appeared like another world. He gazed with disdain at the policeman. As he looked around El Raval, the inspector was aware of Don Gino's importance. It was time for the inspector to stage a retreat. He would do it with style and grace. He knew that Don Gino respected strength. He would show his strength and cunning.

He said: "We have a stalemate."

Don Gino said: "You have two choices. Give up the prisoners. The other choice is to wait for word from your superiors.

"And!"

"Your superiors will not like to be bothered."

"What is in it for me?" The policeman looked nervous.

"Survival." Don Gino ordered a cappuccino. He waited.

"The prisoners are yours." The policeman got up, saluted and prepared to leave."

Don Gino said: "Thank you."

"Remember Commander Domingo-Mercedes is your admirer, Don Gino."

"Commander Domingo-Mercedes, you will be rewarded." The Commander didn't realize that he was about to become a national celebrity. Don Gino was not about to tell him why.

He walked off quickly. When Don Gino walked outside, Smith and his associates were standing near a telephone pole surrounded by six large Samoans. They looked scared.

Don Gino directed the three men into a van. The Samoans climbed in and they left for an undisclosed warehouse. Don Gino followed.

The warehouse located in a side street near the Ramblas had a sign: "Don Gino's Dog Food Plant." A small sign read: "Coming Soon."

The Samoans brought the three men into the warehouse.

Don Gino said: "Gentlemen. Welcome. We need to have a brief discussion."

Smith said: "I will unleash the fury of Allah on you."

Don Gino chuckled. "I don't think so."

"You are some old queer from San Francisco. You can't make me say a word."

"I think we need to keep this civilized." Don Gino lit a small cigar.

The three stood silent and defiant. Aashif and Sayyid looked scared.

One of the Samoans wheeled in the batteries and cables. Another brought a shiny set of small knives into the room. They smiled. A midget in a purple tuxedo walked into the room. He had an evil smile.

Don Gino directed that the three be tied into chairs. He asked them if they were comfortable. They looked at him like he was nuts. They were frightened. In a little more than an hour the depths of the secret al Qaeda cell unraveled Then Don Gino astonished his prisoners.

Don Gino said: "Gentlemen, you are free to go."

They looked bewildered. Don Gino and the Samoans left the warehouse. The three men untied themselves rubbing their sore hands and shaking their dead legs. Hammadi-Smith could barely control his rage. He looked at Aashif and Sayyid.

Smith wiped his forehead. "It is time for us to strike."

Sayyid looked like he was going to get sick. "I need to get some air." Sayyid walked outside and began running down the street. He was hit by a car and killed instantly. The driver in the purple suit lit a small cigar and drove away. The crime remains unsolved.

Smith and Aashif walked out into the street bold and confident. Commander Domingo-Mercedes stood in front smiling.

"Gentleman, we have a reservation for you."

Smith said: "I want a lawyer." Mercedes slapped him across the face. He took his shoe and gouged it into his groin. Smith groaned with pain.

Domingo-Mercedes handcuffed the two men. His men drove them to another of Don Gino's warehouse facilities.

"Greetings Don Gino." Domingo-Mercedes led the men into a dimly lighted room full of machinery. It was another dog food canning plant. One that Don Gino operated for a decade. His dog food brand, Fernando Lamas, brought a quick lawsuit from the American actor. When he found out that Don Gino owned the company, he dropped the legal action and did a commercial for free. No one disrespects the Don.

After Domingo-Mercedes interrogated the two men, he left them. They would be killed and disposed of promptly. He watched as his men took the two terrorists to a soundproof room. They were shot and disposed of in the canned dog food. Smith-Hammadi was done. His plan to blow up Sagrada Familia was nothing more than simple threats by a man with limited brainpower.

Don Gino was pleased. "Thank you Commander Domingo-Mercedes. Your country salutes you."

"My pleasure Don Gino." They sat down to share a bottle of vintage Spanish wine. After finishing the excellent bottle of red wine, Don Gino and Domingo-Mercedes parted company.

They had come to an agreement. One that would help everyone! Don Gino and Inspector Domingo-Mercedes neutralized the impending crime. The terrorist threat was neutralized for the time being in Barcelona. Now it was time to turn their collective attention to San Francisco.

Don Gino visited the Barcelona newspapers. He had a tale of a Spanish patriot who single handedly saved Barcelona from violent crime. He told the story of a courageous Barcelona police inspector. He was a man, said Don Gino, who single handedly saved Barcelona from Muslim extremists. He was a national hero.

The next morning **La Vanguardia**, the leading Barcelona newspaper, prominently displayed a picture of Commander Domingo-Mercedes on the front page. The story detailed his heroism in preventing the destruction of Sagrada Familia. He was promoted to Assistant Commissioner, as well as the head of the newly created internal security force. He was seen that night having dinner at the Restaurant LaSarte in the Hotel des Condes with Don Gino. The chef, Martin Beragategui, came out to make sure that Domingo-Mercedes' dinner was acceptable. It was. The tasting menu was exquisite as he began with trout tartar with orange and a curd cucumber. He followed it with roasted pigeon, ragout of pork, tomato and lemon with apple cream and vegetables. A bottle of Bodegas Vega Sicilia Valbuena 5 was followed by petit fours and brandy. When the Assistant Commissioner left there was no bill. Smith-Hammadi was dead. He would cause them no further problems.

CHAPTER THIRTY-FIVE
Smith Watches And Laughs

"I shall be so brief that I have already finished." Salvador Dali

As Assistant Commissioner Domingo-Mercedes exited La Sarte, a lone figure watched from across the street. The dimly lit street was one filled with shadows. Smith-Hammadi smiled. He had never liked his twin brother. Now the bastard was dead. He deserved it. As Smith gazed from behind a telephone pole, he smelled cigarette smoke. Chastain Johnson came walking down the street. He retreated into the darkness. She would surely complicate matters. He wondered about her role. What the hell was Chastain Johnson doing walking down the street in the middle of nowhere? She was an FBI agent. She was in Barcelona. The FBI didn't have authority to operate outside the U. S. Then he saw Trevor Blake III walk down an opposite street. This inept Private Eye from San Francisco garnered a great deal of positive press. It was like a convention of the absurd. What the hell was going on?

Smith had an ally in Barcelona. He watched as the various figures talked and congratulated themselves on their success. Smith quietly walked to a side street. A car pulled up and he told the driver to take him to see Manuel Vazquez Montalban. The famous Spanish writer had no idea that Smith was a terrorist. They were friends since Smith-Hammadi awarded him a half million-dollar grant for Montalban's novel **Southern Seas**.

When Smith knocked Montalban answered the door. The Spanish mystery writer was a gourmet. He was also an award-winning novelist. He was on his way to San Francisco to accept the International Mystery Writer's Award for **The Stranger**. Not only was Montalban a gourmet, he was an unsuspecting dupe. Smith gave him a small package. It contained the plans for the destruction of one of San Francisco's most prized tourist attractions. This venerated religious site was one that no one suspected could be bombed. It was off the tourist path but visited frequently by good Catholics like Don Gino Landry. The package was to be delivered to Hammadi-Smith's San Francisco partner.

They left Montalban's apartment and went to dinner at Cinco Jotas.

Montalban said: "I am a reputable gourmet. This is not my kind of place."

"Trust me my friend, the best is yet to come." They ordered a meal of barbecued meats, salads and fresh vegetable. Despite his reluctance, Montalban was impressed. He took out his digital camera and took a picture of his salad. It was out of character.

"There is a reason I need your help, Manuel."

Montalban said: "Yes! Tell me what is on your mind."

"You have always been identified with the oppressed, the poor and those Franco tortured until his timely death."

"Ah, timely death, I like that phrase." Montalban smiled and took a bite of his salad. "I think I will use that phrase in my next novel." He made a series of notes.

"Your writing is compared to Raymond Chandler and John LeCarre. Now you have the chance to become a real character in a real crime."

Montalban looked at Smith with astonishment. "You mean commit a crime. No! I am a writer, an intellectual figure, not a common criminal."

"My good friend, you don't understand. You will simply carry some instructions in code." Customs officials will give you little scrutiny. You are the author of award winning mysteries. You are not a criminal."

Montalban said; "You want me to do something criminal or illegal. You are a devil with words Mr. Smith."

"Yes I am, the words ring true."

"We are talking in circles. What do you mean 'the words ring true?"

Smith paused: "You have heard of al Qaeda?"

"Yes, they are pick pockets, they are car thieves and they are petty criminals. They are also not very smart."

"There is a new al Qaeda." Smith paused. He couldn't admit that al Qaeda was composed of only three people and one of them was dead. Smith and his one follower hardly made up an al Qaeda cell. Montalban didn't need to know the truth.

Montalban said: "Tell me more."

"We have a plan to destroy a monument to the Catholic Church as a protest of the arrogance of the American way of life. We will destroy a San Francisco Mafia boss Don Gino Landry."

"Ah," Montalban exclaimed. "Don Gino led a movement to ban my books. He should be ashamed."

"Do we have a deal?"

"Yes, I will do what you like."

This changed things dramatically as Smith could send more than just instructions.

"I will bring a steamer trunk to your house with a false bottom lined with lead. It will contain a simple trigger. Nothing more."

Montalban said: "And this trigger."

"The less you know, my friend, the better it is for you. Trust me."

They shook hands and left Cinco Jotas. Montalban took out a Tums and popped it into his mouth.

As Montalban walked to his car, a tall, handsome police commissioner joined him. They went to a nearby coffee shop. They had known each other since school.

"Commander Domingo-Mercedes it is good to see you or should I say Assistant Commissioner?"

"I am just a humble servant of the people."

"Ah, yes, Commander, I forgot, a humble servant with ambition."

"I do need a favor from a famous writer."

"You've got it."

"I understand the need to carry a letter for your other friend to San Francisco. I have a small packet for Don Gino Landry. He will be appreciative."

"Customs always goes through everything."

"Don Gino and I have arranged a rather quick trip through customs."

Domingo-Mercedes took out a small book of poetry. He opened it to the title page.

"That is my rarest poetry book, **Catalonia Music**, where did you get it?"

"I bought it through e-bay."

Montalban looked perplexed. "What is e-bay?"

"It is a long story my friend but someone sold it with the worst book of poetry every written **Beatle Poems**. For a thousand dollars you received **Catalonia Music**. The cost of **Beatle Poems** was a penny. I felt I overpaid for the Beatles book."

"And to whom do I sign this book?"

Domingo-Mercedes smiled: "To Don Gino Landry a real American."

Montalban signed the book. They shook hands and left the coffee shop.

As they exited the coffee shop, a woman in the shadows snapped pictures of Montalban. She was invisible except for the cigarette smoke.

The next day Montalban flew Lot Airlines to Warsaw. He spent the night at the InterContinental Hotel. He walked into the sports bar for a drink.

"Hello, my friend." Montalban looked to his left. There sat Don Gino Landry. "I have arrived here in Warsaw for one day to prepare you for our San Francisco adventure."

Montalban said: "I suppose no one knows that we are friends."

"That would be correct." Montalban looked to the back of the sports bar and saw six Samoans sipping iced tea.

"I see you are still traveling with your friends."

Don Gino smiled: "A man can never be too careful."

"Or too well informed my friend."

"Yes that is also a necessity."

They talked for hours about Montalban's work with the Unified Socialist Party of Catalonia and his involvement in overthrowing the repressive dictator General Francisco Franco. After they had talked of pleasure, literature and politics, Don Gino got down to business.

"Our friends in al Qaeda are planning a San Francisco attack. We need your help."

"You have it Don Gino." They shook hands and went their separate ways. Now it was up to Assistant Commissioner Domingo-Mercedes to deliver the final intelligence to thwart the San Francisco al Qaeda attack.

No one realized that Montalban, as well as Domingo-Mercedes, worked undercover for the CIA. They were specialized contract agents for the U. S. In Barcelona, they seemed little more than two people interested in local politics. A famous writer and a well-known detective hanging out with each other did not draw attention. They were beyond reproach. That is how the press pictured their foray into the Salvador Dali caper. They were friends getting together for a good time. No one realized that they were integral to solving the Salvador Dali murder.

When Don Gino Landry received the CIA's Distinguished Intelligence Cross, Domingo-Mercedes and Montalban were in attendance. There had been no publicity for this award. Domingo-Mercedes was at the ceremony everyone believed because he was a Spanish policeman. No one could explain Montalban's presence. Maybe he was writing a book about al Qaeda. There was a reason that criminals feared Don Gino Landry. He was an honest criminal with connections. Montalban also received the CIA's Distinguished Intelligence Cross.

Don Gino returned to the Palacette-Continental Hotel. He had to meet with Domingo-Mercedes and Montalban the next day to finalize their part in foiling the San Francisco attack. The next morning Don Gino got up and walked down to the Boqueria Market. As slivers of sun filtered through the open passageway, Don Gino smelled fresh fruits, vegetables and sizzling meats.

As Don Gino walked into the interior, he took a seat at a small seafood bar. A shrimp cocktail appeared followed by a cappuccino. Domingo-Mercedes joined him. They talked for more than an hour.

After he left Domingo-Mercedes, Don Gino walked over to the Ramblas where he met the world famous author, Manuel Vazquez Montalban.

"Hello, Don Gino." Montalban stuck out his big meaty hand. Don Gino shook it.

"Thank you for coming." Don Gino lit a small cigar.

"I have some bad news for you, Don Gino, Mr. Smith is still with us. He had his twin brother in his place."

"Yes Manuel, I know, this case is much like your novel, **Contra los Gourmets**."

"How is that, Don Gino?"

"You concentrate on Spanish cuisine is your marvelous book. You also cover international cuisine. I love that approach. It also suggests how this al Qaeda plot unfolded. I know that Mr. Smith is still free. He needs to think that he has eluded us."

"And why is that?"

Don Gino said: "The al Qaeda attack on San Francisco was so well planned that the CIA, the FBI, the Department of Homeland Security and Spain's Centro Nacional de Intelligencia had no idea how to foil the plot."

The foiling of the plot to blow up the towers at Sagrada Familia caused al Qaeda to revise its plans. The San Francisco plot was discovered. Did they have all the elements? Only time would tell.

Montalban thought a great deal about the San Francisco attack. His friend, Don Gino, had good intelligence. He was missing something. Don Gino requested that he fly into San Francisco to put a final nail in al Qaeda's coffin. He would do so with glee. He loved the city by the bay and what it offered both day and night. His friend, the famous American author and gourmet, Jim Harrison, was meeting him for drinks and dinner. They would party into the night. Both writers would help solve the al Qaeda plot while plying themselves with food and drink. It was a tough job. But someone had to do it.

PART III:
BLOWING UP A SAN
FRANCISCO MONUMENT

"There are some days when I think I am going to die from an overdose of satisfaction." Salvador Dali

CHAPTER THIRTY-SIX

On To San Francisco

"Have no fear of perfection - you'll never reach it."
Salvador Dali

Manuel Vazquez Montalban flew into San Francisco's International Airport. The LOT airline flight was pleasant in first class. The two stewardesses praised his Detective Carvalho novels. They had read all of them. It was the gastronomical references that they loved. Food and sex was a common denominator. LOT Airlines serves steak and lobster in the air. This is the reason Montalban flies LOT, and he knows the stewardesses on a first name basis.

"Ladies, I plan to visit San Francisco's best restaurants. It is my duty as a writer."

"Can you tell us what Pepe Carvalho will do next?" a stewardess asked.

Montalban was a swarthy, handsome man just slightly over-weight. He had the appearance of a Latin lover. He looked at the stewardess lovingly with controlled lust. Unlike other airlines, LOT fired any female who turned twenty-six. The Polish airline was not politically correct. Montalban loved that fact. There were three stewardess huddled around him. They seem to hang on his every word. He didn't want to disappoint them.

"Ladies I promise that Pepe will have his greatest adventure."

The blonde stewardess asked: "And what might that adventure be and where will it take place?"

"Ah, my dear, Pepe and his sidekick, the loyal Biscuter, will embark on a world wind trip to end Muslim violence." The stewardesses looked at each other with confusion.

"How can a fictional private eye end terrorism?" The other two stewardesses looked at the blonde like she was nuts.

Montalban said: "Sometimes fiction becomes real life."

The dark haired stewardess asked: "You mean Pepe is not a real person?"

Montalban realized that these young ladies were not particularly sophisticated. The stewardesses who thought that Pepe was a real person could easily be gotten into bed. He took note. So Montalban decided it was time to stretch the truth. He told the ladies that if they came to his hotel they could have a drink with Pepe Carvalho. They were excited.

Montalban felt guilty. He didn't like talking about Pepe Carvalho, as if he existed. As a good Catholic, albeit a closet one, Montalban didn't go to confession. He might have to admit that he stretched the truth in his writing, as well as in his life. But he would do anything to get these beautiful stewardesses in bed.

"Ladies, Pepe Carvalho is based on an Italian who lives in San Francisco. Don Gino Landry is the model."

"We read about Don Gino in the **San Francisco Chronicle**. Isn't he a criminal? Isn't he gay?"

"No, ladies, he is a patriot, a businessman and a dedicated gourmet. I suspect that he likes the ladies." They didn't look convinced. He was known as a gay man. Carvalho smiled. Things were sometimes not what they seemed.

"Where are you staying?" The three stewardesses smiled.

"I will be at the Fairmont. The penthouse suite." One stewardess wrote down the hotel. She wasn't smart enough to remember it.

She asked: "What is the penthouse."

"Ladies, come visit and see. We will have a gourmet treat." Montalban smiled. They thought he was just talking about dinner. He had other thoughts. Montalban loved San Francisco. The open atmosphere allowed gays and straights to co-exist. The airline stewardesses were among Montalban's San Francisco favorites. They were all over the downtown hotels. They all wanted a good time. Nothing else. He would not disappoint

"Will you have a friend?"

"Oh, yes, ladies I will have more than one friend." The stewardesses giggled.

No one knew that Montalban received his gastronomical education from an American writer Jim Harrison. He was meeting Harrison at Gary Danko's for dinner.

When Harrison sent Montalban a ticket to his winter home in Sonoita, he wondered what the famous writer was doing in the middle of nowhere in Southern Arizona. They regularly talked on the telephone. Harrison is a favorite of the fish, hunt and shoot crowd and Montalban spends a month each year with Harrison in Livingston Montana as well as a few weeks in Arizona.

They tour the Sonoita wineries. There were three local wineries when they started their intense drinking sprees; there are now twelve full-scale wineries. Gilliland Wineries makes a Biscuter Merlot and a Montalban Chardonnay. Everyone is afraid to make a Harrison wine. He might shoot up the place.

Their friendship is based on writing and gourmet dining. Harrison goes hunting while Montalban walks next to him talking literature. It is a strange, but enduring, friendship.

After taking a cab to the Fairmont Hotel, Montalban spends some time taking notes. He was in the middle of an adventure that lent itself to one of his novels. Maybe it would be his next mystery. He couldn't cast Trevor Blake III as the protagonists. He was simply too inept. Don Gino was a friend and dangerous. Maybe he could cast Jim Harrison as the grizzled private eye. Harrison had the grizzled part down. He also had only one eye. As Montalban stared out his penthouse suite he formulated his latest novel. It involved the Mafia and al Qaeda terrorists. Georges Simenon used his life to write crime novels. Why not Montalban? He loved to gaze out the window at the Yerba Buena gardens. His suite was just over 300 square feet, which was twice the size of his Barcelona apartment.

As a former Communist, he felt guilty. There was a knock on the door. Montalban opened it.

"Ah, my friend the famous writer." Harrison and Montalban embraced.

Jim Harrison looked at him askance. Harrison had only one good eye; he dressed like a bum and talked like a longshoreman. Harrison handed Montalban a book, **Jim Harrison: The Raw And The Cooked, Adventures Of A Roving Gourmet**.

Montalban said: "Ah, a favorite of mine. Now I have two copies. The first is dog-eared. Thank you kindly."

Harrison said: "Asshole." Montalban smiled.

"Ah, Jim Harrison has not changed. We need to catch up."

They sat and drank a bottle of Royal Lochnagar twelve year old scotch while talking about literary, if not always, financial fame. Then it was off to Gary Danko's.

The cab ride to 800 North Point went through North Beach, the Italian section of San Francisco that was once home to beat writer Jack Kerouac. Then they entered the restaurant with six 5 star Michelin ratings. The Michelin guide called Gary Danko's: "Perfection by the Bay." They were right.

Jim Harrison is so well known among restaurant aficionados that he has his own table at Gary Danko's. When he walked in, at least a dozen patrons smiled and spontaneously clapped. Before they settled into their table, Harrison talked to five tables. Harrison was well known for writing about Danko's tasting menu. He wrote that it was the best menu in the world. No one disagreed.

"Gentlemen, we have your table." They hadn't identified themselves. The maître'd, Reginald, knew both men by sight. Gary Danko came out from the kitchen. He was smiling in his white chef's jacket.

"Jim and Senor Montalban, welcome."

"Don't I get a title?" Harrison asked.

"You do, Senor Asshole." They all laughed.

They began with a glass of the Pierre Marlet Champaign to accompany their crispy Farm Egg with white polenta, mushrooms, and pancetta followed by a seared filet of beef. The requisite sides and a chocolate praline parfait followed by cappuccinos completed the sumptuous meal. The five wines with the varied courses was an indication why Gary Danko's was the number one San Francisco restaurant.

"I see Jim that you are eating light."

"Yes, I am my friend."

"Should we order more succulent treats?"

"Ah, the Spanish, don't you mean let's sample some more of Gary Danko's cuisine?"

They continued with another meal as they nibbled on Golden Osetra caviar and progressed to Green garlic soup with Duck Rillette and Chive oil, followed by Horseradish crusted salmon and a seared filet of beef with potatoes. Harrison lectured Montalban on the dangers of red meat. Montalban responded by ordering an entre of roast loin of bison with King Trumpet Mushrooms, Cipolline onions and Wild Nettle Spatzle. It was time to stop. They thanked Danko and left to wander down to Ghirardelli Square. They didn't make it.

"Jim, we need an Irish coffee."

Harrison agreed. They walked into the Buena Vista Café. It was packed. There was one table by the window. They grabbed it. The Irish coffees came and the subject of al Qaeda came up. The plot was explained to Harrison. He rubbed his scraggly beard. He looked around the room with his one good eye for women. There were more beautiful women than one eye could handle. He lit a cigarette. He reached into his brief case. He pulled out a book. It was a copy of his acclaimed novel, **Legends of the Fall**. Harrison read from it: "The vulture had just eaten a rattler run over by a truck....more vultures would arrive until the man's dying would have an audience." Harrison continued. "There you have it. The solution to your crime."

Montalban looked perplexed. He said: "Is there a point my friend?"

"The point is very clear. The vulture must think he is in charge and his other vulture friends will flock to the site. You can then kill all of them."

This made sense. Montalban couldn't resist one comment. "You know Jim, Brad Pitt was in the movie from your book. Any thoughts?"

Harrison angrily said: "One thought, those bastards ruined my book. The screenplay was dogshit. It reads like a fairy tale."

"What about Anthony Hopkins?"

Harrison smiled: "There is no better person to have at your side in a drunken brawl."

"What's your complaint Jim?"

"Susan Shilliday and that twit William D. Wittliff ruined the book. The screenplay sucked. I took the money and retreated to Montana. They killed my fucking book."

Montalban reminded Harrison that the movie won an Academy Award for cinematography.

Harrison said: "A pretty picture does not make a masterpiece."

Montalban said: "I hope that you write better than you speak." They laughed.

"You should feel good about the money."

"I feel better about drinking and hanging out with Marlon Brando."

"We need to zero in on the assignment." Montalban pulled out his notes on the al Qaeda San Francisco adventure. Harrison spent an hour looking at the file. They left the Buena Vista after three Irish coffees.

Harrison wandered off toward the North Beach bars. He was later spotted in City Lights Books talking to Lawrence Ferlenghetti. A signed copy of **A Coney Island of the Mind** was under Harrison's arm as he waddled down Broadway to a topless bar. It was all about research. Montalban took a cab to Market Street to sit with the homeless, the party animals and the tourists. They would provide grist for his writing.

Neither Montalban nor Harrison needed to worry about their safety. Three Samoans shadowed each of them. When two young gang bangers began walking behind Harrison making threatening remarks, he turned and laughed at them. Harrison had only one good eye, the other one looked like it could eat you. The gang bangers hollered:

"Hey, old man we gonna kick you scrawny ass." That sounded pretty strange.

Harrison turned around. He was a scrawny two hundred and twenty pounds. He also still liked to fight. He would show the punks. He didn't realize that he was an old man.

"Come on assholes." They advanced toward Harrison.

A group of Samoans appeared to materialize out of nowhere. The Samoans lifted the punks off the street and quietly took them into an alley. They beat them badly. A purple handkerchief was left for them to dab their wounds. The Samoans came out of the alley. They smiled. Harrison was pissed. He didn't need help. He told the Samoans that he would have beaten the shit out of the punks.

Harrison said: "Tell Don Gino thanks. Just like in my book, **Legends of the Fall**, the great feeling of revenge is still with me." Harrison bowed to the Samoans and hailed a cab. It was a short cab ride to the Saloon on lower Grant Street.

He walked into the Saloon and spent the night listening to Ron Thompson and the Resistors. Harrison had a tab at the Saloon for twenty-five years. He racked up a $500 bar bill. He bought two rounds for the one hundred plus patrons. There was no concern. He was good for it. He grabbed a cab back to the St. Francis Hotel and spent the rest of the night in the cocktail lounge singing Irish songs with salesmen from Iowa and Nebraska. He hadn't checked in to his room. When he did the bellhop took him to a penthouse suite. Harrison complained. The bellhop told him that Don Gino insisted he enjoy the penthouse. As he walked into the sumptuous penthouse suite, Harrison noticed a file on the Mission Delores. Don Gino asked for his opinion. Where and when would the terrorists strike? He took notes and opened his computer. An hour later, Harrison sent Don Gino an e-mail suggesting what must be done. He discovered the al Qaeda target.

Harrison realized Don Gino was doing something related to American security. Montalban had gone into great detail about a San Francisco terrorist plot. Harrison thought that this was the book he should be writing.

As Harrison sat down on his penthouse suite balcony, he had an idea. They were all missing a key element of the plot. Follow the money.

The plot was thickening. No one realized that Don Gino had everything in hand.

Montalban knew a great deal about the San Francisco Mafia figure. His name was Don Gino Landry. He was also Montalban's friend. Hammadi asked the Spanish author for his help, he had no idea that Montalban and Don Gino were long time acquaintances. Montalban could see that Don Gino had everything in hand. He also observed that Don Gino was angry. The Don was intent upon revenge. It was not a good thing for the terrorists. It was wonderful for Montalban and Harrison. They would have material for their next books. Life sometimes provides the grist for the writing mill. Montalban had to be careful not to write a sentence that way. It was trite. Then again much of fiction was trite. Much of life was trite.

CHAPTER THIRTY-SEVEN
Trevor Blake III Returns

"Intelligence without ambition is a bird without wings."
Salvador Dali

I t had been a week since Trevor Blake III got off the plane from Barcelona. He was a shadowy figure in the midst of the al Qaeda case. He took a cab to his Chestnut Street apartment. He charged the fare with a nice tip on his Platinum American Express card. There was no sign of Bennie and Bertie. They liked to check the building. After all they owned it. The eight apartments provided a positive cash flow of just over $10,000 a month. Bennie was a financial genius. He began buying houses in San Francisco years ago. He was now a multi-millionaire. Trevor vowed to be nice to him. Bertie was a good cook, a health nut and a black belt. Bennie thought the term "a book" was a country in Eastern Europe. They were wonderful people for white bread conservative Republicans. They would take America back. Mitt Romney failed. Bennie had a plan. He would take America back.

Trevor entered his apartment. There was a note on the kitchen table. "Call Me, Joyce." He threw it away. His sometimes girl friend, Joyce Byers, was not only a San Francisco police officer, but she monitored Trevor's life. He would get in touch with her. But not for some time. He would pretend that he was on a case. He had some idea what was going on with the al Qaeda terrorist case. He still needed to connect some key points.

After making sure the mail was picked up, and the apartment was locked, Trevor changed into his Burberry five-pocket denim trousers. They cost his last girl friend over four hundred dollars. She bought him two pairs and Trevor dumped her. He kept the jeans. A two hundred dollar Tommy Bahama shirt completed the GQ look. No doubt he appeared younger than forty-one. He looked strange walking down Chestnut Street with his box of mail. The famous private eye needed to pay his bills. It was also time to read the fan mail. Or more likely to sort the bills. The Starbucks on Chestnut was full of twenty and thirty something's. This made Trevor nervous. He was forty-one, but he lied about his age. Who doesn't?

After ordering a light mocha, only one hundred thirty calories, Trevor found a seat in the corner. The ladies would get a day free from his amorous intentions. There was work to do. As he went through the mail, Trevor looked up. He had a visitor.

"Hello Dickhead." It was none other than the lovely Chastain Johnson. She looked good. Her tight Versace leggings with her Jimmy Choo spiked high heel boots made her look gorgeous. Her Custo mini cashmere sweater was two sizes too small with a diamond stud in her belly. Her breasts jiggled. The observant private eye notices everything.

"Hello Chastain, the undercover FBI agent dressed as a Versace look a like."

"Trevor, you look like shit. Burberry jeans. That is cool. A Tommy Bahama shirt! You look like every other sixty-year-old guy. I think you are the guy who inspired the name Timmy Bahama."

"There is no Timmy Bahama, Chastain."

"There is for you. Once again, why are you wearing that outfit?"

"I am undercover."

"What do you know about undercover, unless it is with some bimbo under the blankets in that hole you call an apartment. You look like you have a headlight on your face saying 'I'm the moron undercover.'"

"Nasty, nasty, you still haven't forgiven yourself for sleeping with me."

"My one mistake, I am waiting for Mickey Rooney. When he's not available you will be in the mix. Maybe!"

Trevor thought for a moment. It wasn't good to be second to Mickey Rooney. He was ninety-two years old.

"Chastain, do we need to talk? Or did you come in to stare at my body?"

"In your dreams, asshole."

"Actually I prefer Dickhead."

"Let's get done to business." Chastain lit another cigarette. There was a no smoking sign overhead. If you are with the FBI no one will say a word. They didn't.

Trevor said: "I am not sure where the al Qaeda folks are hiding. That Smith fellow was caught. Or so they say. There is someone close to us on the loose."

"Sometimes Trevor, things are more complicated than you are aware. That's because you think with your penis."

"Ah, you get it, penis envy."

Chastain got serious. "Here's what we need to do. The famous Spanish author Manuel Vazquez Montalban is reading at the San Francisco Public Library. You need to find out what he knows."

"The only thing he knows, Chastain, is how to eat a free meal at Gary Danko's with some over the hill writer."

"So you followed him."

"Yes!"

"And."

"It appears that he has some inside information. The plot is to bomb a San Francisco tourist attraction."

"I know that Trevor. Which one?"

"Who knows?"

Chastain said: "We have the Golden Gate Bridge, the Transamerica Building, City Hall, the Ferry Building, Old Saint Mary's Cathedral and the Bank of California building under heavy surveillance. It doesn't appear to be any of these sites."

"I have an idea. I will share it with you tomorrow." Trevor smiled. He took his box of mail and walked back to the apartment. Bertie was driving away. She had a huge vacuum sticking out of the back seat. Not bad. She cleaned the apartment. He breathed a sigh of relief. There would be no lectures on prescription medicines, over the counter pills or Trevor's sex life. Hallelujah. He dropped the mail in his apartment.

Trevor started his car. It was a miracle. It started. It had been sitting for six weeks. Then he saw the charging slip from the San Francisco Police Department. Joyce Byers charged his car while he was away. She also prevented it from being towed. He might have to take Joyce to dinner.

After driving up Fillmore and turning on Haight Street, Trevor felt at home. He parked at Haight and Ashbury and took out his handicapped sign. It was courtesy of Joyce Byers. She joked that he was handicapped in the bedroom. Trevor hoped it was a joke. The two fat guys, Ben and Jerry, stared at him. They were on a large billboard advertising a new ice cream flavor Coffee Coffee, Buzz Buzz. Were these guys kidding?

As he walked up the stairs to his second floor office, Trevor smelled coffee. Not just any coffee. It was a rich, dark roast. He walked in as Guitar Jac filled a brand new Lamborghini Coffee Maker. The sale sticker was still on the side of the machine. It read: "$1750."

"Welcome back, Trevor, my parents bought a better coffee maker, a Siphon Bar."

"Good to see you, Jac. Can I ask what a Siphon Bar costs?"

"It's twenty grand, Trevor."

"Does that come with one or two hookers?"

"I'll ask my mother."

"Come to think of it, don't."

"Have you done some work on the case, Jac?"

"I have it figured out." When Guitar Jac graduated from Stanford, he was a dedicated detective. H was also a Phi Beta Kappa.

"Enlighten me."

Jac took a bulging folder out of his desk. "Here it is, the plan to blow up the Mission Delores." The surprise on Trevor's face was evident. He had missed al Qaeda's most obvious target. Don Gino would not be pleased.

The idea of blowing up the Mission Delores in Don Gino's neighborhood was more than just a slap in the face. It was a means of humiliating the Don. He wouldn't he angry. He would be furious. He would take immediate action. Trevor smiled. The terrorists were toast.

"I have also found a mole, a double agent or should I say a traitor in the mix," Guitar Jac said. There is no doubt that Guitar Jac had too much college. He liked to say things in five sentences and a hundred words when one sentence would do. Trevor looked for an hour at the file. He left his office and walked down to Emilio's for coffee.

The file revealed something he had missed. There was a "three' in the terrorist file. What did it mean? Three kept showing up on encrypted e-mails. There was nothing more just the number three. How weird was that? Trevor couldn't figure it out. Then he noticed that the number three was at times in Spanish. That was even stranger.

Before Trevor drove home, he stopped across the street at Ben and Jerry's and bought a quart of Chocolate Peppermint Crunch. The two fat guys sure knew how to make ice cream. They needed to rethink their pictures on the Haight Ashbury billboard. It was liable to drive people away from drugs and alcohol. It was time to reassess the case.

When he entered the apartment, Trevor noticed the lamp in the front room was moved. He stopped. He looked around. Something was amiss. Then a body slammed into Trevor. The lamp tipped over, a light bulb shattered, glass filled the floor. Trevor raised his right arm; a fist caught him square on the jaw. He threw a light punch as a blackjack hit the side of his head. Then everything went dark.

The sun was setting, a sliver of light entered the front room and Trevor woke to shadows on the wall. He head ached. His body hurt. He had no idea how much time had elapsed. It was getting dark.

Trevor woke up. He rubbed his head. He messaged his neck. He went to the kitchen for a bag of ice. He looked on his desk. The file marked: "Al Qaeda Targets" was missing. Trevor smiled. He had placed his targets material in a file reading: "Bertie's Non Fat, Low Calorie, Sugarless Chocolate Cake." That recipe and others were in the file "Al Qaeda Targets." Trevor laughed. The intruder ran off with Bertie's cake recipe.

After checking the locks, reconnecting the burglar alarm system and looking for electronic bugs, Trevor sat down to business. The al Qaeda file was devastating. It was a roadmap for the imminent attack. No one knew the mastermind. Don Gino wasn't aware of the depth of the duplicity in the terrorists' planning. Trevor would stop the attack.

Trevor drove back to his office. It was time to get Guitar Jac's thoughts on al Qaeda. He knew more about terrorism than most government officials. That was the good news. The bad news is that he wanted to immediately kill the terrorists. Guitar Jac thought justice was a country in Eastern Europe. There was no need for prosecution.

Trevor walked into the office. He looked at the picture of Janis Joplin and smiled. He looked at the Van Morrison poster and frowned. He looked at Guitar Jac.

"What do you think of the file?" No telling what Guitar Jac thought. He was stone faced. "Well, Trevor, does my file help?"

"This plan complicates things, Jac."

"Yes it does. Do you have any idea about the traitor?"

"None." Trevor looked uncomfortable.

"Where did you get the plan Jac?"

"You won't believe it. On the Internet."

"Did you break any laws."

"Yes," Jac smiled.

"Good, let's take a look."

The e-mail read: "Look for moles who are officials, well educated and angry." There was a second page that read: "The police will help." There was another detailed file. There was too much information.

Trevor looked at it for a long time. "Well as far as I can see this e-mail narrows our suspects to about 100,000 San Franciscans."

"What do you make of it, Jac?"

"The traitor is very close to Don Gino. Maybe there is more than one mole or traitor." Guitar Jac got up and left the office.

Trevor pulled out his napkins. He arranged the clues. They had a logical sequence. The traitor was in Barcelona and would come into San Francisco. Trevor wasn't worried. Don Gino would handle it. He had missed something. What was it?

It took some time for Trevor to digest the al Qaeda file on the Mission Delores. They had done their homework. The problem was finding the explosives. There were some people in the mix that Trevor couldn't identify. He believed that they might be locals. The individual that had the depth of knowledge about the twenty-one Missions that made up the famous El Camino Real was Detective Richard Sanchez. He majored in California history at San Francisco State. For his senior thesis, Sanchez visited every Mission. Trevor called him. They talked for an hour. Not only did Trevor figure out what was going on, but also Detective Sanchez was ready to bust the al Qaeda terrorists. Things were coming together. The trail that linked the Missions was a Catholic Shrine to the pioneering Franciscan religious order.

That was the first clue in the file. The second was the suggestion that the al Qaeda terrorists had someone inside. That puzzled Trevor.

Then Trevor realized that the traitor was in his midst. He had figured it out.

Finally.

CHAPTER THIRTY-EIGHT

Don Gino Returns To
San Francisco

"Give me two hours a day of activity, and I'll take the other twenty-two in dreams." Salvador Dali

The U. S. Customs Inspector, Willie Wong, came out and escorted Don Gino Landry to a private lane.

"Good morning, sir." The customs inspector smiled.

"Mr. Wong, it is good to see you. How is the family? Is your boy doing well at LaSalle College Prep?"

"He is and I thank you for the tuition."

"It is my pleasure."

"Did you see that Willie Jr. ran for more than a hundred yards in their last football game? Thanks to you, he is destined for UC, Berkeley."

"If you need another school, I will arrange an interview with Notre Dame. Coach Brian Kelly is a good friend. There are never too many running backs."

"Don Gino, I have a packet for you." Wong handed a bulging folder to the Don. He smiled and stamped his passport.

"Thank you, Mr. Wong."

"My pleasure." Don Gino walked out and a chauffeur in a purple tuxedo held a sign: "Signore Don Gino." It was a nice touch. The respect that Italians demonstrated toward older people was part of the Don's heritage. He followed the chauffeur to a purple limousine.

Don Gino said: "Take me to my other home."

"It's serious business then, boss."

"Yes, it is. We have our work cut out for us."

"We do." Don Gino pulled the large folder out. He began to read.

The road to the Mission District was punctuated by music from Beethoven's 5th and 9th. The Don smiled. He was home. He was overjoyed. This was his business residence. He had serious business to conclude.

After walking into his Lapidge St. home, he turned on the stereo and put on a Vivaldi CD. The music calmed him. He loved it. The five bedrooms, four baths home cost almost three million dollars. It was the Mission District's most expensive residence. It was Don Gino's secret hideaway. His primary residence on Washington Street was being renovated. His was completely redoing and extending the Salvador Dali rooms. He had to forget about his Dali collection. It was time to deal with the terrorists. They would experience his wrath.

The Mission District house was cold. Don Gino turned on the heat. He walked into the kitchen. A note read: "Refrigerator full." He opened it. There was a meal that came directly from Gary Danko's. A note explained how to prepare everything. It was signed "Gary."

After unlocking the door to his private study, Don Gino turned on the computer. The encrypted message told him what he needed to know. Inspector Domingo-Mercedes was arriving the next day to assist in the case. It would not be long before the terrorist cell was destroyed.

It was time for dinner. Don Gino needed to think. He walked out front and asked the Samoans to take the night off. He would be safe. That turned out to be a big mistake. After eating the dinner from Gary Danko, Don Gino put on his purple smoking jacket. He settled in with the new Easy Rawlins novel. Walter Mosley had brought his famous detective back complete with Raymond Alexander known affectionately as Mouse. Don Gino wished that he could affect Mouse's menacing personality. He tried. But he was too good a Catholic.

Just about the time Easy Rawlins was solving the crime. Don Gino's front door exploded. Three men in masks hustled into the house. They grabbed Don Gino, they blindfolded him and took him out the back door to a SUV. They drove toward Golden Gate Park.

After an hour, the SUV stopped at the Japanese Tea Garden. The three men wearing masks untied Don Gino and pointed for him to go into the Tea Garden. They had fear in their eyes. They shivered with thoughts of what might happen to them. Don Gino didn't say a word. He didn't have to as his body language radiated rage. Not fear. Just outright rage. He would deal with these men in due time.

He walked into the Japanese Tea Garden. He was wearing a purple smoking jacket over sleek purple satin pajamas. He had on purple slippers. No one looked twice. This was after all San Francisco.

"Don Gino," a low voice said.

"To what do I owe this inconvenience to and why?" Don Gino glared. He was furious.

"This is to remind you my friend to keep to your own affairs. Allah has a plan for America. If you in any way disrupt it, you will be dealt with accordingly."

Don Gino looked at this little, sniveling, piece of shit from the Middle East. He was going to right this wrong. The small man wore a scarf to hide his face. What was he up to? The little bastard would pay.

The small man continued to speak. After he lectured the Don for ten minutes. He pulled out a Glock 26 handgun.

"I may be going to my maker," Don Gino said. "But, remember my friend, my reach spreads far and wide."

The small man laughed. "I'm pointing a gun at your head getting ready to kill you." The man paused. "You have the nerve to tell me that your influence is far and wide as you prepare to die. You are a sick bastard."

"I don't think you realize your predicament." Don Gino smiled. He didn't look nervous.

The small man looked on angrily. "You are some old faggot destined to die." The man smiled. He raised his gun. He pointed it at Don Gino's face. Suddenly the gunman's head exploded. The man fell to the ground. Don Gino walked over to the street.

A small Asian man left one of the columns in front of the Japanese Tea Garden. He smiled and waved at Don Gino. The small Asian man got into a taxicab. Emilio was more than a cat burglar. He was also an expert marksman.

Don Gino did not suffer fools well. He looked at the small Arab man on the ground. Good riddance.

Don Gino was in Golden Gate Park. He was in a purple bathrobe. There was a dead body nearby. He was alone. He had no wallet. He had no identification. He had no plan. A young kid pulled up in a Volkswagen. After all Don Gino in a purple bathrobe in a park in San Francisco appeared normal.

"Hey, man you need a ride?"

"I do," Don Gino said.

"Hey dude, that is some get up, I'm tripping."

Don Gino said: "What do you do?"

"I'm a D. J., I go to San Francisco State. Marketing man, it's the only way to go."

"Do you have a name young man?"

"Call me M. C. Honky." The kid laughed.

"What is your music like?"

"Here's a free CD, I take the real old stuff like Glenn Miller and mix it with Jay Z. I have a show on KSFS at State. It's bitchin' man. Try to listen. The studio is primitive, I'm cool."

Don Gino looked at the CD. "I see."

When they arrived in the Mission District, Don Gino said: "Wait, just a moment." He went into the house and came out with ten one hundred dollar bills.

"Have a nice time kid."

"Cool." The kid drove off.

A week later M. C. Honky received radio airplay. In a month, he had a contract with Capitol Records. A week later he had a number one rap hit.

San Francisco State's KSFS received a half a million dollar studio make over. The disc jockey's room was wallpapered in a light purple with white stripes, all the new engineering equipment was purple on white panels. It is state of the art. The donor remains anonymous.

Don Gino made a series of phone calls. It was time to call on his old friend Matt Luman. The retired entertainer answered his phone on the first ring.

"Hello my friend, I wondered when you would call?"

Don Gino said: "Thank you, I'm listening to 'I'm Movin' On' as we speak." This was a reference to Luman's top ten hit.

Luman said: "I will have my private plane ready in an hour. I will see you tomorrow morning. I'll be at the Fairmont on Nob Hill. Leave an encrypted flash drive for me at the front desk."

Don Gino said: "Bring the briefing materials. We have a lot of work to do my friend." Matt hung up. He noticed that Don Gino sounded agitated. That was not a good sign.

As he prepared to meet the terrorist's head on, Don Gino spent half the night organizing his plan. He knew exactly what he wanted. It would take Trevor Blake III to set the trap. Trevor would never realize that he was the catalyst to preventing the terrorists from blowing up the historical-religious targets. He would also receive the credit. Don Gino hated the spotlight.

CHAPTER THIRTY-NINE

Zandra Filippi: Cyberspace Protection For Don Gino

"Erotic fantasies take up much of the time I do not devote to painting." Salvador Dali

Zandra Filippi looked out from her office at 1000 California Street. Her dream was to become the most famous cyberspace investigator in the world. When she was stressed, she looked out her twentieth floor window. She loved the view of the Bay Bridge, the downtown business district, and the sight of the Oakland Hills was magnificent. The view of the hills reflected the small forest that obscured Berkley. She got up to read a one-page fax. The message was a clear sign that there was terrorist trouble. Don Gino Landry, the U.S. government, notably the CIA, and the FBI, as well as the famous San Francisco private eye Trevor Blake III needed her help. How could anyone fax her that Trevor was famous or for that matter intelligent? Zandra couldn't figure it out. He was the only person that she had trouble with during an investigation.

Every time Zandra heard from Trevor, there were ridiculous requests for information. That wasn't the problem. It was all the sexual innuendos. Someone needed to teach Trevor manners, protocol, suave behavior as well as a lesson in how to dress. It was too big a job for Zandra. He kept inviting her to do research in his apartment. He didn't understand no. He told Zandra that "no" was a country in Eastern Europe. He laughed at all his lame jokes. This trait was a carry over from hanging out with his brother-in-law Bennie.

Trevor drove her crazy and she hated working with him. Don Gino insisted. When the Don insists everyone listens.

She was being asked to work with Don Gino on a case involving national security. Since leaving her job with the Rolling Stones, Zandra's business, Filippi Security, investigated corporate and government security leaks. She had come a long way since working for the Stones. Her computer expertise, enhanced by a prestigious MIT PHD, was well known in corporate and governmental circles. Now she had to consider working with a friend, Don Gino Landry. He was also her financial benefactor.

Her firm began in 2009 with seed money from the Rolling Stones and Don Gino. While she worked part-time for the Rolling Stones, she was putting her considerable computer skills to work. She consulted as a contract agent with various law enforcement agencies. By early 2010, she was a "special contract agent" with the U. S. Department of Homeland Security, the FBI, the CIA and various state law enforcement agencies. The "special contract agent" status allowed her to wire tap telephones and computers as well as to conduct any type of surveillance that she deemed necessary to American security. Homeland Security officials told her that in the event of a media storm, they would disavow her. She was comfortable with that. Zandra could vanish into cyberspace.

She invented a technology known as metadata, which allows for surveillance on cell phones. Metadata follows texts, photos and e-mails into a series of remote servers that are bounced back to Zandra's sophisticated computer fortress. The National Security Administration hired Filippi to build a computer system to spy on e-mails. She did. Then she resigned. She copyrighted her technology. There were major investors hoping to take her technology into the marketplace. She turned down the venture capitalists. She decided to take on some new clients.

Zandra was hired by corporate entities Apple and Microsoft. She also designed a software program to provide surveillance for designer stores. She became famous when a Cartier watch store in a large Chevy Chase Md. Mall was robbed of 221 watches worth a million dollars. She helped local law enforcement track the cell phone demand from the robbers. Zandra's technological skills allowed her to extract the messages from a series of servers. She became known in the media as the "Dataveillance Queen." Then the FBI, CIA and Homeland Security hired Zandra as a contract consultant. Don Gino desperately needed to implement her skills.

She was uncertain about Don Gino's proposal. Her fee was $250,000 for the month long research and intelligence gathering assignment. Some of what Don Gino required appeared on the edge of the law. That didn't bother her. Zandra was told that she would have to work with Trevor Blake III. That bothered her. She didn't care for him, his investigative skills were minimal and his legendary status with the ladies was in his mind. Trevor was cute and charming. He was intelligent, but he missed the key elements in a crime. If the suspect was a woman, Trevor looked at her breasts not her motives. When he solved the murders of the Start Me Up drummers, he was famous for fifteen minutes. Fortunately, that time had passed.

Filippi Security was a name designed to obscure the corporation's skills. For more than two years Zandra worked with the U. S. Department of Homeland Security to defend against Cyber criminals. At the 2013 Cyber Security Awareness Month celebration, she was presented with a special award for uncovering Julian Assange's Wiki Leaks website. She also alerted the government to the sensitive U. S. military and diplomatic documents that Wiki Leaks released. They were embarrassing to President Barack Obama. Zandra sent a number of explanations for their release. The President's press secretary used Filippi's material verbatim. Zandra didn't receive any credit. She also identified, Bradley Manning, the U. S. Army soldier who was arrested in May 2010 on the suspicion of providing Wiki Leaks with material. Filippi was the unidentified source breaking the case. Since that time she worked extensively as a contract agent for the FBI and the CIA. She uncovered the nefarious deeds of Edward Snowden who leaked information on government surveillance by NSA. It was another of

Filippi's success stories. She identified him to the CIA long before the press broke the story.

There was no one who disgusted Zandra more than Snowden. Unless, of course, you mentioned the name Manning. When she talked about Snowden, Filippi pointed out that he was a high school dropout who wanted notoriety. Snowden was a twenty-nine year old computer geek, who leaked material that resulted in two CIA agents dying. He gave no reason and had no rationale for his leaks. Those agents were Filippi's lovers. She wanted justice for them. They were CIA operatives who went missing in Chechnya and Belarus due to Manning's leaks. Snowden's leaks endangered American security. Filippi helped the U. S. Justice Department in the case that they prepared against Snowden. The little bastard was in hiding in Russia. The little prick deserved cold food, big nasty women and stupid Russian bureaucrats. That was punishment enough. He also had to deal with Vladimir Putin. That was the final insult.

The Attorney General, Eric Holder, came out to San Francisco and spent a day in Zandra's office. She took him and his group of agents to see her secret computer setup in her apartment. They listened and watched as a Russian feed that had Putin ordering dinner. Putin sat like he had a fork up his ass. He looked uptight and uncomfortable. He also acted privileged. When Putin asked for fresh not frozen cabbage, he made a threatening hand gesture. Putin hollered: "It's jail, if it's not fresh." When the food arrived, it was as boring as the Russian leader. Attorney General Holder brought along a dozen agents who then set up a computer network linked to her apartment's super computer. They received more secret worldwide information than the CIA or the National Security Agency provided. President Obama praised her patriotism. The President also told Holder to bring the Attorney General's office outside the scope of the United States. Holder smiled. He had his new source of information. The lovely Zandra Filippi.

She knew everything about Edward Snowden. It didn't take long for Zandra and the Attorney General to identify his leaks. At that point Eric Holder had Zandra sign a confidential agreement as a contract agent. Her newly established fee was in excess of half a million dollars. It was money well spent. Zandra was patriotic. She hated Fox TV News and its right wing moralists. Her job was to expose terrorist activity to help Don Gino and Trevor Blake III solve the crime. The only problem is that she had to work with Trevor Blake III. Yuck!

What troubled Zandra was Snowden's penchant for defining morality. He was one of more than 1.4 million Americans with a top security clearance. Zandra wondered when the government would learn. She spent hours tracking Snowden and helped put the CIA on his trail. Now he was stuck in a Moscow airport. Zandra felt vindicated.

From her apartment on Chestnut Street, two blocks from Trevor, she worked on the sensitive political issues. The 1000 California Street suite was for show not for serious work. No one knew the extent of Filippi's involvement with national security. The thriving business cut into her social life. She would jog down Chestnut Street late at night and see Trevor bringing in beautiful young women into his apartment. They couldn't be very smart. They were young and gorgeous. They were also a little overweight. Trevor liked them that way. They were also clueless.

When Don Gino sent a letter requesting her help, she thought about it for a moment. No one says no to the Purple Don. She called him and accepted his offer. Then when the Attorney General, Eric Holder, called, she neglected to tell him that she was also working for Don Gino. Holder was a controversial figure with a penchant for press leaks. She didn't need any more attention. The less the government knew, the better it was for the investigative process.

As her fax machine buzzed with material sent from Don Gino, Zandra was intrigued She hadn't worked a case involving al Qaeda. This would be exciting. Her only fear was that Trevor Blake III would foul up the investigation. He had solved the murder of the Start Me Up drummers and earned praise from the Rolling Stones. How had he solved a case? Zandra couldn't figure it out. He was a good-looking, lightweight whose only strength was seducing young Barbie's with store bought breasts and no brains.

Zandra walked out into her small kitchen. She fixed a cup of green tea. After spending more than two hours going over Don Gino's files, she had a good idea about how and where the al Qaeda cell targeted a local landmark. She walked down to her garage. Her Lexus roared to life and she drove off to the Mission District. She parked near Mission Delores. She took out her I pad and began taking notes. She didn't see the small Asian man standing behind a tree. He smiled. The terrorists were in for a surprise. Emilio was ready to help the beautiful young girl. She could take care of herself. If she needed help Emilio was in the shadows. He cracked his knuckles. He flexed his arms. He couldn't wait to help the young lady.

CHAPTER FORTY

Don Gino Calls A Meeting

"A true artist is not one who is inspired, but one who inspires others." Salvador Dali

When Don Gino woke up from a long nap, he was well rested. He recovered from the Golden Gate Park nightmare. He also forwarded a one hundred thousand dollar donation to upgrade the Japanese Tea Garden. They painted a wall for purple Japanese plants. It was call the DGL wall. His psyche remained outraged. He looked at the notes on the table next to his bed. He had written his notes in a series of poems: "The End." He smiled. The title was fitting.

He took a series of papers with the copious notes in poetic form and prepared his plan. He had carefully analyzed the threat. Now he would neutralize it.

Don Gino went directly to the phone and made a call. He informed the person who answered the phone that he would require certain supplies. He dictated the list. He required small nails, a specialized rope, and a number of ties for the hands and feet as well as large hoods. The person on the other end said: "This order is our privilege to fill. There will be no charge." Don Gino smiled. He had work to do.

Don Gino had his driver take him to the 3rd Street Warehouse. The Irvington Brothers owned it, and after their untimely death everyone was surprised that the warehouse was left in their will to Don Gino Landry. The family protested. The will was ironclad. The Purple Don owned the 3rd Street Warehouse.

He loved the 3rd Street Warehouse in the old days. It was full of longshoremen, union workers who loaded and unloaded trucks of fruits, vegetable, beer, wine and imported meats. Now it is the land of the yuppie. It is called South Beach. The San Francisco Giants built a ballpark, condo developments threatened the view and there were more Starbucks in this part of San Francisco than anyplace else.

Red's Java House was the only remaining place serving good food and bad coffee. The rehab people had a restaurant that they called Delancey Street. It served some of the best food in the city and gave the drunks and drug addicts a second chance. Don Gino anonymously donated a million dollars a year to the Delancey Street Foundation. The Don hated publicity. He also hated yuppies, developers, new age folks, vegans and gluten free types. He made an exception for Bennie and Bertie. This was after all San Francisco. Those people didn't belong in the City. Jack Kerouac was turning over in his grave.

Don Gino spent an hour in his 3rd Street Warehouse keeping track of people on his encrypted Internet devices. The meeting was set at the Boulevard Restaurant a few blocks from the 3rd Street Warehouse. After stuffing a batch of papers in a large briefcase, Don Gino walked over to Market Street and down to the Boulevard restaurant. He loved walking in San Francisco. The fresh air, the people walking dogs, the scent of the sea and the sunlight filtering through the downtown buildings created a euphoric paradise.

As Don Gino walked into 1 Mission Street, Nancy Oakes came to greet him. When she opened the Boulevard in 1993, she had no idea that, other than Gary Danko, she had opened San Francisco's best restaurant.

"Greetings Don Gino."

He hugged her. "How is my favorite owner?"

"Things are going well thanks to Pat Kuleto."

"Ah," Don Gino said. "Mr. Kuleto the fashion designer turned restaurateur."

Don Gino looked around at Kuleto's timeless Belle Epoque inspired design. It was magnificent. The art nouveau at Boulevard evoked images of Barcelona.

"Do you still approve of the décor?"

"I do, Mr. Kuleto refurbished my humble second home in the Mission."

"Yes, I heard."

"Is the private room ready, Nancy?"

"It is. Follow me." She led Don Gino to the back of the restaurant where a door that looked like it was out of a Paris restaurant led to a brilliantly designed room. A table filled with white and red wines from Pat Kuleto's private winery highlighted the tables filled with hors d'ouvres. The bottles were breathing and ready to drink. Don Gino walked over to a couch where a sixteen-year-old bottle of Lagavulin Single Malt Scotch sat regally on a special table ready for the guests. Don Gino smiled in appreciation.

The head waiter, Edsel Ford, worked for three decades in San Francisco's finest restaurants. "Hello Don Gino." Edsel smiled and bowed.

"It's nice to see you Edsel." Don Gino gave him two hundred dollar bills.

"I will have my usual."

"Yes sir," Edsel went off to get more scotch.

Trevor Blake III arrived dressed in a Ralph Lauren leather jacket and his stylish five pocket Marc Jacobs's jeans were finished off with Tommy Bahama loafers. Trevor shaved closely to look younger. He loved to tell people that he was thirty-five. It sounded better than forty-one.

Don Gino said: "You have the over forty GQ look."

"Hello, my friend. I am here to bed Chastain Johnson."

"She will shoot your balls off before bedding you."

Like magic, Chastain walked into the room.

"Hello, Don Gino." She ignored Trevor.

"My dear young lady, please join us. Do you know Trevor?"

She looked with disdain. She smiled. "Yes. Unfortunately. He has on clothes that match. That in itself is a miracle."

Trevor said: "Don't you approve of my GQ look?"

"By G. Q. you mean genital quotient. You have a low rating in that area. Look at your colors, blue and black, you look like a god damned salesman."

323

"I am, I'm selling my body. Would you like to buy a small part of it?"

"I would. You can sell me your brain. It is the smallest thing in your body. What a minute, it is bigger than the penis. I won't purchase that. It doesn't work."

"Ah, Chastain, always the joker. You do remember our famous night."

"What I remember is my unmitigated bad judgment. I am Catholic, Trevor, guilt is my enemy. There is a special level of Dante's hell for my lack of judgment."

Don Gino said: "Spoken like a poet."

Trevor said: "Maybe, God was trying to tell you something."

Chastain said: "What, that I should give up bad sex."

Trevor smiled: "Isn't it better than no sex?"

"Sex, Trevor is in the mind of the beholder. Me, I love it long and exciting. Words that you need to look up in a fucking dictionary."

"You sound like a truck driver who has read too much Bukowski."

"Is he on Facebook?" Chastain looked stumped.

"You can't be that unaware or maybe you speak Spanish."

"Can you translate kiss my ass into English?"

Don Gino said: "Children, Children we have important business. Be civil. I understand that Matt Luman is helping you Chastain."

She smiled: "Yes he is a detecting genius." Chastain looked at Trevor. "Unlike some poseurs."

Trevor said: "Too much college, Chastain, too little time in bed with a real man."

"Remember Trevor I am still waiting for Mickey Rooney."

"Sounds like your speed, Chastain."

"Ok, how does kiss my ass sound the second time?"

"It sounds like you."

Don Gino said: "Shall we end the banter and work on the case? Chastain you have a meeting at a nearby location with Matt Luman. Go quickly. Learn the new facts and return." She left.

Matt and Zandra had a brief meeting scheduled. This impromptu meeting was hastily arranged near the Boulevard Restaurant, There was material on the San Francisco attack that needed assimilation. No one noticed Matt and Zandra talking quietly in the corner. Her phone rang. She had the location for the quick meeting.

The festive party atmosphere at the Boulevard continued with plentiful food and drink. No one paid attention to Zandra as she took a file from Don Gino and grabbed Matt to walk to the bar.

Zandra said: "We need to exit quickly." Matt looked at his sixteen-year-old Scotch. Some of it would go to waste. Oh, well it was for national security.

They left the Boulevard restaurant. No one noticed. Don Gino told Zandra to make it quick. Zandra jumped into a cab with Matt still complaining about leaving the Scotch behind. They were driven a few blocks to Red's Java House.

Zandra and Matt discussed the information on the CIA. What were they doing with the case? Why? They had information from four undercover CIA agents working with Luman and Filippi. The CIA realized that the San Francisco bombing was one that they had to help Don Gino and his crew solve.

They spent more than two hours going over the files. Then officials from Homeland Security entered Red's Java House. This small hamburger coffee emporium is a greasy spoon with a large group of open-air tables out back. The Homeland Security people ordered hamburgers and fries as Luman and Filipe took out their extensive files.

Homeland Security was transfixed by Filippi's beauty. She had lips like Mick Jagger. She had a body like Sofia Vergara. She had clothes from the Stella McCartney collection. Her figure was perfect. The plastic surgeon must have made a fortune.

She also had a warm, disarming personality. There was silence as the government official's oogled Zandra. Not a good idea. Her cooperation came from respect. Matt decided to set the record straight with a proper introduction for Miss Filippi.

Luman said: "Let me introduce Zandra Filippi. She is a PhD in Middle Eastern History and Computer studies. Then she left academic life to work for the Rolling Stones. She was fired. She is now my personal assistant. She also owns a security consulting firm."

The Homeland Security official looked surprised. He thought that Zandra was little more than a secretary. He was shocked that she was Luman's assistant.

Luman said; "Let me correct you, she is the brains. I am the brawn." Zandra smiled. Matt continued: "I work for her and she works for me." Zandra frowned.

The Homeland Security official said: "Matt you don't have a job, you don't record, you don't tour. What does she do mow the lawn?"

"No, She mows me." Matt laughed. Zandra didn't.

Zandra said: "Let me fill you in on how I can help." Zandra talked for a half an hour. She made the point that radical Muslims were not predictable. They often didn't look like radical Muslims. Some were African American. There was such a politically correct mania in the U. S. that it was virtually impossible to accuse an African American of terrorism. She emphasized that James Smith smiled every time he realized that President Barack Obama helped to cover his nefarious deeds. Zandra knew all of Smith's thoughts, his texts and even his encrypted messages. She had surreptitiously bugged his home, his office, his cell phone and a courier examined his snail mail. She knew everything about him. She shared this information with Matt and the Homeland Security official. James Smith was toast.

Zandra and Matt took a cab back to Boulevard. As they left Homeland Security officials stood in awe watching her walk to the cab.

It had only been an hour since they left Boulevard. They were hardly missed. The cocktail and hors d'ouvres hour wasn't over and people were still talking. Boulevard's fine wines and tapas were so plentiful that the party atmosphere escalated into a drunken feast. At this point Don Gino noticed what he had missed. He knew one of the moles. He had missed the most obvious traitor. Much like the customs agent who betrayed him, Don Gino observed a Boulevard employee acting as the eyes and ears for al Qaeda. He would take care of this person.

After Matt and Zandra spent an hour with an FBI and Department of Homeland Security official at Red's Java House, they verified much of what Trevor told them They now fully understood the plot to bomb the Mission Delores.

Zandra said: "Matt we need to look carefully at those around Smith-Hammadi."

"Yes, we do, there is something we are missing."

When Zandra and Matt quietly returned to the Boulevard party, an elegantly dressed man with a Spanish accent entered the private room.

Don Gino said: "Commander Domingo-Mercedes let me introduce you to my friends." Mercedes kissed Chastain's hands and bowed so he could get a better view of her magnificent breasts. She stepped on his toe. He lurched back. He smiled. She looked disgusted.

Domingo-Mercedes said: "Ah, the lovely young FBI lady."

"Hello, sir." There was a hint of disdain in her voice. She lit a cigarette.

Then Assistant Commissioner Domingo-Mercedes found Zandra Filippi sitting on the couch drinking scotch. He recognized her.

"Are you the young lady who has a PhD studying political extremism in Spain?"

"Busted." She continued. "You do remember that we had drinks down in the Ramblas when I spoke at the American Consulate."

"How could I forget?" He bowed and kissed her hand.

Zandra said: "Your new responsibilities in Barcelona, do they include terrorist infiltration?"

Chastain walked over to Zandra. They embraced.

Chastain said: "You were saying Commissioner Domingo-Mercedes that you are now concentrating on terrorists. Is that correct?"

Domingo-Mercedes paused. He looked long and hard at Chastain. He did not like being questioned by a woman. That was an American trait. He detested it.

"Yes." Domingo-Mercedes paused. "I have special information." He smiled. "Here are some files Miss FBI lady." He winked at her. Mr. Winkey was also alert.

Chastain said: "Do you have complete confidence in your materials?"

He looked chagrined. What the hell was going on? How could this big-breasted woman continue to question him? Who the hell did she think she was?

Chastain had to admit that Domingo-Mercedes was a handsome man with a smooth air. He was also a macho asshole. "I thank you Commissioner for the privilege of working with you."

"I have been promoted. Perhaps we could talk about it over dinner."

Chastain said: "We can. Mickey Rooney will have to take a rain check."

"Who is Mickey Rooney?" Domingo-Mercedes looked perplexed.

The last person arrived. It was Emilio. He owned the donut shop near Trevor Blake III's office. The Blake Detective Agency was located nearby at Haight and Ashbury. When Emilio graduated with an MA in English literature from San Francisco State no one suspected that he was a former North Vietnamese high-ranking military officer. He was also a successful local businessman.

He was also a published author and a rich man. Rumor had it that he was a cat burglary. The high-end jewelry robberies on Nob Hill were Emilio's work. The San Francisco Police Department tried to catch him without results. Don Gino and Emilio were frequently seen at dinner at Gary Danko's. Emilio had skills in surveillance, hand-to-hand combat and counter intelligence. He was well past sixty but looked and acted thirty years younger. He was also one of Don Gino's closest friends.

Don Gino tapped the table. Everyone looked up. They all looked at Zandra Filippi. Who was she? They wondered what she was doing at the meeting. Trevor kept smiling at her. Matt Luman combed his hair and sang a few lines of his hit "I'm Movin' On." Zandra smiled. She licked her lips.

Don Gino said: "Please say hello to Miss Filippi. She coordinates our research. Her files on al Qaeda are the key to our eventual success."

Matt said: "She is the inspiration for my biggest hit 'I'm Movin' On.'"

Zandra said: "Matt I was born in 1979. Your hit was 1963. My parents were being toilet trained." For once Matt was lost for words.

He kept looking at her breasts. They were magnificent. They looked store bought. That was ok. Matt wondered if Mick Jagger or Keith Richards enjoyed them.

Don Gino took Zandra aside. He explained to her about James Smith. He outlined the Hammadi alias. He also needed Smith's phone tapped. There were three other taps that he needed. They were all illegal. She agreed instantly. No one turns down the Don.

While everyone talked, Nancy Oakes came in to instruct the wait staff. Trays of crispy Maryland soft-shell crab, an Ahi Tuna Tartare with hummus and a lacquered King Quail in the dimly lit private room provided more hors d'ouvres. The eight bottles of Chateau Sociando-Mallet (Haut Medoc) 2000 and two pitchers of Boulevard's home made sangria, as well as assorted wines, made for relaxing conversation. There was a large ice bin with bottles of Bollinger Blanc de Noris Vielles Vignes Francaises 1977 made with the finest pinot noir grapes. At $650 a bottle, Trevor quietly took one bottle to his car. There was a young lady somewhere who would be impressed.

Edsel Ford cleared the drinks quickly. He replenished them silently. No one noticed the small recorder attached to Ford's belt. That is except for one man. Edsel noticed a small Chinese man standing in the corner. He was dressed as a bus boy. He was too old to be a bus boy.

Edsel walked over and said: "Sir, what are you doing here?"

"So sorry boss, I need Mr. Don Gino." At that moment Don Gino walked over.

"Don't worry I will handle this beggar." Don Gino put a hundred dollar bill in Emilio's hand. No one saw the note that Emilio slipped to the Don. Emilio left. He was no more than a common beggar to the assembled throng. Most of the people in attendance were intelligence analysts who had little knowledge of the real world. Fortunately, everyone at this private dinner had some idea about the terrorist plot. They would provide Don Gino with even more information. The plan to end Hammadi's well-planned attack was taking final shape.

But the food and drink remained the star attraction. Boulevard had a reputation for innovation as Nancy Oakes re-entered the room.

She was a brilliant woman. Oakes realized that the assembled throng was in the process of solving a major terrorist plot. She still wanted to treat them right. All good deeds come from a full palate.

Nancy Oakes said: "We are experimenting with a sangria, I hope you all like it. Let us know what you think, as we may add it to the menu." After she left the room, the sangria was emptied. Like magic, two more pitchers appeared in the comfortable, dimly lit private dining room. Then the five-course dinner took place with animated conversation. As the baked Alaska, coffee and brandy finished the sumptuous dinner, the conversation turned to solving the terrorist plot. The Boulevard rivaled Gary Danko's for five star cuisines. Everyone looked full and happy. Don Gino stood up and thanked his guests.

"We need to talk about goals."

Chastain Johnson said; "And that goal is?"

He smiled: "Miss FBI lady, we need to find out what the al Qaeda terrorists will bomb here in San Francisco."

There was a lively discussion. Matt Luman asked about targets. The Transamerica Pyramid, Ghirardelli Square, the U. S. Consulate, the Federal Building on Golden Gate, the SF Police Headquarters, the City Hall, the Ferry Building or the Embarcadero Center were all on the list. None appeared threatened.

Trevor said: "Stop, I have the answer. Don Gino will not like it." After taking a large envelope out of his brief case, Trevor took out an architectural drawing of the Mission Delores.

"The Mission San Francisco de Asis is the oldest surviving structure in the city. It was the sixth Mission constructed and it is now known as the Mission Delores." Trevor laid out a large drawing. Everyone looked at it.

Chastain Johnson said: "Trevor are we getting a history lesson or do you have a point?" She smiled. Always the wiseass FBI agent!

"Listen to me Chastain."

"I need you to get to the point."

Don Gino said: "Stop it, let Trevor have his say as long winded and convoluted as it is." Everyone looked at the Don and said nothing. When the Don talks people listen. They don't contradict the Don.

"Thank you, Don Gino," Trevor continued. "The mission was named for St. Francis of Assisi. Our Muslim friends believe that its destruction will strike a multi-pronged blow. This is meant to embarrass you Don Gino."

Don Gino said: "Continue Trevor, I know some of this but not everything."

Trevor said: "There is another facet to the plan. You will not like it."

Don Gino said: "You mentioned another blow. What's that?" Don Gino lit a small cigar. He looked agitated. Not a good sign.

Trevor looked nervous. He hesitated. "They are going to eliminate you." There was dead silence in the room. Everyone looked nervous. The Don's eyes burned with anger. He quietly seethed. He recovered.

"Thank you Trevor," Don Gino smiled. "I have anticipated their moves. We are taking care of it. I appreciate your forthright opinion." The Don glared at everyone in the room. "I will also eliminate the mole in our midst." Don Gino looked menacingly around the room.

Trevor said: "I have a plan to prevent the destruction of the Mission Delores. To catch the perpetrators, we must not act until the last minute. There will be no more details until later."

Don Gino said: "Thank you all for coming. I will be in touch."

Don Gino shook everyone's hand and left the room. There was a stunned silence. The Don walked outside and quickly entered his purple limousine. Emilio was already in the back seat. Trevor quickly jumped into the front seat.

Trevor said: "I guess we are the new Three Musketeers." There was a dead silence. Don Gino and Emilio were not amused.

Don Gino said: "Well, Emilio and Trevor did we smoke out the mole?"

Emilio said: "Yes Don Gino, I watched him with interest. He was in the room and I have seen him in Barcelona. There was no reason for Edsel Ford to be in Barcelona. He is coming to destroy the Mission Delores. He thinks we are stupid. We now know his accomplices."

"I see," Don Gino continued. "Emilio would you like to personally take care of this matter?"

"Yes, Don Gino, it would be my pleasure." He was smiling and sharpening a small knife.

Trevor said: "What do you see during the Boulevard lunch? Was there anything suspicious?"

"Emilio said: "Do you think anyone in the room suspected that there was a traitor?"

"Yes, Emilio. I think that Matt Luman got it. I hope Trevor did but his hormones get in the way of his common sense."

Trevor said: "I not only got it, Don Gino, I have the note with the number '3' on it. That is the key to finding our three friends."

Emilio said: "Plus two, Trevor, there are five of them. The plot is thickening."

Don Gino said: "This sounds like one of my many mystery books where the plot is fun but convoluted.

Don Gino, Trevor and Emilio talked strategy as the purple limousine rolled slowly down Lombard Street. When two SFPD Motorcycle policemen rolled up next to the limousine, they saluted.

"I see my friend that you are still connected," Trevor said.

"Only for the common sense things in San Francisco."

Trevor laughed: "What is common sense in San Francisco?" They both laughed. The purple limousine stopped at the Hi Fi Lounge. Lombard Street was filled with cars and people. There was a parking place reserved for Don Gino in front of the club. The demographics placed twenty something's and early thirty partygoers in this bar. It was the easiest place to get laid in San Francisco. Don Gino, Trevor and Emilio were out of their element but they needed to meet someone. Emilio walked across Lombard Street and took up a position where he could watch the Hi Fi entrance. Don Gino and Trevor walked toward the entrance.

There was a long waiting line as they approached the entrance. The two muscle bound bouncers-doormen in purple tuxedos bowed and Don Gino walked in to find Detective Sgt. Richard Sanchez sitting at his table. A large full scale drawing of Steve McQueen stared down at the table. The Hi Fi Lounge had purple velvet walls and purple velvet seats with white and purple tables. The rumor was that Don Gino had a share in the Hi Fi ownership. He denied it.

The waitresses were dressed in purple tuxedos that revealed plenty of cleavage.

"Hello my friend," Detective Sanchez stood up smiling and shook Don Gino's hand.

"Ah, Detective, once again it is good to see you."

"You know my friend, Trevor?"

Sanchez said: "Yes, he has helped to gather most of the major intelligence."

Don Gino said: "Good. Gentlemen, we need to get down to business."

They talked for an hour. Three cocktail waitresses slipped Sanchez a napkin with their phone number. The waitresses continually interrupted with drinks and hors d'ouvres. Don Gino got up; they shook hands and left the Hi Fi. The plan to catch and take care of the al Qaeda terrorists was in place. Detective Sanchez left the Hi Fi. He looked back at the entrance and recognized a solitary figure standing near Lombard Street. The meeting had other eyes. That was good, Sanchez thought. It was time to deceive the al Qaeda plotters. He smiled. Don Gino had a foolproof plan. One that would make Trevor Blake III once again a hero. Trevor walked home. No one would know that he was a nice kid; he is an oaf as a private detective. He has no sense when it comes to unraveling a crime.

That is fine. Detective Sanchez would be nearby to insure that Trevor was the hero in the plot unfolding. Detective Sanchez followed the case from the beginning. He was aware of everything. Don Gino would solve the crime. Trevor Blake III would get the credit. Detective Sanchez would make sure that the perpetrators wound up in Don Gino's dog food cans. He knew who they were and why they were committing an act of terrorism. The lesson in their punishment would be not only to terrorists but also to Americans who helped the despicable Muslims.

The case was special as Detective Sanchez worked once again with Zandra Filippi. He loved her beauty. He was wary of her brains. She could not easily be fooled. He depended on her for key information that the FBI, the CIA and Homeland Security could not obtain. She was a valuable asset. She was also easy on the eyes.

CHAPTER FORTY-ONE

Zandra Filippi: Freedom Of Information

"I am surrealism." Salvador Dali

Alan Rushbridger sat in his office at the **San Francisco Mail**. He was on the phone with Eric Holder, the Attorney General of the United States. Holder was threatening to charge Rushbridger with national security crimes.

Holder said: "President Obama is concerned with your cavalier attitude toward national security."

"I beg your pardon, Mr. Attorney General. We report the news. I don't understand your concern."

"I will make it as simple as possible. You are violating U. S. law by reporting on national security concerns."

Rushbridger was silent. Holder said nothing.

"I beg your pardon, Mr. Attorney General. All we are doing is publishing Edward Snowden's material. Is that a crime?"

"Yes, it is. The documents are classified and stolen by Mr. Snowden."

"What if the documents reveal illegal American surveillance of its citizens?"

Eric Holder was silent. Then he said: "There is no such thing as illegal surveillance. We are a democracy with safeguards."

Rushbridger asked: "And what are those safeguards?"

"We are a constitutional government."

Rushbridger laughed. The Attorney General didn't know a thing about democracy. He kept those thoughts to himself.

Rushbridger said: "What if I send along documents that demonstrate that an FBI official is operating in Barcelona? I have photos of a beautiful blonde smoking a cigarette and tailing terrorists. She is FBI."

Holder looked astonished. "There is no such person." Holder continued. "She is impersonating an FBI agent. We don't allow excessive smoking. We don't allow provocative dress. How could she be an agent?"

"I beg to differ Mr. Attorney General."

"That is impossible," Holder continued. "I need proof."

"I will send it along." Rushbridger hung up. He called the **San Francisco Mail** legal office, they told him to back off. He didn't know what to do. He had evidence that the Obama Administration was spying on U. S. citizens. They were simply collecting e-mails and phone messages. There was no rhyme or reason for this violation of the First Amendment.

Warren Huckings, the **San Francisco Mail** editor, called: "Back off asshole or be fired." The reporter was furious. Huckings was a liberal, excessive left Obama supporter. What was happening to the free press? Rushbridger couldn't believe the turn of events. What the hell was happening with a socialist president, an Attorney General peeping into your bedroom and an FBI agent who looked like a hooker?

Against his better judgment, Rushbridger wrote a detailed memo to Holder pointing out that citizens needed to know when the government was collecting too much information. Then he shipped off the documents.

The next night the FBI raided Rushbridger's Chestnut Street apartment. They found nothing. He went to work at his 5th and Mission Street office and walked around the **Mail** printing plant. There were some new employees. They didn't look like print shop people. Rushbridger knew that he had a problem. The Obama Administration was trying to scare him. They were doing a good job.

The next night Rushbridger went to the Chestnut Street Starbucks. He made a phone call. He needed help. Zandra Filippi walked into Starbucks looking radiant and as always beautiful.

"Hello Alan," She gave him a big hug.

"Zandra, I need your help."

"Anything for you, I do remember you hired me when no one thought I had a brain, only a body." He explained the illegal government surveillance and Attorney General Holder's threats.

"What can I do?"

"I'm going to give you a file. If anything happens to me, give the file to Paul Steiger who will publish it on ProPublica."

"Whoa, this is big time."

"It is."

Zandra thought for a moment. "I need to look at your computer. There is something I need to search for in the FBI, CIA and Homeland Security confidential files." She knew that one of the agencies bugged his computer. She took Rushbridger outside and put him in a cab.

"I have a pass to the **S. F. Mail** office. I will be there shortly."

"Good." Rushbridger looked relieved.

Zandra said: "Go to Don Gino's. We will meet shortly." She grabbed a cab to the **Mail** office as Rushbridger sped away. The three hundred pound Samoan driver played Hawaiian music. He said: "We'll be at Don Gino's shortly." Rushbridger realized that he was dealing with professionals. Fuck Eric Holder. Fuck Warren Huckings. Rushbridger realized that he needed to control his emotions.

Zandra entered the 5th and Mission **San Francisco Mail** offices. She opened Rushbridger's computer and released the **Mail's** encrypted files. Who was behind the Sagrada Familia and Mission Delores terrorist attacks? Zandra found what she needed in a minute. The terrorists not only had Edsel Ford, the waiter at Boulevard, as their employee, they had other important people working undercover. Money worked wonders. The key to all aspects of evil was an endless supply of money. She wondered how San Francisco's major metropolitan newspaper had this information. Something was wrong.

Someone was sending out false information to the **San Francisco Mail**. Or maybe it was two people, Edsel Ford and Willie Wong. Zandra downloaded everything on a zip drive. She noticed the number "3" then a few sentences later highlighted with the number "2." She was puzzled.

When the San Francisco based Customs Inspector Willie Wong was on duty the Three Amigos always went through his line. When Edsel Ford traveled to Barcelona on vacation, Willie Wong stamped his passport. Wong was seen vacationing in Barcelona Zandra now knew what the numbers "3" and "2" meant. She identified the five terrorists.

Zandra left the **Mail** office. She called Don Gino. It was two in the morning. He was up listening to Judy Henske's **"Hooka Tooka"** with Rushbridger. When he got time, Don Gino vowed to bring Henske back to commercial prominence. Then "Wade in the Water" came on as Henske's husky voice inspired the Don. The phone rang.

Don Gino said: "Miss Filippi, to what do I owe the honor of this late night call? I know it is important."

"Yes, it is. I need to talk to you about another traitor. Is Mr. Rushbridger there?"

"Yes," Don Gino asked. "Where are you?"

"I'm at the **San Francisco Mail**."

"Walk out front in ten minutes, a purple limousine will pick you up."

"I'll be there."

Every light was on in Don Gino's Washington Street mansion. There was a visitor at Don Gino's home. He looked nerdy with his horn-rimmed glasses. He had his pencils and pens in a holder in his shirt pocket and a swatch of black hair that was a mess. He arrived an hour before Filippi. Alan Rushbridger was fifty-nine years old. He had been the **San Francisco Mail's** political editor for eighteen years. He was tough as nails, and he had gone to war in the courts with the federal government.

Rushbridger had a brief case full of documents. He was intent on publishing them. He wanted to demonstrate Attorney General Eric Holder's inability to monitor or control terrorists. He entered Don Gino's home in a rage.

Rushbridger said: "The God damned Socialist-Commie President needs to be exposed." Don Gino looked flummoxed.

"My friend, President Obama is doing his best as is Attorney General Holder. Don't write your story for a few days. You don't have all the facts." Don Gino lit a small cigar.

Not only did Rushbridger respect Don Gino, he knew that the Mafia Don had inside information. Rushbridger was still bothered.

He was concerned over the abuse of first amendment rights. Freedom of information was under siege and Rushbridger was determined to publicize the government's illegal collection of e-mails, telephone calls and personal mail.

"I will wait on the story."

"Thank you, Mr. Rushbridger, I appreciate your willingness to come here and help me at this late hour."

"For you Don Gino anything."

"Thank you again. I won't forget your kindness."

Don Gino said: "Remember a Pulitzer is in your future."

"I hope so." Rushbridger felt better.

"In a moment Ms. Zandra Filippi will arrive. We need to talk." The Don clapped his hands and a glass of Aberlour single malt scotch was placed in front of Rushbridger. He took a small sip, closed his eyes and smiled. Don Gino knew everyone's favorite drink. Or for that matter everyone's favorite vice.

Zandra Filippi arrived. She took off her coat and settled into a big, soft chair. A cup of chai tea was brought to her.

"We need to get down to business. I want to thank you both for coming."

"How did you know I found new information?" Filippi asked.

"The tone of your voice."

"Don Gino and Zandra, what am I doing here?"

"Mr. Rushbridger. Thank you again for holding off publishing your material on government intrusion into the lives of our citizens."

"The documents will appear in a special Sunday edition of the-mail in two weeks."

"Does this cause a hardship?" Don Gino asked.

"Yes, we will lose $100,000 in preparation coasts by delaying the material."

"I see." Don Gino took out a checkbook and wrote a $125,000 check.

"Thank you," Rushbridger continued. "Why the extra sum of money?"

"Convenience money." Don Gino lit another small cigar.

Zandra said: "What is my role Don Gino?"

"I need you to find as much as you can on Edsel Ford and the Three Amigos."

"Consider it done." She got up and left the house.

Don Gino looked at Rushbridger. "Why did you agree so easily to delay publication of such explosive material? It is unlike you."

"I have the feeling a bigger scope is coming my way."

"You do, it will happen. I see a Pulitzer Prize in your future."

Rushbridger finished his scotch and left.

Don Gino sat by the window looking out on Washington Street. It was dark, cold and quiet. So was the Don's mood.

He walked down to his garage. Don Gino put on a leather jacket. He started up his Harley Davidson and placed some folders in his saddlebags. He drove the seven blocks to Lombard Street. It was four in the morning. He wanted the IHOP steak and eggs special. The restaurant was virtually empty. There were two tables with couples drowsily eating eggs, pancakes and bacon.

He sat in the back at his private table. The coffee arrived. The steak and eggs came in minutes, and he continued to look over his files. Don Gino looked at the front door. There were two men in dark suits, crew cuts and wingtip shoes. The Don was furious. Someone was shadowing him. One was tall and looked like he had eaten too many pieces of pie. The short one was muscular and worked out. Brains and brawn! A good combination!

Don Gino took out his cell phone. He called Attorney General Eric Holder. They talked for five minutes. Holder had no idea what was going on. The Don believed him. The men weren't looking his way. The Don dialed Emilio. He explained what he needed. To everyone's surprise, Don Gino ordered apple pie a la mode. He had another cappuccino and left the restaurant. The two men followed discreetly. They failed to see the small Vietnamese man with a tazer.

When the two men woke up they were in the back of an SUV in the Marina Green. Don Gino called Detective Sgt. Richard Sanchez. He requested no police patrols in or near the Marina Green for an hour. Sanchez took care of the request.

The men awoke tied up. They blinked. One sneered: "An old Chinaman and a faggot. When we get out of here you are toast."

Don Gino stared for five minutes saying nothing. Even Emilio looked nervous.

"I will ask you only once. Are you planning to blow up the Mission Delores?"

They laughed. Don Gino pulled out a gun. He shot the small one in the middle of the forehead. "Get the body bag in the trunk, Emilio and throw him off the Golden Gate Bridge."

"It's done, boss."

"Do I have to repeat the question?"

"No." The big guy spilled the whole scenario. Willie Wong was toast. So was everyone else.

"Thank you, my friend." Don Gino raised the gun and shot the big fat guy in the forehead. "Sorry my friend there is no more pie." Emilio appeared and got rid of the body. Don Gino reminded himself to go to confession.

Twice. The burden of being a good Catholic weighed heavily on Don Gino's soul. It was a tough burden. He would endure it. Don Gino said: "Father I have sinned, forgive me."

He knew that he was forgiven. Don Gino was an integral part of God's army.

CHAPTER FORTY-TWO

Father I Have Sinned: Forgive Me

"My aim is to have absolutely nothing in common with anyone."
Salvador Dali

D on Gino returned to his Washington Street mansion. He had a heavy heart. Murder was not his forte. Despite his reputation, he hated violence. He walked into the kitchen. His valet had a date. The au pair was at Perry's with her boyfriend. Helga, a Swedish beauty, was also a fitness instructor. No one realized that she was much more than an au pair. She was also a bodyguard. Danielle Steel complained to Don Gino that the only people who hired au pair's were couples with kids. Don Gino ignored her. The au pair was a trained killer. Nice to have her around.

There was no one in the house. Don Gino put on a kettle of hot water. He made a hot chocolate. The Dali room awaited his visit. He walked in and sat in the purple fur lined chair. The Dali's were exquisite. He took out a copy of Andre Parinaud's book **The Unspeakable Confessions of Salvador Dali**. He tore out the pages and lit a fire in the large fireplace. Don Gino hated the pompous and imperious French journalist. He smiled as Parinaud's burning tome heated the room. He sipped his hot chocolate. Don Gino was deep in thought.

The sun was coming up over San Francisco Bay. Don Gino gazed at the glistening Golden Gate Bridge. He would see the outline of Sausalito's magnificent homes and Alcatraz stood out like a sore thumb. There is a purity to the San Francisco landscape. Don Gino never tired of it. His mood improved.

Sin, salvation and redemption were the elements that Don Gino had in mind. He loved to identify and isolate evil. This is what he was doing in the Salvador Dali murder. His religious fervor was absolute and brought the evil forces to their end. The stability of law was not something that Don Gino could count on. He would provide stability with his own law. It was the only way to deal with the terrorists. He would kill them. Then he would go to confession.

He looked at a small envelope on his desk in his Dali room. He didn't remember a letter. The postmark said: "Barcelona." Strange! Don Gino's valet, the maid, the au pair and the butler were out for the day. How did the letter get on his desk? In of all places his special Dali room. He looked up. James Smith, aka Omar Abdul Hammadi, stood holding a small revolver. Don Gino wasn't worried. He had his faith. He looked up. Smith-Hammadi smiled.

"Don Gino we meet."

"Yes, we do." When Don Gino reached for the purple and gold box with his small cigars, Smith-Hammadi screamed: "Stop."

Don Gino smiled. "I am having my final small cigar."

"So you know I'm about to kill you."

"As you say." Don Gino lit the small cigar. "Your brother died needlessly."

Hammadi looked angry: "Don't mention my brother."

"Why not? He is a noble man. You are a piece of shit." Don Gino smiled.

"I have a surprise for you." Smith-Hammadi smiled.

"That is!" Don Gino smiled. He had no fear. He realized that this man was weak. He was a coward and confused. Don Gino would have another day.

"I am leaving. Turn around." Don Gino did. Smith slowly and silently came up behind Don Gino and hit him on the head. That was the last thing Don Gino remembered. He woke up two hours later. Don Gino caressed his head. He smiled. He wasn't upset. Smith-Hammadi had revealed his weakness. It was time to prepare for the final showdown. The anger would come. It would be slow and seep into his soul. He would act in rage. A very quiet but firm rage. A killing rage. Then he would once again go to confession.

He had been attacked twice solving this case. Maybe Trevor shouldn't get the credit. All he ever did was go to bed with the young ladies. The criminals were about to find out that Don Gino wasn't benevolent. He rubbed his sore head.

Don Gino walked into his kitchen. He took out a plastic bag and filled it with ice. His head hurt. He was not happy. He took out his cell phone.

"Hello Trevor, I need a favor."

"Anything for you Don Gino."

For ten minutes Don Gino provided Trevor with a list of things he needed done. Trevor said that he would have Guitar Jac take care of half the tasks, and he would finish the rest.

"Thank you, Trevor. I knew I could count on you."

Don Gino dressed and took his S-Class Mercedes sedan out of the garage. He put his heavy briefcase into the trunk. He drove to St. Patrick's Catholic church at 756 Mission Street near the Opera. He took the briefcase and walked into St Patrick's. The church surrounded by restaurants, hotels, businesses and public transportation has a pristine cleanliness. Father Patrick O'Brian stood out front smoking a cigarette. Father Pat was a star pitcher for the University of San Francisco. After pitching two no hitters, he was drafted in the first round of the Major League Baseball Draft in 2000. He elected to become a priest. He still pitches for the Mission Delores Padres, a group of Priests who play charity games. They had lost only one game since 2001. They faced Ronald "Fast Ball" Brockins when the Texas Rangers played an exhibition game. The charity event sold out San Francisco's Candlestick Park. Father Pat was still complaining about a call that lost the Padres the game. After Father Pat pitched a no hitter for eight innings. He walked a Ranger in the ninth who promptly stole second and third. Then Father Pat balked the run home. He commented that God must live in Texas. After a rebuke from the Catholic hierarch, he apologized to "Fast Ball" Brockins who gave him the finger. The game did raise $200,000 for Catholic charities.

"Hello Father Pat."

"Don Gino, what brings you to St. Patrick's?"

"I need to have someone hear my confession."

"I can't imagine that you have any sins. You are the best Catholic in the City."

"Thank you, Father."

"Come this way, my son."

They walked into St. Patrick's. Don Gino looked at the confessional with a red light. A minute later the green light goes on. A priest enters. The Sacrament of Penance is an important part of Don Gino's personality. It cleanses his soul. He enters the confessional.

"I will hear your confession my son."

"I have sinned. I need absolution. I have killed two men just hours ago. I will kill four more in the next day or two. Is there any chance for salvation, Father?" Don Gino wiped his sweaty brow with a purple handkerchief.

"My son you have a healthy or realistic sense of your sinfulness. This in itself is a good thing. Remember God embraces foreword forgiveness."

"Father is it true that my sins stand between myself and God?"

"Yes and no."

"What do you mean Father?"

"You need to prepare your confession by remembering that God is the fount of grace, and the purveyor of wisdom. He is generous in his forgiveness." The cigarette smoke made Don Gino cough. He caught his breath.

"Father I am about to nail a man to a cross."

"Christ was nailed to a cross."

"What does that have to do with me?"

"You are nailing someone to a cross for a good reason. God will forgive you."

"Thank you Father."

"Go in peace Don Gino and come visit again."

Before Don Gino walked out of St. Patrick's, he stopped at the church's ornate door. Father Daniel Ortega was standing out front. He was a thirty-year-old priest who looked like a movie star. He had been a television and movie actor before finding God. There was a third priest, Father Jose Rizal, who served the largely Filipino congregation. But it was Father Daniel who was responsible for the upsurge of young ladies attending St. Patrick's. Thanks to Don Gino, St. Patrick's is the only San Francisco Catholic Church serving cappuccinos before and after Mass.

"Hello Father Daniel."

"Don Gino, it is nice to see you."

"I have a gift for the parish."

"Thank you Don Gino."

Father Daniel took the brief case.

When Father Daniel opened the briefcase, he found $100,000 in small bills. Don Gino's note suggested that it was a donation for the CYO basketball league. But Father Daniel could do with the money as he pleased. He didn't. The money went to St. Patrick's for its basketball program. The 6th grade team was important in keeping kids off the street.

The Don was hungry. It was time for lunch. He walked down to Café Claude. The French knew how to do lunch. Don Gino was sore. The blow to his head still hurt. It was a mild pain. The blow to his pride was more hurtful. He was also hungry. He would remain calm. He would have his revenge. It was God's will.

The Café Claude menu was brilliant. Don Gino started with onion soup, and it was followed by the French cassoulet. Then steak and pommes frites finished the main courses. There was one thing left. He ended the meal with a crème Brule. He didn't have wine. A large bottle of Perrier allowed Don Gino to think. He had a plan. As he nursed his second cappuccino, he concluded that Trevor Blake III was the key to quietly solving the Salvador Dali Murder.

CHAPTER FORTY-THREE
Trevor Rethinks His Role

"What shall we be? When we aren't what we are?" Derek Raymond

Trevor sat down in his Chestnut street apartment with Derek Raymond's first novel in the Factory series, **He Died With His Eyes Open**. Trevor loved Raymond's minimalist fiction. He read for almost two hours. The Raymond novel opened Trevor's eyes to what he had missed in the Salvador Dali case. He had become too involved in Dali's life. He needed to look beyond Dali to the al Qaeda terrorists. They were in his midst. They also had no idea that he knew their identity.

Raymond provided another clue. One that he had missed. Trevor knew that someone at Gary Danko's was a mole. There was more than one insider. Trevor shuttered at the number of people that Don Gino would eliminate. The terrorists' weren't safe.

Trevor was reading when Don Gino called. The Don explained about James Smith, aka Omar Abdul Hammadi. It sounded like he was describing a fictional character. He wasn't. Don Gino asked Trevor to meet him.

Thinking about the case, Trevor wondered if he was chasing fictional characters? Then Trevor realized that he had caught the Chef who was a serial killer. Trevor looked around his dreadful bachelor pad. It reeked of a depressing life. Although he was never happily married to Marilyn, she kept the house clean and cooked. She also brought home a six-figure salary. Marilyn's Chinese name was "bitch, bitch, bitch." Trevor quickly got a divorce. What could be worse than Marilyn? Bennie and Bertie for starters.

Now he was married to Bennie and Bertie's budget apartment. It did come with a perk. The rent was low. The best part was the location. Chestnut Street is the center of social life for thirty something's and forty something's who tell people they are in their thirties. Trevor was in the later class. Trevor was depressed. He was forty-one. He was tired of renting from Bennie and Bertie. It was like living in your parent's basement. He was famous for catching the serial killer poisoning the Start Me Up rock band drummers, but he was still at loose ends. Fame and money did not equal happiness. It did bring young ladies.

Then he thought about his family. He had a brother who was dead. The problem is that one of the brothers, Herman, was a famous lawyer with the six-figure salary. He also reflected on his oldest brother, Dempster. He is a highly intelligent, personally abusive sociopath who still worked at age sixty-six, because he might go on a drunken binge and kill himself. He was a sick man. He called Trevor once a week to verbally abuse him. Since Trevor only had two cases, the calls were frenetic explanations of Dempster's record collection. Dempster liked to tell Trevor the he didn't know that Jimi Hendrix played a concert in Hawaii. Dempster was nuts. Trevor felt sorry for him. Why was he thinking about Dempster? He might be a psychotic nutcase like his brother if he didn't find the killer. He would. Then he remembered something that Dempster said: "Trevor when you look for the criminal, remember he is a friend of many friends." That was it. It didn't make a lot of sense. Then he got it. The message was clear. Trevor needed to make three more napkins. He had found three more of Hammadi's cohorts.

The accumulated files and napkins were on Trevor's kitchen table. He put on a pot of coffee. He sat down and arranged the more than sixty napkins. They told a story. One that Trevor didn't fully understand. Then he added the three napkins. These napkins unwittingly solved the crime.

There was a solution to the crime. He had found it. The notes on the three napkins sealed his evidence. Trevor realized that he was unable to identify James Smith as not just a killer but also an al Qaeda operative. It was time to solve the Salvador Dali case.

Trevor's mistake was concentrating solely on James Smith. He was the puppet master. It was the puppets that were carrying out the crime. There were three puppets. They were the clue to the perpetrators in what was a strange encrypted message that read simply "3." Zandra Filippi found the message as she monitored James Smith's e-mails. The same number came up on Edsel Ford's computer and the e-mails of the Three Amigos. Trevor now had firm proof it was the Three Amigos who were part of the terrorist clan. There was more to discover.

For more than two hours, Trevor studied and rearranged the napkins. He wanted to make sure that he had it right. He did. What he couldn't understand was the mentality of the homegrown American terrorists. There were more of them than just the innocuous James Smith.

A sociopath, James Smith, lacked a conscience and any sense of morality. He had other flaws. He also had the requisite mental agility to take on two well-planned terrorist attacks and complete them.

Trevor wondered how this weakling could lead a group of al Qaeda terrorists. The irony, Trevor thought, is that there is not a solution to the Salvador Dali Murder. There needs to be the quick death of those involved. The details must never come to light.

Trevor realized that Smith was a visionary with a warped sense of his intellect. Trevor was set to catch the al Qaeda terrorists. He had figured out the case. Don Gino was wrong. It would be tough to tell the Don. He would. Trevor recalled a chance remark during dinner at Gary Danko's. How could he have ignored the comment?

Edsel Ford made a verbal mistake. Trevor caught it. He wondered if Don Gino picked up on Ford's faux pas?

As Trevor walked out to his car, he had a mission. He drove to San Francisco International Airport. It was time to catch the al Qaeda operatives. Don Gino was not going to like the inside moles. They were as good as dead.

CHAPTER FORTY-FOUR

Don Gino Learns The Truth

"I like it, murder, because this is courage. It is anti-bourgeois. Murder is closer to heaven...one opens the sky, and the angels say 'Good Morning." Salvador Dali

In one week Don Gino put a few observations together and realized that the al Qaeda terrorists were connected to the Three Amigos. When the author Jim Harrison was at his ranch in Sonoita one winter, the Three Amigos arrived in Southern Arizona. They had no idea that he was a famous writer. They thought he was no more than some kind of homeless guy. When they set off explosives in the remote Arizona desert, Harrison came out and threatened them with a shotgun. They laughed at him. That was a mistake.

They thought that he was a one-eyed crazy man. They ignored him. Then Harrison snapped almost a hundred pictures. He had just given them to Don Gino. The Don knew how and why the Three Amigos were involved. It was money.

The meeting at Gary Danko's exposed a truth. There was another traitor in their midst. One who was so close that he was beyond suspicion? Don Gino pondered the seemingly innocuous questions asked by the Three Amigos. They were too curious. They knew too much. They acted like a disinterested party while gleaming every bit of information. They gave themselves away. They were too curious. They knew too much. Now it was time for Don Gino to learn the truth.

On the Carnivolet cruise, Don Gino recalled that they were talk-ing to a large African American man. It was Smith-Hammadi. There was no reason for them to talk to him. Something was amiss. Then Don Gino remembered that he had a tape of conversations between the Three Amigos.

As Don Gino listened to the tape, there was one question that troubled him. Jorge said: "What does the law in Spain say about the desecration of religious artifacts?" Juan and Carlos had no answer. Jorge pointed out that the desecration of religious artifacts was an accepted part of the Spanish way of life.

Zandra Filippi provided another tape, which indicated that the Three Amigos were in touch with Edsel Ford. The headwaiter at the Boulevard was Hammadi's San Francisco contact. But why? The Three Amigos were professionals, rich and well thought of in San Francisco social circles. Something didn't make sense. Don Gino real-ized that the Three Amigos were broke. They were in it for the money.

After Zandra Filippi accessed their e-mails, tapped their phones and arranged for their personal mail to be read, there was no doubt one amigo was the key terrorist. The others simply went along. It didn't take long to identify that he reported to James Smith. The other two amigos were accomplices for a five million dollar payment to a bank in Grand Cayman. Which one was the head amigo? Who was the person responsible for unprecedented terror? Don Gino knew the culprit.

Jorge was a judge. His file points to three divorces, two pali-mony suits, a foreclosure on his Pacific Heights mansion and Las Vegas gambling debts. He was on the edge of bankruptcy and then he mysteriously paid off his home and all debts. Where did the money originate? That was the unanswered question. As a judge his salary was $180,000 a year. There was something wrong. Don Gino had the answer. Zandra Filippi's file traced his bank accounts, his spending habits and his sudden wealth.

Jorge would be dealt with in a novel manner. He would be allowed to live. He would serve Don Gino's ultimate purpose. The others would meet an unexpected end. They would be comingling with the dog food. They didn't realize that they were in danger. Arrogance made a man easy to find. It was even easier to kill him. He believed that he fooled everyone. Revenge was sweet.

Don Gino thought long and hard about the dinner at Boulevard. Fortunately, he hadn't missed all the signs of imminent terrorism. There was one remark that he couldn't get out of his mind. Edsel Ford had unwittingly made a note. Don Gino saw it on his drink order pad: "3." To most people "3" meant nothing. It was the answer to the San Francisco plot. The Don realized that the plan to blow up the Mission Delores was not the work of one person. It was a brilliant plan by a small cadre of al Qaeda converts. It was the work of fanatics. The homegrown al Qaeda terrorists were good Catholics. They were well known in the Mission District. They could move easily in and around the Mission Delores. They were also friendly with the priests. They were graduates of St. Ignatius College Prep. How had Don Gino missed the obvious signs? He prepared to deal with the terrorists who called themselves the Three Amigos.

The Three Amigos were college educated Catholics with a hatred for affirmative action, the Pope, the Democratic Party and President Barack Obama. The renounced their Catholic roots for Muslim radicalism. There was no rationale for their actions. Don Gino vowed to end their blasphemous behavior.

The Don ordered a cadre of six limousines. He called the **San Francisco Chronicle** and notified Steve Muncini. The ace reporter was the Don's good friend. Muncini could be counted on to spin the story. This was necessary for ending the terrorist plot. There were other things to put in order.

After talking with Trevor Blake III, Don Gino went to a hardware store. Then he called Emilio. They met in the Haight Ashbury at Emilio's donut shop. They talked for hours about strategy. They knew what they had missed. Don Gino could finally put his finger on it. Then it dawned on Don Gino. He had the answer to his dilemma. He told Emilio to wait for the phone call. He bid Emilio good-by and drove home.

Once Don Gino entered his Washington Street mansion, he went to the small library in the back of the house. The Don was aware that having a collection of rare mystery books was not the image that a Mafia Don projected. He kept this hobby quiet. Only Emilio knew about the book collection. There was a book scout, Harvey, who was responsible for half of the Don's rare mystery and espionage books. He only collected first editions.

Harvey, the book scout, concentrated recently on works by Daniel Silva and Barry Eisler. He had a studio apartment near Chinatown on Monroe Place filled with books. Harvey lived a half a block from Chinatown.

Don Gino showed up at Harvey's small apartment. He walked in and sniffed. The place smelled. Don Gino looked at the bookcase. Books by Richard Hofstadter, Arthur Link and George Mowry were prominent. He wondered who in God's grace were these obscure authors? Harvey, the book scout, was physically fit at one hundred eighteen pounds and he had wrestled for Stanford University. He was a typical San Francisco character.

"How can you live in this tin can?" Don Gino continued: "I can find you something comfortable in the Mission with a real bedroom. Not a bed that comes out of the wall."

Harvey said: "I'm fine. I love this place."

Why don't you live in the middle of Chinatown?"

Harvey thought for a moment. "This is the best I can do" Harvey continued. "I have a Murphy bed and no girl friends. The Chinese girls won't give me the time of day."

"Harvey, you are a book scout, you make two thousand dollars a month. The Chinese girls want a Stanford doctor."

"I'm a Stanford history graduate."

"Case closed."

"What can I find for you Don Gino?"

"Get rid of the Murphy bed and find me a first edition of Edgar Allan Poe's **The Raven**. I have a reprint. That is unacceptable."

Harvey said: "Can I get that on kindle?' Harvey laughed. "Sorry Don Gino I know that an 1845 book, a first edition, is not on kindle." He hoped that the Don had a sense of humor. Harvey sweated profusely. He had to tell Don Gino the truth. Harvey stuttered and then explained.

Don Gino said: "I said a first edition."

Harvey said: "Edgar Allen Poe died in 1849, sorry Don Gino, I will find a January 1845 first edition." Harvey waited for Don Gino to pull out a gun and shoot him. Don Gino reached into his suit pocket. Harvey said a little prayer. He closed his eyes. He waited. He was still alive. He opened his eyes to see Don Gino place ten one hundred dollar bills on his Formica dining room table.

Harvey said: "Thank you, the money goes to a good cause. Don Gino I hope that I didn't upset you, Poe first editions are almost impossible to find."

"I appreciate your honesty. Your humor is noted. Fill in my espionage books. I will talk to you soon." Don Gino left Harvey's apartment and walked down to Broadway and Columbus. He took a seat at the bar at Vesuvio's. A large cappuccino arrived. Don Gino took out his notes. He kept a small notebook on his mystery and espionage book collection. He believed that there was a clue in one of the mysteries.

Don Gino devoured these espionage thrillers. The answer to the Salvador Dali murder was found not in one of his books, but in a Barry Eisler blog. When Eisler wrote: "We have more than 80,000 people held in solitary confinement, and the government's treatment of whistleblower Bradley Manning has been cruel and inhuman...." Don Gino had his answer. The James Smith plan to blow up the Mission Delores was a protest against these confinements. Don Gino realized there was more to the plot.

When Zandra Filippi penetrated Smith's computer, Don Gino received a daily print out. He scanned it, and he looked for a clue in his library. He had the three books that Smith was reading. The answer to Smith's warped consciousness was in these books.

Looking at his early Americana collection, Don Gino pulled out the three disparate books. The first was James Fennimore Cooper's **The Spy**, published in 1821. It told the story of a double agent working for President George Washington. The next book was a recent one. Maria Ressa's, **Seeds of Terror: An Eyewitness Account of al Qaeda's Newest Center of Operations in Southeast Asia**. It provided another clue. Ressa wrote: "The typical al Qaeda terrorist is a pseudo patriot. One who ingrains himself with those who least suspect him." That was not only the final clue. It was a perfect description of the culprit, James Smith, aka Omar Abdul Hammadi.

The last book that Smith read was a curious choice. It was Alexandre Dumas' **The Three Musketeers**. What could this book possibly tell one about the al Qaeda plot? Don Gino opened it, and he read about the three merry men whose motto was "all for one, one for all." He heard this phrase on the ship. The Three Amigos uttered it repeatedly. They were returning to San Francisco from a legal conference in Pakistan. How convenient.

The next stop was the San Francisco International Airport. Don Gino was in the front of the six purple limousines parked for arriving passengers. Detective Richard Sanchez was already in place. He had two men stationed in U. S. Customs, an undercover detective was disguised as a porter, and there was a taxi driver waiting for the Three Amigos. Sanchez shook his head. Why did Don Gino come to the San Francisco International Airport in six purple limos? He wouldn't mention it to the Don. But he knew that there was a plan. Trevor stood in the shadows. He wasn't needed.

No one noticed Customs Inspector Willie Wong. He was handcuffed and led to an unmarked van. Inside, Detective Sgt. Sanchez began talking to Wong. He had questions. Wong would have answers. Or else!

When Wong asked for a lawyer. Sanchez slapped him. Then he pistol-whipped him. Wong talked.

When Don Gino walked into SFO there were reporters, television cameras, a crew from TMZ and Director George Lucas. They filmed the purple limousines, as they pulled into a private parking area adjacent to the terminal. Don Gino smiled and waved to the cameras. He walked over to a private charter plane embarkation area. His entourage included a small Asian man, six Samoans, a midget and twenty assorted guests. None were identified. They walked into the plane. The paparazzi went away. Don Gino sat for a time.

There was an inordinate amount of publicity as Don Gino organized a party of his friends for the Broadway premiere of a play,

Don Gino: An American Life. Not only would Don Gino attend the premiere, he would be available for interviews. The Three Amigos knew this and they were returning to San Francisco to complete the destruction of the Mission Delores. Don Gino would surprise them.

Don Gino said: "Ladies and gentlemen, we will be served a light snack and some drinks." There was applause. They began their snack, which was a recipe that Michelle Obama sent to Don Gino. The president's wife created the snack for New York's Waldorf Astoria Hotel. The people on the plane loved it.

Don Gino said: "We are having a brief party on the plane. Then I have arranged for all of you to have suites in New York at the Waldorf Astoria. I have to remain in San Francisco. Business has come up." He smiled.

Danielle Steel asked: "Don Gino are you remaining in San Francisco?"

"Yes, Madame, I am."

"Could you feed my cat?"

"Of course." The Don smiled. Someday he would tie her up and hire someone to read her books to her. It would be a fitting punishment.

After an hour the private jet took off without Don Gino. He had business to conduct. There were no purple limousines meeting them. As an SUV pulled up, Don Gino said: "We are going to mass at the Mission Delores." The Samoans looked confused. Emilio smiled. The end was in sight.

PART IV:
WHAT DOES IT ALL MEAN?

"According to Vladimir Nabokov, Salvador Dali was really Norman Rockwell's twin brother kidnapped by gypsies in babyhood." Margaret Atwood

CHAPTER FORTY-FIVE

The Three Amigos:
The Real Terrorists

"It is a very pleasant sensation, this admiration, that flows over me in magic waves." Salvador Dali

The Three Amigos got off the Iberia flight from Barcelona. They had been in Pakistan for a week on a judicial conference. At least this was their cover story. In reality, they were putting final touches on the plan to destroy San Francisco's Mission Delores. They listened to a variety of al Qaeda terrorists, they also spent time with a group of noted Imams and the Three Amigos left Pakistan on a short flight to Barcelona. They were hailed as heroes.

To cover their tracks they booked a holiday in Spain. They would contact Smith-Hammadi with final instructions in what looked to be an innocent holiday. They checked into the Palacette-Continental Hotel. They didn't notice the new bell hop. He was a small Asian man. He smiled. He bowed.

He took their luggage to separate rooms. "Jorge, give the Chinaman ten Euros, we might as well be big tippers." The other two laughed. "It's not our money. We are all rich."

"Thank you, Sir." Emilio smiled and bowed. They would soon experience his wrath. After the Three Amigos unpacked they decided to do some drinking on the Ramblas. It was cold out. They felt like sitting in a sidewalk café and drinking some Spanish wine. That way they could look at the beautiful young ladies who strolled the promenade.

Even in the cold weather the slinky leggings and slit skirts showed enough leg to excite the Three Amigos. The high heels accentuated the Spanish beauties figures and stylish clothing. Their breasts jiggled as they walked. They joked about going to confession.

Jorge said: "We never see anything like this on Telegraph in Berkeley." They chanted "Here Here."

Carlos said: "Does she have underpants on?" They shouted: "Here Here." They looked at each other with seriousness.

Juan said: "That fucking Mission, I can't wait to blow it up. Every Christmas we went there to sing carols. Yuck! Now I will get my revenge."

They laughed. The Three Amigos got up and began walking down the Ramblas. They wanted to visit one more neighborhood.

Jorge said: "Gentlemen to the hood." They began a slow, tourist stroll down the Ramblas. No one suspected them. Just three wide-eyed tourists out for fun.

"Terrorists out for fun," Juan said. They laughed uproariously.

Las Ramblas is a three quarter mile street for strolling and the tree-lined streets make the shops intimate. The Opera House Liceu built in 1847 adds elegance to the small shops, restaurants and bars. The Three Amigos walked to the nearby El Raval ghetto and entered the Ambard for mojitos. "Here Here" was heard coming from the Ambard and then the Three Amigos walked over to their favorite pub, La Ovella Negra, where the girls were all under thirty and the drinks were less than three Euros. For millionaires, they weren't spending any money. They still had the mentality like they lived in the hood. They were oblivious to those around them. They would soon be retired spending their well-earned al Qaeda blood money.

Then as they were celebrating in the cheap bars on the side streets off Las Ramblas they walked into the Manchester Bar on Carrer Valldonzella and there sat Omar Abdul Hammadi. He smiled. They moved to a rear table. Hammadi sat with his back to the wall. He gave each of them an envelope.

Hammadi said: "When you land in San Francisco follow the instructions. There is an envelope with $9,999 for expenses. That amount does not interest the IRS or Customs." The Three Amigos smiled. Hammadi continued: "This is a bonus gentlemen. Spend it wisely." Smith Hammadi got up and left. He was disgusted with the Three Amigos. He needed them. They would sever his ends.

Emilio followed the Three Amigos around Barcelona, and he witnessed their meeting with Smith-Hammadi. He found out the last part of their plan. He e-mailed Don Gino the information. There was other information coming from Zandra Filippi about Willie Wong.

Customs Inspector Willie Wong, just before he was arrested, e-mailed the Three Amigos that Don Gino and his entourage had left San Francisco for a New York Broadway premiere. The truth was that Don Gino's guests flew to New York, while he returned to his Washington Street home. He was waiting for the Three Amigos. They would pay for their nefarious deeds.

Zandra Filippi printed an e-mail detailing Wong's involvement. She sent it to Detective Sanchez. An hour later Wong was in hand-cuffs. The Three Amigos were too focused on pleasure and their impending terrorist act to realize they were in danger. They were also too focused on wealth.

The weekend in Barcelona was one that the Three Amigos wouldn't forget. They also had a brief trip, in the midst of this holiday, where they were feted by Islamabad based al Qaeda terrorists. They hated Pakistan but loved the acclaim. They also didn't believe in 300 Virgins. They had a stronger belief in money.

They converted to Islam at Stanford University. It was a youthful flirtation. They blamed it on liberal professors. James Smith, aka Hammadi, was simply a pawn. He was used by al Zawahiri to recruit American al Qaeda members. The poor bastard never realized it. What a fool! Then they realized that they could make millions from radical al Qaeda terrorists. They would take expenses for their terrorist activities. The travel, the acclaim, the money was important. Equally significant was revenge. The politically correct, race conscious, affirmative action types would be punished. It wasn't Islam and Allah that the Three Amigos protested, it was the liberal, political correct types like the Socialist President Barack Obama that they detested. Revenge was on the horizon.

They became greedy after they cut a deal with Ayman al-Zawahiri to bomb the Sagrada Familia and the Mission Delores. The Three Amigos had neither ethics nor integrity. Somewhere along the line they had never left the ghetto. At least in their minds. Who would suspect them? What a perfect cover. They were affirmative action babies who went on to become celebrated lawyers, one was now a judge, one was a famed defense attorney and one was a city prosecutor. They were all advisers to the Republican and Democratic parties. They supported both political parties as a matter of necessity and expediency. They were also good Catholics. They were handsome and articulate. They were an American success story. They were also traitors.

When Smith-Hammadi contacted the Three Amigos, he offered money. That was all they needed. They already had too much prestige. You couldn't spend prestige. They would have enough money to quietly retire to Argentina, Uruguay or any other South American country with Nazis. They looked patriotic, they acted patriotic and their politics reeked of patriotism. The reality was something different. They hated America. The special affirmative action treatment galled them. They would take their revenge.

Since 9-11, they had gone from secret Muslims to active terrorists. When the media reported in July 2013 that there were at least thirty-six Muslim terrorist training camps in the U. S., a picture of the terrorist's camp had a slight shadow of three men wearing sombreros. Not exactly typical of the al Qaeda dress code. It was an indication to Don Gino, who had this picture, that they were dangerous.

Zandra Filippi identified the picture of the Three Amigos. She had a huge file demonstrating that they trained with Ayman al-Zawahiri. They provided legal counsel to al-Zawahiri, and in April 2009 the Three Amigos provided intelligence for al Zawahiri, as he planned future attacks. The 2011 death of Osama bin Laden brought al-Zawahiri unprecedented power. He counted on the Three Amigos to continue to manipulate the American media.

Zandra Filippi e-mailed an encrypted file to Don Gino. It contained the information necessary in ending the terrorist plot and eliminating the Three Amigos. Don Gino spent hours digesting the information. He seldom got angry. He was angry.

The Three Amigos were instrumental in organizing an al Qaeda terrorist camp in a seaside villa in an area of Somalia. It was from this remote base that the Three Amigos met with Smith-Hammadi and learned about their tasks in the Sagrada Familia and Mission Delores attacks.

That base in Somalia no longer existed. President Barack Obama ordered Navy Seals to attack and there was a successful operation that led to the capture of Abu Anas al-Liby, the terrorist responsible for the 1998 bombings of U. S. Embassies in Kenya and Tanzania. At a press conference, President Obama thanked one special San Francisco citizen for his help. He failed to identify that citizen. Gino Landry smiled in the background as Obama concluded his press conference. The President wore a purple handkerchief in his black suit pocket. No one noticed his purple socks.

When the Obama administration found out about the plots to bomb Sagrada Familia and the Mission Delores, the CIA and FBI came to the president. He told them to stand down. He had a personal solution. The President called his good friend Don Gino Landry. They had a brief conversation.

Don Gino told Emilio that he worried about the president. He was too soft on Muslims; he was too vague in his public statements. His policies bordered on socialism. Don Gino couldn't vote for a Republican. So he listened and acted on the president's orders.

President Obama sent Don Gino a private message. "Take care of it." He also sent Don Gino a diplomatic passport. The Don smiled. He didn't need to go to confession. The President had given him the authority to act. In fact, President Obama gave him the authority to kill. Even the Pope and God would understand.

Don Gino had proof of the Three Amigos deception. He also documented their treacherous and treasonous activity. It was more widespread than he realized. Trevor Blake III had given Don Gino files that contained all the essential information. People didn't give Trevor enough credit. He had solved the crime. It was Trevor who exposed the Three Amigo's duplicitous behavior.

The Three Amigos convinced the State Department that al-Zawahiri was a scholar and not a violent radical. This turned out to be a big mistake. The Three Amigos convinced the Obama administration that the threat to U. S. soil was not real. Had it not been for Don Gino, Zandra Filippi and Trevor Blake III, the U. S. would not have been able to take action to meet the world wide al Qaeda threat in Barcelona and San Francisco.

When Don Gino met with President Obama in July 2013, he convinced the Chief Executive to reassess his policies on American Embassies. He educated the president on the dangers that a multitude of embassies faced. Obama believed that only one Embassy, Benghazi, was in danger. Don Gino convinced the president otherwise.

President Obama said: "Your intelligence is flawless Don Gino."

"Thank you Mr. President."

"Can I ask your source?"

"No, Mr. President." President Obama smiled and steered the conversation toward his revised U. S. Embassy policies.

In August 2013, the U. S. State Department closed nineteen embassies in the Middle East. The **New York Times** alleged that the Three Amigos met with Juan Zarate, President Obama's Deputy National Security Adviser, and they convinced him that al-Zawahiri remained a minor player in the al Qaeda network. This not only proved to be a terrible error, but it allowed al Qaeda to plan the Familia Sagrada attack as well as the destruction of San Francisco's Mission Delores.

As the Three Amigos left Pakistan and prepared for a brief return to Barcelona, they felt like supreme Muslim warriors. They were told that local al Qaeda members would fete them in a private dining room. The Three Amigos were surprised that there was only one al Qaeda follower in Barcelona. The rest had been killed. The Three Amigos didn't care. They weren't suicide bombers. In fact, they really weren't good Muslims. The leader of the Syrian al Qaeda faction, Issa Ibrahim Hiso, paid the Three Amigos five million dollars each. The money was transferred to Grand Cayman accounts on July 29. The next day Hiso was assassinated. A small Asian man was seen following Hiso the day before he died. The case remains unsolved.

The Three Amigos didn't realize that only one of them received the five million. Hiso's henchmen made it appear like everyone got the money. They were so greedy that only one of them checked. He was the only one to receive the money.

The Three Amigos weren't the only ones who knew about the bribe. Zandra Filippi had a complete dossier on their activity. They didn't say a word after Hiso was terminated. Everything was going right for them. Soon they would retire. With five million dollars each and freedom in the Muslim world, they would live a good life with five or six wives. They didn't believe in 300 Virgins. They were ready to drink and party in Barcelona. Even a Muslim needed some fun. After the three days in Barcelona they flew to San Francisco.

They had toasted each other with hundreds of "Here Here's." In Barcelona life was good and no one suspected them. To alloy any fears they flew home coach. They bitched all the way to San Francisco about bad food, only two glasses of wine and old stewardesses. They joked about blowing up the plane. Than Juan reminded them that they were on the plane. The Three Amigos said: "Here, Here." They laughed.

In the back of the plane, Emilio watched. He felt like calling the Department of Homeland Security. No sense alerting the authorities to the Three Amigos new found wealth. They believed that they were going to blow up the Mission Delores. Emilio and Don Gino had other plans for them. Emilio cracked his knuckles. He would have his revenge. They would be dead.

While they were in Barcelona, Emilio not only watched the Three Amigos, he collected information necessary to ending their nefarious plot. He crept in the shadows. When they slept, he quietly came into each room and searched it. He found the incriminating evidence. It was not difficult. They were arrogant and unaware.

The Three Amigos were overconfident. They believed that Don Gino was in New York. They laughed about the Haight Ashbury detective Trevor Blake III. They believed that he didn't know what he was doing. The FBI lady, Chastain Johnson, was a liberal and didn't believe that they were dangerous. She thought they were three handsome Hispanics. She never used the term Mexican, as it wasn't politically correct. She had no idea they were violent. She would soon find out. They also would eliminate Detective Sanchez. That vile womanizer gave every Mexican a bad name. The Three Amigos couldn't wait to land at San Francisco International and rain down havoc upon the Mission Delores.

CHAPTER FORTY-SIX

The Three Amigos Plot
In San Francisco

**"It is difficult to hold the world's interest
for more than half an hour."
Salvador Dali**

The San Francisco International Airport was filled with media types as the Three Amigos flew in from Barcelona. They exited the terminal and looked for a cab. They had carried on their luggage, and it was a quick trip through customs. They quickly made their way to the warehouse to get the explosives ready. They were nervous and indecisive.

A taxi pulled up to pick up the Three Amigos. They got into it quickly. They looked nervous. There was a strong police presence. They wondered what was going on? The Samoan cab driver had difficulty fitting into the front seat. He was sweating and looked uncomfortable. His passengers didn't seem to notice. They noticed that he was a terrible driver. Oh well, immigrants.

Juan said: "You think that big Chinese guy can understand us?"

Carlos said: "No!"

Juan said: "We need to get to the warehouse and finalize the plan."

The big Samoan smiled: "Where to boss?"

"We need to go to South of Market near the Third Street Warehouse."

They didn't like anyone knowing the place where they kept their explosives. Even a foreign cab driver that didn't understand English could remember the Third Street Warehouse.

Jorge said: "We might need a change of plans." They were all nervous.

Juan said: "The Don is lurking in the shadows and that fucking little Chinaman seems to be everywhere. That FBI woman with the big tits is hiding and that stupid midget was ever present." The Three Amigos were nervous. They weren't thinking clearly. There was too much pressure.

Carlos said: "Take us to the San Francisco Giants stadium." The two other amigos looked at him strangely.

Carlos whispered: "We can't let anyone, even this stupid cabbie, know where the C4 is located." The microphone in the back seat sent every word to Zandra Filippi. Don Gino was also listening.

The Samoan felt good. These turds were about to find out that they weren't so smart. They were nothing more asinine than affirmative action assholes. Not even degrees from Stanford and U. C. Berkeley guaranteed brains. Or for that matter manners.

Jorge said: "We need to work on the C4 explosives in our warehouse. This guy can't understand anything. Let's stick with the original plan." They directed the driver to go to Third and Brannan. The Third Street Warehouse was in the middle of a redevelopment revolution. They had no idea that Don Gino owned the building. He rented them a space through his company Don's Storage. Their storage space was the site of a company they chartered under an LLC as "The Three Musketeers." The cab dropped them off. The large Samoan driver eased out of the cab to help with the luggage.

Carlos said: "Bring the trunk upstairs."

"Yes sir," the Samoan smiled. The Three Amigos ignored the Samoan cab driver. They walked quickly in the building. They had an arrogance that was grating.

The cab driver wondered how they could blow up anything. They couldn't decide on their destination. Did college produce stupid people? Or was it just Stanford and Berkeley?

They walked up the stairs with their suitcases. Only the small trunk that they had trouble carrying was left for the cab driver.

Jorge said: "Bring up the trunk, now."

The Cab driver said: "Just a minute gentleman, I need to turn off the cab."

A small van pulled up and unloaded a trunk exactly like that of the Three Amigos. The van loaded the Three Amigos trunk into their vehicle and roared away. Soon they would look like the Three Stooges. Their C4 explosives were now in the hands of the SFPD. Detective Sanchez smiled as he sat in the front seat of the small van. He decided not to arrest the Three Amigos. Detective Sanchez knew that Don Gino had his own brand of justice. Sanchez preferred instant justice. The Don had an easier and more efficient way of taking care of criminals. Sanchez preferred that brand of justice.

Sanchez called the Three Amigos "the worst excuse for affirmative action." They were elitists who forgot their roots. Sanchez would make sure that Don Gino taught them humility. Sanchez wasn't alone. Emilio was waiting in the wings. They would rue the day that they called him "a little Chinaman." He knew how to teach humility.

A small Asian man watched from across the street. He watched as the Samoan cab driver laboriously lugged the trunk up three flights of stairs. He quietly went around to the back of the Third Street Warehouse. He was dressed as a cleaning person. When the Three Amigos left their warehouse, he would enter and clean it. There would be no trace of the Three Amigos in the warehouse. Soon there would be no trace of them anywhere. Emilio smiled. He liked to be the cleanup man.

The Samoan cab driver grunted as he lugged the trunk to the third floor. He took out a handkerchief and went through an elaborate ritual of wiping his forehead. The truth was that he had barely broken a sweat. He was wiping off his fingerprints.

Juan, Carlos and Jorge were hunched over a table looking at a large blueprint. The title: "Mission Delores" was prominently displayed at the top of the blueprint. The Three Amigos tipped the cabbie twenty dollars and went back to their work. They didn't notice the small pen camera that he placed on the desk next to the map. They also didn't notice that it was a different trunk.

The Three Amigos called their friends Jose and Nilo. The two illegal immigrants had no idea that they were in the midst of a terrorist crime. They were in it for the money.

They were instructed to be a block from the Mission Delores in an hour. The large trunk was opened. The C4 explosives were in place. They didn't notice some minor changes in the explosives. They were in fact plaster copies. The weight was the same due to iron bars.

The Three Amigos drove to the Mission District. They had to hurry to implement their plan. They realized that Don Gino could show up at any moment. He was supposed to be in New York. They weren't so sure.

Jorge said: "What do we do about Jose and Nilo?" Juan answered: "We let them take the fall." They laughed.

Carlos said: "One for all and all for one."

Juan: "No, no, it's five million for each of us."

It had been two hours since Jose and Nilo were instructed to stand at 19th and Army Street. They were afraid to leave. The Three Amigos gave them each $500 and strict instructions to stand on the corner. They looked bewildered. They weren't the smartest guys in the Mission. Five hundred dollars made them pliable.

As a large purple limousine cruised the area for an hour, a small Asian man dressed as a street cleaner said: "Could you gentlemen move to the side please, I need to sweep the sidewalk." Emilio smiled. He bowed deferentially. Jose and Nilo moved away from the curve. The Three Amigos arrived.

As Jorge, Carlos and Juan got out of their SUV. They were wearing black suits, black shirts, black shoes and sunglasses. The perfect disguise for the hoodlum Chicano turned al Qaeda terrorist. They pulled the trunk out of the back of the SUV. That is the last thing that they remembered. Something hit the Three Amigos in the back of their heads. They were out like a light. Jose and Nilo stood there transfixed. A man in a purple velour suit came up and gave them each a hundred dollars. A cab pulled up and they were told that they would be dropped off at 5th and Mission. They looked flustered. The rage in the man's eyes made him look as purple as his workout outfit. Jose and Nilo got in the cab. They were scared.

The Three Amigos woke up in a dimly lit church. At least it looked like a church. It wasn't the Mission Delores. Juan said: "We are in the basilica." They focused and realized that they were tied to three crosses.

Carlos said: "There aren't three crosses in the basilica."

Juan said: "What the hell is going on? What are we doing here? Where are we? Is this some part of the Mission Delores?"

Jorge said: "The Mission Church is full of people. Boyle Heights is a community where everyone goes to church daily. There is no one here. We are alone."

Emilio said: "Unfortunately, you are not alone." The Three Amigos looked at a small Asian man.

Juan said: "It's that fucking Chinaman." Emilio pulled out a long knife and began sharpening it.

"Gentlemen welcome," Don Gino smiled. "I hope that you are comfortable. I have personally built these crosses to make a point."

Jorge said: "I hope you realize that you have kidnapped a judge. You may be an important businessman but to us you are simply an old faggot."

Juan said: "Do you now who we are? Do you realize our importance?"

"Yes, he knows," a voice said from the shadows. Detective Sanchez walked to the front of the basilica. "Juan, Carlos and Jorge you are a disgrace. You are the affirmative action babies with no brains, no balls and no brawn. The three b's what a joke."

"We will have your job, Detective," Carlos said.

"I don't think so. You are about to experience a new form of justice." Sanchez pulled out a shiny, sharp nail file. He smiled. I will watch as things get more difficult."

Detective Sanchez said: "I have some papers for you to sign."

They looked at him in disbelief.

"Our lawyer will end your little charade." The Three Amigos smiled.

"We won't sign a damned thing." They looked at Don Gino defiantly.

Sanchez walked over and kicked each man in the balls.

Don Gino said: "Please take them off the crosses."

Jorge said: "You finally understand that we need our rights."

"You do, gentlemen, you have the right to meet my friend Emilio."

Emilio walked over with a large tub of water. He began water boarding the Three Amigos. They didn't sign the papers. The six Samoans moved menacingly into the Three Amigos vision. They looked terrified. They were terrified.

Don Gino said: "Please, spare these men detective. We have a plan for them."

The six Samoans backed away looking disappointed.

Sanchez looked at Don Gino. He was bewildered.

"Detective I believe that you are too hard on the Three Amigos."

Sanchez said: "As I have said, they are affirmative action babies with no brains. I see a definite end for them. One that eludes survival. They are the scum of the earth."

The Samoans walked back into the room with a battery, some cables and little knifes. The Three Amigos looked on in horror. Emilio slowly, but efficiently, began to work on them. The agony was brief but effective as they howled from the pain.

After an hour of gruesome torture, they signed Detective Sanchez' documents.

Carlos said: "You have broken the law Detective Sanchez. We will put you in jail." Trevor Blake III walked into the church.

"Ah, the Three Amigos." Trevor looked at them with disdain.

"Does Don Gino think that he can deal with us? He is nothing more than a miserable old faggot who is a career criminal. Does he have political connections?"

Don Gino didn't say a word. He didn't have to as the rage in his eyes made everyone nervous.

Detective Sanchez said: "You have disrespected the Don. No one disrespects Don Gino."

Jorge said; "I asked does he have political connections?" Jorge smiled.

"Yes, he does," Trevor Blake III, continued. "Don Gino may I take these gentlemen with me? I would like to teach them some manners and then take care of them."

Don Gino smiled. The Three Amigos had charisma, political connections and professional careers. That didn't mean that they had brains. He looked at Trevor.

"Yes, Trevor, be my guest." The Three Amigos couldn't believe it. Trevor Blake III was San Francisco's most inept private investigator. They could escape in a minute. They smiled. They said nothing. They would be in Brazil or Argentina in a couple of days. Had Don Gino lost his mind?

The Samoans loaded the Three Amigos into a SUV. They were still tied up. Trevor got in and started driving. Jorge said: "Where are you taking us?" Trevor smiled. He didn't respond. Carlos said: "We have millions, we will share it with you." Trevor didn't answer. They drove south for an hour. Trevor turned off when the road sign said San Mateo. He drove into an area of exclusive homes in a densely wooded enclave. The million dollars homes were the small ones. Probably for the maids or the gardeners.

There were a large number of BMWs, Mercedes, Cadillac's, Lexus' and Bentleys. There was one Ford and an old Mini Cooper in the parking lot. These cars were probably the butlers or the stable hands. There were horses out back.

Trevor stopped in front of a large two-story home. There were two columns out front. In front of each column a Greek statue stood out. One was Alcestis, the wife of Ademetus, who was much braver than her husband. She faced death fearlessly. The other Greek statue was of Cassandra, who was a princess that Apollo gives the gift of prophecy. The Three Amigos were taken toward the statues. They looked at the two figures quizzically. What the hell was Trevor doing? Did he drive them all this way to look at two fucking Greek statues? Had he lost his goddamned mind?

The front door of the large home opened and ten hooded men dressed as monks walked to the SUV. They bowed. They didn't say a word. They took the Three Amigos out of the SUV. Trevor drove off.

The Three Amigos realized that they were in the company of Opus Dei. They were frightened. It was a different Opus Dei. The hooded men were women. They were taken into a large hall in the sumptuous house.

Jorge said: "This is Shirley Temple's house."

Carlos said: "Who is Shirley Temple?"

Juan said: "Would you guys shut up? We need a plan."

"Welcome gentleman." The voice was soft and feminine. Carlos, Jorge and Juan relaxed. Why would women wear hoods? The answer was obvious. This was a radical feminist enclave. Even worse they were educated. Even worse they appeared vicious.

The chorus of female voices erupted in an angry hue. The large bay windows had light flit in and draw shadows upon the walls. There were candles burning. The smell of incense wafted through the room. The Three Amigos thought it was some kind of hippie ritual. They weren't terrified. They should have been scared to death. Then they noticed the intensity. They realized that they were in danger. The quiet and the eerie sense of foreboding made the Three Amigos sweat profusely.

Everyone was masked or hooded. The Three Amigos were confused. Opus Die was a male organization. No one had ever talked of a female Opus Dei. It was a secret organization. The organization was dedicated to finding happiness in daily life. What kind of horseshit was this? The Three Amigos didn't feel threatened or for that matter terrified. They should have been. They were about to experience a roller coaster of horror.

Juan, Carlos and Jorge were brought to the center of the large ballroom. At least two hundred masked women stood around them.

"Gentlemen, we are a secret society. We plan to remain as such."

Carlos said: "What is this about?" He also noted that the Opus Dei ladies spoke like they had matriculated at Stanford. That made it even worse. They were highly intelligent.

"It is about your future, your survival."

A woman with a youthful voice brought out a cell phone, a fax machine and some instructions. "You will fax your account in the Grand Cayman."

"And," Carlos said.

"You will send five million dollars to the Chestnut Center For Women at 89 Hillcrest Road, Berkeley California."

"If I don't!" The young woman kicked him in the balls.

"That's only the beginning." She spent an hour working on him with little more than her fists. Carlos wired the money.

Then it was Jorge's turn. He smiled.

"You bitch, I am prepared to die."

"You are dead already."

"Then why should I do or say anything?"

She brought out a picture of his ex-wife and kids. He looked at it for a long time.

"So. I am divorced and I could care less."

She smiled. "Here is another picture." It showed his parents tied up in a motel room. Then another picture of two of his girl friends showed them tied up and crying.

She continued: "They are all friends now you little weasel."

Jorge looked horrified. "You would punish my parents for my acts? Even more hideous is going after my girl friends."

"No. I will kill them." Jorge wired what he had left of his saving and checking accounts. It was a paltry $100,000. He was broke. The five million dollars that the terrorist promised Jorge was never sent. The others assumed that he had deposited the money for them. Never trust a rag head.

Juan looked on in horror. He was San Francisco's leading public prosecutor. He had dealt with fanatics. These people were off the grid. He didn't have any money. He didn't have anything to barter.

"Hello Juan." The young lady in front of him smiled.

"Hello." He looked puzzled. She smiled. She appeared friendly. What in the hell was going on?"

"We are going to let you go."

"What?"

"You are an honest man. Your prosecution of rapists, wife beaters, homeless ladies and radical political feminists has been fair. You have also dismissed too many rape cases. You will continue as a prosecutor. We will be in touch on your level and intensity of prosecution. Do you understand?"

"Yes I do."

"Keep in touch about all your cases. You are free to go." He couldn't believe it.

"Thank you." He looked speechless.

Juan was taken outside. He was put in a car. He was dropped off on the Bayshore Highway. He had no identification. No money. He was freezing. The peninsula was cold. Those fucking women would rue the day that they did this to him.

Juan hitchhiked. Two ugly white guys with bad moustaches, smelly clothes and pock marked faces picked him up. They let him in the back seat.

"Drop me anywhere in the city, fellas."

"Do you recognize us?"

Juan looked at them. He didn't have a clue. He didn't hang out with scum. They looked even lower.

"We are the Cochran brothers, Eddie and Hank."

Oh shit, Juan had prosecuted them for a double murder. They received a life sentence. They had escaped. They were also innocent.

"I have money."

"There is no amount of money we need. Revenge. That is our motive."

They drove in silence. Juan knew his life was about to end.

They turned off the 101 and drove to Army Street. Juan was pulled out of the car.

"We have an apartment. You, my friend, are going to be tortured."

A man walking down Army Street in a purple tuxedo approached. "Gentleman. Can I ask you a question?"

"No, aren't you lost, the Castro is just a few blocks away."

"Let us be civil."

"We have guns pulled. We are taking this scumbag into our apartment for a little recreational torture." They smiled.

"What if I told you that I wanted him released?"

They laughed. "Some old faggot approaches us with a stupid request. Get lost. Or we shot you. Or we torture you. Or we make you have sex with a woman." They laughed again.

A small midget with a purple suit came out of the shadows.

"Is this your lover?"

Don Gino lit a small cigar. "You will not be reasonable?"

"No. Now get your ass out of here, you miserable old queer."

"You may want to look behind you."

"Sure we take our eyes off you. No way." Silently six Samoans appeared. The Cochran brothers didn't hear a thing.

The purple garrotes kill them instantly.

Juan turned to Don Gino. "Thank you."

"I will hope that you thank me in court, my friend." Don Gino reached into his pocket and gave Juan five one hundred dollar bills. A purple limousine pulled up. He got in it and the chauffeur drove him home to Twin Peaks.

When Juan got out of the limousine, he saw an African American standing across the street from his palatial home. He couldn't remember who he was and then it dawned on him. James Smith, aka Hammadi, had gotten away. Juan shut the door and looked back at the corner. The tall African American was gone.

Don Gino followed the limousine. He stood watching in the shadows.

Don Gino said: "We have solved the problem."

"Boss, why didn't you kill him?"

"He is more useful alive." Don Gino got into the purple limousine and arrived at Perry's on Union Street for a hamburger. The simple pleasures in life still appealed to him. Don Gino now had San Francisco's premier legal minds in his pocket. He would have to go to confession. The death of the Cochran brothers bothered him. As he left Perry's "Summertime Blues" came out of the sound system. It was a fitting tribute to an interesting night. Don Gino stood outside Perry's smoking a small cigar. He was a lucky man. The Pope was about to recognize him. His businesses were profitable and his country was safe. He was in good health. No one could ask for any more. He had solved two major crimes and allowed Trevor Blake III and Inspector Domingo-Mercedes to take credit for this heroism. He preferred to remain in the background. A small Asian man drove up in front of Perry's. He was dressed in a dark tuxedo. Emilio never looked better. Emilio and Don Gino left for Vesuvio's and an Irish coffee.

When they entered Vesuvio's the famous writer Richard Brautigan was sitting at the bar holding court. At least it looked like Brautigan.

"Emilio didn't Richard Brautigan die in 1984?"

"Yes, he did."

"Who the hell is that?"

"His name is Irving Israel. He makes his living as a Brautigan impersonator. He rents himself out for parties."

"Well, Emilio, this is after all San Francisco."

"I know boss."

"Emilio, we need to take a brief trip to Paris. I still have a task or two to clean up this Dali mess. The loose ends bother me."

"Whenever you are ready, boss, I am packed." They left and went home to get ready for a Paris adventure. It was one that would avenge Salvador Dali's reputation and solve the riddle of the fake Dali's.

CHAPTER FORTY-SEVEN

Righting A Wrong: Don Gino Robs
The Paris Dali

"You know the worst thing is freedom. Freedom of any kind is the worst for creativity." Salvador Dali

The threat to Sagrada Familia and the Mission Delores ended. Don Gino had one more task to complete. He flew to Paris. Trevor Blake III was the key to this final nail in al Qaeda's coffin. The police, the politicians, the FBI, the CIA and Homeland Security missed the hidden element in al Qaeda fund raising. Although al Qaeda was counterfeiting paintings at the Paris Dali Museum, the word on the street was that these priceless Dali's were for sale. Don Gino heard the rumors. He was incensed. It was time to right a wrong at the Paris Dali.

After checking into the George V Hotel with Emilio in an adjoining room, Don Gino took a cab to Maxim's. It was time for a fine Paris dinner. After he finished his sumptuous repast the cab dropped him at Montmartre. The Dali museum was down a small side street. He lit a small cigar and walked past the small, poorly lighted museum. Perfect. It would be easy to use a small knife to open the door. Or perhaps even better, there were skylights on the roof for easy access.

The Paris Dali Museum was filled with fakes. James Smith had stolen a dozen priceless Dali's. He was in the process of selling them to Arab sheiks. It was all done quietly to raise money for his nefarious terrorist activities. After they purchased the rare art items, the Arab

Sheiks sent the Dali's to a Paris warehouse for Don Gino. There was no charge. The word on the street was that Don Gino made them a deal. Donate the paintings and live. No one ignored Don Gino's requests.

Don Gino needed a map for the Paris Dali. He made a call. Within an hour an architectural schematic was delivered to his hotel. He spent the evening pouring over the architectural plan. He found his way into the museum. It was a skylight on the roof. Emilio also looked at the schematic, he pointed to the skylight entryway that he would open up for Don Gino.

Emilio took a cab to the Paris Dali. He quietly hopped onto the roof. It took him less than five minutes to pry the skylight open. He would wait a day to steal the fake Dali's and replace them with originals. Emilio made detailed drawings of the Paris Dali. He also had a small tube with a carefully folded sketch of **Christ In Egypt**. This rare Dali wasn't catalogued by the Paris museum. There was no record of it. The provenance was missing. Emilio placed it in the tube; it was a gift for Don Gino.

There was one other task that Don Gino had in mind. He went to bed that night thinking about his visit to Paris' famous cemetery. He had a mission to pay tribute to two of his idols.

The next morning Don Gino got up and took a cab to the 118-acre Pere-Lachaise Cemetery. He wanted to see two graves. The ride to the 20th arrondissement gave him time to think. He wanted to pay tribute to the Doors' lead singer Jim Morrison. The other grave he wanted to visit was Guillaume Apollinaire's. He had given birth to surrealism.

The Apollinaire Monument was a fitting tribute to the avant-garde poet. Don Gino stood in front of the tall headstone admiring it. He placed a purple rose on the grave. He walked over to a crowd of about twenty people laying roach clips on Jim Morrison's grave. He placed a small purple guitar on the grave. Then a bouquet of purple roses was set on the left side of the grave. No one touched them for a week.

As Don Gino walked out of the cemetery, he noticed the small metal signs. Not everyone had a flamboyant headstone. He liked the humble gravesites. There was one more task that Don Gino needed to finish. Dali's friend, Robert Descharnes, had been vilified by a number of Parisians. Don Gino sent Emilio to take care of this injustice. It took Emilio the better part of an afternoon to beat up the three critics who questioned Descharnes work. That night Emilio took out a portion of the skylight and he removed the fake paintings that Descharnes identified.

An hour later, Don Gino quietly eased through the Paris Dali Museum skylight and into the darken museum. Emilio followed Don Gino. They had a mission. A truck was parked out front with six Samoans. A small Asian man came out of the Paris Dali with fake paintings. He put them in the spacious truck as the six Samoans quickly replaced them with originals. It didn't take long. The beat policeman was having a nice dinner nearby at Au Clair de Lune. This small, cozy African restaurant provided a goat cheese salad and snails in a puff pastry. When he finished the policeman looked at the thousand Euros. The main in the purple cape asked the policeman to wait an hour before examining the Paris Dali. He did so after the gentleman handed the policeman an envelope. The policeman saluted.

An hour and a half later, the policeman walked by the Dali museum as a small van came out of the side street and onto the main thoroughfare. It was full of tourists from another country. They looked like large Chinese people. The policeman wondered what they were doing in the neighborhood. He tipped his hat. The large tourists smiled and bowed as the van sped away. An elegantly dressed man walked up the street and tipped his hat to the policemen. The tourists were getting to know the area.

The next day Don Gino went to the Salon du Livres where he heard San Francisco poet Richard Brautigan read from **Trout Fishing In America**. Only in France could a book with a title about fishing, that had little to do with the sport, become a perpetually popular French book. But then again there was no explaining the French. The speaker who looked like Richard Brautigan had a droopy mustache. He looked like the author on Brautigan's book. He wasn't. The fake Brautigan looked nervous. He didn't take compliments well. The problem is that he was Irving Israel the world's foremost Brautigan impersonator.

Richard Brautigan had been dead since the 1980s. After all it was Paris. Even a Brautigan impersonator was acceptable. All you had to do was look and talk like Brautigan. One wondered if Irving Israel could write his name. He probably could on one of his checks.

Don Gino had one more day in Paris. He decided to visit Anne Guidicelli, the founder of the Paris-based security risk company Terrorist Inc. Guidicelli, a Filipino-Italian, became famous when she stopped assassination attempts on Carla Bruni. When Bruni was France's first lady, during the Sarkozy regime, there was a hit put out on her. Guidicelli investigated Rolling Stone lead singer Mick Jagger for the hit. He was innocent. He had banged Bruni not killed her.

Guidicelli prevented three Muslim terrorist attacks in Paris. As a result, her firm became internationally famous. She was also a wealthy woman. She was also a Dali collector and a friend of Don Gino Landry.

She talked daily with Zandra Filippi who gave the Don a large packet to deliver to Guidicelli. Don Gino made a lunch date with her. They met in front of the Meurice Hotel and Don Gino asked if she had time for a long lunch. She did.

Don Gino said: "I would like to dine in Dali's favorite restaurant."

Guidicelli said: "As you wish." They stood out front the Meurice Hotel and admired the 5 Star masterpiece. They looked over at the Tulleries Garden, the Place de la Concorde and the Musee du Louvre.

Don Gino said: "I could stand here forever, magnificent."

"Ah, yes," Guidicelli paused. "We both appreciate the finer things." They walked back inside the Meurice Hotel. The plush, newly installed purple carpet led the way to Dali's favorite restaurant.

The Restaurant le Dali is Don Gino's favorite Paris eatery. When the Don walked in, he admired the Ara Starck ceiling. When Philippe Starck remodeled Le Dali in 2007, he included one booth with plush purple velvet cushions and white contrast pillows. The result was a unique creation. Le Dali is a tribute to Dali's genius.

Don Gino is able to relax amidst some of Dali's greatest works. The maître'd, Pierre, sat Don Gino and Ms. Guidicelli in a private corner. Franka Holtmann, the General Manager, walked over with a bottle of a 2004 Louis Roderer Cristal Brut Millesime, Champaign. They drank a toast to the Dali art.

The service is flawless. The duck is the best in Paris and Don Gino always begins his meal with the fresh tomatoes, mozzarella and strawberries salad. The Saint Pierre with eggplant mousse is the light and tasty dish that Don Gino recommends.

They shared an appetizer of roasted Duck Foie Gras with pomegranate molasses, candied cherries and raisins with groundnut. A bottle of Domaine Roger Sabon Chaneauneuf du Pape le Secret de Sabon, 2006, was placed on the table. Don Gino smiled. It was compliments of the chef. Don Gino loved this magnificent wine that was produced from a secret family recipe.

Guidicelli ordered the sliced breast of pigeon with Pigeon Foie Gras and Hazelnuts. She smiled when the sumptuous platter was served.

"I take it Ms. Guidicelli that you approve?"

"Yes, Don Gino, I am envious of your gastronomic knowledge. You always order a dinner to delight the palate."

The waiter placed a purple plate with a roasted fillet of Turbot with Glasswort and cockles fed with apple petals.

"Don Gino, I believe that you have ordered the most succulent meal." She smiled. They toasted and quietly ate making small talk. Guidicelli never tired of looking around the Meurice Hotel. She gazed dreamily at the ceiling.

When Starck's daughter, Ara, painted the giant ceiling the gold and ochre hues, it prompted Don Gino to fund a book on the restoration. Suddenly Dali's work, particularly the Dalinien chair with feet in the form of ladies shoes, became a tourist draw. There were many other eclectic art pieces including a beautiful lamp with drawers and Le Meurice's recognizable lobster talking on a telephone.

"I want to thank you Don Gino for a perfect day." She smiled. The soft Chocolate Cream with Hazelnut Praline topped with crunchy mousse with frozen lemon arrived. Don Gino was served the Puffed Egg Whites with a Strawberry Heart over egg white melted in the oven. He dug into his desert as cappuccinos arrived.

Don Gino pointed out the unique design of the Dalinien chair, as well as the other art pieces. He gave Ms. Guidicelli a brief history of each item. She appeared interested. She sat with rapt attention as Don Gino continued his lengthy, but fascinating, history of Salvador Dali's Paris visits.

Don Gino explained that Dali spent one month a year at Le Meurice. During one stay, Dali demanded that a herd of sheep be brought to his room. The hotel obliged. He pulled out a pistol and shot at them. What did Le Meurice receive for his eccentric behavior? They didn't charge him for his room. He provided the hotel with art. He designed chairs that were so heavy they couldn't be lifted. They are Dali's. They are worth millions. He also created Le Meurice's avant-garde reputation. The hotel room prices were adjusted to cover Dali's eccentricities. He was also a one-man public relations figure for Le Meurice.

At Christmas, Dali autographed lithographs as gifts. This was in lieu of tips to the staff. There are half a dozen instant millionaires created from the Dali lithographs who live in Paris and worked at the Meurice. No one complained about the lack of tips.

After Don Gino and Ms. Guidicelli finished lunch they walked down the Rue de Rivoli.

"Are you going home soon, Don Gino? I would love to show you a little more of Paris."

"Sorry, the invitation is tempting. I still have some business in Spain."

"Do I have some time to send a gift to your hotel?"

"Yes, of course, how kind."

"What is your itinerary, Don Gino and when do you leave Paris?"

"In two more days, I have some unfinished business."

"Thank you for the lunch."

"My pleasure." He put the young lady in a cab and took a long walk. Don Gino needed to take care of a couple of tasks.

There is magic to the Paris Metro. Nothing beats the Paris Metro experience. Don Gino walked under the Rue de Rivoli and caught line 12 to Montmartre. He got off at the Rue de Bac stop.

The warehouse was nearby. He walked into it. The six Samoans sat around a small room. The midget valet was filing his nails. He looked unhappy. In the middle of the room the counterfeit Dali's surrounded a man tied to a stake. He was a little man. He had a pronounced Spanish accent.

"Hello, Pip."

"Who are you?"

"It is not who I am. It is what I want."

"I know nothing. I am a simple guide at the Sagrada Familia. My vacation in Paris was interrupted by these awful men."

"I need to know if James Smith is alive."

"Yes you do, you need to keep me alive to tell you." Pip smiled.

"My friend, my patience is wearing thin." Don Gino lit a small cigar.

"I will tell you nothing."

"As you please." Don Gino snapped his fingers. The six Samoans placed the fake Dali's around Pip. They poured gasoline on the paintings. Then all over the room. The little man looked terrified. He was also horrified.

"You are going to burn those originals." Pip couldn't believe it. He was transfixed on the paintings surrounding him.

"Pip, you have one last chance."

"You don't scare me you old faggot. You will never destroy these originals. I know that you are a Dali collector. You are just trying to frighten me." Pip smiled. He had no idea that the paintings were authentic fakes. "I will take my secrets to the grave."

"Yes, you will."

Don Gino looked angry. People were dead. People were injured. This little bastard was worried about the paintings. Disgusting. There was still a terrorist on the loose. Or perhaps there was more than one terrorist running around. The Don couldn't be certain. He was certain of one thing. Pip would die.

"Good bye my friend." Don Gino tossed his small cigar on the floor. The fire started slowly. By the time the purple limousine was down the hill from Montmartre a five-alarm fire prompted three Paris fire trucks to arrive. It didn't pay to make the Don mad. When the Don asked a question. You answered.

The limousine stopped at La Coupole. The Montparnasse art décor brasserie was Don Gino's favorite place to relax outside the Meurice Hotel. He sat down at a small table and ordered a glass of champagne. It would not taste as good as previous glasses at the Meurice Hotel. He drank it slowly. Thinking. It was time to walk and plan for the future. He also had to rid his conscience of his recent behavior. There was no time to confess. He would have to consider a self-confession.

Don Gino walked around Paris. He always felt bad when he burned someone to death. His Catholic conscience took a day or two to recover. It was three o'clock in the morning. He loved the smell and the sights around Paris. The Montparnasse area that surrounded La Coupole was an art deco jewel that brought images of the old Paris to mind. Don Gino could relax. He could think. It was time for some French onion soup. The aroma of onion soup seeped into the streets.

Don Gino took a cab to the Café Montparnasse and as he got out in front of the Gare Montparnasse, he noticed an African American watching him. He walked into a small bistro that was still open. He sat by the window with a small bowl of aromatic onion soup and a glass of red wine. He had some business to conclude with those who thought that they had fooled him.

The changes in world affairs bothered Don Gino. He remembered reading Andre Malraux's notion that people were revolting and ideology was consuming them. This is why he gave large sums to political charities. Malraux was a French novelist who predicted the triumph of the socialist movement in Paris and the surrounding countryside. Socialism bred revolution. Everyone ignored justice. Don Gino had to return to Spain to pursue justice. Don Gino was worried that President Obama was a Socialist. He would set the president straight.

There were still some loose ends. Don Gino didn't like to leave things to chance. He pulled out a book by his favorite author, Joyce Carol Oates. He turned to one of her beautiful sentences. It was another key to making the loose ends go away. "Nothing is accidental in the universe," Oates continued. "This is one of my Laws of Physics-except the entire universe itself, which is Pure Accident, pure divinity." Don Gino smiled. This quote from a legendary writer, Joyce Carol Oates, made him realize he had to pursue final justice in Spain. That justice is based on destroying a home. He also had to learn more about American Muslim's. The ones that he knew were good people. What had gone wrong?

When Don Gino purchased Denise A. Spielberg's book **Thomas Jefferson's Qur'an: Islam and the Founders**, he learned another truth. He read about anti-Muslim sentiment from sixteenth century Europe to the present day migration to America. He realized that toleration and equality toward Muslims would go a long way to ending the political radicalism of people like James Smith, aka Hammadi. Don Gino went to his bookshelf and pulled out a John Locke treatise where the political philosopher wrote of "civic equality" for Muslims. The Don realized that hatred toward Catholics was much like that directed toward Muslims. Or for that matter a religious nonconformist, like President Thomas Jefferson, who was criticized for defending deism. It was Jefferson's words that urged toleration toward Muslims. Don Gino was frustrated. No one listened to Jefferson in the 21st century. Then Don Gino pulled out a biography of President George Washington who urged tolerance toward Muslim laborers. What was it about history that people ignored? Don Gino made a note to donate a million dollars to the University of California's Bancroft Library for a study of Muslim rights in America. Don Gino thought about what had turned James Smith into Hammadi. He didn't have a clue. What turned the Three Amigos into terrorists? That was easy. Greed!

Tolerance. That was a subject that Don Gino needed to explore. He went to confession. He needed to ask the Catholic Priest about tolerance.

CHAPTER FORTY-EIGHT

Don Gino Goes To Rotteredam's Kunsthal Museum

"Do not dwell in the past, do not dream of the future, concentrate the mind on the present moment." Salvador Dali

Don Gino was preparing to leave Paris. There was never enough time. A loud knock on his door surprised him. This had never happened. He instructed the staff that he needed privacy. He pulled out a small Glock. He looked through the peephole. There were two well-dressed men in dark suits. Behind them stood the six Samoans. Don Gino opened the door.

"Gentleman, can I help you?"

They pulled out large shiny badges. "I'm Inspector Claude Francois with Interpol and this is my colleague Absolon Abelard. "We need your help. It is a matter of some urgency." They looked uncomfortable. Interpol did not like asking for help.

"My help in what?" Don Gino looked quizzical.

"Yes, we need you to come to Rotterdam. It is an art theft case with profits from the sales linked to al Qaeda. We understand that you may know something about this type of crime."

Don Gino smiled. They had done their homework. "I'm at your disposal gentlemen."

"We have two SUVs to take you, your six bodyguards, the small Chinese man and that reprehensible valet to Rotterdam. The little bastard stomped on our feet."

Don Gino smiled: "It is simply the small man's way. He means nothing. My apologies."

"There is an Interpol plane waiting at the DeGaulle Airport." An hour later they were in the air.

'I'll be ready." Don Gino e-mailed Zandra Filippi. He needed some intelligence on the Kunsthal robbery. He didn't realize that an obscure Dali was stolen. No one steals Dali's. That is unless they want to deal with Don Gino Landry. The Don was concerned about only a few of the Dali's. Particularly, those that are rare or virtually unknown. They are not easy to acquire. They also interest him. Then Don Gino took out his encrypted cell phone. He called Rome. He talked to the Pope's secretary. He was told to contact the Mafia's Don Carlo. An hour later, Don Gino dialed the Mafia Don.

"Hello Don Carlo."

"My good friend, Don Gino, to what do I owe this pleasure?" Don Gino explained for almost half an hour.

Don Carlo said: "I see. I will send a team to Rotterdam. Let me know where the other team needs to arrive." An hour later, three gentlemen took off for Rotterdam. They had Don Gino's back. The Pope made it clear. Don Gino Landry had special privileges.

Don Carlo hung up. Don Gino picked up a virtually empty large bag. He would need it in Rotterdam.

The Rotterdam Hague Airport is the smallest and least conspicuous Dutch airport. Don Gino observed the landing at the edge of the tarmac farthest from the terminal. There were two SUV's waiting. The Interpol agent directed the driver to the Mainport Design Hotel in the heart of the city. This 5 Star hotel is quiet, discreet and a short distance from the Kunsthal.

That afternoon they entered Rotterdam's Kunsthal Museum. Don Gino watched a video of two men wearing hoods stealing eight paintings by Monet, Dali, Gauguin, Picasso and Matisse. These paintings were part of the "Avant Gardes: The Collection of the Triton Foundation" which was a special exhibition. One of the Kunsthal Museum Curators, Fred Leeman, told Don Gino that it appeared to be "a shoplifting crime." Don Gino agreed. It was the work of amateurs.

When they sent out a message they said they were Mafia. Don Gino privately laughed. Mafia! Not really!

Then the museum director put on a second DVD. It showed a Greek man stealing Dali's "Queen Ant Gala With Sharp Pincers." This painting was done late in Dali's life as a tribute to Gala's influence.

It took the Don one day to figure out the crime. It wasn't difficult. Amateurs robbed the Kunsthal Museum. They took the Dali painting at the last moment. When they tried to sell their art, the two robbers said that they would throw in the Dali for free, if someone bought the two Monet's. This was the final insult for Don Gino. He directed Emilio and the six Samoans to London.

Zandra Filippi e-mailed Don Gino a map of an area underneath London's Waterloo Bridge. It was here that one of the robbers buried Monet's pastels **Waterloo Bridge** and **Charing Cross Bridge**. The robber, David Churchill Williams, was apprehended and the paintings returned.

Williams cut a deal with one of the City of London's Prosecutors. The chief prosecutor, Fazal Arvin, was hard nosed on terrorism. But Williams pointed to his lineage to Winston Churchill. Williams also had Rolling Stones' lead singer, Mick Jagger, testify to William's patriotism. In a mirthful moment, Jagger said: "Mr. Williams also has every Muddy Waters record."

Fazal Arvin said: "Who is Muddy Waters?"

Despite the tense exchange, Williams was given community service. He was sent to Guildford, a London suburb, where he directs tourists to local pubs. He also serves pro bono as an usher for Queen's Park Ranger soccer games. Williams told the **London Times** that this was severe punishment as QPR was relegated from the premier league to the championship division. The judge threatened Arvin and Williams for not taking the threats seriously. They apologized to the Court.

Williams did have the last laugh. The profits from the Guildford tours went to the David Churchill Williams Foundation to preserve Salvador Dali's art. Richard Branson donated a million pounds to the cause. The British government then awarded Williams the OBE. He is now Sir David Churchill Williams. He proved that crime does pay.

Don Gino still had work to do on his own. There were clues in the heart of Rotterdam, according to another e-mail from Zandra Filippi.

Don Gino walked alone into the heart of Rotterdam. He had a coffee and asked if there was a red light district. To his surprise, Rotterdam didn't have one. He was directed to the privehuizen or private houses that served as houses of prostitution. It was here that Don Gino met Dan Carlo's small band of men.

"Hello gentlemen."

"Don Gino, we are here to serve you. Don Carlo said to extend every courtesy."

"Thank you. This is a crime of amateurs. Sometimes these crimes are more difficult to solve."

"What can we do?"

"Be my eyes and ears, this is the work of immigrants." The men left quickly to cover Rotterdam's less savory places. They soon found that Afghan food and the Rumanian Mafia were the keys to recovering the stolen art. The Italian Mafia members e-mailed the Don this information and a packet came in from Zandra Filippi. She traced a part of the crime to Rumania.

Don Gino went into another coffee shop and learned that Rotterdam's Bar Tender on Coolsingel was where Afghan cuisine was served. It was also Rotterdam's hip spot for music and dancing. He spent an hour in the Bar Tender. The final clue became apparent. Don Gino returned to the hotel.

He was ready to solve the art theft from the Kunsthal Museum. He needed an art expert. Don Gino contacted the best person for the job.

Don Gino waited for Chris Marinello, who directed the Art Loss Register. They talked at length about the robbery. Marinello was also an undercover Rotterdam police officer. The heist was the most costly in the history of the Netherlands. Kunsthal director, Emily Ansenk, met the press and attempted to mollify them. The questions about inadequate security didn't have an answer. Then Don Gino strode to the podium.

"Gentlemen of the press, my name is Gino Landry, I represent a private consulting firm, Trevor Blake III Investigations. We will have the case solved in three days. Thank you for your time." Don Gino left the press area and took Ms. Ansenk with him.'

"Have you lost your mind?" Ms. Ansenk said.

"My apologies madam, I need two days and I will bring you the thieves. Trust me."

"What about the missing art?"

"It will arrive with me. I have a special plan."

She looked on speechless. Don Gino left the Kunsthal Museum and walked out to a limousine. The large Samoan driver left for the airport. That night Don Gino landed his private plane in Romania. He went to the Bucharest Hilton where three well-known Italian businessmen met him. There was also a local judge. That night a special court session prompted the judge to issue an arrest warrant for three Rumanian citizens.

The next morning Rumanian police arrested three men. The arresting officer was from Rotterdam. His name was Chris Marinello, and he received international praise.

The news conference announcing the arrest of the Romanians showed a tall elegantly dressed man in a purple suit unobtrusively standing behind the police. When a reporter asked if the Monet's, the Picasso's, the lone Dali and the Gaugin's were recovered. The answer was an unequivocal yes. The only painting missing or destroyed was Salvador Dali's **Queen Ant Gala With Sharp Pincers**. The Rumanian police pointed out that the worth and provenance of this Dali had not been established. They viewed it as a minimal loss. No one was concerned about the Dali. It was small and its value undetermined. Don Gino stood in the back holding a large suitcase. The Dali was inside.

That night Don Gino returned to Rotterdam. He was in a private plane with Chris Marinello, and they talked at length about the criminal activity of the robbers.

Don Gino said: "The robbers were so stupid that they didn't know how or where to sell the paintings."

"I still can't believe it." Marinello took a drink of the champagne served by the leggy stewardess. He ate a meatball and continued: "How did you discover the problem with sales Don Gino?"

"I went to the best art fence in the world and he led me directly to the three criminals. My friend Don Carlo was instrumental." The plane landed and Don Gino left for his hotel.

That night in Rotterdam, Don Gino had a private dinner with Ms. Ansenk and apologized for his boorish behavior. "I took over that press conference and upstaged you, my apologies." He took out a gold Cartier watch. "I would like you to have this as a token of my appreciation."

Ms. Ansenk said: "For what?"

"For your kindness and understanding."

As Don Gino packed his luggage, he had the problem of placing a small painting in a proper receptacle. He took off the frame, he had a large tube, and he rolled up the painting and put it in the tube. He smiled. It was another rare Dali. He hoped that Danielle Steel wouldn't ask what it was or where he purchased it. Sharon Stone never asked these questions.

Chris Marinello showed up to drive Don Gino to the airport. While six Samoans in a large purple limousine followed his police car closely, the press waited at the airport to give Don Gino a fond farewell. He was an international hero. The Don was nervous about praise. He would make sure that Marinello was the hero.

"Don Gino, I would like to thank you."

"My friend, you are an extraordinary policeman."

"I don't see how you solved the crime so quickly?"

"My associates in Rumania are of Italian descent. We have similar interests and goals. Contrary to public opinion, we are law abiding. If we find someone who is not law abiding, we make a decision about the future. We usually kill them. We simply had the art thieves arrested."

"Well Don Gino, that is civilized."

"Perhaps! Perhaps not!" In truth the Don believed in instant justice.

`As Don Gino flew back to the United States, he was troubled by what he had seen in Barcelona. The American Ambassador was holding meetings in the Raval district and apologizing to Muslims. This was not acceptable. It was time to have a talk with President Barack Obama. The Democrat's waffling foreign policy was unacceptable. The idea of mollifying Muslims was ridiculous. They wanted to take away our holidays, replace our legal system with Sharia law and force women into a secondary or subservient role. Someone had to stand up to the Muslim threat. Don Gino directed his plane to Dulles International Airport. It was time to set President Obama straight. The bombing at the conclusion of the Boston Marathon was the latest example of Obama coddling Muslim radicals.

CHAPTER FORTY-NINE

Don Gino Feels Defeated:
U. S. State Department Promoting
Islam In Barcelona

"Very few people know who I really am." Salvador Dali

After he finished cleaning up the Rotterdam Dali thefts, Don Gino felt relieved. He had done his job. The Barcelona and San Francisco Muslims were defeated. The Muslim threat was over. Then he received an encrypted e-mail from Zandra Filippi. It read: "U. S. State Department Actively Promoting Islam in Europe." Don Gino couldn't believe it. Zandra must have it wrong. She didn't. The accompanying material included a speech by U. S. Ambassador Alan Solomont in which he said: "The Obama Administration wants to practice Muslim outreach." Solomont went on to apologize for America's anti-Muslim policies.

Don Gino realized he had one more goal. He had to straighten out President Obama about the al Qaeda threat. He made copious notes. He drafted a mock bill for better Embassy security. He was still on his private plane flying to Washington D.C. He was prepared to argue for strong American action. The facts were a big part of Don Gino's intellectual argument. The president was a good listener. Don Gino was a non-stop talker. Don Gino voted twice for Obama. He worried that the president was indecisive. He was having trouble making the right decisions. Don Gino drew up a mock bill on military protection for American Embassies. He quietly presented it to President Obama. He wrote a memo to the president that Ambassador Solomont was a good man who couldn't do the job. Don Gino underplayed his concerns and couched his argument for Solomont's removal in gentlemanly tones.

He e-mailed his notes to President Obama. In two hours, Don Gino's plane would land and he would meet with the president. While he crafted his arguments, Ambassador Solomont continued to represent American interests in Spain. When Solomont spoke he failed to notice the small Asian man in the back of the room. Emilio took copious notes. He e-mailed them daily to Don Gino. His reports frustrated Don Gino. It was time to take action. The president had to understand the danger.

When Solomont spoke in the Barcelona Raval, he was preaching to those who wanted to bring the Muslim way of life into the Spanish mainstream. Sharia law, Solomont suggested, needed to be a part of Spanish law. Don Gino was outraged.

After Don Gino's plane landed at Dulles International, he went to the U. S. State Department. He had a friend at State that provided intelligence. They went out for a quick cup of coffee. There was a folder under the State Department officials arm. They talked at length. The Don shook the officials hand and left with the folder. The folder contained another loose end. The al Qaeda terrorists and the U. S. State Department were both making mistakes. Don Gino would set the State Department straight. The terrorists, he would simply terminate them. The State Department needed to be educated to the al Qaeda menace as did the president.

The file told Don Gino that he needed a brief visit to Barcelona. He was tired, the six Samoans were tired and the valet was sleeping. The return to Barcelona was to be quick and decisive.

Don Gino flew back to Barcelona. He couldn't believe it. He and his men had risked their lives, they had spent an inordinate amount of his money to defeat the al Qaeda terrorists and now that two-faced bastard in the White House was working behind their backs. Muslim Outreach incensed Don Gino.

When Don Gino stormed into Ambassador Solomont's office, he was asked to wait. The picture on the wall showed a reed thin man with the face of an aristocrat and the glasses of an intellectual. Don Gino was nervous. Here was a man who would coddle Muslims. This was not a good sign. Don Gino cracked his knuckles. He tried to look calm. He wasn't. He was furious.

After an hour, the Don excused himself. He realized that the Ambassador had no intention of seeing him. His secretary said that the Ambassador was busy. No one makes Don Gino wait. No one disrespects the Don.

He took a cab to the Raval district. He found two Muslims who Don Carlo directed to talk to him. Don Gino met the two Muslims at his favorite Italian restaurant, Ca I'Sidre, where the owner Isidre Girones had his Don Gino capriccioso pizza ready. The Don had a lengthy meeting over a nice lunch.

The two Muslims informed Don Gino that the ambassador apologized for American policy toward the Middle East. Don Gino sat in stony silence. He couldn't believe it. They told him of a $750 million soccer field built quietly at Gitmo for detainees. Then they pulled out detailed payoff lists to keep local Muslims happy. They also showed the Don cashier's checks they received to proselytize for American interests. Don Gino believed that President Obama's allegiance to America was in question. Don Gino envisioned this strange turn of events as a major turning point in American foreign policy. Were the historic checks and balances fading? The Don hoped not. He would talk to the president.

Then Don Gino called his good friend, Secretary of State, John Kerry. They talked at length. Kerry told the Don that the Obama Administration was embarking on a policy of appeasing European Muslims. The Don couldn't believe it. He called Kerry.

Secretary John Kerry: "My friend, Don Gino, thanks for the call."

"What is going on with the State Department and European Muslims?" Don Gino lit a small cigar.

Secretary Kerry paused: "We are beginning a program of Muslim Outreach."

"I beg to differ, Secretary Kerry." Don Gino continued: "You are enabling a group of radicals with appeasement. How can you defend that?"

"I am the instrument of President Obama."

"I see. This Muslim Outreach will it be continued?"

"Oh, yes, make no mistake, we must live with the Muslim world."

Secretary Kerry hung up. Don Gino sat thinking. Nothing has changed. He had risked his life. He had risked his men. He had risked his life. He had spent two million dollars of his own money combating al Qaeda. President Obama rewarded him with the Muslim Outreach program. Now he knew why so many people couldn't trust the president.

Don Gino made another phone call to San Diego. On the Marina a retired ceiling contractor and former Navy Seal sat on his sixty-foot Carver boat lifting weights and working out.

His boat the King Claudius X was the party boat on the San Diego pier. His phone rang. He had to rush up to the front to answer the phone.

"Let me speak to the El Sereno Phantom."

"Don Gino is that you?"

"Yes, it is, how is the Phantom?"

"I suspect that I am coming out of retirement."

"Yes, you need to fly into Barcelona. I have a job for you."

"Can I say no?"

"See you tomorrow, I am sending a private plane it will be at San Diego International at nine in the morning. I know you still spend late nights with the ladies. See you in two days."

"I'll be there Don Gino."

The El Sereno Phantom looked in the mirror. For a sixty-year-old former Navy Seal, he looked great. He grew a beard to look older. It didn't work. He looked forty and distinguished. He vowed to get some girl friends over thirty. Well, maybe next year. The El Sereno Phantom packed a large trunk. He would need his supplies. It was good to be back in the game. He loaded a machine gun, two glocks and packed a rocket launcher. There would be no customs. He knew that Don Gino had taken care of any official intrusion into the mission. Then the El Sereno Phantom placed two specialized knifes in his luggage. The El Sereno Phantom smiled. He was back.

When he landed in Barcelona, at the El Prat airport, it was full of tourists. He wasn't looking forward to customs. The El Sereno Phantom wore a dark Savile Row suit and sunglasses. He was an imposing figure. He watched as two large Samoans carried his trunk away. He didn't have to worry.

"Sir." He turned and looked at a distinguished man in a dark suit. Obviously, police. "I am Inspector Domingo-Mercedes, would you come with me? We have a special exit for you. It is courtesy of Don Gino."

The El Sereno Phantom walked out a side door. Don Gino stood on the curb. He leaned against a purple limousine.

"Thank you my friend for coming."

"Don Gino, it has been too long." They shook hands and embraced.

On the ride to the Palacette Continental Hotel, Don Gino outlined his plan. The El Sereno Phantom smiled. He hadn't blown up a building in a decade. He was looking forward to using his old explosive secrets.

Don Gino said: "I thought that President Obama was using his Muslim Outreach program to integrate Muslims into the European community."

"Why is this important?" The El Sereno Phantom wasn't sure what was going on.

Don Gino said: "Muslims can't become Europeans. Sharia law and their attitude toward women are just two negative factors. Our president has stabbed us in the back by appeasing the very bastards we have hunted down and killed. It is time to turn the tables." Don Gino smiled. He would have the ultimate revenge. No one disrespected Don Gino. He was also incensed when American values weren't respected.

After they settled in for a lengthy dinner at Cinco Jotas, Don Gino outlined his plan. They would bomb the Barcelona based Muslim's For Moderation storefront in the Raval ghetto.

That night the El Sereno Phantom walked around the storefront of Muslim's For Moderation. Piece of cake! He could destroy the building and not touch the businesses on either side. The rag head bastards were in for a surprise.

It took another day to place the C4 around the building. In two days the Barcelona based newspaper, **La Vanguardia**, reported the destruction of the Muslim's For Moderation storefront. There were two members inside conducting a meeting. They were killed. The police had no leads. The case remains unsolved.

Inspector Domingo-Mercedes announced a week later that a Muslim radical, known as Aashif, was arrested for the bombing. There was a problem. Domingo-Mercedes informed the press that Aashif committed suicide with a purple rope used to hold up jail pants. There was no next of kin. There was a strange request. The body was to be shipped to Alabama for burial. No one could figure out why.

Don Gino and the El Sereno Phantom returned to Washington D. C. They were picked up at Dulles International by a presidential limousine.

Don Gino said: "This is a 2009 GM model called 'The Beast."

The Phantom said: "The damn thing is heavily armored. Are we in danger?"

"I contributed ten million to the Obama Reelection campaign. Maybe Karl Rove wants me offed." The El Sereno Phantom laughed.

The drive from Dulles International took a half an hour. The traffic parted as four police motorcycles stopped traffic. The El Sereno Phantom said: "I guess we are important."

"More than you know, my friend."

They entered the Oval House and spent an hour talking with President Obama. The secret service looked on nervously.

"Don Gino, my apologies, you know I am not a Muslim supporter."

"Mr. President, I have confidence in you."

"Thank you, now who is our friend who solved this Barcelona Muslim situation?"

"We call him the El Sereno Phantom. He was at one time our greatest Navy Seal. Now he is San Diego's favorite bachelor."

President Obama said: "What is his name?"

"In Poland, he is known simply as Edualc."

"That is a strange name." The President looked perplexed.

"Mr. President, it is the name they use in Poland to describe those who install ceilings."

"Well, I am learning something." The President smiled.

Don Gino looked uncomfortable. "Mr. President, what are you doing about our current Muslim policy? I'm not happy with Muslim Outreach."

"I have made some mistakes regarding Muslims. There is a new bill that gives our Embassies and Consulates more fire power. They will be protected. There will be no more Benghazi's."

"Thank you Mr. President."

"It is all due to you Don Gino. I don't know how the electorate would react to a San Francisco Mafia boss advising the president."

"You would be like President Kennedy. He had Mafia folks everywhere." Don Gino laughed. So did the President.

President Obama stood up and shook the El Sereno Phantom's hand. "Please gentlemen, follow me out for a quick press conference. This is because of your good work." President Obama went down a small corridor. Don Gino, the El Sereno Phantom and six Secret Service agents followed. The small walk way led to the pressroom. The lights blared and the announcement said: "The President of the United States."

President Barack Obama strode to the presidential press podium. He announced that his administration was ending the appeasement of Muslim's in Europe. He apologized for his overzealous foreign policy. President Obama signed a new bill to combat terrorism by allowing U. S. Embassies to have greater police power. He signed the bill with a purple pen that he presented to a San Francisco businessman, Gino Landry. Nearby a former Navy Seal with a well-trimmed beard stood smiling. When one of the secret service agents asked him his name, there was an uncomfortable moment of silence. "They call me the El Sereno Phantom." President Obama shook his hand. Don Gino had killed Barcelona's last terrorist. The Phantom blew up the al Qaeda organizational center. The President came to his senses. He ended his coddling of European Muslims.

Don Gino had a long conversation with President Obama about Ambassador Solomont. The Don emphasized that Solomont had raised more money in 1997 than any previous National Finance Chairman of the Democratic National Committee. The Don said that was a good thing and a bad omen.

"Mr. President, let me be frank, Ambassador Solomont is a low level political appointee. He looks like an ambassador. He dresses like an ambassador. He talks like an ambassador. The problem is that he has little knowledge of world affairs."

The President listened intently. When they finished President Obama shook Don Gino's hand. "My friend I will take care of the problem."

"You sound like me, Mr. President." They laughed

Ambassador Solomont resigned as the Ambassador to Spain and accepted the presidency of Tufts University. Ambassador Solomont announced that he was accepting the Tuft's presidency because of a ten million dollar anonymous grant from a San Francisco businessman to established a School of Muslim Studies. This new Tufts University department would concentrate upon solving terrorist plots. The anonymous donor made only one stipulation. All the rooms in the School of Muslim Studies would be painted purple. Tufts agreed.

Don Gino returned to Barcelona. The case hadn't ended. The Don needed to find justice for his friend Inspector Domingo-Mercedes. There was still need for another form of justice in Barcelona.

As he prepared to leave for another trip to Barcelona, Don Gino made some notes on Salvador Dali. He realized that the Catalan artist blended talent and character. He saw it. James Smith, aka Omar Abdul Hammadi, could envision Dali's terrorist talent. It was sad.

What Don Gino appreciated about Dali was that he challenged the goddamned modernists who in 1923 dominated the art world. Then along came T. S. Eliot's **Waste Land** and James Joyce's **Ulysses**. Their art and literature created what was known as modernism. By the time Salvador Dali emerged a decade later, he was the antidote to modernism. Don Gino appreciated Dali's surrealistic rebellion. Those

God damned Muslims, every one of them, would be exterminated for setting up a Dali al Qaeda cell. There was more work for Don Gino.

Don Gino took a small file out of his brief case. He was waiting for his private jet to be fueled. He looked over the file on Inspector Domingo-Mercedes. He was not only a good policeman; he was a staunch supporter of Democracy. Some right wing political lunatic in Barcelona was attempting to end Domingo-Mercedes career. No one disrespects the Don's friends. He was on his way to Barcelona. It was time to secure justice in Spain for Domingo-Mercedes.

Inspector Domingo-Mercedes was vacationing in San Francisco. He called Don Gino.

"I'm sorry Don Gino, I was having a last minute bit of fun with Jim Harrison."

"Be careful, if you remember Harrison loves to go to the Upper Michigan peninsula and hang out by the Sucker River."

"The Sucker River?" Domingo-Mercedes sounded quizzical.

"It is an American thing, a peaceful river in Northern Michigan. We all need peace."

"Ah, I see, well Jim Harrison is not peaceful in San Francisco," Domingo-Mercedes asked: "Do I need to return to Barcelona?"

"Yes, my friend immediately."

"I'll be there tomorrow."

"Well, let's have a comfortable ride to Barcelona." Don Gino smiled. The Spanish government would soon rue the day that some officious bastard would cause the Don and one of his friends trouble. Domingo-Mercedes was about to find out how loyal Don Gino was to those who helped him.

Domingo-Mercedes had no idea that trouble was waiting at home. Don Gino knew of the trouble. He looked forward to putting the politicians who were after Inspector Domingo-Mercedes in their place. Justice was imminent. No one insulted the Don's friends.

CHAPTER FIFTY

Don Gino Secures Justice In Spain

"Mistakes are almost always of a sacred nature. Never try to correct them. On the contrary, rationalize them, understand them thoroughly. After that it will be possible for you to sublimate them." Salvador Dali.

Don Gino landed at the Barcelona Airport. The Don waited two hours for Domingo-Mercedes to land inside the customs area. Inspector Domingo-Mercedes was unusually quiet as he greeted Don Gino. Something was up. He didn't know. The Don did. A representative of Spain's National Court met them at customs. They quickly exited the area. When they walked outside the Barcelona El Prat Airport, there were six armed policemen. There were also two detectives. They handcuffed Domingo-Mercedes and read him his rights.

Don Gino lit a small cigar. There was no disguising his volcanic rage. His crimson face matched his dark velvet purple suit. He was not smiling. The six Samoans standing discreetly in the background frowned. The midget valet glared.

Inspector Domingo-Mercedes looked puzzled. The Don failed to inform the esteemed Inspector why the National Court was interested in the case. Or for that matter, why he was being arrested? Domingo-Mercedes wondered if Don Gino knew about the arrest? The Don did.

The Don obviously had something on his mind. Otherwise he would protest. He didn't. The inspector wasn't worried. Something was up. Don Gino looked angry.

There was someone inside Spanish government who had it in for the Inspector. Don Gino was getting the information that would allow Domingo-Mercedes to clear his name. The Don was not happy with the bureaucrat who wanted Domingo-Mercedes tried for disclosing national secrets. He would soon become an ex-bureaucrat.

When they walked outside the airport, Don Gino and the hand-cuffed Inspector Domingo-Mercedes were taken in a limousine to see Judge Pablo Rustic. The reason was a simple one. Judge Rustic was about to replace Spain's most famous investigative Judge, Balman Garstone. Rustic hoped to make his reputation by making an example of Domingo-Mercedes. Judge Rustic was in for a surprise.

There were internal politics in Spain tearing the judicial system apart. Inspector Domingo-Mercedes was in the middle of it. One of his enemies looked to end his career. Don Gino would not allow this travesty of justice.

Inspector Hector Diaz filed espionage charges against Inspector Domingo-Mercedes. The files that Domingo-Mercedes provided to Don Gino were the crux of the Spanish government's case. Don Gino and his band of men single handedly prevented the destruction of a part of Sagrada Familia and the Mission Delores. The official Spanish government files were rewritten. The credit for preventing a terrorist attack on Sagrada Familio was attributed to Inspector Domingo-Mercedes. The report was a strange one. It was written in purple ink.

There was a Spanish law preventing foreign agents from being involved in or the police assisting in domestic crimes. Domingo-Mercedes was charged with violating that law with his relationship to Don Gino.

Unbeknownst to Inspector Domingo-Mercedes, he was about to be indicted on espionage charges. Don Gino was aware of what the Spanish government thought. He quickly took action and contacted the proper officials. They had to go through a court procedure that looked fair. Inspector Domingo-Mercedes was about to be acquitted and promoted.

The issue was whether or not the Inspector exceeded his power by helping Don Gino solve the Sagrada Familia bombing plot as well as the equally abortive attempt on San Francisco's Mission Delores. Did he violate Spanish law? The Don worried that politics might get in the way of justice. Judge Rustic was out to make a name for himself and at thirty-five he hoped to become Spain's youngest investigative judge.

After Don Gino checked into the Palacette Continental Hotel, he walked down the Ramblas for a dinner at Cinco Jotas. He thought a great deal about his friend Domingo-Mercedes. He was a good man. Someone was trying to ruin his reputation. The Don did get bail for Domingo-Mercedes.

The next morning a nervous Inspector Domingo-Mercedes met Don Gino for breakfast.

Inspector Domingo-Mercedes said: "What is going on?"

"Someone is after your reputation."

"Who?"

"I have no idea."

They talked for an hour and then they took a cab to the Barcelona National Courthouse. They walked in and sat down. A few minutes later Judge Pablo Rustic walked out in an elaborate flowing robe. He looked unhappy. There was no one else in the court. No attorneys, no stenographer, no bailiff. There were two national policemen standing outside the locked courtroom.

Judge Rustic said: "Gentleman, will you approach the bench?" They got up and walked to the Judge's docket.

"Good morning." They said it in unison and looked puzzled. Inspector Domingo-Mercedes whispered: "What the hell is going on?"

Don Gino said: "I don't have a clue."

They approached the judge. There was a strained silence.

Judge Rustic said: "Gentleman, we have a very strange situation. The American CIA has requested that Inspector Domingo-Mercedes be decorated for his heroism. What the Spanish government thought was treason turns out to be an act of patriotism."

Inspector Domingo-Mercedes said: "What do you mean?" He looked perplexed.

"Your friend, Don Gino, informed the CIA, the Spanish government and our court system that you single handedly prevented the al Qaeda terror cell from blowing up two of the Familia Sagrada towers. For that we are eternally grateful. There will be no treason charges. You are to be promoted to head the Barcelona Internal Security Unit on Terrorism."

"I have never heard of the unit."

"That's because the Spanish government established it last week. I would also like to thank Don Gino for helping our country escape the ravages of terrorism."

"Thank you your honor, may I suggest that we all go to Cinco Jotas for lunch?"

The Judge, Inspector Domingo-Mercedes and Don Gino walked down the Ramblas laughing. They had a long lunch and laughed about the inept Barcelona al Qaeda terrorists.

As they ate their sumptuous lunch, a tall African American watched from across the street. A small alcove hid him. He hated these men. He would be back. James Smith, aka Hammadi, was blunted in his attempt to bring Muslim justice to Barcelona and San Francisco. His days as a terrorist were not over. He needed to find out where there were radical Muslims. He considered going to the Far East. Perhaps to Hong Kong. The Chinese were the least likely terrorists. He would change that perception. A Hong Kong al Qaeda cell would be a first. James Smith couldn't wait.

As Don Gino prepared to fly home, Inspector Domingo-Mercedes drove him to the airport.

"Thank you, my friend, for clearing my name."

"It was nothing."

"You have a friend for life, Don Gino, I will not forget you."

They shook hands. Don Gino walked into the airport. Don Gino was carrying a backpack. This was not characteristic of the Don. There was a priceless work of art stashed in his backpack. Don Gino wasn't getting paid for solving the Salvador Dali Murder. He took his pay in the form of two Dali drawings. They would be preserved and displayed properly. The Catholic Church said that they did not exist.

The Don was safe to show them publicly. He smiled. The drawings were enough pay for two lifetimes.

There was a front-page story. The assistant head of Barcelona's Office of Political Performance, Inspector Hector Diaz, was found dead. He was robbed and strangled with a purple garrote. The police have no leads. The case remains unsolved.

The Spanish press heralded Domingo-Mercedes for his eye to detail, his ability to identify a terrorist plot and his use of key information. He appeared to have eyes everywhere. When he held a news conference, there was a slight, but muscular, older Asian man smiling in the background. He was dressed as a janitor. As he left the building, when the press conference ended, Emilio walked over to the janitor's closet. He stepped in. He locked the door. Ten minutes later he came out wearing a suit cut by a London Seville Row tailor. He was ready to return to San Francisco.

CHAPTER FIFTY-ONE
Late Night With David Letterman

"It is not necessary for the public to know whether I am serious, just as it is not necessary for me to know it myself."
Salvador Dali

The **San Francisco Chronicle** headlined: "Trevor Blake III Single Handedly Saves The Mission Delores." Trevor looked at the paper nervously. He helped. He hadn't saved it. Once again Don Gino provided the press releases that made Trevor a hero.

Trevor sat in his apartment. He looked out the window as the sun filtered through the Golden Gate Bridges steel girders. The noise of young Indian computer geeks playing cricket in the park across the street reminded Trevor why he loved San Francisco. It was cool. It was eclectic. It was multi-cultural. He poured a glass of Jordan Merlot. The Don bought the wine. The phone rang.

"You need to put on some camera clothes."

"What do you mean camera clothes, Don Gino?"

"A limousine will be out front in five minutes."

"Why?" The Don hung up. When Don Gino makes a request. You follow it. I put on my best GQ clothes and walked out to Chestnut Street.

In exactly five minutes the limousine arrived. Trevor put on his best young English gentlemen's clothes. They were his only such clothes. The limousines horn sounded. Trevor walked out onto

Chestnut Street. The midget gave him the finger from the front seat. Some things don't change.

As the purple limousine slowly arrived in front of San Francisco's City Hall, no one noticed Trevor. He exited the limo and walked to the edge of the crowd. A policeman showed up and escorted him to the temporary platform in front of City Hall. Trevor watched as the police arrested nude rights activist Gypsy Johnson who was attempting to marry for the fifth time in the nude. It was hard to have a serious press conference in the City. As the nude activist protest ended, so did the crowd. Instead of a major crowd the press conference drew a few reporters, a couple of drunks, a guy with a sign reading: "Support the United Negro Cheeseburger Fund." He was not just a character from the past, he was out of touch with the present. This was after all San Francisco. Then Trevor noticed Don Gino standing nearby.

The hastily called press conference on the steps of San Francisco's City Hall drew such a small crowd there was no need for a speaker system. Mayor Edwin M. Lee praised Trevor Blake III and Emilio for solving the Mission Delores planned attack. Emilio was absent. He was robbing Danielle Steel's house. Then Mayor Lee turned the stage over to Detective Richard Sanchez who talked briefly about Trevor Blake III's heroism. Chastain Johnson stood to his side scowling and smoking a cigarette. Zandra Filippi was scowling so hard that permanent lines appeared on her beautiful face. They couldn't stand the praise for Trevor. Don Gino stood in the background smiling. Trevor was dressed in a dark Savile Row three button traditional suit. He looked out of place. He also looked uncomfortable.

The press conference continued as a love fest. Detective Sanchez said: "We need to hear from the man of the hour, Trevor Blake III." There was weak applause.

Trevor waved to the crowd. He walked to the microphone: "Thank you." He stepped back.

"The foresight and heroism of Trevor Blake III," Sanchez told the assembled news people, "is what makes our country great." There were numerous questions about others involved." Sanchez concluded:

"The San Francisco private eye who operates out of the Haight Ashbury is a special breed of investigator." Then Sanchez left the interview platform and vanished into the bowels of San Francisco's City Hall. Trevor nervously drove home.

When he entered his Chestnut Street apartment, Trevor turned on Channel 5 and watched a recap of the press conference. He was nervous about the accolades. He hadn't solved the terrorist plot. Oh well, the world's second most famous private eye once again became national news. At least he could pay the rent. It was time to celebrate with a burger. It was also happy hour.

Trevor walked over to Fillmore and up to Union Street. He walked into Perry's. Everyone at the bar stood and chanted: "Trevor, Trevor, Trevor." He waved and sat at the end of the bar.

"Myles, can I have a turkey burger and fries?"

"It's on the house, Trevor." Myles also poured a glass of Cakebread Merlot

"I hope the twenty dollar glass of wine is on the house."

Chastain Johnson walked into the bar and sat down. She smiled: "A turkey burger for the turkey, I'll have one too." Suddenly three men were talking to her. She lit a cigarette. They left. Even with a great body and good looks, the politically correct San Francisco men couldn't stand a smoker. Go figure.

Myles passed Trevor two napkins. "Your fans are giving you their phone numbers." He smiled and walked to the other end of the bar. Two young ladies smiled at Trevor. He finished the burger and walked down to Lombard Street. It was time to have a happy hour drink at the Hi Fi Lounge. He hated the purple décor. He wouldn't mention that to Don Gino.

At the Hi Fi a few girls as young as twenty-five talked to him. This was not the norm. He was once again a famous private eye. Shell Scott eat your heart out. As Trevor left the Hi Fi Lounge, everyone stood and clapped. Damn! He could get used to the accolades.

He walked to his apartment. On the doorstep, Bennie and Bertie placed a basket of fruit. The card said: "You may be an asshole, Trevor but we are proud of you." There was also a large purple box. Trevor opened it and found $10,000 in twenty dollar bills. A note in purple paper and white ink read: "A token of my gratitude. A patriot."

Trevor felt good. He was once again a hero. He also had some money. It was a nice feeling. Even faint praise or misdirected praise was better than none.

After he was home for a week, the producer for Late Night With David Letterman called with a spot on the next Friday night show. The producer sent via overnight FedEx a first class plane ticket, reservations at New York's Waldorf Astoria and a card for all drinks and meals.

There was also a packet of notes suggesting Trevor's role on the show. Letterman's producer wrote a note that said at age forty-one Trevor still had demographic appeal. He gave Trevor a list of clothes to wear. He also stated that he needed to appeal to the boomer demographics. The producer wrote: "Trevor you need the casual under forty English style." He was forty-one, it would be tough to create the boomer style. Trevor wasn't sure what the rest of the message meant, but he e-mailed him thanks for the plane ticket and hotel-food voucher. There were too many freebies to ask questions.

As Trevor prepared for his second visit to Late Night With David Letterman, he was nervous. The first show was a three-minute appearance. Letterman didn't think that Trevor had much to say. This time Trevor would have a great deal to say. He would also arrive dressed in the London casual look.

Trevor went down to Cable Car Clothiers and bought some casual clothes. Since 1954 this traditional British clothing outlet served the needs of charming young men. It was the place to shop for the English look. He liked the British clothing lines that they carried. He purchased a fur-felt fedora for $258. It was the most stylish hat that Trevor had ever seen. He selected a bar stripped tie in blue and red for $95 and a $148 blue spread shirt with the U. K. look. He gave the clerk his Platinum American Express Card. The clerk mentioned that they had a suit sale. Trevor purchased a suit. Why not? The Don was paying. He was determined to make a good impressed on Late Night With David Letterman. Or at least make some type of impression as he was barely on during the earlier show. He almost didn't survive Late Night With David Letterman.

Last time on the show, he wore a suit. David Letterman made fun of him. Then again Letterman made fun of everyone. This time Trevor opted for the casual, but well dressed, young Englishman's look. He would lie about his age and be a thirties dandy in the Big Apple.

The flight to New York was on United Airlines and it was First Class. The stewardess, Trish, had seen better days. The steak was perfect. The drinks were good. He had three glasses of Cakebread Merlot. The plane was new. Only the stewardesses were old. Trish handed Trevor a note with her phone number. It read: "Call me, Trish the Dish, 555-Fuck-Me-1. She said: "If you can't figure it out Trevor the phone is 555-382-5631. I live on Chestnut Street. My apartment is over the Starbuck's off Fillmore. Look up I have a Lady Gaga picture in the window." Trevor decided he would forgive her for bad taste in music. He eagerly awaited his visit to the plush New York Hotel and the fine food.

After checking into the Waldorf Astoria, Trevor took a cab to Greenwich Village. There were still some musical remnants from the past. He walked into the Village Vanguard and watched a smooth jazz trio recreate the John Coltrane sound. It was magic. Then he went next door and heard a set by Dean and Brita.

After catching a cab, Trevor had the driver drop him off at 1600 Broadway. This was down the block from where Late Night With David Letterman was taped. Trevor walked to the theater. No one noticed him. He was disappointed. The Ed Sullivan Theater is a historic one. Trevor stood outside and recalled that this was where the Beatles made their American television debut. He walked inside. An intern took him down to a small dressing room. It was one with a single star. Another dressing room had five stars and a custom door painted purple. Don Gino's name was on the door. The Don was in Letterman's private office. Trevor could hear them talking and laughing. Cigar smoke wafted from the room and a Lady Gaga song played loudly. Something was wrong. They couldn't have such bad musical taste.

Then it was time for the show. Letterman came out to the side of the stage. An intern sprayed something in his mouth. The famous host couldn't have bad breath. Don Gino went into his dressing room and a few months later came out in a conservative black pin striped suit. The gangster as TV personality.

The Letterman show began with Paul Shaffer leading the orchestra with Ringo Starr on drums. The former Beatle looked bored and sober. He also looked twenty years younger than the last time Trevor saw him. Ringo went into a drum solo and Letterman appeared to thunderous applause. Someone held up a sign. It read: "Thunderous applause."

Letterman went through a monologue that was not really funny. Then he brought out his first guest. Don Gino Landry was introduced. He spent ten minutes laughing and talking with Letterman. Then Dave brought out Emilio. He was dressed in a tuxedo and the audience cheered. He read from his latest book of poems. Zandra Filippi and Chastain Johnson came out with Matt Luman. The audience stood and applauded.

Letterman spent almost ten minutes talking to Filippi and Johnson about catching the terrorists. He asked Matt Luman to play a song. Matt walked over. Ringo Starr stood up: "My good friend Matt is a great drummer." Ringo pointed to the drums. The audience burst into applause. Matt sat at the drums and Ringo went to the microphone and began singing "Honey Don't." Ringo stopped in the middle of the song and Matt took over the vocals. The audience stood and cheered. Then half a dozen young girls rushed the stage. They stopped and urged Matt and Ringo to do another song. They did a quick version of Starr's solo hit "It Don't Come Easy."

Letterman said: "If these young ladies came after me, I would sing any song they wanted."

Shaffer said: "Dave you can't sing."

"I would learn."

Paul Shaffer frantically waved his arms. It was time for another musical number.

Luman sat at the piano and Shaffer stood up to lead the band. The crowd cheered Luman's brief version of "I'm Movin' On." He stood and bowed. He walked over and chatted up Letterman. An assistant director frantically waved his arms and held up three fingers. There were only three minutes left.

"Ladies and Gentleman," Letterman announced: "The guest of honor Trevor Blake III."

Trevor walked out smiling. The audience stood and cheered.

Letterman said: "A true patriot, he single handedly saved us from the terrorists." There was a minute and a half of applause. Trevor basked in it. The applause continued for more than two minutes.

"There is no time, folks. We will talk to Trevor when he solves his next case. Good night folks," Letterman continued. "You will be seeing more of Trevor Blake III."

Bennie was backstage seething. He was supposed to close the show with his vanishing trick. He hoped that Trevor vanished permanently. No chance.

Everyone got up and shook Trevor's hand. He didn't have time to say a word. The good news is that he was a hero. Once again there would be money to pay the bills.

Trevor walked backstage with a smile. Chastain Johnson sat on a chair smoking a cigarette. Zandra Filippi was standing next to her scowling.

"Ladies would you like the autograph from the world's second greatest detective? My apologies to Elvis Cole."

Zandra said: "What part of fuck off don't you understand?"

"My charm precedes me."

Chastain said: "No, your arrogance and your abject stupidity precedes you. As well as your inept ways." She smiled.

I wondered did Elvis Cole get this degree of disrespect? Joe Pike wouldn't stand for it.

As Trevor walked out of the studio where Late Night With David Letterman was recorded, he looked up and down Broadway. It was the early evening and Trevor decided to wander off to dinner alone. He didn't notice the tall African American standing in a nearby alley. James Smith vowed to get his revenge. He walked down the alley into the twilight. Don Gino and Trevor Blake III hadn't heard the last of the man known as Hammadi. They would meet him again.

Epilogue

**"I seated ugliness on my knees. And almost immediately
I tired of it." Salvador Dali**

**"Fiction is better at the truth than a factual record."
Doris Lessing**

Trevor walked up the steps to his office. He turned on the light and looked out the window. The fat guys, Ben and Jerry, had put up a new sign. They had invented a new ice cream flavor. They were multi-millionaires and had nothing else to do. Janis Joplin smiled at me from the wall. Van Morrison frowned. Maybe he was giving me the finger. Van was doing his best imitation of Don Gino's reprehensible midget. The office was unusually tidy. That happened when I was gone solving a case.

Guitar Jac was on vacation. He was performing in Monaco. Princess Charlene brought him over every year for her birthday. Princess Charlene was 5' 10' as was Guitar Jac. She joked that they were soul mates. Prince Charlene was a South African Olympic swimmer and she met Guitar Jac at the 2000 Sydney Olympics. He was playing a concert with Ritchie Havens at the Sydney Opera House. They talked sports and music. She couldn't believe the things they had in common. There was some truth to it. She was right wing, they both loved George Bush, she was entitled, and she was a pain in the ass. Remind me to share these scientific observations with Guitar Jac. Whatever happened to blues in the ghetto? I guess it had been replaced by rap and hip-hop.

I put Van Morrison's CD **No Plan B** into the sound system and sat down. Van's blues vocals soothed me. I needed it. Trevor Blake III Investigations once again had a nice financial nest egg. Don Gino sent a large sum of money, the federal government sent a reward and I was paid $100 to give a speech at Professor Fillmore Schwarz's criminal justice class at U. C. Berkeley. Now there was enough to pay the bills.

My desk was filled with bills. I organized them and wrote checks. There were forty requests for interviews. I only did the Late Night With David Letterman Show. Nothing else mattered. I was once again the world's second greatest detective. Eat your heart out Elvis Cole. I heard that someone stole his Pinocchio clock. I looked at my new Pinocchio clock. It was a dead ringer for Elvis Cole's. I looked up when I heard feet shuffling on the stairs.

Emilio walked in. He bowed. He smiled. I think it is an Asian thing. He was dressed in an Armani suit. How does a guy who owns a donut shop afford Armani suits?

"Trevor I brought you donuts, private eye needs donuts for pretty girl."

"There is no pretty girl in sight, Emilio." I picked up a chocolate frosted and downed it in two bites. I quickly ate a custard filled. I wondered what Emilio wanted. I wasn't going to ask. The third donut filled me to the brim. It was time to be polite.

"Thank you, Emilio. To what do I owe this visit?"

"I need you to help my cousin, Susan Wong."

"That name sounds Hong Kong Chinese."

"It is. My sister married into the Kang family. I'm afraid they are gangsters."

"I wouldn't want you hanging out with gangsters, Emilio."

He glared at me. No sense of humor.

Emilio had a large paper bag. He dipped into it. He pulled out $20,000. "This is a down payment Trevor on your next case. You are off to Hong Kong."

"What am I supposed to do?"

"It is simple. Find out who Yuhay Kang is and what he does for a living?"

"He married your sister."

"Yes."

"You don't know anything about him."

"Correct. I don't know much. He runs an entertainment business providing Chinese Elvis Presley impersonators."

"What?"

"Trevor, it is simple, he uses his Elvis business to run drugs, booze, weapons and prostitutes into Hong Kong and Memphis. They are also looking to sell illicit products to North Korea. The dictator there is an Elvis fan."

"Am I missing something here? I am looking for a gangster who is breaking the law in North Korea, Hong Kong and Memphis. Dennis Rodman is not going to like this."

"Who is Dennis Rodman?"

"Never mind Emilio."

"Trevor, I have a list of people involved, the list of goods sold, a list of Yuhay's bank accounts and complete dossiers on those who work for him. Hunter S. Thompson said: 'In a closed society where everybody's guilty, the only crime is getting caught.' I agree with Mr. Thompson." Where in the hell did Emilio get this Hunter S. Thompson quote?

"Emilio, why am I getting perfect English? As well as literary illusions. That is if Hunter S. Thompson is literary."

"Trevor, this is serious family business."

What am I supposed to do in the Yuhay Kang investigation?" I didn't have a clue.

"I may want the son of a bitch dead." Emilio looked like he wanted to break my arms and legs.

"Why do you want him dead?"

"Asian people do not get divorced."

"What if I send him to jail. I just don't know on what charge. Providing inept Elvis impersonators who are Chinese is not a crime."

Emilio said: "It should be."

"Answer my question, Emilio. What charge will bring him down?"

Emilio looked uncomfortable. "I think that he is a drug dealer. There are Hong Kong Chinese showing up in San Francisco's Mission district."

"And what does this mean?"

"There is every indication that a Chinese drug cartel is organizing." Emilio paused and pulled out a file.

I said: "Does Don Gino know this?"

"No."

"The Don will not be happy."

"No, he won't." Emilio handed me the file.

I read it over and told Emilio that Don Gino will quickly take action.

"Yes," Emilio said. "I need my sister out of Hong Kong."

"How do you suggest that Trevor Blake III do this?"

"You are the world's greatest detective, Trevor, you will figure it out."

"Will I?"

Emilio smiled. He left.

I sat down at my desk. Hong Kong. I couldn't wait. I looked at the money. I will fly coach. The world's greatest detective is also the world's cheapest man.

I pulled out a copy of Elmore Leonard's **Get Shorty**. I would read it on the plane to Hong Kong. I needed to learn to act like a tough guy. There were more mobsters in Honk Kong than in Las Vegas. There were also more Chinese. There are also more dead people in the streets.

I couldn't wait for my next case. I had solved two of the highest profile mysteries in San Francisco history. This is why they call me the world's greatest detective. The Hong Kong Chinese beware. Trevor Blake III is coming.

I wandered into the San Francisco Mystery Book Store. I asked for a Charlie Chan mystery. I was thrown out. I guess I had a lot to learn about Hong Kong. Or maybe Charlie Chan was out of the mystery loop.

I picked up a Joyce Carol Oates book. She wrote: "Anything I've encountered in the world is never as interesting as a novel...What you find out there is never as exciting as your own creation." What did this message say to me? Maybe Don Gino knew. I wasn't sure. I was off to Hong Kong.

A Note On Sources And Methods

Salvador Dali Murder is a work of fiction. The names, characters and incidents are the product of the author's imagination or have been used factiously. None of the characters are based on friends, family, relatives or anyone else. Matt Luman is a friend and he has consented to use his career and name in a work of fiction. His real name is Matt Lucas. Keep in mind; this is a work of fiction employing real hotels, real cities and real tourist sites. Not real people. Some of my relatives seem themselves in the book. Thanks for the compliment but you are not a character.

In using the life of Salvador Dali in a fictional tome, I have tried to represent the historical record as accurately as possible, but remember that this is a fictional work. It is not history but a fictional art creation; other aspects of Dali's life and the forces around him have been invented. For me a novel is a form of invention that allows the author to follow his or her mantra. I have followed mine. Flannery O'Connor said it best "writing is an act of discovery." I was raised in a house without books by alcoholic parents and my imagination was my saving grace. Much of the tension in this book is from the alcoholic parents and one dysfunctional brother who remains a psychological mess. Thanks for drinking and raging as you have provided me with my fictional direction.

The three preliminary sketches for Dali's **Persistence of Memory** as far as I know do not exist. They were added as a fictional part of the story.

The cruise ship line is fictitious. The characters are not based on real people. The Salvador Dali material is based on fact and biography.

I have added some fictional sketches that Dali never completed. The basic Dali story runs through the mystery.

The line drawing and finished product for **Portrait of A Pope**, that Dali drew does not exist. I have used the Ecumenical Council painting that Dali completed in 1960 and I have combined it with the fictional portrait used in this novel. The statistics and information regarding art theft in this novel are accurate. But **Portrait of A Pope** could not have been stolen, as it never existed. It is integral to the novel. The fictional **Portrait of a Pope** is based on a real life 1960 Dali work **The Ecumenical Council**.

The hotels, the tourist sites and the Dali homes are as close to reality as possible. The Carnivolet Line is a fictional cruise company and it is not based on fact. Nor is it based on any other cruise line. The Park Avenue Artists are also fictionalized. I have found all the art dealers on cruise ships to be honest and above board as well as the art contractors being honest to a fault.

A chance conversation with author and filmmaker Paul Perry provided the inspiration for Trevor Blake III to tackle a Salvador Dali mystery. Mr. Perry had no input into the book, so bad writing, poor thought, historical errors and statements about art that aren't correct can't be attributed to him. When I mentioned to Mr. Perry that I had completed the book, Mr. Perry denied any involvement in the project.

The original idea came from Mr. Perry's fertile mind and a documentary, **Dali's Greatest Secret**. This is perhaps Paul Perry's best documentary. His tales about Dali and those around him caught my attention. After I read what I could find on Dali, it was the inspiration for this novel. Thank you Paul. His documentary on Dali is the inspiration for much of this book. His best selling **New York Times** books provided great reading and inspiration. There are also numerous others books and articles important to this mystery.

The characters are fictionalized with the exception of my good friend and extraordinary musician, Matt Luman. He is a real person. He is not only one of the most talented musicians in the world. He is a wonderful human being. I have his permission to place him playing the piano throughout the book. He is a drummer. So much of his appearance is fictionalized. He is not a piano player except for this novel. His real name is Matt Lucas. He remains one of America's most creative and vibrant musicians.

Daniel Silva's **The Rembrandt Affair** is the best novel on art fraud. Much of the material in Silva's historical sketch of this theft is employed. There were a number of books that were important and these included Dawn Ades, **Dali And Surrealism**, (New York, 1983). The Ades volume deserves a new printing. For explanations of Dali's art see Paul Moorhouse, **Dali** (Mallard Fine Art Series, New York, 2002).

See Salvador Dali's **The Secret Life of Salvador Dali**, published in 1942, for an honest and compelling autobiography. This book deals with his early life and work through the 1930s. It is a rare window into his life, his talent and his thought processes. Charles Stuckey in an article in **Art In America** observed that Dali's autobiography "arguably revolutionized a literary genre." This was a brilliant deduction as Dali crafted a new path for other artists to follow.

The Secret Life of Salvador Dali was not only a hit in America but **Time** magazine called it "one of the most irresistible books of the year." **Time** also said that Dali's book was "a wild jungle of fantasy, posturing, belly laughs, narcissist and sadist confessions." The critics concluded that Dali was crazy as a fox. He knew how to use publicity to generate huge sums of money from his art and writing. He needed every penny as Gala spent his money as soon as it came into the coffers. She was beautiful, crazy, unpredictable and great in bed. Dali was never concerned about the money.

Trevor took the book and opened it to search for one last clue. He found it in the middle of the autobiography. He found the clue in an unlikely page.

A Cook Who Wants To Be Napoleon is integral to the Dali mystery. In the novel, terrorists destroyed it during the commission of the crime. This is fine, as the painting does not exist. It is a figment of my imagination. The Dali autobiography **The Secret Life of Salvador Dali** is real, and it is a roadmap for the mystery. The majority of the fictional paintings are based in facts surrounding Dali's life. **A Life**

Long Romance is another Dali that does not exist and the Provenance listing is a figment of my imagination. The same goes for Gala's gun. I don't believe that she owned one. **Christ In Mecca** is a Dali destroyed by the Catholic Church. That is fine, as the painting never existed. It is another figment of my imagination.

The material on terrorism was written during the time of the terrorist attack at the Boston Marathon.

The Italian Friar Gabriele Maria Berardi and the Dali sculpture that he received, as a gift is a real piece of art The Dali sculpture discovered after Berardi's was known as **Christ On The Cross**. Since this is fiction, I have had Berardi's Dali sculpture found the year before he died. My invention. Friar Berardi claimed that Dali gave it to him because he performed on exorcism on Dali. This is the true story. The Friar and the sculpture have another fate in this novel and it is a fictional one. The Dali article "Muslim Life In A Catholic Heaven" did not sell at auction for millions of dollars as it doesn't' exist. It is a figment of my imagination. The depictions of Figueres are based on fact with a bit of literary license.

Dali at the Perpignan train station is covered in "The Dali Murder Mystery," **London Guardian**, March 8, 2000 and Audrey Arthur, "Salvador Dali Leaves Legacy In Perpignan," http://inperpignan. net/2010/?p=1167 Don Gino did not show up at the train station that is a figment of my imagination. The act of Dali's teacher Esteban Trayter Colomer, having him secretly read the Quran is a fictional account.

The material on Ayman al-Zawahiri is biographically accurate; the plot to blow up Sagrada Familia in Barcelona and the Mission Delores in San Francisco is the product of the author's imagination.

Manuel Vazquez Montalban is a Spanish mystery novelist who died in 2003. His book **The Strangler** was an award-winning book. He did not win the International Mystery Writer's Award Hammett prize, as there is no such award. There is an International Mystery Writers' organization, which met in Owensboro, Kentucky October 10-13, 2013. It is primarily a venue for mystery plays, movies and television. For purposes of fiction it was moved to San Francisco as the Hammett Award is an invention of the author essential to the plot.

For the history of the Mission Delores see Howard A. DeWitt, **The California Dream** (Dubuque, 1996). Also see, Howard A. DeWitt, **Readings in California Civilization** (Dubuque, 1981).

Jim Harrison, the late Manuel Vazquez Montalban and various others writers are used for fictional purposes. Their books are real and fun to read. Buy some. Harrison's best book is **Legends of The Fall** followed by **The River Swimmer**. For Montalban's books see **Tattoo: A Pepe Carvalho Mystery**, which was published in, 1976 but remains the classic Spanish noir mystery.

The material on Ayman al-Zawahiri is factually correct as are the scientific inventions from the Arabic world. Mohammad Chaib is a Muslim who is an elected Spanish official and he is accurately described.

For Dali's religious faith see Matthew J. Milliner. "God In the Gallery," December 12, 2007 http://www.firstthings.com/onthesquare/2007/12/god-in-the-gallery The U. S. does have a Muslim Outreach program. This is accurately described, as is Ambassador Alan Solomont's role.

The San Francisco restaurants and bars are legitimate ones. I owe a special thanks to the Hi Fi Lounge and its patrons for color and atmosphere. The San Francisco restaurants, Gary Danko's and Boulevard, are real and I have enjoyed many meals in these fine establishments. I hope that I am not banned from future meals. The material on Julian Assange, Bradley Manning, Wiki Leaks and Edward Snowden is based on fact. The interpretation of the events surrounding their actions is my fictional nod to their deeds. The French writer, Andre Parinaud, used a series of interviews to complete his book, **The Unspeakable Confessions of Salvador Dali**. Published in 1950 it was a fictional window into Dali's life The English translation by Harold J. Salemson is brilliant. Salemson was a film and book critic who also translated biographies of Pablo Picasso and Georges Simenon. This dreadful book attempted to make money from Dali's penchant for overstatement. Don Gino purchases and burns all copies of this, but remember this is fiction. Pick up Parinaud's volume and decide for yourself. This volume is an eye opener.

The Insider Threat Program discussed in chapter 11 and throughout the remainder of the book is a real government program. Novelist Barry Eisler, a former CIA operative, is one of the key figures in bringing this program to the general public.

The material on al Qaeda terrorists is aided by a wide number of books, these include Howard A. DeWitt, **The Road To Baghdad** (Dubuque, 2003).

The material on California history depends upon my teaching the subject for thirty years at Ohlone College and writing three textbooks, a multicultural book, **The Fragmented Dream: Multicultural California** as well as books on political radicalism I wrote about California in the 1920s and 1930s. The material on Don Gino comes largely from the multicultural book and is historically accurate. Don Gino is of course a fictional character.

Bennie and Bertie are modeled after the careers of the legendary San Francisco lawyer Melvin Belli and the Bertie character is based on Pat Montandon. Belli's loose biography is Bennie and Montandon is Bertie. Remember it is fiction. Bernard Ewell is a real person. He is the foremost Dali Detective who has authenticated more of Dali's work than anyone.

Kate Atkinson's four detective novels, which are really literary tomes, helped in structuring this book. Her 2004 introduction of Detective Jackson Brodie was particularly inspirational. While Dali's **Christ In Mecca** is a fictional painting the story is based upon al Qaeda operatives who believed in a similar alleged painting. All reference to paranoia comes from Dali's paranoid critical approach to the art world. Unless noted here the historical facts are accurate and the interpretation sometimes leads to bit of drama. It is all for a good story.

The changes to the structure and the symbols on Sagrada Familia are my invention. The history is accurate. Or at least as accurate as I could make it. Maybe! Maybe not!

Opus Dei operates the Chestnut Center for Women in San Francisco. I have fictionalized a female branch of the organization known as The Prelate of the Holy Mother. The homeless shelter for women in the tenderloin is an invention for the novel.

The quote from the Mike Wallace-Salvador Dali 1958 American TV interview is an accurate one. Sayyid Qutb is the intellectual father of al Qaeda and **Milestones** is the book that gave birth to the Muslim Brotherhood. Dali didn't know Qutb or his work.

If the Devil had an Egyptian name, it is Sayyid Qutb. He personified evil. See my book **A Blow To America's Heart: England Reacts To 9-11** (Dubuque 2002) for a look at Qutb's sordid career as well as his radical influence.

The material on Ayman al-Zawahiri is factually correct in chapter 44 but the Three Amigos did not take Juan Zarate, who was one of President Obama's terror advisers, to lunch. The obvious conclusion is that my description bears a great resemblance to the realities of the American al Qaeda problem in the latter part of 2013. Salim Benarama is an Imam who is a strong, but not radical, voice of Muslim rights.

The material on the Paris Dali Museum is factually accurate. The counterfeited paintings removed from the museum by Don Gino and replaced with the originals remains a product of fiction not fact.

Chapter 41 on Zandra Filippi's global investigations of terrorism is influenced by real life events. The character came at the suggestion of J. Alexander who bears no responsibility for the action in Zandra's life. See Ken Auletta, Freedom of Information," **The New Yorker**, October 7, 2013, pp. 46-57 for information on how the British newspaper, the **Guardian**, blew the whistle on U. S. government surveillance on its citizens and the world. I have placed Zandra Filippi in the role of British newspaper editor, Alan Rushbridger, and I created a character based on him. That character, Arnold Rushbridger, will help Zandra gather information.

The story of a sail painted by Dali to support a group of explorers who were sailing rafts from Ecuador to Australia is true. Don Gino purchasing the sail is fiction.

There were two trips to Barcelona that helped the novel. For forty years I lived in and around San Francisco and the material from the City bears forty years of eating and drinking in the City By The-bay. I taught California history at the college level for more than four decades and much of the historical material comes from my best selling textbooks and a marvelous diversity history **The Fragmented Dream: Multicultural California**.

The intent in this book is to have a ring of truth about Dali using fiction. When we visited Figueres there was no doubt that many myths and legends about Dali had a ring of truth.

See Rachel Cohen, **Bernard Berenson** (New York 2013) for a biography of a pioneering scholar in the art world. Berenson is the figure who provides the background for the fictional character Dr. Harold Weinstein.

The idea of replanting the Mission Delores with Middle Eastern plants is fictional aided by a wonderful book by Kamal H. Batanouny, **Plants In the Deserts In The Middle East** (New York, 2001).

A very interesting and useful book is Denise A. Speilberg, **Thomas Jefferson's Qur'an: Islam and Founders** (New York 2013). The Speilberg volume is beautifully written and suggests a level of tolerance toward Muslims in America that would go a long way to combating terrorism.

Ian Gibson's, **The Shameful Life of Salvador Dali** (New York, 1997) is a well researched, beautifully written, but flawed, biography that was instrumental to this novel. Also see, Meryle Secrest, **Salvador Dali: A Biography** (New York, 1986) for an interesting and well-written view of Dali's life.

Salvador Dali's **Diary of A Genius** (New York, 1965) is an interesting, eccentric, iconoclastic book that most people do not take seriously. They should. Dali casts a great deal of light upon his career, his thought process, his writing style, his ego, his influences, his life and those around him. This book is often dismissed because of its over the top approach. Much of what he writes seems to be putting the reader on. After all is this not Dali?

The Dali painting that Don Gino Landry stole for his collection is "Queen Ant Gala With Sharp Pincers." It is a Dali that does not exist, as it is a fictional painting. Danielle Steel thinks it is real. The Rotterdam Art Museum robbery and the Muslim Outreach program in Barcelona are described accurately and the people involved are placed within the context of the events. Don Gino Landry did not solve either problem. The readers hope that his advice is taken.

For the Kunsthal Museum robbery there were seven painting taken. There was not a Dali in the crime. The Dali in this novel, **Queen Ant Gala With Sharp Pincers**, is a fictional painting necessary to the novel. The rest of the story is factually correct with the exception of Don Gino Landry not solving the crime. The book on Dali and surrealism by Sacha Fourier, **Salvador Dali: The Fake Surrealist**, is a fictional one. It does not exist. Fourier and his volume are necessary to the plot.

About The Author

Howard A. DeWitt is Professor Emeritus of History at Ohlone College, Fremont, California. He received his B. A. from Western Washington State University, the M. A. from the University of Oregon and a PhD from the University of Arizona. He also studied at the University of Paris, Sorbonne and the City University in Rome. Professor DeWitt is the author of twenty-two books and has published over 200 articles and more than 200 reviews in a wide variety of popular and scholarly magazines.

DeWitt has also been a member of a number of organizations to promote the study of history. The most prestigious is the Organization of American Historians.

For more than forty-five years he has taught full and part time at a number of U. S. colleges. He is best known for teaching two college level courses in the History of Rock n Roll music. He continued to teach the History of Rock and Roll music on the Internet until 2011. Among people he brought to class were Bo Diddley, Mike Bloomfield, Jimmy McCracklin, Paul Butterfield, George Palmerton and Pee Wee Thomas. In a distinguished academic career, he has also taught at the University of California, Davis, the University of Arizona, Cochise College and Chabot College. In addition to these teaching assignments, Professor DeWitt is a regular speaker at the Popular Culture Association annual convention and at the National Social Science Association meetings. He has delivered a number of addresses to the Organization of American Historians.

He wrote the first book on Chuck Berry, which was published by Pierian Press under the title **Chuck Berry: Rock N Roll Music** in

1985. DeWitt's earlier brief biography, **Van Morrison: The Mystic's Music**, published in 1983, received universally excellent reviews. On the English side of the music business DeWitt's, **The Beatles: Untold Tales**, originally published in 1985, was picked up by the Kendall Hunt Publishing Company in the 1990s and is used regularly in a wide variety of college courses on the history of rock music. Kendall Hunt also published **Stranger in Town: The Musical Life of Del Shannon** with co-author Dennis M. DeWitt in 2001. In 1993's **Paul McCartney: From Liverpool To Let It Be** concentrated on the Beatle years. He also co-authored **Jailhouse Rock: The Bootleg Records of Elvis Presley** with Lee Cotten in 1983.

Professor DeWitt's many awards in the field of history include founding the Cochise County Historical Society and his scholarship has been recognized by a number of state and local government organizations. DeWitt's book, **Sun Elvis: Presley In The 1950s**, published by Popular Culture Ink. was a finalist for the Deems-ASCAP Award for the best academic rock and roll book.

Professor DeWitt is a renaissance scholar who publishes in a wide variety of outlets that are both academic and popular. He is one of the few college professors who bridge the gap between scholarly and popular publications. His articles and reviews have appeared in **Blue Suede News, DISCoveries, Rock 'N' Blues News**, the **Journal of Popular Culture**, the **Journal of American History, California History**, the **Southern California Quarterly**, the **Pacific Historian, Amerasia**, the **Western Pennsylvania Historical Magazine**, the **Annals of Iowa**, the **Journal of the West, Arizona and the West**, the **North Beach Review, Ohio History**, the **Oregon Historical Quarterly**, the **Community College Social Science Quarterly, Montana: The Magazine of the West, Record Profile Magazine, Audio Trader**, the **Seattle Post-Intelligencer** and **Juke Box Digest**.

For forty plus years DeWitt has combined popular and academic writing. He has been nominated for numerous writing awards. His reviews are combined with articles to form a body of scholarship and popular writing that is frequently footnoted in major work. As a political scientist, Professor DeWitt authored three books that questioned

American foreign policy and its direction. In the Philippines, DeWitt is recognized as one of the foremost biographers of their political leader Jose Rizal. His three books on Filipino farm workers remain the standard in the field.

During his high school and college years, DeWitt promoted dances in and around Seattle, Washington. Such groups as Little Bill and the Bluenotes, Ron Holden and the Playboys, the Frantics, the Wailers and George Palmerton and the Night People among others played at such Seattle venues as the Eagle's Auditorium and Dick Parker's Ballroom. DeWitt was a hyperactive kid in those days roaming the Seattle streets and hanging out at Birdland. He now roams the word processor and hangs out in coffee shops writing furtively.

Howard has two grown children. They both live in Los Angeles. His wife of forty plus years, Carolyn, is an educator, an artist and she continues to raise Howard. She is presently retired and vacationing around the world. The DeWitt's divide their time between Scottsdale, Arizona and the Silver Lake area of Los Angeles. That is when they are not in Paris looking for art, books and music. Howard is working on a book on Paris. That is a year away and a study of Sixto Rodriguez is on the horizon.

His book on the president **Obama Detractor's: In The Right Wing Nut House** is a marvelous look at the radical right. **Stone Murder** features a San Francisco P.I. Trevor Blake III, and much of the story line will evolve around crimes that DeWitt witnessed while working four years and two days as an agent with the Bureau of Alcohol, Tobacco and Firearms. He was a street agent for the BATF and his tales of those years are in manuscript waiting for publication. He was also a key figure in the BATF Union.

He is currently working on a series of rock and roll mystery novels featuring Trevor Blake III, a private eye in San Francisco. The first novel **Stone Dead**, published in 2012, can be ordered through Amazon. He also writes fiction under another name.

Any corrections or additions to this or the subsequent volumes that will follow this study can be sent to Horizon Books, P. O. Box 4342, Scottsdale, Arizona 85258. DeWitt can be reached via e-mail at Howard217@aol.com

25204322R00252

Printed in Great Britain
by Amazon